D0168651

Stories and Poems
Cuentos y poesías

A Dual-Language Book

Rubén Darío

Edited and translated by
STANLEY APPELBAUM

DOVER PUBLICATIONS, INC.
Mineola, New York

Copyright

Bibliographical Note

This Dover edition, first published in 2002, contains a new selection of stories and poems by Rubén Darío (extensive information on original periodical and volume publications will be found in the "Introduction and Annotations"), together with new English translations by Stanley Appelbaum, who also supplied the introductory matter and the footnotes.

Library of Congress Cataloging-in-Publication Data

Darío, Rubén, 1867–1916.
    [Selections. English & Spanish]
    Stories and poems = Cuentos y poesías : a dual-language book / Rubén Darío ; edited and translated by Stanley Appelbaum.
    p. cm.
    Includes bibliographical references and indexes.
    ISBN-13: 978-0-486-42065-3
    ISBN-10: 0-486-42065-5
    1. Darío, Rubén, 1867–1916—Translations into English. I. Appelbaum, Stanley. II. Title: Cuentos y poesías.

PQ7519.D3 A227 2002
861'.5—dc21

2002025986

Manufactured in the United States by Courier Corporation
42065505   2015
www.doverpublications.com

Contents

Introduction and Annotations

Rubén Darío

Rubén Darío was the nom de plume (adopted as early as 1880) of Félix Rubén García Sarmiento, who was born in 1867 in the Nicaraguan town of Metapa (now called Ciudad Darío in his honor). His parents separated when he was two, and he was adopted by Colonel Félix Ramírez, husband of the boy's *"tía abuela"* (she was both an aunt and the adoptive mother of the boy's mother). The future poet grew up in their comfortable home in the town of León, where he imbibed local legends and wonder tales. The colonel died in 1871. The boy, a prodigy, could read at the age of three, and began writing verse at age eleven, while a pupil in a Jesuit-run school; his first publications, in local newspapers, were in 1880.

In 1881 he moved to the capital, Managua, where he fell in love with Rosario Murillo, the "brown heron" of his autobiographical story "Palomas blancas y garzas morenas." To prevent an undesirable marriage with her, his friends bundled him off to El Salvador in 1882. As a bohemian there, he first became acquainted with the French literature of the day. In 1883 he returned to Nicaragua, where he resumed contact with Rosario and worked as a journalist and as a librarian, writing all the while.

The single most important change in his life occurred in 1886. Disgusted by Rosario's infidelities, he moved to Chile (on advice, and with recommendations). That nation was then enjoying unprecedented peace and prosperity, and was wide open to progressive European influences. Darío had his first taste of big-city life while on the staff of the Santiago paper *La Época*. He made friends with the son of the country's president, and had access to a vast collection of current French books. In 1887, during a cholera outbreak in Santiago, he briefly worked as a customs inspector in Valparaíso. That same year he published a volume of verse and received first prize in a contest for poems in honor of Chile. He kept *La Época* and other papers supplied with poems and stories.

A landmark year for Darío personally, and for the *modernismo* movement, of which he was now chief representative, was 1888, when he published the first edition of *Azul* . . . . Critical acclaim in Spain itself put Darío and *modernismo* on the international map. In the same year he became associated with the important Buenos Aires newspaper *La Nación* as their Santiago correspondent.

Nevertheless, Darío was homesick, and in 1889 he returned to Nicaragua, and then to El Salvador, where that country's political boss made him director of the paper *La Unión*. (Darío's life contains a recurring pattern of reliance on political favors, which were notoriously unreliable in the volatile politics of the day.) In 1890 he married Rafaela Contreras, who appears as "Stella" in his poetry. His position in El Salvador became untenable, and he moved on to Guatemala, where he directed another paper and brought out the substantially enlarged second edition of *Azul* . . . . In 1891, his new paper was shut down, and he moved on to Costa Rica for a while.

In 1892, he tried unsuccessfully to find more work in Guatemala. The uncertainty of his situation was temporarily relieved when the Nicaraguan government sent him to Spain as their delegate at the celebration of the four-hundredth anniversary of Columbus's discovery of America. There he met a number of major Spanish writers.

In 1893 Darío's wife died; this event is seen as the immediate cause of his alcoholism, which grew progressively worse over the years, often numbing his faculties, making him prematurely old, and eventually killing him before his time. Almost immediately after his loss, he was forced into what was virtually a shotgun wedding with Rosario. Life with her soon became impossible for him, and for the rest of his days he tried his best to avoid her, while she hunted him down implacably. Still in 1893, he visited New York, where he met José Martí, the Cuban patriot and pioneer of *modernismo*; then he proceeded to Paris (a city he had long loved from afar), where he met Verlaine, one of his heroes; and finally he was sent to Argentina as Colombian consul. In Buenos Aires, one of the centers of *modernismo*, he became a staff member of *La Nación*, and an important new phase of his career began. (The consulship expired in 1895, but Darío's journalistic work and writing of poetry continued apace.)

In 1896, he published in Buenos Aires the first edition of his next major volume of verse (which many critics consider his best), *Prosas profanas y otros poemas*. His foreword to this book was a prideful manifesto for *modernismo*, which here reached its pinnacle.

Darío's long residence in Europe began in 1898, after the Spanish-

American War, when *La Nación* assigned him as its correspondent in
Spain, to report on the local reaction to the loss of prestige and
colonies. Darío was quickly accepted into progressive intellectual cir-
cles. In 1899 he began a long relationship with a simple country girl,
Francisca Sánchez, who bore him several children. In 1900, *La
Nación* sent him as correspondent to the magnificent World's Fair in
Paris and to the Holy Year celebrations in Rome. Around this time,
Paris became his chief headquarters.

In 1901 Darío published two volumes of reportage on his European
travels, and the second, enlarged edition of *Poesías profanas*. In the
same year he visited England and Belgium. Recurrent money worries
became serious around this time. In 1903 he was appointed
Nicaraguan consul in Paris; he made trips to Spain; and Francisca
gave him the son he poetically dubbed "Phocas" (who unfortunately
died two years later). In 1904 Darío journeyed to Morocco, Germany,
Austria, Hungary, and Italy, and published a travel account.

In 1905 he returned to Spain, where he published his next major
volume of verse, *Cantos de vida y esperanza*, which some critics re-
gard as his supreme achievement, more mellow, mature, and varied
than *Prosas profanas.* By this time, Darío's alcoholism was well ad-
vanced; he had grown pursy and old-looking, and was often confused.
His younger friend, the major Spanish poet Juan Ramón Jiménez, was
instrumental in seeing the new volume through the press, and Darío
dedicated the four-poem subdivision of the book called "Cisnes" to
Jiménez.

In 1906 the Nicaraguan government appointed Darío as a delegate
to the important Third Interamerican Conference in Rio. Returning
by way of Buenos Aires and Paris, Darío spent some time in Majorca.
In 1907, Darío's prestige in his native Nicaragua reached epic pro-
portions, and a special law was passed there to enable him to get a
much-wanted divorce from his persecutress Rosario, but the divorce
failed to come about. In the same year, Darío published a new volume
of verse, *El canto errante,* in Madrid, and was named Nicaraguan
envoy to Spain. In 1909 he visited Italy and his beloved Paris.

In 1910 he published in Madrid the volume of verse *Poema del
otoño y otros poemas,* and was named the Nicaraguan delegate to the
centennial celebration of independence in Mexico, but while he was
en route a revolution in Nicaragua vitiated his credentials, and he re-
turned to Europe via Havana. By 1911, Darío's financial distress had
become acute, and he reluctantly accepted the direction of a journal
financed by two Uruguayan brothers. (Around this time, he suspected

that his talents and fame were being largely exploited.) In 1912 his employers sent him on a huge publicity tour through Spain, Portugal, and Latin America, but his health broke down and he returned to Paris. In 1913 his alcoholism produced mystic visions (he had long toyed with theosophy and occultism). He spent some time on Majorca.

In 1914, the year that the First World War broke out, he made a pacifist tour of the Americas, and was bed-ridden with pneumonia in New York. His last volume of verse, *Canto a la Argentina y otros poemas,* was published in Madrid that year.

In 1915 he accepted the local dictator's invitation to Guatemala to write a panegyric. Very ill, he was whisked away to Managua by the relentlessly possessive Rosario. In 1916 some friends brought him to León, the town of his boyhood, where, after two operations, he died of cirrhosis of the liver. He was buried in León Cathedral.

Modernismo and Darío's Major Publications

The movement in Spanish literature known as *modernismo*[1] lasted roughly from 1880 to 1910 (though some historians make it last as long as 1940). Never a "school," but rather a common approach to the practice of writing verse in particular, but also prose, *modernismo* was originally a New World, Latin American phenomenon that was only later acknowledged in Spain, thereupon entering the mainstream of Spanish-language literature. First making its appearance in a sporadic way, *modernismo* eventually became centered in Mexico and Argentina. Important early practitioners were the Cuban José Martí and the Mexican Manuel Gutiérrez Nájera, who are considered as belonging to the "first generation" of *modernistas.*

These young Latin Americans had lost their allegiance to the outworn modalities of late Romanticism, and were alive to the new movements arising in Europe, particularly in France. *Modernismo* was influenced first by the French Parnassian poets, who aimed at descriptive verse of great clarity, associated psychologically with the visual arts, especially sculpture. Later, *modernismo* incorporated the literary methods of the French Symbolist poets, who strove for the kind of suggestion, transcending verbal information, that is inherent in the art

---

[1]The term *modernismo* is also used in Spanish art history, where it corresponds by and large to "Art Nouveau" in English.

of music. But the *modernistas* were also influenced by such French Romantics as Gautier and Hugo, and even by Naturalists such as Zola. They were not necessarily aloof from social concerns, though their so-called "decadent" art was imbued with eroticism, encyclopedism, and cosmopolitanism. Musicality of language and prosodic virtuosity were primary concerns.

Darío has been seen either as the link between the first two generations of *modernismo* or as the chief representative of the second generation, but he has never lost his standing as the preeminent figure of the entire movement. He was influenced by the French Romantics, Parnassians, and Symbolists, but also by the classical verse of antiquity and by Spanish verse: medieval, Renaissance, Baroque (Góngora), and Neo-Romantic (Bécquer). His huge vocabulary includes Grecisms, Gallicisms, local Latin American words, and bold new coinages. He commands an impressive array of meters (37 by one count, including classical hexameters and—a great favorite—French-inspired 14-syllable alexandrines), which he combines into a vast number of different stanzas (136). His primary concern in verse (and, by extension, in life) is rhythm. His writings, both verse and stories, form a sort of para-religious Revelation, in which dreams, occultism, and angst play a large part. His numerous personal symbols include the centaur, the forest, and the swan. The centaur combines human and bestial traits. In the forest, gross animals feed on the ground, while more ethereal creatures feed in the treetops, near the sky. The swan (which had already been a favorite symbol in Vigny, Baudelaire, and Mallarmé, with different sets of references) in Darío stands for both the purity of whiteness and for eroticism (as the lover of Leda); moreover, the curve of its neck forms an eternal question mark.

Darío's breakthrough volume, *Azul* . . . (Blue . . .), was first published in 1888, in Valparaíso, by the Imprenta y Litografía Excelsior; this first edition contained 9 stories, 6 poems, and some prose sketches about Chile. More stories and many more poems were added to the second edition, published in 1890, in Guatemala (city), by the Imprenta de la Unión. The third edition, which some critics consider definitive because it was the last in Darío's lifetime (though many of its readings are simplified and less flavorful), was published in 1905, in Buenos Aires, by the Imprenta de la Nación.

Although the "blue" of the title may have been inspired by reminiscences of Hugo and Mallarmé, Darío later maintained that it represented the clear, pure sky and sea of his native land, with associations of infinity, beauty, freedom, and imagination. After its

successful reception in Spain, the book became the flagship of *modernismo*. Never again in his lifetime did Darío publish a volume that was entirely or largely comprised of stories, but at this point in his development his prose was still more assured and more significant than his poetry. For this reason, nine of the ten stories in this anthology have been selected from *Azul* . . . (first and second editions), but only three poems (all from the second edition). (Subsequently, poetry was his chief medium of imaginative writing, and the ratio of poetry in this anthology reflects that fact.)

Prosas profanas y otros poemas (Worldly Hymns, and Other Poems) was first published in 1896, in Buenos Aires, by the Imprenta Pablo E. Coni y hijo; this edition contained 33 poems. The enlarged second edition, with 21 additional poems, was published in 1901, in Paris, by the Veuve (widow) de Ch. Bouret.

The word *prosas* in the title denotes certain major hymns (or, sequences), such as the Dies Irae or the Stabat Mater, which are sung during solemn Masses. Thus, the phrase "worldly hymns" is a defiant provocation right from the outset. Nor do the individual poems palliate matters: a number of them boldly combine erotic material with the language of Christian ritual. In *Prosas profanas*, Darío is at his most extravagantly innovative, with recherché vocabulary, ethereally beautiful versification, and wide-ranging thought. To many, this volume is the summit of his own achievement, and of *modernismo* in general.

But there will always be partisans of his next verse collection, *Cantos de vida y esperanza* (Songs of Life and Hope). The choice is between youthful ardor (and even impudence) and the more fully rounded (and equally well expressed) experience of life as an older man with increased responsibilities and wider commitments. *Cantos de vida y esperanza* was first published in 1905, in Madrid, by the Tipografía de la Revista de Archivos, Bibliotecas y Museos (the book largely assembled, overseen, and even reconstructed from memory, by Juan Ramón Jiménez while Darío was largely incapacitated by drink); no significant changes were ever made.

In this volume, Darío often assumes the role of an elder statesman and a spokesman for Spain who is often *plus royaliste que le roi*. But there are also many notes of personal anguish, and his private mythology is still very much in evidence. His poetic powers show no signs of falling off.

El canto errante (The Wandering Song; or, more archly, The Song-Errant) was first published in 1907, in Madrid, by the Biblioteca

Nueva de Escritores Españoles, M. Pérez de Villavicencio Editor. This is more of a grab-bag volume than its predecessors, with poems from various periods of Darío's life, and of more varying quality, though a fair number are still outstanding and even unique.

The volume *Poema del otoño y otros poemas* (Poem of Autumn, and Other Poems) was first published in 1910, in Madrid, by the Biblioteca Ateneo. It did not contain much new material, and is chiefly remarkable for its title poem, which forms a fitting close to any Darío anthology.

Annotations to the Individual Stories and Poems

In addition to providing an accurate, "no-frills" translation (line-for-line in the poetry section) in modern American English (but striving to match the lexical level of the Spanish at all points), the present translator's biggest task was to identify the best Spanish texts of the items selected.[2] This was done by carefully collating all the currently available commercial Spanish-language editions that he could find, no one of which is totally free of typographical errors, and one or two of which are totally disfigured by the most grotesque misrepresentations of the words that Darío obviously had in mind (besides mispunctuation that distorts the syntax, etc., etc.). (Even so, the translator did not feel competent, or even called upon, to decide among all the choices in punctuation, indentations, capitalization, and stanza divisions that the various editions offer; he limited himself to making this volume as internally consistent as possible.)

The currently available Spanish editions just mentioned are also characterized by great skimpiness in factual annotation (as opposed to literary analysis); moreover, even the best of them, though edited by academics, contain one or two silly errors in their annotation, such as calling Monsieur Prudhomme a French author! The annotation section that follows immediately, based on the best information in the Spanish editions, but, even more, on the translator's knowledge and new research, is incomparably larger. Even so, to keep it from being

---

[2]The best texts, not *the* (definitive) text! For one thing, there are differences between editions published during Darío's lifetime, especially in the *Azul* . . . stories, where simpler words were sometimes substituted for rarer ones (e.g., *esmeraldas* for *esmaragdina* in "El Rey Burgués"), or duller generalized terms for specific ones (e.g., *cementerio* for *Playa-Ancha* [the paupers' graveyard in Valparaíso] in "El fardo"). The translator tends to favor more colorful original readings over flatter later ones.

infinitely large, the translator has assumed that the reader has access to a good one-volume dictionary and a good desk reference, and/or possesses at least the first rudiments of Bible history and Greco-Roman mythology, and a familiarity with the outstanding names in political and cultural history.

The basic sequence of this book is: story section, then poetry section. Within each section, the sequence is chronological by date of first publication of Darío's various volume collections, and, within each such volume, the original sequence of the items. The annotations also indicate, for the poems, under which subdivisions of the original volumes each poem appeared. For every item (with two regrettable exceptions) the annotations indicate its first appearance in print (before it was gathered into a volume), including (again with two exceptions) the (rare) information as to the *city* of that first publication.

Stories

"El Rey Burgués": first published in *La Época* (Santiago, Chile), November 4, 1887; then collected in the first (1888) edition of *Azul* . . . . The "king" Darío had in mind was Eduardo MacClure, owner of *La Época*, where he worked. Ohnet: Georges Ohnet, a very popular French novelist of the period. Hermosilla: José Gómez Hermosilla (1771–1837), a very finicky Spanish literary critic. Goncourt: the French brothers Edmond (1822–1896) and Jules (1830–1870) Goncourt were not only novelists but trend-setting art collectors.

"El sátiro sordo": first published in *La Libertad Electoral* (Valparaíso, Chile), October 15, 1888; then incorporated into the second (1890) edition of *Azul* . . . . Kant: the theme of the donkey conversing with the philosopher Kant (a recurring one in Darío's work) is based on Victor Hugo's poem "L'âne" (The Donkey). Daniel Heinsius: a seventeenth-century Dutch Latinist. Passerat: Jean Passerat, a sixteenth-century French poet. Buffon: the great eighteenth-century French naturalist (Georges-Louis Leclerc, conte de Buffon). Posada: Joaquín Pablo Posada, a nineteenth-century Colombian writer. Valderrama: Adolfo Valderrama (1834–1902), a Chilean physician.

"La ninfa": first published in *La Época* (Santiago), November 25, 1887; then in the first edition of *Azul* . . . . Some of Darío's early readers were amazed that, in this and other stories in *Azul . . .*, he had captured so much Parisian atmosphere before he ever visited Europe; Santiago was the big city that inspired him, along with his reading of

French books. Aspasia: the highly cultured courtesan of fifth-century B.C. Athens who was the mistress of Pericles. Frémiet: Emmanuel Frémiet (1824–1910), French sculptor of animals. Myron: Greek sculptor, fifth century B.C. Heinrich Kornmann: a seventeenth-century German scholar (a good guess at identifying the "Enrico Zormano" of Darío's text). Vincentius: a thirteenth-century French monk. Phlegon (not "Philegon"!) of Tralles: a second-century A.D. Greek writer on the wonders of nature. Numa: a legendary king of Rome (ca. 700 B.C.) who was advised by the nymph Egeria. Tartarin: the comic hero of novels by Alphonse Daudet.

"El fardo": first published in *La Revista de Artes y Letras* (Santiago), April 15, 1887; then in the first edition of *Azul* . . . . Based on Darío's brief experience as customs inspector on the Valparaíso docks, and supposedly a true story, this *cuento* shows Darío experimentally flirting with Zolaesque Naturalism, a trend that he didn't continue. Bulnes: Manuel Bulnes (1799–1866), a general who became president of Chile. Miraflores: an 1881 battle in the Pacific War between Chile and the combined forces of Peru and Bolivia.

"El velo de la reina Mab": first published in *La Época* (Santiago), October 2, 1887; then in the first edition of *Azul* . . . . Darío's Mab is more Shakespeare's (Mercutio's speech in *Romeo and Juliet*) than Shelley's. Terpander: a legendary Greek musician of the seventh century B.C.

"La canción del oro": first published in *La Revista de Artes y Letras* (Santiago), February 15, 1888; then in the first edition of *Azul* . . . . Inspired by Jean Richepin's volume of poems *La chanson des gueux* (The Beggars' Song; 1876). Duran(d): the French painter Carolus Duran (1838–1917). Bonnat: the French painter Joseph-Léon Bonnat (1833–1922). "The pin that wounds the slave girl's breast": refers to a slave girl dressing the hair of a cruel ancient Roman matron. Anthony, Macarius, Hilarion, Paul the Hermit: some of the earliest Christian anchorites (third and fourth centuries).

"El pájaro azul": first published in *La Época* (Santiago), December 7, 1886; then in the first edition of *Azul* . . . . The influence of Henri Murger's *Scènes de la vie de Bohême* (1847–8) is evident. Clay: Jan Carel Clay, a nineteenth-century Belgian painter of seascapes.

"Palomas blancas y garzas morenas": first published in *La Libertad Electoral* (Valparaíso), June 23, 1888; then in the first edition of *Azul* . . . . Highly autobiographical; Darío did have a female cousin in León, Nicaragua, who first aroused him sexually (the "white dove"); the "brown heron" was Rosario Murillo, whom he met in Managua, and

eventually married and shunned. *Paul et Virginie:* the famous 1787 French novel by Bernardin de Saint-Pierre about two chaste young lovers on a tropical island. Solomon: the biblical Song of Songs, traditionally attributed to Solomon, is here quoted in the Latin Vulgate version (chapter 4, verse 11). The kiss "all a-tremble" is a reference to the love between Paolo and Francesca in Canto V of "Inferno" in Dante's *Divine Comedy,* as is the line "That day we no longer merely dreamed" (a counterpart to Dante's "That day we read no further").

"La muerte de la emperatriz de la China": first published in *La República* (Santiago), March 15, 1890; then in the second edition of *Azul* . . . . The characters Recaredo and Robert were modeled on friends of Darío's; Recaredo was a sixth-century Visigothic king of Spain. Some editions bear a dedication of the story to "Duque Job," a nickname of the Mexican *modernista* Manuel Gutiérrez Nájera (1859–1895). Ayesha: the *She* of Rider Haggard's famous novel of that name, an imperious, mysterious ruler who "must be obeyed."

"El caso de la señorita Amelia": first published in *La Nación* (Buenos Aires), January 1, 1894 (hence, the New Year's setting). This is a highly regarded example of the several fantasy stories Darío wrote subsequently to *Azul* . . . . Hirsch: Maurice, baron de Hirsch (1831–1896), a French Jewish philanthropist who devised a plan for the ill-used Russian Jews to found a colony in Argentina. Apollonius of Tyana: a Greek thaumaturge of the first century A.D. Paracelsus: the famous sixteenth-century Swiss-German alchemist (Theophrast von Hohenheim). Crookes: William Crookes (1832–1919), an English chemist. *Grupa, jiba, . . . atma:* except for the peculiar *"grupa,"* these are normal Sanskrit words used in theosophy in special extended meanings. Literally, *jīva* = "life, living being"; *linga* = "token, sign; phallus"; *śarīra* = "body, person"; *kāma* = "desire, sexual love"; *rūpa* = "phenomenon, form, figure"; *manas* = "mind, intellect"; *buddhi* = "intelligence, reason"; *ātman* = "soul, self." Rosas: Juan Manuel de Rosas, dictator of Argentina from 1835 to 1852. Mansilla: Lucio Mansilla, nineteenth-century Argentine general and travel writer. Keherpas, Kalep, . . . Limbuz: apparently a variety of elemental or universal principles; the translator has been unable to make firm identifications, or even verify the spellings (though he suspects that "Keherpas" may be Keresaspa, or Garshasp, a hero who will conquer a major evil force in the final days of the world, and that "Archoen[o]" is Archaeus, or Arkhaios, an imaginary being, with astral force, located in the human body, whose functions it regulates). Satan, Lucifer, . . . Baal: various demons (many of them Canaanite deities discredited by

the Hebrews); the only one that may not be presented in a proper English form in the translation is the unidentified "Mabema." Colonel Olcott: H. S. Olcott, who, with Madame Blavatsky, founded the New York chapter of theosophy in 1875.

Poems

From *Azul* **. . .**

"Caupolicán": first published in *La Época* (Santiago), November 11, 1888; then placed as the first of the three "Sonetos áureos" (Golden Sonnets) in the second edition (1890) of *Azul* . . . . The dedicatee was a Cuban poet. Caupolicán (died 1558) led the Araucanian Indians' resistance to the Spanish conquerors of Chile. The sonnet is based on a legend reported in the epic poem *La Araucana* (1569 ff.) by the Spanish poet Alonso de Ercilla: a tree-carrying endurance contest was a prerequisite for being chosen tribal chief (*toqui*).

"Venus": first published in the *Repertorio Salvadoreño* (San Salvador), July 1889; then, as the second of the three "Sonetos áureos" (see "Caupolicán," just above).

"Walt Whitman": no known publication earlier than the second edition of *Azul* . . . , where it appears as the third item in the section "Medallones" (Medallions). The sonnet may have been inspired by José Martí's noteworthy article on Whitman, which appeared in a Mexican periodical in 1887.

From *Prosas profanas*

"'Era un aire suave . . .'": first published in *La Revista Nacional* (Buenos Aires), September 1893; then included in the first edition (1896) of *Prosas profanas*, in the volume's first subdivision, which had the same title as the volume. The opening poem of the volume, this piece owes a great debt to Verlaine's *fête-galante* poems. Terminus: a Roman guardian god of field boundaries. Giambologna: the most common designation of the Flemish sculptor Jean de Boulogne, whose famous Mercury, poised on one foot, dates from 1580. Cypris: Venus (Aphrodite). Omphale: a Lydian queen for the love of whom Herakles donned female garb and plied the spinning wheel. Thyrsis: a conventional shepherdess's name.

"Divagación": first published in *La Nación* (Buenos Aires), December 7, 1894; then included in the first subdivision of the first edition of the volume. Again, we are very close to Verlaine. Clodion:

The French sculptor Claude Michel (1738–1814). Arsène Houssaye: nineteenth-century French art critic and minor novelist. Monsieur Prudhomme: a character, representing the foolish self-importance of the bourgeoisie, created by the cartoonist, playwright, and actor Henry Monnier (1799–1877). Homais: the dull pharmacist in Flaubert's *Madame Bovary* (1857). Cypruses (etc.): locations of major shrines of Aphrodite; the singular of "Amathuntes" is Amathus, the *u* being long (= Greek *ou*). Wolfgang: Mozart? Goethe?? Li Bai: this is the currently most acceptable form of the name of this superb eighth-century Chinese poet (in the past, commonly: Li T'ai-po). Yamagata: a city in northern Japan, far from Kyoto. Handsome king: Solomon; the reference is to the swarthy but comely woman in the Song of Songs (1:5).

"Sonatina": first published in *La Nación* (Buenos Aires), June 17, 1895; then included in the first subdivision of the first edition of the volume. Delicate, musical, and easy to understand, this may be Darío's most frequently anthologized poem—and justifiably so, since it is a perfect introduction to his art. "Butterfly": the *hipsipila* of the original comes from the name of Hypsipyle, a woman loved and abandoned by the argonaut Jason; she became a symbol of the human soul longing for love, and souls were associated with butterflies.

"Blasón": first published in *El Siglo XX* (Madrid), late in 1892. Vinci: Leonardo did a famous painting of Leda and the swan. Ludwig of Bavaria: Ludwig II (1845–1886), enamored of Wagner's characters, including Lohengrin, the knight of the swan.

"Ite, missa est": presumably not published before the first edition of the volume, where it is located in the first subdivision. The words of the title are those with which the officiating priest dismisses the congregation at the end of the Roman Catholic Mass. The poem is a prime example of Darío's almost insolent combination of erotic and religious motifs.

"Coloquio de los centauros": first published in *La Biblioteca* (Buenos Aires), July 1896 (the dedicatee was the director of that monthly); then included in the first edition of the volume as the entire second subdivision. The noble structure of this long piece, its unflagging elegance of diction, its breadth of imagination, and its depth of thought make it very possibly Darío's finest single poem. The poet derived most of the names of his centaurs from Book XII of Ovid's *Metamorphoses*, which recounts their epic battle against the (human) Lapiths at the wedding of Pirithous and Hippodamia, after the centaur Eurytus attempted to rape the bride; the forms of the names in

the translation are in the correct Latin nominative case! Chiron: the chief of the centaurs, he was the wise tutor of Achilles, Jason, and even of the god of medicine, Aesculapius; after being killed by Herakles, Chiron became the constellation Sagittarius. Aeolus: the guardian of the winds; here, he himself acts like a wind, puffing out his cheeks. Ixion: male ancestor (here, father) of the centaurs, whom he begot on Nephele (Cloud). Dejanira: a woman loved by Herakles; he killed the centaur Nessus during an attempted abduction. Anadyomene: "she who rises (from the sea)," that is, Venus (Aphrodite) at the moment of her creation from a body part of the mutilated Uranus. Acheron, Charon: respectively, an underworld (afterlife) river, and the ferryman of the souls of the dead. Caenis and Caeneus: in this myth, which Ovid associates with the battle of centaurs and Lapiths, the woman Caenis was permitted by the god Neptune to change sex, at her urgent request; as a man, she assumed the name Caeneus. Deiphobe: the personal name of the oracular Sibyl who had her grotto at Cumae, near Naples. Pasiphae: a queen of Crete who copulated with a bull and gave birth to the Minotaur. Deucalion (the Greco-Roman Noah) and his wife Pyrrha repopulated the world by throwing stones (which became people) after the universal flood. Atys: there was more than one Atys who had sorrow in forests, but the shepherd loved by the goddess Cybele is most likely the one that Darío intended.

"El poeta pregunta por Stella": first published in *La Tribuna* (Buenos Aires), October 9, 1893; then included in the first edition of the volume, in the third subdivision, "Varia." "Stella" was Darío's poetic name for his first wife, who had died earlier in 1893. Ligeia: the eponymous heroine of Poe's story.

"Sinfonía en gris mayor": information on first publication not located; included in the subdivision "Varia" of the first edition of the volume. The poem has strong reminiscences of Baudelaire, Verlaine, and especially Théophile Gautier, who wrote a celebrated "Symphonie en blanc majeur."

"Verlaine: Responso": first published in *Argentina* (Buenos Aires), January 15, 1896 (seven days after Verlaine's death); then it formed the entire fourth subdivision in the first edition of the volume. Acanthus: a plant used as a funerary offering. Cythera: an island sacred to Aphrodite. The recondite vocabulary of this poem gave some early readers a sort of culture shock; one proclaimed that, in the verse *"Que púberes canéforas te ofrenden el acanto,"* the only word he understood was *"Que"*!

"El reino interior": no publication is known earlier than the first edition of the volume, where it is included in a subdivision with the same title as the poem. Critics have pointed to the influence of Dante Gabriel Rossetti on this piece. The epigraph is from Poe's poem "Ulalume." Domenico Cavalca: an Italian ascetic writer (died 1342). Papemor: an imaginary bird. Bulbul: an Asian songbird, the counterpart of the European nightingale in Persian and Persian-influenced poetry. Sandro: the fifteenth-century Italian painter Botticelli. Satans: the reference is to Verlaine's poem "Crimen Amoris."

"'Ama tu ritmo . . .'": first published in *La Revista Nueva* (Madrid), either August 5 or August 15, 1899; then included in the second edition (1901) of the volume *Prosas profanas*, in the subdivision titled "Ánforas" (Amphoras), or "Las ánforas de Epicuro" (The Amphoras of Epicurus).

"Alma mía": apparently never published before the second edition of the volume, where it is in the subdivision "Ánforas." Triptolemus: the ancient Greek culture hero credited with the invention of agriculture.

"'Yo persigo una forma . . .'": apparently never published before the second edition of the volume, where it is in the subdivision "Ánforas." This poem was the last in the second edition of the volume. In addition to showing the influence of Baudelaire, it is highly reminiscent of the great visionary sonnets of Gérard de Nerval.

From *Cantos de vida y esperanza*

(Note: "Cantos de vida y esperanza" is also the title of the volume's first subdivision, which includes the first 8 selections that follow, through "Marcha triunfal." After its initial publication in 1905, there were no changes to the volume that would affect this anthology.)

"'Yo soy aquel . . .'": first published in *Alma Española* (presumably Madrid, but this is not certain), February 7, 1904. This poem, placed first in the volume, is obviously a continuation of the "Yo . . ." poem that concluded the previous volume, *Prosas profanas*. Galatea: a character in Góngora's major poem "Fábula de Polifemo y Galatea." *Ego sum lux*: the Vulgate text, from John 14:6, actually says "*Ego sum via*" ("I am the *way*"), but it was necessary to keep Darío's word, "light," in the translation because of what follows in the next stanza.

"Salutación del optimista": first published in *La Revista Hispano-Americana* (Madrid), April 1905. The poem had already been recited on March 28 at a meeting of the Spanish-American League. The meter is based on Greco-Roman dactylic hexameters (as in Homer,

Vergil's *Aeneid*, etc.). Two-headed eagles: this refers to the defeat of Russia in its war against Japan.

"Al rey Óscar": first published in *La Ilustración Española y Americana* (Madrid), April 8, 1899. Oscar II, the king of Sweden and Norway, was a man of high culture. Hendaye and Fuenterrabia: the towns on the French and Spanish sides of the common border on the Côte Basque; the latter town appears on current maps as Hondarribia. Segismundo: the hero of Calderón's play *La vida es sueño*. Lepanto: site of a great victory of Spain and her allies over the Turks in 1571. Otumba: site of a victory over the Aztecs in 1520. The symbolic lion and the Cross: this refers to the Swedish royal arms. "After the tempest . . . to the dwelling saddened": this refers to Spain's crushing defeat, loss of face, and loss of colonies in 1898, the year before the king's encouraging words.

"Cyrano en España": first published in *La Vida Literaria* (presumably Madrid [?]), January 28, 1899. This poem was commissioned from Darío on the occasion of the Spanish première of Rostand's 1897 play, which had occurred on January 25 in Madrid, with Cyrano portrayed by Fernando Díaz de Mendoza, conte de Balazote, and Roxane by María Guerrero, Spain's counterpart to her contemporaries Sarah Bernhardt and Eleonora Duse. Clavileño: a wooden horse ridden by Don Quixote, who thinks he's riding in the sky. The castle of the Foolish Virgins: said to be a reference to Gabriele D'Annunzio's novel *Le vergini delle rocce* (The Virgins of the Rocks; 1895). Durandal: Roland's sword in the Old French heroic epics. Tizona: one of the swords wielded by El Cid. Pacheca courtyard: in Madrid; one of the courtyard theaters typical of play performance in Spain's Golden Age, it retained its old name until the early nineteenth century, later becoming the Teatro Español. Tirso: the Golden Age Spanish playwright Tirso de Molina.

"A Roosevelt": first published in *Helios* (Madrid), February 1904. A cautionary address to U.S. President Theodore Roosevelt, who in 1903 had crowed: "I took Panama!" Hugo . . . Grant: this refers either to Hugo's 1872 poem "Le message de Grant" or to remarks made when Grant visited France in 1877. The sun of Argentina . . . and the star of Chile: this refers to emblems on their national flags. "Our America": an appreciative echo of Martí's stirring essay "Nuestra América" (1891). Netzahualcoyotl: a fifteenth-century Aztec ruler. Bacchus: this refers to a legend that the god Bacchus, roaming the world before reaching Greece from India, reached the New World, where the alphabet, the invention of Pan, was then introduced.

Cuauhtemoc: this last Aztec emperor is said to have made his famous remark while undergoing Spanish torture.

"¡Torres de Dios! . . .'": apparently not published before its appearance in the volume.

"Canto de esperanza": apparently not published previously. The Far East: another reference to the Russo-Japanese War. The visionary: St. John on Patmos, reputed author of *Revelation*.

"Marcha triunfal": first published in *La Nación* (Buenos Aires), May 25, 1895. The occasion was a military parade on the Argentine national holiday.

"¿Qué signo haces . . . ?" ("Cisnes" I). This poem and the next three constitute the volume's subdivision "Cisnes" (Swans); the first, third, and fourth were not published before their appearance in the volume. Garcilaso: the Spanish pastoral poet Garcilaso de la Vega (1503–1536). Rodrigo . . . Nuño: Spanish rulers and conquerors of yesteryear; Rodrigo is most likely the Cid; Jaime is Jaime I of Aragon (1208–1276), who recovered Valencia and the Balearic Islands from the Moors; Alfonso was the name of several highly effective medieval kings of Castile and Aragon; Nuño probably refers to the semilegendary mighty warrior Alfonso Nuño of the mid-twelfth century.

"En la muerte de Rafael Núñez" ("Cisnes" II): first published in *La Revista de América* (Buenos Aires), October 1, 1894. Núñez (1825–1894) was a poet who had served as president of Colombia several times; he had referred to Montaigne's famous motto, "*Que sais-je?*," in one of his poems; late in life, he had become religious; hence, the looming Cross of the last stanza.

"Por un momento . . ." ("Cisnes" III). The Dioscuri (the constellation Gemini) are Castor and Pollux, twin sons of Leda and of Zeus, who seduced her in the form of a swan.

"Antes de todo . . ." ("Cisnes" IV). Dioscuri: see just above.

"'La dulzura del ángelus . . .'": first published in *La Revista Hispano-Americana* (Madrid), April 1905. Note: This poem, as well as all the remaining selections from *Cantos de vida y esperanza*, is located in its final subdivision, "Otros poemas" (Other Poems).

"Tarde del trópico": first published in *El Diario de Centroamérica* (Ciudad Guatemala), June 4, 1892. Verlaine's influence is extremely strong.

"Nocturno" ("Quiero expresar . . ."): apparently not published before the volume. Darío refers to death euphemistically (and terrifyingly) as "*Ella*" (She; *muerte* is feminine in Spanish).

"Canción de otoño en primavera": apparently not published before

the volume. The dedicatee, Gregorio Martínez Sierra (1881–1947), was a friend of Darío's, as well as the founder of the Madrid magazine *Helios* to which Darío contributed, and a major playwright.

"Trébol": first published in *La Ilustración Española y Americana* (Madrid), June 15, 1899, on the occasion of the 300th anniversary of Velázquez's birth. Angelica and Medoro, a pair of lovers, were characters in Ludovico Ariosto's *Orlando furioso* (1516), but Góngora wrote a poem about them, too. His "Fábula de Polifemo y Galatea," alluded to in the last line of subsection II, was already mentioned in the opening poem of *Cantos de vida y esperanza*, "'Yo soy aquel . . . .'" The ancient Greek poet Theocritus and the seventeenth-century French painter Poussin also treated the theme of Polyphemus. The expression *"pace estrellas"* in subsection III is a quotation from Góngora's *Soledad* I. *Las Meninas* (The Maids of Honor) is one of Velázquez's greatest paintings.

"Leda": first published in *Guatemala Ilustrada* (Ciudad Guatemala) in its issue for the first half of September 1892.

"'Divina Psiquis . . .'": apparently not published before the volume. Hugo: Victor Hugo discussed the saints in question in his book *William Shakespeare* (1864). Edgar: Poe; the reference is to his poem "Ulalume," which Darío had already (mis)quoted in the epigraph to "El reino interior" in *Prosas profanas*.

"A Phocás el campesino": apparently not published before the volume. The title words were the nickname Darío gave to the second child borne to him by his loyal Spanish mistress Francisca Sánchez. The association came from a story (1895) by the French writer Remy de Gourmont (1858–1915) about a Byzantine emperor raised among shepherds (if the story was based on a historical emperor Phocas, it would almost have to be the ruler of humble origins who died in 610, rather than others in later centuries; in some editions of Darío, "Phocas" has no accent mark—at any rate, the normal Spanish form of the name is "Focas"). The link to Darío's situation is that the baby was tended far from Madrid, in the countryside with Francisca's relatives, making him a "peasant." Born in 1903, the boy died only two years later.

"'¡Carne, celeste carne . . . !'": apparently not published before the volume. The poem is based on a line in Hugo's poem "Le sacre de la Femme" (The Celebration of Woman).

"'En el país de las Alegorías . . .'": apparently not published before the volume.

"Augurios": apparently not published before the volume. The

dedicatee, Eugenio Días Romero (1877–1927), was an Argentine *modernista* poet.

"Melancolía": first published in *El Cojo Ilustrado* (Caracas, Venezuela), December 1, 1905. Domingo Bolívar was a painter (more likely Venezuelan than Colombian, as Darío later remembered him to be) who killed himself in 1903; thus, he already "possessed light."

"Nocturno" ("Los que auscultasteis . . ."): apparently not published before the volume. The dedicatee, Mariano de Cavia (1855–1920), was a Spanish journalist.

"Letanía de nuestro señor don Quijote": apparently not published before the volume. The poem was written for the celebration, at the Ateneo of Madrid, on May 13, 1905, of the 300th anniversary of the publication of Part One of *Don Quixote*. The dedicatee, Francisco Navarro Ledesma (1869–1905), was an eminent literary critic. The Orpheus pun is impossible to translate; the term *Orphéon* for a choral society came from a school of vocal music by that name founded in Paris in 1833. *Pro nobis ora:* Latin for "pray for us." Clavileño: see notes to "Cyrano en España." Segismundo: see notes to "Al rey Óscar."

"Lo fatal": apparently not published before *Cantos de vida y esperanza,* in which it is the final poem. The dedicatee, René Pérez Mascayano, was a South American composer.

From *El canto errante*

"Momotombo": first published in *Blanco y Negro* (Madrid), October 17, 1907; then placed in the volume's subdivision "Intensidad." The epigraph is from Canto XXVII of Hugo's *La légende des siècles*. Squier (not Squire!): the preeminent U.S. archeologist Ephraim George Squier (1821–1888). Oviedo: most likely, Gonzalo Fernández de Oviedo (1478–1577), author of *Summary of the Natural and General History of the Indies* (1526). Gómara (with an accent): most likely, Francisco López de Gómara (1512–1572), author of *The History of the Indies and Conquest of Mexico* (1552).

"Salutación al águila": first published in *La Nación* (Buenos Aires), March 10, 1906; then placed in the subdivision "Intensidad." Written on the occasion of the Third Interamerican Conference, held in Rio in 1906, to which Darío was a Nicaraguan delegate. The author of the epigraph was Antônio de Fontoura Xavier, a Brazilian poet and Brazilian consul in New York. Palenque: site of spectacular Mayan ruins in Mexico.

"¡Eheu!": first published in *El Renacimiento* (Madrid), October

1907; then placed in the subdivision "Ensueño" (Dream). The setting is Majorca, where Darío spent the winter of 1906–07. The Latin title, meaning "Alas!," may possibly refer to a famous ode by Horace, beginning with that word, which laments the all-too-rapid passing of time.

"Nocturno" ("Silencio de la noche . . ."): first published in *El Renacimiento* (Madrid), June 1907; then placed in the subdivision "Lira alerta" (Alert Lyre).

"Epístola": apparently not published prior to the volume, where it is placed in the subdivision "Lira alerta." Many serious poets have found it beneficial to "unwind" in poetic letters to friends. In this poem (which may have been a response to an epistle by the Argentine Lugones, an old friend of Darío's and a leading *modernista* [1874–1938]), the open-ended structure, the easygoing versification, the playful rhymes, and the frank self-evaluation leave us wishing that Darío had written many more of the kind. The second half of the first line, and the entire second line, are in French, as are the words *surmenage, sauvage,* and *poire* (disguised as Spanish *pera*) later on in the poem. Rodenbach: the Belgian Symbolist poet Georges Rodenbach (1855–1898). Rio: Darío went there for the Interamerican Conference in 1906 (see "Salutación al águila," three poems above). *Arcades ambo:* a Latin phrase meaning literally "[we are] both from Arcadia"; the translation on page 209 of this volume conveys the proper connotation. Tijuca: a lushly tropical suburb of Rio; presumably this was the specific site of the Conference. Nabuco: Joaquim Nabuco de Araújo (1849–1910), a Brazilian statesman and writer who was appointed ambassador to the United States in 1905; he was in favor of cooperation among all American nations. Garcilaso: see notes to "¿Qué signo haces . . . ?" Root: Elihu Root, Theodore Roosevelt's secretary of state, who improved U.S. relations with Latin America after the forced creation of Panama. The phrases *la terra dels foners* and *bon di tengui* are in Catalan, which is spoken on Majorca. Mossen Cinto: "Mister 'Cynth," the nickname of endearment of the poet Jacinto Verdaguer (1845–1902), who was largely responsible for the renaissance of Catalan as a literary language. Coppée: the popular nineteenth-century poet François Coppée. Madame Noailles and Francis Jammes: Anna, contesse de Noailles, and Jammes were, like Coppée, highly successful and widely read French minor poets of the day. Ramón Lull (or Llull; ca. 1232–ca. 1315): possibly the greatest medieval Catalan author—a poet, novelist, philosopher, theologian, mathematician, and scientist. Jean Orth: pseudonym assumed by the

disillusioned Austrian archduke Johann Salvator (born 1852), who re-
nounced his titles in 1889 and sailed for South America; his where-
abouts (if he was still alive) remained a mystery, and a number of
people claimed to have "spotted" him. Santiago Rusiñol: Catalan
painter (1861–1931). Aurore Dupin: the real name of George Sand.
Kant and the donkey: see notes to the story "El sátiro sordo."

   "Balada en honor de las musas de carne y hueso": previous publi-
cation, if any, not found by translator; located in the volume's subdivi-
sion "Lira alerta." On the dedicatee, see notes to "Canción de otoño
en primavera" in *Cantos de vida y esperanza*. The poem is in the form
of the medieval French *ballade*, as perfected by Villon (and imitated
by Rostand in Cyrano), with its four-line tag (*envoi*) addressed directly
to the dedicatee. Armida: the mighty enchantress in Tasso's
Gerusalemme liberata (Jerusalem Delivered; 1575). Orlando's mount:
probably refers to the hippogriff ridden by Ruggiero in Ariosto's
Orlando furioso (1516). Clio (etc.): names of the Greek Muses; Clio is
the muse of history; Euterpe, of music; Thalia, of comedy;
Melpomene, of tragedy; Terpsichore, of dance; Erato, of lyric poetry;
Polyhymnia, of singing and rhetoric; Calliope, of epic poetry; and
Urania, of astronomy.

From *Poema del otoño*

"Poema del otoño": first published in *El Cojo Ilustrado* (Caracas)
sometime in 1908; then it constituted the entire first subdivision of
the 1910 volume. The translator has been unable to identify Zingua,
queen of Angola, any more closely. Phryne: a fourth-century B.C.
Athenian courtesan who modeled for her lover, the sculptor
Praxiteles, *not* (fifth-century) Phidias.

Cuentos
Stories

El Rey Burgués

(Cuento alegre)

¡Amigo! El cielo está opaco, el aire frío, el día triste. Un cuento alegre . . . , así como para distraer las brumosas y grises melancolías, helo aquí:

Había en una ciudad inmensa y brillante un rey muy poderoso que tenía trajes caprichosos y ricos, esclavas desnudas, blancas y negras, caballos de largas crines, armas flamantísimas, galgos rápidos y monteros con cuernos de bronce, que llenaban el viento con sus fanfarrias. ¿Era un rey poeta? No, amigo mío: era el Rey Burgués.

Era muy aficionado a las artes el soberano, y favorecía con gran largueza a sus músicos, a sus hacedores de ditirambos, pintores, escultores, boticarios, barberos y maestros de esgrima.

Cuando iba a la floresta, junto al corzo o jabalí herido y sangriento, hacía improvisar a sus profesores de retórica canciones alusivas; los criados llenaban las copas de vino de oro que hierve, y las mujeres batían palmas con movimientos rítmicos y gallardos. Era un rey sol, en su Babilonia llena de músicas, de carcajadas y de ruido de festín. Cuando se hastiaba de la ciudad bullente iba de caza atronando el bosque con sus tropeles, y hacía salir de sus nidos a las aves asustadas, y el vocerío repercutía en lo más escondido de las cavernas. Los perros de patas elásticas iban rompiendo la maleza en la carrera, y los cazadores, inclinados sobre el pescuezo de los caballos, hacían ondear los mantos purpúreos y llevaban las caras encendidas y las cabelleras al viento.

The Bourgeois King

(A Merry Tale)

Friend! The sky is leaden, the air cold, the day sad. A merry tale . . .
one that will dispel foggy, gray melancholy . . . here it is:

In a vast, brilliant city there lived a very mighty king who possessed
fanciful, rich clothing, nude slave-girls both white and black, long-
maned horses, brightly gleaming weapons,[1] swift hunting hounds, and
huntsmen with bronze horns who filled the breeze with their fanfares.
Was he a poet king? No, my friend: he was the Bourgeois King.

The sovereign was very fond of the arts, and was extremely gener-
ous to his musicians, his makers of dithyrambs, painters, sculptors,
pharmacists, barbers, and fencing masters.
When he went to the forest, alongside the stricken roebuck or boar
he had his professors of rhetoric improvise songs on the subject; his
servants would fill the goblets with wine like seething gold, and the
women would clap hands with rhythmic, elegant movements. He was
a sun king, in his Babylon filled with music, laughter, and festive
sounds. Whenever he tired of the bustle of the city, he went hunting,
deafening the woods with his throngs of followers, making the fright-
ened birds leave their nests, while their shouts echoed in the remotest
recesses of the caves. The dogs on their springy paws went about
trampling the underbrush in their wild race, and the huntsmen, bent
over their horses' necks, made their purple capes billow out, with
flushed faces and their hair streaming in the wind.

---

[1]Could also be construed as: "a brand-new coat-of-arms."

El rey tenía un palacio soberbio donde había acumulado riquezas y objetos de arte maravillosos. Llegaba a él por entre grupos de lilas y extensos estanques, siendo saludado por los cisnes de cuellos blancos antes que por los lacayos estirados. Buen gusto. Subía por una escalera llena de columnas de alabastro y de esmaragdina, que tenía a los dos lados leones de mármol, como los de los tronos salomónicos. Refinamiento. A más de los cisnes, tenía una vasta pajarera, como amante de la armonía, del arrullo, del trino; y cerca de ella iba a ensanchar su espíritu, leyendo novelas de M. Ohnet, o bellos libros sobre cuestiones gramaticales, o críticas hermosillescas. Eso sí, defensor acérrimo de la corrección académica en letras y del modo lamido en artes; alma sublime, amante de la lija y de la ortografía.

—¡Japonerías! ¡Chinerías! Por lujo y nada más.

Bien podía darse el placer de un salón digno del gusto de un Goncourt y de los millones de un Creso; quimeras de bronce con las fauces abiertas y las colas enroscadas, en grupos fantásticos y maravillosos; lacas de Kioto con incrustaciones de hojas y ramas de una flora monstruosa, y animales de una fauna desconocida; mariposas de raros abanicos junto a las paredes; peces y gallos de colores; máscaras de gestos infernales y con ojos como si fuesen vivos; partesanas de hojas antiquísimas y empuñaduras con dragones devorando flores de loto; y en conchas de huevo, túnicas de seda amarilla como tejidas con hilos de araña, sembradas de garzas rojas y de verdes matas de arroz; y tibores, porcelanas de muchos siglos, de aquellas en que hay guerreros tártaros con una piel que les cubre los riñones y que llevan arcos estirados y manojos de flechas.

Por lo demás, había el salón griego lleno de mármoles: diosas, musas, ninfas y sátiros; el salón de los tiempos galantes, con cuadros del gran Watteau y de Chardin: dos, tres, cuatro, ¡cuántos salones!

Y Mecenas se paseaba por todos, con la cara inundada de cierta majestad, el vientre feliz y la corona en la cabeza, como un rey de naipe.

Un día le llevaron una rara especie de hombre ante su trono, donde se hallaba rodeado de cortesanos, de retóricos y de maestros de equitación y de baile.

—¿Qué es esto? —preguntó.

—Señor, es un poeta.

The king owned a magnificent palace, in which he had amassed riches and marvelous art objects. He would arrive there passing between clumps of lilacs and wide pools, being greeted by the white-necked swans even before the haughty lackeys greeted him. Good taste. He would climb a flight of stairs filled with columns of alabaster and smaragdite, which had marble lions at its two sides, like the ones on Solomon's thrones. Refinement. Besides the swans, he had a huge aviary, since he loved harmony, cooing, warbling; near it, he would expand his spirit, reading novels by Monsieur Ohnet, or beautiful books on questions of grammar, or literary criticism by Hermosilla. Yes, indeed, he was a staunch defender of academic correctness in literature and an excessively fastidious style in the arts; a sublime soul, a lover of polishing with sandpaper, and of proper spelling.

"Japonaiserie! Chinoiserie! Give me luxury, and that's all!"

He was well able to indulge himself in a salon worthy of the taste of a Goncourt and the millions of a Croesus: bronze chimeras with open jaws and coiled tails, in fantastic, wondrous groupings; Kyoto lacquers inlaid with the leaves and branches of a monstrous flora, and animals of an unknown fauna; butterfly arrangements of rare fans on the walls; multicolored fish and cockerels; masks with infernal expressions and seemingly living eyes; partizans with age-old blades and handles with dragons that were devouring lotus blossoms; and, in eggshells, tunics of yellow silk as if woven from cobwebs, with a repeat pattern of red herons and green rice paddies; and tall Oriental vases, porcelains many centuries old, the type that depict Tartar warriors, wearing an animal skin over their loins and carrying tautened bows and handfuls of arrows.

In addition, there was the Greek salon, filled with marble statues: goddesses, muses, nymphs, and satyrs; the salon of the gallant era, with paintings by the great Watteau and by Chardin; two, three, four, any number of salons!

And Maecenas would walk through all of them, his face bathed in a certain majesty, his stomach sated and his crown on his head, like the king in a deck of cards.

One day a rare breed of man was brought before his throne, where he sat surrounded by courtiers, rhetoricians, and riding and dancing masters.

"What is this?" he asked.

"Highness, it's a poet."

El rey tenía cisnes en el estanque, canarios, gorriones, sinsontes en la pajarera; un poeta era algo nuevo y extraño.

—Dejadle aquí.

Y el poeta:

—Señor, no he comido.

Y el rey:

Habla y comerás.

Comenzó:

—Señor, ha tiempo que yo canto el verbo del porvenir. He tenido mis alas al huracán, he nacido en el tiempo de la aurora; busco la raza escogida que debe inspirar, con el himno en la boca y la lira en la mano, la salida del gran sol. He abandonado la inspiración de la ciudad malsana, la alcoba llena de perfumes, la musa de carne que llena el alma de pequeñez y el rostro de polvos de arroz. He roto el arpa adulona de las cuerdas débiles contra las copas de Bohemia y las jarras donde espumea el vino que embriaga sin dar fortaleza; he arrojado el manto que me hacía parecer histrión o mujer, y he vestido de modo salvaje y espléndido; mi harapo es de púrpura. He ido a la selva, donde he quedado vigoroso y ahíto de leche fecunda y licor de nueva vida; y en la ribera del mar áspero, sacudiendo la cabeza bajo la fuerte y negra tempestad, como un ángel soberbio, o como un semidiós olímpico, he ensayado el yambo dando al olvido el madrigal.

He acariciado a la gran Naturaleza, y he buscado el calor ideal, el verso que está en el astro en el fondo del cielo, y el que está en la perla en lo profundo del océano. ¡He querido ser pujante! Porque viene el tiempo de las grandes revoluciones, con un Mesías todo luz, todo agitación y potencia, y es preciso recibir su espíritu con el poema que sea arco triunfal, de estrofas de acero, de estrofas de oro, de estrofas de amor.

¡Señor, el arte no está en los fríos envoltorios de mármol, ni en los cuadros lamidos; ni en el excelente señor Ohnet! ¡Señor! El arte no viste pantalones, ni habla burgués, ni pone los puntos en todas las íes. Él es augusto, tiene mantos de oro, o de llamas, o anda desnudo, y amasa la greda con fiebre, y pinta con luz, y es opulento, y da golpes de ala como las águilas o zarpazos como los leones. Señor, entre un Apolo y un ganso, preferid el Apolo, aunque el uno sea de tierra cocida y el otro de marfil.

¡Oh la poesía!

¡Y bien! Los ritmos se prostituyen, se cantan los lunares de las

   The king possessed swans in his pool, canaries, sparrows, mocking-
birds in his aviary; a poet was something new and strange.
   "Leave him here."
   And the poet said:
   "Highness, I haven't eaten."
   And the king said:
   "Speak and you'll eat."
   He began:

   "Highness, for some time now I've been singing the words of the fu-
ture. I've spread my wings in the hurricane, I was born at the time of
dawning; I seek the chosen race which, a hymn on its lips and a lyre in
its hands, is to inspire the rising of the great sun. I have abandoned the
inspiration of the unhealthful city, the bedroom filled with perfumes,
the flesh-and-blood muse who fills one's soul with pettiness and one's
face with rice powder. I have broken the groveling, weak-stringed harp
against the Bohemian goblets and the pitchers of foaming wine that in-
toxicates without giving fortitude; I have cast away the mantle that
made me resemble an actor or a woman, and I have dressed in a wild,
splendid way; my tatters are of purple. I have gone to the forest, where
I have become vigorous, satiated with rich milk and the fluid of new
life; and on the shore of the rugged sea, shaking my head in the strong,
dark tempest, like a haughty angel or an Olympian demigod, I have es-
sayed the iamb of satire, while abandoning the ingratiating madrigal.
   "I have caressed great Nature, and I have sought the heat of the
Idea, the verses to be found in the heavenly bodies in the highest
reaches of the sky, and in the pearl at the bottom of the sea. I have
tried to be forceful! Because the era of great revolutions is at hand,
with a Messiah who is all light, all restlessness and potency, and his
spirit must be welcomed with a poem that is a triumphal arch, with
strophes of steel, strophes of gold, strophes of love.
   "Highness, art is not contained in cold marble claddings, or in finicky
paintings, or in the excellent Mister Ohnet! Highness! Art doesn't wear
trousers, use bourgeois vocabulary, or dot every *i*. It is an august figure
that either wears mantles of gold or flame, or else goes nude; it kneads
cleansing fuller's earth feverishly, it paints with light, it is opulent, and
strikes you with its wings as eagles do, or with its paws as lions do.
Highness, between an Apollo and a goose, prefer the Apollo, even if one
of them is made of terra-cotta and the other of ivory.
   "O poetry!
   "Well, then! Rhythms are being prostituted, people write about

mujeres y se fabrican jarabes poéticos. Además, señor, el zapatero critica mis endecasílabos, y el señor profesor de farmacia pone puntos y comas a mi inspiración. Señor, ¡y vos les autorizáis todo esto! . . . El ideal, el ideal . . .

El rey interrumpió:

—Ya habéis oído. ¿Qué hacer?

Y un filósofo al uso:

—Si lo permitís, señor, puede ganarse la comida con una caja de música; podemos colocarla en el jardín, cerca de los cisnes, para cuando os paseéis.

—Sí —dijo el rey; y dirigiéndose al poeta—: Daréis vueltas a un manubrio. Cerraréis la boca. Haréis sonar una caja de música que toca valses, cuadrillas y galopas, como no prefiráis moriros de hambre. Pieza de música por pedazo de pan. Nada de jerigonzas, ni de ideales. Id.

Y desde aquel día pudo verse, a la orilla del estanque de los cisnes, al poeta, tiriririn, tiriririn . . . ¡avergonzado a las miradas del gran sol! ¿Pasaba el rey por las cercanías? Tiriririn, tiriririn . . . ¿Había que llenar el estómago? ¡Tiriririn! Todo entre las burlas de los pájaros libres que llegaban a beber el rocío en las lilas floridas; entre el zumbido de las abejas que le picaban el rostro y le llenaban los ojos de lágrimas . . . , ¡lágrimas amargas que rodaban por sus mejillas y que caían a la tierra negra!

Y llegó el invierno, y el pobre sintió frío en el cuerpo y en el alma. Y su cerebro estaba como petrificado, y los grandes himnos estaban en el olvido, y el poeta de la montaña coronada de águilas no era sino un pobre diablo que daba vueltas al manubrio: ¡tiriririn!

Y cuando cayó la nieve se olvidaron de él el rey y sus vasallos: a los pájaros se les abrigó, y a él se le dejó al aire glacial que le mordía las carnes y le azotaba el rostro.

Y una noche en que caía de lo alto la lluvia blanca de plumillas cristalizadas, en el palacio había festín, y la luz de las arañas reía alegre sobre los mármoles, sobre el oro y sobre las túnicas de los mandarines de las viejas porcelanas. Y se aplaudían hasta la locura los brindis del señor profesor de retórica, cuajados de dáctilos, de anapestos y de pirriquios, mientras en las copas cristalinas hervía el champaña con su burbujeo luminoso y fugaz. ¡Noche de invierno, noche de fiesta! ¡Y el infeliz, cubierto de nieve, cerca del estanque, daba vueltas al manubrio para calentarse, tembloroso y aterido, insultado por el cierzo, bajo la blancura implacable y helada en la noche sombría, haciendo resonar entre los árboles sin hojas la música loca de

women's moles, and poetic syrups are being manufactured. What's more, Highness, the cobbler criticizes my hendecasyllables, and the professor of pharmacy adds periods and commas to my inspiration. And, Highness, you authorize them to do all that! . . . The ideal, the ideal . . ."

The king interrupted:

"You've all heard him. What's to be done?"

And a philosopher said, as customary:

"If you permit it, Highness, he can earn his food with a barrel organ; we can place it in the garden, near the swans, for the times when you stroll by there."

"Yes," said the king, and, addressing the poet: "You'll turn a crank. You'll shut your mouth. You'll operate a barrel organ that plays waltzes, quadrilles, and galops, unless you prefer to die of hunger. A piece of music for a chunk of bread. No gibberish, no talk of ideals. Go."

And from that day on, the poet could be seen at the edge of the swans' pool, deedle-deedle-dum, deedle-deedle-dum . . . ashamed to have the great sun behold him! If the king strolled nearby: deedle-deedle-dum, deedle-deedle-dum . . . If he had to fill his belly: deedle-deedle-dum! All this amid the mockery of the free birds that came to drink the dew from the lilac blossoms; amid the buzzing of the bees that stung his face and made his eyes fill with tears . . . bitter tears that rolled down his cheeks and fell upon the black earth!

And winter came, and the poor man felt the cold in his body and soul. And his brain seemed to have turned to stone, and the great hymns were forgotten, and the poet of the eagle-crowned mountain was nothing but a poor devil turning the crank: deedle-deedle-dum!

And when the snow fell, the king and his vassals forgot about him; he gave shelter to the birds, but him he left in the freezing air that nipped his flesh and lashed his face.

And one night when the white shower of little crystal feathers was falling from above, there was a feast in the palace, and the light from the chandeliers laughed merrily over the marble, the gold, and the tunics of the mandarins of antique porcelain. And there was applause bordering on madness for the toasts given by the professor of rhetoric, chock-full of dactyls, anapests, and pyrrhics, while the champagne frothed in the crystal goblets with its luminous, fleeting bubbles. A winter night, a festive night! And the unhappy man, covered with snow, near the pool, kept turning the crank to get warm; he was shivering, perishing with the cold, buffeted by the north wind, beneath the implacable, frozen whiteness in that dark night, making the mad

las galopas y cuadrillas; y se quedó muerto, pensando en que nacería
el sol del día venidero, y con él el ideal . . . y en que el arte no vestiría
pantalones, sino manto de llamas o de oro . . . Hasta que al día si-
guiente lo hallaron el rey y sus cortesanos, al pobre diablo de poeta,
como un gorrión que mata el hielo, con una sonrisa amarga en los
labios, y todavía con la mano en el manubrio.

—¡Oh, mi amigo! El cielo está opaco, el aire frío, el día triste.
Flotan brumosas y grises melancolías . . .
Pero ¡cuánto calienta el alma una frase, un apretón de manos a
tiempo! Hasta la vista.

El sátiro sordo

(Cuento griego)

Habitaba cerca del Olimpo un sátiro, y era el viejo rey de su selva. Los
dioses le habían dicho: «Goza, el bosque es tuyo; sé un feliz bribón,
persigue ninfas y suena tu flauta.» El sátiro se divertía.

Un día que el padre Apolo estaba tañendo la divina lira, el sátiro
salió de sus dominios y fue osado a subir el sacro monte y sorpren-
der al dios crinado. Éste le castigó, tornándole sordo como una roca.
En balde de las espesuras de la selva llena de pájaros se derramaban
los trinos y emergían los arrullos. El sátiro no oía nada. Filomela lle-
gaba a cantarle, sobre su cabeza enmarañada y coronada de pám-
panos, canciones que hacían detenerse los arroyos y enrojecerse las
rosas pálidas. Él permanecía impasible, o lanzaba sus carcajadas sal-
vajes, y saltaba lascivo y alegre cuando percibía por el ramaje lleno
de brechas alguna cadera blanca y rotunda que acariciaba el sol con
su luz rubia. Todos los animales le rodeaban como a un amo a quien
se obedece.
A su vista, para distraerle, danzaban coros de bacantes encendidas
en su fiebre loca, y acompañaban la armonía, cerca de él, faunos ado-
lescentes, como hermosos efebos, que le acariciaban reverentemente
con su sonrisa; y aunque no escuchaba ninguna voz, ni el ruido de los
crótalos, gozaba de distintas maneras. Así pasaba la vida de este rey
barbudo, que tenía patas de cabra.

music of the galops and quadrilles resound amid the leafless trees; and he finally died, thinking that the sun of the coming day would rise, and with it the Ideal . . . and that art would no longer wear trousers but a mantle of flames or of gold. . . . Until, on the following day, the king and his courtiers found the poor devil of a poet, like a sparrow killed by the frost, a bitter smile on his lips, and his hand still on the crank.

—Oh, my friend! The sky is leaden, the air cold, the day sad. Foggy, gray melancholy is afloat. . . .

But, how an opportune phrase or handshake warms the soul! So long!

The Deaf Satyr

(A Greek Tale)

Near Olympus there lived a satyr, and he was the old king of his forest. The gods had told him: "Enjoy yourself, the woods are yours; be a jolly rogue, pursue nymphs, and play your flute." The satyr was having a good time.

One day when Father Apollo was playing his sacred lyre, the satyr left his own territory and was emboldened to climb the holy mountain and take the long-haired god by surprise. The god punished him by making him deaf as a post. It was in vain that, in the dense, bird-filled forest, warbling was poured forth and cooings were uttered. The satyr couldn't hear a thing. Philomel would come to sing to him, perched above his tousled, vineleaf-crowned head, songs that made the brooks stand still and the pale roses turn red. He remained unaffected, or emitted his wild guffaws, and leaped lustfully and happily whenever he caught sight, through the gap-filled branches, of some white, rounded hip that the sun caressed with its blond light. All the animals encircled him like a master to be obeyed.

When he appeared, in order to divert him, choruses of bacchantes blazing with their mad fever would dance, and, near him, that harmony would be accompanied by teenage Fauns, like handsome ephebes, who caressed him reverently with their smiles; and, even though he couldn't hear any voice, or the clicking of their castanets, he would derive pleasure in various ways. Thus was spent the life of this bearded, goat-footed king.

Era sátiro caprichoso.

Tenía dos consejeros áulicos: una alondra y un asno. La primera perdió su prestigio cuando el sátiro se volvió sordo. Antes, si cansado de su lascivia soplaba su flauta dulcemente, la alondra le acompañaba. Después en su gran bosque, donde no oía ni la voz del olímpico trueno, el paciente animal de las largas orejas le servía para cabalgar, en tanto que la alondra, en los apogeos del alba, se le iba de las manos, cantando camino de los cielos.

La selva era enorme. De ella tocaba a la alondra la cumbre; al asno, el pasto. La alondra era saludada por los primeros rayos de la aurora, bebía rocío en los retoños; despertaba al roble diciéndole: «Viejo roble, despiértate.» Se deleitaba con un beso del sol; era amada por el lucero de la mañana. Y el hondo azul, tan grande, sabía que ella, tan chica, existía bajo su inmensidad. El asno (aunque entonces no había conversado con Kant) era experto en filosofía, según el decir común. El sátiro, que le veía ramonear en la pastura, moviendo las orejas con aire grave, tenía alta idea de tal pensador. En aquellos días el asno no tenía como hoy tan larga fama. Moviendo sus mandíbulas, no se habría imaginado que escribiesen en su loa Daniel Heinsius, en latín; Passerat, Buffon y el gran Hugo, en francés; Posada y mi amigo el doctor Valderrama, en español.

Él, pacienzudo, si le picaban las moscas, las espantaba con el rabo, daba coces de cuando en cuando y lanzaba bajo la bóveda del bosque el acorde extraño de su garganta. Y era mimado allí. Al dormir su siesta sobre la tierra negra y amable, le daban su olor las hierbas y las flores. Y los grandes árboles inclinaban sus follajes para hacerle sombra.

Por aquellos días, Orfeo, poeta, espantado de la miseria de los hombres, pensó huir a los bosques, donde los troncos y las piedras le comprenderían y escucharían con éxtasis, y donde él podría temblar de armonía y fuego de amor y de vida al sonar de su instrumento.

Cuando Orfeo tañía su lira había sonrisa en el rostro apolíneo. Deméter sentía gozo. Las palmeras derramaban su polen, las semillas reventaban, los leones movían blandamente su crin. Una vez voló un clavel de su tallo hecho mariposa roja, y una estrella descendió fascinada y se tornó flor de lis.

¿Qué selva mejor que la del sátiro, a quien él encantaría, donde sería tenido como un semidiós; selva toda alegría y danza, belleza y lujuria; donde ninfas y bacantes eran siempre acariciadas y siempre

He was a capricious satyr.

He had two royal counselors: a lark and a donkey. The first of these lost its authority when the satyr became deaf. Formerly, whenever he was exhausted by his lust and blew softly into his flute, the lark would accompany him. Afterward, in his great forest, where he heard not even the sound of the thunder from Olympus, the patient animal with long ears served him as a mount, while the lark, at the summit of the dawn, would fly out of his hands and sing as it headed skyward.

The forest was huge. Its treetops belonged to the lark, its grazing land to the donkey. The lark was greeted by the first rays of daybreak, and drank dew from the sprouting shoots; it used to awaken the oak with the words: "Old oak, wake up." It was delighted by a kiss from the sun; it was loved by the morning star. And the deep blue sky, which was so vast, knew that the lark, which was so small, existed beneath its immensity. The donkey (although at that time it hadn't conversed with Kant) was an expert in philosophy, according to common report. The satyr, watching it browse in the pasture, moving its ears gravely, had great respect for such a thinker. In those days the donkey wasn't as widely recognized as it is today. As it moved its jaws, it would never have imagined that things would be written in its praise by Daniel Heinsius in Latin; Passerat, Buffon, and the great Hugo in French; Posada and my friend Dr. Valderrama in Spanish.

If that patient beast was bitten by flies, it would scare them off with its tail; it would kick out from time to time, and would utter its strange vocal sound beneath the forest vault. And it was pampered there. When it took its nap on the friendly black earth, the grasses and flowers would send it their fragrance. And the tall trees would bend their foliage over it to shade it.

At that time the poet Orpheus, alarmed by the pettiness of mankind, decided to escape into the woods, where the trees and stones would understand him and listen to him in rapture, and where he would be able to tremble with harmony and the flame of love and life as he played his instrument.

When Orpheus used to play his lyre, there was a smile on Apollo's face. Demeter felt joy. The palm trees would spread their pollen, seeds would burst open, lions would softly shake their manes. Once a carnation turned into a red butterfly and flew off its stem, and a fascinated star came down and became a fleur-de-lis.

What better forest than the one belonging to the satyr, whom he would charm, where he would be treated like a demigod; a forest that was all gladness and dance, beauty and lust; where nymphs and bacchantes were

vírgenes; donde el rey caprípedo bailaba delante de sus faunos beodos y haciendo gestos como Sileno?

Fue con su corona de laurel, su lira, su frente de poeta orgulloso, erguido y radiante.
Llegó hasta donde estaba el sátiro velludo y montaraz, y para pedirle hospitalidad, cantó. Cantó del gran Jove, de Eros y de Afrodita, de los centauros gallardos y de las bacantes ardientes; cantó la copa de Dionisio, y el tirso que hiere el aire alegre y al Pan Emperador de las montañas, Soberano de los bosques, dios sátiro que también sabía cantar. Cantó de las intimidades del aire y de la tierra, gran madre. Así explicó la melodía de un arpa eólica, el susurrro de una arboleda, el ruido de un tronco de caracol y las notas armónicas que brotan de una siringa. Cantó del verso que baja del cielo y place a los dioses, del que acompaña el bárbitos en la oda y el tímpano en el peán. Cantó los senos de nieve tibia y las copas del oro labrado, y el buche del pájaro y la gloria del sol.
Y desde el principio del cántico brilló la luz con más fulgores. Los enormes troncos se conmovieron, y hubo rosas que se deshojaron y lirios que se inclinaron lánguidamente como en un dulce desmayo. Porque Orfeo hacía gemir los leones y llorar los guijarros con la música de su lira rítmica. Las bacantes más furiosas habían callado y le oían como en un sueño. Una náyade virgen a quien nunca ni una sola mirada del sátiro había profanado, se acercó tímida al cantor y le dijo:
—Yo te amo.
Filomela había volado a posarse en la lira como la paloma anacreóntica. No hubo más eco que la voz de Orfeo. Naturaleza sentía el himno. Venus, que pasaba por las cercanías, preguntó de lejos con su divina voz:
—¿Estáis aquí, acaso, Apolo?
Y en toda aquella inmensidad de maravillosa armonía, el único que no oía nada era el sátiro sordo.
Cuando el poeta concluyó, dijo a éste:
—¿Os place mi canto? Si es así me quedaré con vos en la selva.
El sátiro dirigió una mirada a sus dos consejeros. Era preciso que ellos resolviesen lo que no podía comprender él. Aquella mirada pedía una opinión.

—Señor —dijo la alondra, esforzándose en producir la voz más fuerte de su buche—, quédese quien así ha cantado con nosotros. He

always caressed and always remained virgins; where the goat-footed king danced in front of his drunken Fauns, who made faces like Silenus?

He went there with his laurel wreath, his lyre, his proud poet's brow erect and radiant.

He came all the way up to the shaggy, savage satyr, and, in order to ask him for hospitality, he sang. He sang of great Zeus, Eros, and Aphrodite, about the elegant centaurs and the ardent bacchantes; he sang of Dionysus's goblet and the thyrsus that strikes both the happy air and Pan, emperor of the mountains, sovereign of the forests, a satyr god who also knew how to sing. He sang of the intimate relations between the air and the earth, the great mother. In that way he explained the melody of an Aeolian harp, the murmuring of a copse of trees, the sound of a truncated seashell, and the harmonious notes that issue from a reed flute. He sang of the verse that descends from heaven and pleases the gods, of the one that the barbitos accompanies in an ode, and the tympanum in a paean. He sang of warm snowy breasts and chased gold goblets, and the throats of songbirds and the glory of the sun.

And from the beginning of his canticle, the light shone with greater brightness. The enormous tree trunks were stirred, and there were roses that shed their petals and lilies that stooped languidly as if in a gentle swoon. Because Orpheus used to make lions moan and pebbles weep with the music of his rhythmic lyre. The most furious bacchantes had fallen silent and were listening to him as if lost in dreams. A virgin naiad who had never been sullied by even a single glance of the satyr, approached the singer timidly and said:

"I love you."

Philomel had flown down and perched on the lyre as the dove did in Anacreon's poem. There was no echo besides Orpheus's voice. Nature felt his hymn. Aphrodite, who was passing nearby, asked from the distance with her divine voice:

"Apollo, are you here by any chance?"

And in all that immensity of marvelous harmony, the only one who heard nothing was the deaf satyr.

When the poet was done, he asked him:

"Do you like my singing? If you do, I'll remain here in the forest with you."

The satyr looked at his two counselors. They had to resolve that which he was unable to understand. That glance solicited a judgment.

"Highness," said the lark, straining to produce the loudest volume of

aquí que su lira es bella y potente. Te ha ofrecido la grandeza y la luz rara que hoy se ha visto en tu selva. Te ha dado su armonía. Señor, yo sé de estas cosas. Cuando viene el alba desnuda y se despierta el mundo, yo me remonto a los profundos cielos y vierto desde la altura las perlas invisibles de mis trinos, y es el regocijo del espacio. Pues yo te digo que Orfeo ha cantado bien, y es un elegido de los dioses. Su música embriagó el bosque entero. Las águilas se han acercado a revolar sobre nuestras cabezas, los arbustos floridos han agitado suavemente sus incensarios misteriosos, las abejas han dejado sus celdillas para venir a escuchar. En cuanto a mí, ¡oh señor!, si yo estuviese en lugar tuyo, le daría mi guirnalda de pámpanos y mi tirso. Existen dos potencias: la real y la ideal. Lo que Hércules haría con sus muñecas, Orfeo lo hace con su inspiración. El dios robusto despedazaría de un puñetazo al mismo Athos. Orfeo les amansaría, con la eficacia de su voz triunfante, a Nemea su león y a Erimanto su jabalí. De los hombres, unos han nacido para forjar metales, otros para arrancar del suelo fértil las espigas del trigo, otros para enseñar, glorificar y cantar. Si soy tu copero y te doy vino, goza tu paladar; si te ofrezco un himno, goza tu alma.

Mientras cantaba la alondra, Orfeo le acompañaba con su instrumento, y un vasto y dominante soplo lírico se escapaba del bosque verde y fragante. El sátiro sordo comenzaba a impacientarse. ¿Quién era aquel extraño visitante? ¿Por qué ante él había cesado la danza loca y voluptuosa? ¿Qué decían sus dos consejeros?

—¡Ah! ¡La alondra había cantado; pero el sátiro no oía! Por fin, dirigió su vista al asno.

¿Faltaba su opinión? Pues bien; ante la selva enorme y sonora, bajo el azul sagrado, el asno movió la cabeza de un lado a otro, grave, terco, silencioso, como el sabio que medita.

Entonces con su pie hendido, hirió el sátiro el suelo, arrugó su frente con enojo, y, sin darse cuenta de nada, exclamó, señalando a Orfeo la salida de la selva:

—¡No! . . .

Al vecino Olimpo llegó el eco, y resonó allá, donde los dioses estaban de broma, un coro de carcajadas formidables que después se llamaron homéricas.

Orfeo salió triste de la selva del sátiro sordo y casi dispuesto a ahorcarse del primer laurel que hallase en su camino.

No se ahorcó, pero se casó con Eurídice.

sound that its throat permitted, "let the man who has sung so well remain with us. His lyre is beautiful and powerful. He has bestowed on you the grandeur and the rare light that has been seen today in your forest. He has given you his harmony. Highness, I know about such things. When the naked dawn comes and the world awakens, I rise up to the high heavens and from that height I pour forth the invisible pearls of my trills, and the atmosphere rejoices. And so I tell you that Orpheus has sung well, and that he is a chosen one of the gods. His music intoxicated the entire forest. The eagles approached and circled over our heads, the flowering shrubs gently waved their mysterious censers, the bees left their cells to come and listen. As for me, Highness, if I were in your place, I'd give him my vineleaf wreath and my thyrsus. There are two powers: the real and the ideal. What Herakles would accomplish with his wrists, Orpheus accomplishes with his inspiration. The burly god would break even Mount Athos into pieces with one punch. Orpheus, with the power of his triumphant voice, would tame the Nemean lion and the Erymanthian boar. Among men, some were born to forge metals, others to wring ears of grain from the fertile soil, others to teach, glorify, and sing. If I am your cupbearer and give you wine, your palate enjoys it; if I offer you a hymn, your soul enjoys it."

While the lark was singing, Orpheus accompanied it with his instrument, and a vast, dominating lyrical gust emanated from the fragrant green woods. The deaf satyr started to get impatient. Who was that strange visitor? Why had his presence put a stop to the wild, voluptuous dance? What were his two counselors saying?

—Ah! The lark had sung, but the satyr couldn't hear! Finally he directed his gaze at the donkey.

Its judgment was still wanted? All right; in the enormous, echoing forest, beneath the sacred blue sky, the donkey shook its head from side to side, gravely, stubbornly, silently, like a meditating sage.

Then with his split hoof the satyr struck the ground, furrowed his brow in vexation, and, paying no attention to anything else, exclaimed, as he pointed the way out of the forest to Orpheus:

"No! . . ."

The echo reached nearby Olympus, and there, where the gods were in a joking mood, there resounded a chorus of tremendous guffaws which were later referred to as Homeric laughter.

Orpheus left the deaf satyr's forest sadly and nearly ready to hang himself from the first laurel he encountered along the way.

He didn't hang himself, but he married Eurydice.

La ninfa

(Cuento parisiense)

En el castillo que últimamente acababa de adquirir Lesbia, esa actriz caprichosa y endiablada que tanto ha dado que decir al mundo por sus extravagancias, nos hallábamos hasta seis amigos. Presidía nuestra Aspasia, quien a la sazón se entretenía en chupar, como niña golosa, un terrón de azúcar húmedo, blanco, entre las yemas sonrosadas. Era la hora del *chartreuse*. Se veía en los cristales de la mesa como una disolución de piedras preciosas, y la luz de los candeleros se descomponía en las copas medio vacías, donde quedaba algo de la púrpura del borgoña, del oro hirviente del champaña, de las líquidas esmeraldas de la menta.

Se hablaba con el entusiasmo de artistas de buena pasta, tras una buena comida. Éramos todos artistas, quién más quién menos, y aun había un sabio obeso que ostentaba en la albura de una pechera inmaculada el gran nudo de una corbata monstruosa.

Alguien dijo:

—¡Ah, sí, Fremiet!

Y de Fremiet se pasó a sus animales, a su cincel maestro, a dos perros de bronce que, cerca de nosotros, uno buscaba la pista de la pieza, y otro, como mirando al cazador, alzaba el pescuezo y arbolaba la delgadez de su cola tiesa y erecta. ¿Quién habló de Mirón? El sabio, que recitó en griego el epigrama de Anacreonte: «Pastor, lleva a pastar más lejos tu boyada, no sea que creyendo que respira la vaca de Mirón, la quieras llevar contigo . . .»

Lesbia acabó de chupar su azúcar, y con una carcajada:

—¡Bah! Para mí los sátiros. Yo quisiera dar vida a mis bronces, y si esto fuese posible, mi amante sería uno de esos velludos semidioses. Os advierto que más que a los sátiros adoro a los centauros; y que me dejaría robar por uno de esos monstruos robustos, sólo por oír las quejas del engañado, que tocaría su flauta lleno de tristeza.

El sabio interrumpió:

—Los sátiros y los faunos, los hipocentauros y las sirenas han existido como las salamandras y el ave Fénix.

Todos reímos; pero entre el coro de carcajadas se oía irresistible, encantadora, la de Lesbia, cuyo rostro encendido de mujer hermosa estaba como resplandeciente de placer.

The Nymph

(A Parisian Tale)

In the château that had just recently been purchased by Lesbia, that capricious and mischievous actress who has given society so many subjects for gossip with her eccentricities, we six friends had assembled. We were presided over by our Aspasia, who at the moment was busy, like a greedy child, sucking a lump of moist white sugar from the pinkish egg-yolk dessert. It was time for the chartreuse liqueur. There was to be seen in the table glassware something like precious gems dissolving, and the light from the candlesticks was refracted in the half-empty goblets, in which there remained some of the purple of the burgundy, the molten gold of the champagne, the emerald liquid of the crème de menthe.

The conversation was conducted with the enthusiasm of good-natured artists after a good meal. We were all artists, some more, some less, and there was also an obese scholar who displayed on the whiteness of an immaculate shirtfront the large knot of a monstrous tie.

Somebody said:

"Oh, yes, Frémiet!"

And from Frémiet the topic shifted to his animals, to his masterly chisel, to two bronze dogs near us, one of which was seeking the spoor of a hunted animal while the other, as if looking up at the hunter, raised its neck and hoisted its thin tail, tense and extended. Which one of us mentioned Myron? The scholar, who recited in Greek Anacreon's epigram: "Oxherd, take your drove to graze farther off, so that you don't believe that Myron's cow is really breathing, and try to take her with you. . . ."

Lesbia finished sucking on her sugar, and said with a loud laugh:

"Bah! Give me satyrs. I'd like to make my bronzes come alive, and if that were possible, my lover would be one of those shaggy demigods. I warn you that, even more than satyrs, I adore centaurs, and I'd let myself be abducted by one of those sturdy monsters, if only to hear the laments of the disappointed satyr, who'd play his flute, full of sadness."

The scholar interrupted:

"Satyrs and Fauns, hippocentaurs and sirens really existed, just like salamanders and the phoenix."

We all laughed; but amid the chorus of guffaws was heard the irresistible, enchanting laughter of Lesbia, whose flushed face, that of a beautiful woman, was virtually radiant with pleasure.

—Sí —continuó el sabio—: ¿con qué derecho negamos los modernos, hechos que afirman los antiguos? El perro gigantesco que vio Alejandro, alto como un hombre, es tan real como la araña Kraken que vive en el fondo de los mares. San Antonio Abad, de edad de noventa años, fue en busca del viejo ermitaño Pablo, que vivía en una cueva. Lesbia, no te rías. Iba el santo por el yermo, apoyado en su báculo, sin saber dónde encontrar a quien buscaba. A mucho andar, ¿sabéis quién le dio las señas del camino que debía seguir? Un centauro; «medio hombre y medio caballo» —dice un autor—. Hablaba como enojado; huyó tan velozmente, que pronto le perdió de vista el santo; así iba galopando el monstruo, cabellos al aire y vientre a tierra.

En ese mismo viaje, San Antonio vio un sátiro, «hombrecillo de extraña figura, estaba junto a un arroyuelo, tenía las narices corvas, frente áspera y arrugada, y la última parte de su contrahecho cuerpo remataba con pies de cabra».

—Ni más ni menos —dijo Lesbia—. ¡M. de Cocureau, futuro miembro del Instituto!

Siguió el sabio:

—Afirma San Jerónimo que en tiempo de Constantino Magno se condujo a Alejandría un sátiro vivo, siendo conservado su cuerpo cuando murió.

Además, vióle el emperador de Antioquía.

Lesbia había vuelto a llenar su copa de menta, y humedecía su lengua en el licor verde como lo haría un animal felino.

—Dice Alberto Magno que en su tiempo cogieron a dos sátiros en los montes de Sajonia. Enrico Zormano asegura que en tierras de Tartaria había hombres con un solo pie y sólo un brazo en el pecho. Vincencio vio en su época un monstruo, que trajeron al rey de Francia; tenía cabeza de perro (Lesbia reía). Los muslos, brazos y manos tan sin vello como los nuestros (Lesbia se agitaba como una chicuela a quien hiciesen cosquillas); comía carne cocida y bebía vino con todas ganas.

—¡Colombine! —gritó Lesbia.

Y llegó Colombine; una falderilla que parecía un copo de algodón. Tomóla su ama, y entre las explosiones de risa de todos:

—¡Toma, el monstruo que tenía tu cara!

Y le dio un beso en la boca, mientras el animal se estremecía e inflaba las narices como lleno de voluptuosidad.

—Y Filegón Traliano —concluyó el sabio elegante— afirma la existencia de dos clases de hipocentauros: una de ellas como elefantes.

"Yes," the scholar continued, "what right do we moderns have to deny facts which the ancients affirm? The gigantic dog, tall as a man, seen by Alexander the Great, is just as real as the spidery kraken that lives at the bottom of the sea. Saint Anthony Abbot, at the age of ninety, went in search of the aged hermit Paul, who lived in a cave. Don't laugh, Lesbia! The saint was wandering in the desert, with the aid of his staff, not knowing where to find the man he sought. After much traveling, do you know who pointed out to him the path he needed to take? A centaur, 'half-man and half-horse,' one author states. It spoke as if it were angry, and it dashed away so swiftly that the saint quickly lost sight of it; that's how the monster went galloping off, its hair in the wind and its belly nearly touching the ground.

"On that same journey, Saint Anthony saw a satyr, 'a little man of odd appearance; he was standing beside a brook; he had a curved nose and a rugged, wrinkled brow, and the bottom of his misshapen body ended in goat's feet.'"

"Exactly as you've described it, eh?" said Lesbia. "You, Monsieur de Cocureau, future member of the French Institute!"

The scholar proceeded:

"Saint Jerome declares that in the reign of Constantine the Great a living satyr was brought to Alexandria, and his body was preserved after he died.

"What's more, the emperor of Antioch saw him."

Lesbia had refilled her goblet with crème de menthe, and was moistening her tongue with the green liquid just as a feline would.

"Albertus Magnus states that in his day two satyrs were caught in the mountains of Saxony. Heinrich Kornmann assures us that in the Tartar lands there were men with only one foot and with only one arm on their breast. Vincentius, in his own day, saw a monster that was being brought to the king of France; it had a dog's head." (Lesbia laughed.) "Its thighs, arms, and hands were as lightly haired as ours." (Lesbia was fidgeting like a little girl being tickled.) "It ate cooked meat and drank wine with great pleasure."

"Colombine!" Lesbia called.

And Colombine came: a lapdog resembling a cotton boll. Her mistress picked her up, and amid bursts of laughter from everyone, said:

"There, the monster had your face!"

And she gave her a kiss on the mouth, while the animal wriggled and puffed out its nostrils as if filled with voluptuousness.

"And Phlegon of Tralles," the elegant philosopher concluded, "affirms the existence of two classes of hippocentaurs, one of them as big as elephants."

—Basta de sabiduría —dijo Lesbia, y acabó de beber la menta.
Yo estaba feliz. No había despegado mis labios.

—¡Oh —exclamé—, para mí las ninfas! Yo desearía contemplar
esas desnudeces de los bosques y de las fuentes, aunque, como
Acteón, fuese despedazado por los perros. ¡Pero las ninfas no
existen!

Concluyó aquel concierto alegre con una gran fuga de risas y de
personas.

—¡Y qué! —dijo Lesbia, quemándome con sus ojos de faunesa; y
con voz callada para que sólo yo la oyera—: ¡Las ninfas existen, tú las
verás!

Era un día primaveral. Yo vagaba por el parque del castillo, con el
aire de un soñador empedernido. Los gorriones chillaban sobre las
lilas nuevas y atacaban a los escarabajos, que se defendían del pico-
tazo con sus corazas de esmeralda, con sus petos de oro y acero. En
las rosas el carmín, el bermellón, la onda penetrante de perfumes
dulces; más allá las violetas, en grandes grupos, con su color apacible
y su olor a virgen. Después, los altos árboles, los ramajes tupidos,
llenos de mil abejeos, las estatuas en la penumbra, los discóbolos de
bronce, los gladiadores musculosos en sus soberbias posturas gímni-
cas, las glorietas perfumadas cubiertas de enredaderas, los pórticos,
bellas imitaciones jónicas, cariátides todas blancas y lascivas, y vigo-
rosos telamones del orden atlántico, con anchas espaldas y muslos
gigantescos. Vagaba por el laberinto de tales encantos cuando oí un
ruido, allá en lo oscuro de la arboleda, en el estanque donde hay
cisnes blancos como cincelados en alabastro, y otros que tienen la
mitad del cuello del color del ébano, como una pierna alba con media
negra.

Llegué más cerca. ¿Soñaba? ¡Oh, Numa! Yo sentí lo que tú, cuando
viste en su gruta por primera vez a Egeria.

Estaba en el centro del estanque, entre la inquietud de los cisnes
espantados, una ninfa, una verdadera ninfa, que hundía su carne de
rosa en el agua cristalina. La cadera, a flor de espuma, parecía a veces
como dorada por la luz opaca que alcanzaba a llegar por las brechas
de las hojas. ¡Ah! Yo vi lirios, rosas, nieve, oro; vi un ideal con vida y
forma y oí, entre el burbujeo sonoro de la linfa herida, como una risa
burlesca y armoniosa que me encendía la sangre.

"Enough scholarship," said Lesbia, and she drank the rest of her crème de menthe.

I was happy. I hadn't opened my mouth.

"Oh," I now exclaimed, "give me nymphs! I'd like to gaze on those nude beauties of woods and fountains, even if I were torn apart by dogs, like Actaeon. But nymphs don't exist!"

That merry consort ended with a great fugue[2] of laughter and flight of guests.

"Oh, no?" said Lesbia, burning me with her eyes like those of a female Faun. In a low voice meant for my hearing alone, she said: "Nymphs do exist, you'll see them!"

It was a spring day. I was roaming through the park of the château, with the air of a hardened dreamer. The sparrows were chirping on the fresh lilacs, and attacking the beetles, which protected themselves from their pecks with their emerald cuirasses, their breastplates of gold and steel. Among the roses, the crimson, the vermilion, the pungent wave of sweet fragrance; beyond them, the violets, in large clumps, with their peaceful color and virginal scent. Next, the tall trees, the dense branches, filled with a thousand swarms of bees, the statues in the shade, the bronze discus throwers, the muscular gladiators in their proud gymnastic poses, the fragrant arbors covered with bindweed, the porticos, beautiful imitations of the Ionic order, caryatids all white and lascivious, and vigorous telamons of atlantean type, with broad shoulders and gigantic thighs. I was roaming through the maze of these enchantments when I heard a sound, there in the darkness of the copse, by the pool that housed white swans, as if sculpted in alabaster, and others that have necks half ebony-colored, like a white leg in a black stocking.

I came closer. Was I dreaming? Oh, Numa! I had the same sensation that you had when you first saw Egeria in her grotto.

In the center of the pool, amid the restlessness of the frightened swans, stood a nymph, a real nymph, plunging her pink flesh into the crystalline water. Her hip, awash in foam, seemed at moments to be gilded by the dense light that managed to penetrate the gaps in the foliage. Ah! I saw lilies, roses, snow, gold; I saw an Idea clothed in life and form, and, amid the loud gurgling of the stricken watery element, I heard what sounded like a mocking, harmonious laugh that set my blood on fire.

---

[2]Or "escaping."

De pronto huyó la visión, surgió la ninfa del estanque, semejante a Citerea en su onda, y recogiendo sus cabellos, que goteaban brillantes, corrió por los rosales, tras las lilas y violetas, más allá de los tupidos arbolares, hasta perderse, ¡ay!, por un recodo; y quedé yo, poeta lírico, fauno burlado, viendo a las grandes aves alabastrinas como mofándose de mí, tendiéndome sus largos cuellos en cuyo extremo brillaba bruñida el ágata de sus picos.

Después almorzábamos juntos aquellos amigos de la noche pasada; entre todos, triunfante, con su pechera y su gran corbata oscura, el sabio obeso, futuro miembro del Instituto.

Y de repente, mientras todos charlaban de la última obra de Fremiet en el salón, exclamó Lesbia con su alegre voz de parisiense:

—¡Té!, como dice Tartarín: ¡El poeta ha visto ninfas! . . .

La contemplaron todos asombrados, y ella me miraba como una gata, y se reía, como una chiquilla a quien se le hiciesen cosquillas.

El fardo

Allá lejos, en la línea como trazada con un lápiz azul, que separa las aguas y los cielos, se iba hundiendo el sol, con sus polvos de oro y sus torbellinos de chispas purpuradas, como un gran disco de hierro candente. Ya el muelle fiscal iba quedando en quietud; los guardas pasaban de un punto a otro, las gorras metidas hasta las cejas, dando aquí y allá sus vistazos. Inmóvil el enorme brazo de los pescantes, los jornaleros se encaminaban a las casas. El agua murmuraba debajo del muelle, y el húmedo viento salado, que sopla de mar afuera a la hora en que la noche sube, mantenía las lanchas cercanas en un continuo cabeceo.

Todos los lancheros se habían ido ya; solamente el viejo tío Lucas, que por la mañana se estropeara un pie al subir una barrica a un carretón y que, aunque cojín cojeando, había trabajado todo el día, estaba sentado en una piedra, y, con la pipa en la boca, veía, triste, el mar.

—¡Eh, tío Lucas! ¿Se descansa?

—Sí, pues, patroncito.

Y empezó la charla, esa charla agradable y suelta que me place entablar con los bravos hombres toscos que viven la vida del trabajo fortificante, la que da la buena salud y la fuerza del músculo, y se nutre con el grano del poroto y la sangre hirviente de la viña.

The vision soon fled; the nymph emerged from the pool, like Cytherea from the waves, and, gathering up her hair, which shone with water droplets, she ran through the rosebushes, past the lilacs and violets, beyond the dense groves of trees, until, alas, she was lost to view around a bend. And I, lyric poet, mocked Faun, stood there watching the large alabaster birds seemingly making fun of me, extending toward me their long necks, at the end of which shone the burnished agate of their bills.

Later, all the friends of the night before lunched together; triumphant among us, with his shirtfront and his dark tie, sat the obese scholar, future member of the Institute.

And suddenly, while everyone was talking about Frémiet's latest sculpture exhibited at the Salon, Lesbia exclaimed in her merry Parisienne's voice:

"What do you know—as Tartarin says—the poet has seen nymphs! . . ."

Everyone gazed at her in amazement, while she looked at me like a cat and laughed like a little girl being tickled.

The Bale

Far off there, on the line, seemingly drawn in blue pencil, that separates sea and sky, the sun was setting, with its powdery gold and its whorls of purplish sparks, like a huge disk of white-hot iron. The customs dock was now being left in repose; the guards were walking from one place to another, their caps pulled down to their eyebrows, casting glances here and there. The enormous arms of the cranes were motionless; the day laborers were on their way home. The water was murmuring below the dock, and the damp, salty wind that blows off the sea when night falls kept the nearby lighters rocking constantly.

All the lightermen had already gone; only old man Lucas, who had sprained a foot that morning while hoisting a barrel onto a cart, but who had gone on working all day long even with a limp, was sitting on a stone and, pipe in mouth, was watching the sea sadly.

"Hey, old man Lucas! Taking a rest?"

"Yes, young boss."

And the chat began, that pleasant, easygoing sort of chat that I enjoy engaging in with the good, rough men who lead lives of fortifying labor, the life that gives good health and strong muscles and is nourished by beans for grain and the seething blood of the grapevine.

Yo veía con cariño a aquel rudo viejo, y le oía con interés sus relaciones, así, todas cortadas, todas como un hombre basto, pero de pecho ingenuo. ¡Ah, conque fue militar! ¡Conque de mozo fue soldado de Bulnes! ¡Conque todavía tuvo resistencia para ir con su rifle hasta Miraflores! Y es casado, y tuvo un hijo, y . . .

Y aquí el tío Lucas:

—Sí, patrón, ¡hace dos años que se me murió!

Aquellos ojos, chicos y relumbrantes bajo las cejas grises y peludas, se humedecieron entonces.

—¿Que cómo se murió? En el oficio, por darnos de comer a todos, a mi mujer, a los chiquillos y a mí, patrón, que entonces me hallaba enfermo.

Y todo me lo refirió al comenzar aquella noche, mientras las olas se cubrían de brumas y la ciudad encendía sus luces; él, en la piedra que le servía de asiento, después de apagar su negra pipa y de colocársela en la oreja y de estirar y cruzar sus piernas flacas y musculosas, cubiertas por los sucios pantalones arremangados hasta el tobillo.

El muchacho era muy honrado y muy de trabajo. Se quiso ponerlo a la escuela desde grandecito; ¡pero los miserables no deben aprender a leer cuando se llora de hambre en el cuartucho!

El tío Lucas era casado, tenía muchos hijos.

Su mujer llevaba la maldición del vientre de los pobres: la fecundidad. Había, pues, mucha boca abierta que pedía pan; mucho chico sucio que se revolcaba en la basura, mucho cuerpo magro que temblaba de frío; era preciso ir a llevar que comer, a buscar harapos, y para eso, quedar sin alimento y trabajar como un buey.

Cuando el hijo creció, ayudó al padre. Un vecino, el herrero, quiso enseñarle su industria; pero como entonces era tan débil, casi un armazón de huesos, y en el fuelle tenía que echar el bofe, se puso enfermo y volvió al conventillo. ¡Ah, estuvo muy enfermo! Pero no murió. ¡No murió! Y eso que vivían en uno de esos hacinamientos humanos, entre cuatro paredes destartaladas, viejas, feas, en la callejuela inmunda de las mujeres perdidas, hedionda a todas horas, alumbrada de noche por escasos faroles, y donde resuenan en perpetua llamada a las zambas de echacorvería, las arpas y los acordeones, y el ruido de los marineros que llegan al burdel, desesperados con la castidad de las largas travesías, a emborracharse como cubas y a gritar y patalear como condenados. ¡Sí! Entre la podredumbre, al estrépito de las fiestas tunantescas, el chico vivió, y pronto estuvo sano y en pie.

I was fond of seeing that unvarnished old man, and listened with interest to his stories, all told in a jerky style, all befitting the plain man that he was, but all betokening a sincere heart. Ah, so he had been a soldier! So, as a lad, he had fought under Bulnes! So he had still felt an urge to take his rifle and head for Miraflores! And he's married, and he had a son, and . . .

At this point old man Lucas said:

"Yes, boss, it's two years since he died on me!"

The eyes, small and shiny beneath his hairy gray eyebrows, became moist.

"How did he die? At work, so he could feed all of us, my wife, the little ones, and me, boss, because I was sick at the time."

And he told me the whole story as that night fell, while the waves were covered with mist and the city turned on its lights, as he sat there on the stone, after putting out his blackened pipe, thrusting it behind his ear, and stretching out and crossing his thin, muscular legs, which were covered by dirty trousers rolled up to the ankle.

The boy was very respectable and very hard-working. They had wanted to send him to school as soon as he was old enough, but poor people shouldn't learn to read when their family weeps with hunger in their hovel!

Old man Lucas was married and had many children.

His wife had the physical curse of the poor: fecundity. So, there was many an open mouth clamoring for bread, many a dirty child wallowing in the filth, many a scrawny body shivering with cold; it was necessary to bring in some food, to accumulate a few tatters of clothing, and in order to do so, to be undernourished while working like an ox.

When the boy grew up, he helped his father. A neighbor, the blacksmith, was willing to teach him his trade, but since he was so weak at the time, just a bundle of bones, and it was necessary to slog away at the bellows, he got sick and returned to his tenement. Oh, he was very sick! But he didn't die. He didn't die! In spite of the fact that they lived in one of those human sardine cans, between four ramshackle, old, ugly walls, in the vile alley of fallen women, which was malodorous at all hours and lit at night by just a few streetlamps, a street where a perpetual call to prostitutes' shindigs is sounded by harps and accordions, and by the shouts of sailors arriving at the bordello fed up with the enforced chastity of long voyages, aiming to get dead drunk, and to yell and stamp their feet like condemned criminals. Yes! Amid the rot, amid the racket of the rascally festivities, the boy lived and was soon well and up and about.

Luego llegaron sus quince años.

El tío Lucas había logrado, tras mil privaciones, comprar una canoa. Se hizo pescador.

Al venir el alba, iba con su mocetón al agua, llevando los enseres de la pesca. El uno remaba, el otro ponía en los anzuelos la carnada. Volvían a la costa con buena esperanza de vender lo hallado, entre la brisa fría y las opacidades de la neblina, cantando en baja voz algún «triste», y enhiesto el remo triunfante que chorreaba espuma.

Si había buena venta, otra salida por la tarde.

Una de invierno, había temporal. Padre e hijo en la pequeña embarcación, sufrían en el mar la locura de la ola y del viento. Difícil era llegar a tierra. Pesca y todo se fue al agua, y se pensó en librar el pellejo. Luchaban como desesperados por ganar la playa. Cerca de ella estaban; pero una racha maldita les empujó contra una roca, y la canoa se hizo astillas. Ellos salieron sólo magullados, ¡gracias a Dios!, como decía el tío Lucas al narrarlo. Después, ya son ambos lancheros.

Sí, lancheros; sobre las grandes embarcaciones chatas y negras; colgándose de la cadena que rechina pendiente como una sierpe de hierro del macizo pescante que semeja una horca; remando de pie y a compás; yendo con la lancha del muelle al vapor y del vapor al muelle; gritando ¡bhiooeep! cuando se empujan los pesados bultos para engancharlos en la uña potente que los levanta balanceándolos como un péndulo, ¡sí!, lancheros; el viejo y el muchacho, el padre y el hijo; ambos a horcajadas sobre un cajón, ambos forcejeando, ambos ganando su jornal, para ellos y para sus queridas sanguijuelas del conventillo.

Íbanse todos los días al trabajo, vestidos de viejo, fajadas las cinturas con sendas bandas coloradas y haciendo sonar a una sus zapatos groseros y pesados que se quitaban al comenzar la tarea, tirándolos en un rincón de la lancha.

Empezaba el trajín, el cargar y descargar. El padre era cuidadoso:

—¡Muchacho, que te rompes la cabeza! ¡Que te coge la mano el chicote! ¡Que vas a perder una canilla!

Y enseñaba, adiestraba, dirigía al hijo, con su modo, con bruscas palabras de roto viejo y de padre encariñado.

Then he turned fifteen.

After a thousand privations, old man Lucas had managed to buy a boat. He became a fisherman.

When dawn came, he'd head for the water with his big boy, taking along his fishing tackle. One of them rowed, the other one baited the hooks. They returned to shore in high hopes of selling their catch, in the cool breeze and the density of the mist, quietly singing some popular song about unfortunate lovers, with their triumphant oars raised upright and dripping with foam.

If they made a good sale, they'd go out again in the afternoon.

On one winter afternoon there was a storm. Asea in their small boat, father and son suffered from the madness of waves and wind. It was hard to reach shore. Their catch and everything else was lost in the water, and their only thought was to save their own hide. They struggled desperately to get to the beach. They were already near it when one accursed gust drove them against a rock, and the boat broke into smithereens. They got out of the incident merely bruised, thank God, as old man Lucas said when narrating it. After that they both became lightermen.

Yes, lightermen; borne on those large, flat, black vessels; clinging to the creaking chain that hangs like an iron snake from the massive crane that resembles a gallows; rowing in rhythm while standing; traveling in the lighter from the dock to the cargo ship and from the ship to the dock; yelling "hup!" when the heavy loads are shoved so they can be hooked onto the powerful claw that raises them while they swing like a pendulum. Yes, lightermen: the old man and the boy, father and son; both of them straddling a packing case, both of them struggling, both of them earning their day's wages for themselves and for their beloved bloodsuckers back in the tenement.

Every day they went to work dressed in old clothes, their waists encircled by red sashes, and their rough, heavy shoes clattering in unison—shoes that they took off when starting their job, tossing them into a corner of the lighter.

The hustle and bustle, the loading and unloading began. The father was worried:

"Son, you'll break your head open that way! The rope end will snarl your hand! You're going to break a shinbone!"

And he'd teach, train, direct his son in his own fashion, with the brusque words of an impoverished old workingman and a loving father.

Hasta que un día el tío Lucas no pudo moverse de la cama, porque el reumatismo le hinchaba las coyunturas y le taladraba los huesos.

¡Oh! Y había que comprar medicinas y alimentos; eso sí.

—Hijo, al trabajo, a buscar plata; hoy es sábado.

Y se fue el hijo, solo, casi corriendo, sin desayunarse, a la faena diaria.

Era un bello día de luz clara, de sol de oro. En el muelle rondaban los carros sobre sus rieles, crujían las poleas, chocaban las cadenas. Era la gran confusión del trabajo que da vértigos, el son de hierro, traqueteos por doquiera, y el viento pasando por el bosque de árboles y jarcias de los navíos en grupo.

Debajo de uno de los pescantes del muelle estaba el hijo del tío Lucas con otros lancheros, descargando a toda prisa. Había que vaciar la lancha repleta de fardos. De tiempo en tiempo bajaba la larga cadena que remata en un garfio, sonando como una matraca al correr de la roldana; los mozos amarraban los bultos con una cuerda doblada en dos, los enganchaban en el garfio, y entonces éstos subían a la manera de un pez en un anzuelo, o del plomo de una sonda, ya quietos, ya agitándose de un lado a otro, como un badajo en el vacío.

La carga estaba amontonada. La ola movía pausadamente de cuando en cuando la embarcación colmada de fardos. Éstos formaban una a modo de pirámide en el centro. Había uno muy pesado, muy pesado. Era el más grande de todos, ancho, gordo y oloroso a brea. Venía en el fondo de la lancha. Un hombre, de pie sobre él, era pequeña figura para el grueso zócalo.

Era algo como todos los prosaísmos de la importación envueltos en lona y fajados con correas de hierro. Sobre sus costados, en medio de líneas y de triángulos negros, había letras que miraban como ojos.

—Letras en «diamante» —decía el tío Lucas. Sus cintas de hierro estaban apretadas con clavos cabezudos y ásperos; y en las entrañas tendría el monstruo, cuando menos, linones y percales.

Sólo él faltaba.

—¡Se va el bruto! —dijo uno de los lancheros.

—¡El barrigón! —agregó otro.

El hijo del tío Lucas, que estaba ansioso de acabar pronto, se alistaba para ir a cobrar y desayunarse, anudándose un pañuelo de cuadros al pescuezo.

Bajó la cadena danzando en el aire. Se amarró un gran lazo al fardo, se probó si estaba bien seguro, y se gritó: «¡Iza!», mientras la cadena tiraba de la masa chirriando y levantándola en vilo.

Until, one day, old man Lucas was unable to get out of bed, because his rheumatism had swollen his joints and was piercing his bones.

Oh! And food and medicine had to be bought; *that* was necessary.

"Son, to work, to earn some silver; today is Saturday."

And his son departed, alone, almost at a run, without breakfast, for his daily tasks.

It was a lovely day, bright with golden sunshine. On the dock the carts were rolling about on their rails, the pulleys were creaking, the chains were clanking together. It was the great confusion of the dizzying job, the sound of iron, clatter everywhere, and the wind blowing through the forest of masts and rigging of the group of ships.

Below one of the cranes on the dock stood the son of old man Lucas with other lightermen, unloading in great haste. The lighter, filled with bales, had to be emptied. From time to time the long chain that ended in a hook descended, making a noise like a rattle as the pulley wheel turned; the men were tying up the bales with a doubled rope and attaching them to the hook; then the bales rose like a fish on a hook, or the lead of a sounding line, now steady, now shaking from side to side, like a clapper in the void.

The cargo was piled up. The waves occasionally rocked the bale-laden vessel gently. The bales formed a sort of pyramid in the center. There was one that was very heavy, very heavy. It was the biggest one of all, wide, fat, and smelling of tar. It was at the bottom of the lighter. One man, standing on it, was like a small statue on a huge base.

It resembled all those routine import items wrapped in canvas and trussed with iron bands. On its sides, in the midst of black lines and triangles, it bore lettering that looked at you like eyes.

"Diamond" lettering, old man Lucas used to call it. Its iron bands were fastened with rough, large-headed nails. In its bowels the monster probably contained muslins and percales.

It was the only one left.

"Here comes the beast!" said one of the lightermen.

"Potbellied, isn't it?" added another.

The son of old man Lucas, who was eager to finish quickly, got ready to go pick up his pay and have breakfast; he knotted a checked bandanna around his neck.

The chain descended, dancing in the air. A big loop of rope was fastened to the bale, they tested it to see whether it was firm, and they shouted "Hoist!" while the creaking chain hauled the heavy mass, lifting it into the air.

Los lancheros, de pie, miraban subir el enorme peso, y se prepararon para ir a tierra, cuando se vio una cosa horrible. El fardo, el grueso fardo, se zafó del lazo, como de un collar holgado saca un perro la cabeza, y cayó sobre el hijo del tío Lucas, que entre el filo de la lancha y el gran bulto quedó con los riñones rotos, el espinazo desencajado y echando sangre negra por la boca.

Aquel día no hubo pan ni medicinas en casa del tío Lucas, sino el muchacho destrozado, al que se abrazaba llorando el reumático, entre la gritería de la mujer y de los chicos, cuando llevaban el cadáver a Playa-Ancha.

Me despedí del viejo lanchero, y a paso elástico dejé el muelle, tomando el camino de la casa y haciendo filosofía con toda la cachaza de un poeta, en tanto que una brisa glacial, que venía de mar afuera, pellizcaba tenazmente las narices y las orejas.

El velo de la reina Mab

La reina Mab, en su carro hecho de una sola perla, tirado por cuatro coleópteros de petos dorados y alas de pedrería, caminando sobre un rayo de sol, se coló por la ventana de una buhardilla donde estaban cuatro hombres flacos, barbudos e impertinentes, lamentándose como unos desdichados.

Por aquel tiempo, las hadas habían repartido sus dones a los mortales. A unos habían dado las varitas misteriosas que llenan de oro las pesadas cajas del comercio; a otros, unas espigas maravillosas que al desgranarlas colmaban las trojes de riqueza; a otros, unos cristales que hacían ver en el riñón de la madre tierra, oro y piedras preciosas; a quiénes, cabelleras espesas y músculos de Goliat, y mazas enormes para machacar el hierro encendido, y a quiénes, talones fuertes y piernas ágiles para montar en las rápidas caballerías que se beben el viento y que tienden las crines en la carrera.

Los cuatro hombres se quejaban. Al uno le había tocado en suerte una cantera, al otro el iris, al otro el ritmo, al otro el cielo azul.

La reina Mab oyó sus palabras. Decía el primero:

—¡Y bien! ¡Heme aquí en la gran lucha de mis sueños de mármol! Yo he arrancado el bloque y tengo el cincel. Todos tenéis, unos el oro, otros la armonía, otros la luz; yo pienso en la blanca y divina Venus,

The lightermen, on their feet, watched the enormous weight rising, and prepared to go ashore, when a terrible sight was seen. The bale, the huge bale, came undone from the loop of rope, the way that a dog slips its head out of a loose collar, and fell onto the son of old man Lucas, who, between the edge of the lighter and the big load, had his lower back broken and his spine twisted; dark blood was oozing from his mouth.

On that day there was neither bread nor medicine in old man Lucas's house, but the shattered boy, whom the rheumatic man embraced weeping, while his wife and little children screamed, when the body was taken to the potter's field at Playa-Ancha.

I took leave of the old lighterman and with springy steps I left the dock, heading homeward and philosophizing with all the phlegmatic coolness of a poet, while a glacial breeze, blowing off the sea, tenaciously pinched my nose and my ears.

The Veil of Queen Mab

Queen Mab, in her chariot made of a single pearl, drawn by four beetles with gilded breastplates and wings of precious gems, traveling on a sunbeam, squeezed through the window of a garret that contained four thin, bearded, impertinent men who were lamenting like sufferers from misfortune.

At that time the fairies had distributed their gifts among mortals. To some they had given the mysterious wands which fill the heavy tills of business with gold; to others, miraculous ears of grain which, when shelled, heaped their granaries with riches; to others, crystals which allowed them to see gold and precious stones in the depths of mother earth; to some, thick heads of hair and muscles like Goliath's, and enormous mallets for striking white-hot iron; and to some, strong heels and agile legs for riding the swift steeds that drink the wind and spread out their manes as they race along.

The four men were complaining. To the lot of one had fallen a stone quarry; to another's, the rainbow; to another's rhythm; to another's, the blue sky.

Queen Mab heard their words. The first man was saying:
"All right! Here I am engaged in the great battle of my marble dreams! I have hewn out the block and I hold the chisel. All of you have something, some have gold, others harmony, others light; I think

que muestra su desnudez bajo el plafón color del cielo. Yo quiero dar a la masa la línea y la hermosura plástica; y que circule por las venas de la estatua una sangre incolora como la de los dioses. Yo tengo el espíritu de Grecia en el cerebro, y amo los desnudos en que la ninfa huye y el fauno tiende los brazos. ¡Oh Fidias! Tú eres para mí soberbio y augusto como un semidiós en el recinto de la eterna belleza, rey ante un ejército de hermosuras que a tus ojos arrojan el magnífico Kiton, mostrando la esplendidez de la forma en sus cuerpos de rosa y de nieve.

Tú golpeas, hieres y domas el mármol, y suena el golpe armónico como un verso, y te adula la cigarra, amante del sol, oculta entre los pámpanos de la viña virgen. Para ti son los Apolos rubios y luminosos, las Minervas severas y soberanas. Tú, como un mago, conviertes la roca en simulacro y el colmillo del elefante en copa del festín. Y al ver tu grandeza siento el martirio de mi pequeñez. Porque pasaron los tiempos gloriosos. Porque tiemblo ante las miradas de hoy. Porque contemplo el ideal inmenso y las fuerzas exhaustas. Porque a medida que cincelo el bloque me ataraza el desaliento.

Y decía el otro:

—Lo que es hoy romperé mis pinceles. ¿Para qué quiero el iris y esta gran paleta de campo florido, si a la postre mi cuadro no será admitido en el salón? ¿Qué abordaré? He recorrido todas las escuelas, todas las inspiraciones artísticas. He pintado el torso de Diana y el rostro de la Madona. He pedido a las campiñas sus colores, sus matices; he adulado a la luz como a una amada, y la he abrazado como a una querida. He sido adorador del desnudo con sus magnificencias, con los tonos de sus carnaciones y con sus fugaces medias tintas. He trazado en mis lienzos los nimbos de los santos y las alas de los querubines. ¡Ah!, pero siempre el terrible desencanto. ¡El porvenir! ¡Vender una Cleopatra en dos pesetas para poder almorzar!

Y yo, ¡que podría en el estremecimiento de mi inspiración trazar el gran cuadro que tengo aquí dentro!

Y decía el otro:

—Perdida mi alma en la gran ilusión de mis sinfonías, temo todas las decepciones. Yo escucho todas las armonías, desde la lira de Terpandro hasta las fantasías orquestales de Wagner. Mis ideales brillan en medio de mis audacias de inspirado. Yo tengo la percepción

of the divine white Venus displaying her nudity beneath the sky-colored ceiling. I wish to give the mass line and sculptural beauty, so that a colorless blood, like that of the gods, will circulate in the statue's veins. I have the spirit of Greece in my veins, and I love the artistic nudes in which the nymph flees and the Faun holds out his arms. O Phidias! For me, you are as superb and reverend as a demigod in the realm of eternal beauty, a king fronting an army of beauties who before your eyes cast off their splendid chitons, revealing the majesty of form in their bodies of rose and snow.

"You strike, wound, and tame the marble, and the stroke sounds as harmonious as a line of poetry, and you are praised by the cicada, lover of the sun, hidden amid the leaves of the virginal grapevine. For you, Apollos are blond and luminous, Minervas severe and majestic. You, like a magician, turn rock into a likeness and the elephant's tusk into a festive goblet. And, viewing your greatness, I feel the torture of my smallness. Because the glorious days have passed. Because I tremble before the gaze of today's people. Because I contemplate the immensity of my vision and the exhaustion of my strength. Because as I continue to ply my chisel, I am tormented more and more by discouragement."

And the next man said:
"This very day I shall break my brushes. Why do I wish for the rainbow and this extensive palette like a flowering field, if in the end my picture won't be accepted in the Salon? Where shall I begin? I've run through every artistic school and inspiration. I've painted the torso of Diana and the face of the Madonna. I've asked the countryside to lend me its colors, its shadings; I have flattered light as if it were a beloved woman, and I've embraced it like a woman I adored. I have worshipped the nude with its splendors, with the tones of its flesh colors and with its evanescent demitints. I have drawn on my canvases the haloes of saints and the wings of cherubim. Ah, but always the same terrible disenchantment! The future! To sell a Cleopatra for two pesetas in order to eat lunch!

"And I, who in the tremor of my inspiration could paint the great picture I have here inside me!"

And the next man said:
"My soul having been lost in the great hopeful dreams of my symphonies, I fear all disappointments. I listen to all harmonies, from Terpander's lyre to Wagner's orchestral fantasies. My ideals shine in the midst of my audacities, those of a man inspired. I possess the

del filósofo que oyó la música de los astros. Todos los ruidos pueden aprisionarse, todos los ecos son susceptibles de combinaciones. Todo cabe en la línea de mis escalas cromáticas.

La luz vibrante es himno, y la melodía de la selva halla un eco en mi corazón. Desde el ruido de la tempestad hasta el canto del pájaro, todo se confunde y enlaza en la infinita cadencia.

Entre tanto, no diviso sino la muchedumbre que befa, y la celda del manicomio.

Y el último:

—Todos bebemos del agua clara de la fuente de Jonia. Pero el ideal flota en el azul; y para que los espíritus gocen de la luz suprema es preciso que asciendan. Yo tengo el verso que es de miel, y el que es de oro, y el que es de hierro candente.

Yo soy el ánfora del celeste perfume: tengo el amor. Paloma, estrella, nido, lirio, vosotros conocéis mi morada. Para los vuelos inconmensurables tengo alas de águila que parten a golpes mágicos el huracán. Y para hallar consonantes, las busco en dos bocas que se juntan; y estalla el beso, y escribo la estrofa, y entonces, si veis mi alma, conoceréis a mi musa. Amo las epopeyas, porque de ellas brota el soplo heroico que agita las banderas que ondean sobre las lanzas y los penachos que tiemblan sobre los cascos; los cantos líricos, porque hablan de las diosas y de los amores; y las églogas, porque son olorosas a verbena y tomillo, y el sano aliento del buey coronado de rosas. Yo escribiría algo inmortal; mas me abruma un porvenir de miseria y de hambre.

Entonces, la reina Mab, del fondo de su carro hecho de una sola perla, tomó un velo azul, casi impalpable, como formado de suspiros, o de miradas de ángeles rubios y pensativos. Y aquel velo era el velo de los sueños, de los dulces sueños, que hacen ver la vida de color de rosa. Y con él envolvió a los cuatro hombres flacos, barbudos e impertinentes. Los cuales cesaron de estar tristes, porque penetró en su pecho la esperanza, y en su cabeza el sol alegre, con el diablillo de la vanidad, que consuela en sus profundas decepciones a los pobres artistas.

Y desde entonces, en las buhardillas de los brillantes infelices, donde flota el sueño azul, se piensa en el porvenir como en la aurora, y se oyen risas que quitan la tristeza, y se bailan extrañas farándulas alrededor de un blanco Apolo, de un lindo paisaje, de un violín viejo, de un amarillento manuscrito.

perceptiveness of the philosopher who heard the music of the spheres. All sounds can be captured, all echoes are susceptible of being combined. Everything finds its place within the line of my chromatic scales.

"Vibrant light is a hymn, and the melody of the forest finds an echo in my heart. From the roar of the tempest to the song of the bird, everything is blended and intertwined in the infinite cadence.

"But in the meantime, all I can discern is the mob jeering at me, and a cell in a madhouse."

And the last man said:

"All of us drink of the clear water of the Ionian spring. But the Ideal floats in the blue; and if spirits are to enjoy the supreme light, they must ascend. I possess the line of poetry made of honey, the one made of gold, and the one made of white-hot iron.

"I am the amphora of heavenly fragrance: I possess love. Dove, star, nest, lily, you all know my dwelling place. For immeasurable flights I have eagle's wings that cut through the hurricane with magical beats. To find rhymes, I seek them in two mouths joining; and the kiss resounds, and I write the stanza, and then, if you see my soul, you'll recognize my muse. I love poetic epics, because they are the source of the heroic gust that stirs the banners waving atop lances and the plumes quivering atop helmets; I love lyric poems, because they speak of goddesses and love; and pastoral poems, because they are fragrant with vervain and thyme, and the healthy breath of the rose-garlanded ox. I would write something immortal, but I am overwhelmed by a future full of poverty and hunger."

Then, from the bottom of her chariot made of a single pearl, Queen Mab took a blue veil, all but impalpable, as if it had been woven of sighs, or of the gaze of blond, meditating angels. And that veil was the veil of dreams, of sweet dreams that make you see life as rose-colored. And with it she enveloped the four thin, bearded, and impertinent men, who ceased being sad because hope entered their hearts and merry sunshine entered their heads, along with the little imp of vanity, who consoles poor artists in their deep disappointments.

And from that time on, in the garrets of brilliant but unfortunate people, where the blue dream floats, the future is looked forward to as if it were the dawn, and laughter is heard that dispels sadness, and strange farandoles are danced around a white Apollo, a pretty landscape, an old violin, and a yellowing manuscript.

La canción del oro

Aquel día, un harapiento, por las trazas un mendigo, tal vez un pere-grino, quizá un poeta, llegó bajo la sombra de los altos álamos a la gran calle de los palacios, donde hay desafíos de soberbia entre el ónix y el pórfido, el ágata y el mármol; en donde las altas columnas, los her-mosos frisos, las cúpulas doradas, reciben la caricia pálida del sol moribundo.

Había tras los vidrios de las ventanas, en los vastos edificios de la riqueza, rostros de mujeres gallardas o de niños encantadores. Tras las rejas se adivinaban extensos jardines, grandes verdores salpicados de rosas y ramas que se balanceaban acompasada y blandamente como bajo la ley de un ritmo. Y allá en los grandes salones debía de estar el tapiz purpurado y lleno de oro, la blanca estatua, el bronce chino, el tibor cubierto de campos azules y de arrozales tupidos, la gran cortina recogida como una falda, ornada de flores opulentas, donde el ocre oriental hace vibrar la luz en la seda que resplandece. Luego las lunas venecianas, los palisandros y los cedros, los nácares y los ébanos, y el piano negro y abierto, que ríe mostrando sus teclas como una linda dentadura; y las arañas cristalinas, donde alzan las velas profusas la aristocracia de su blanca cera. ¡Oh, y más allá! Más allá el cuadro valioso, dorado por el tiempo, el retrato que firma Durand o Bonnat, y las preciosas acuarelas en que el tono rosado parece que emerge de un cielo puro y envuelve en una onda dulce desde el lejano horizonte hasta la hiedra trémula y humilde. Y más allá . . .

(Muere la tarde.

Llega a las puertas del palacio un break flamante y charolado. Baja una pareja y entra con tal soberbia en la mansión, que el mendigo piensa: Decididamente, el aguilucho y su hembra van al nido. El tronco, ruidoso y azogado, a un golpe de fusta, arrastra el carruaje ha-ciendo relampaguear las piedras. Noche.)

Entonces en aquel cerebro de loco que ocultaba un sombrero raído, brotó como el germen de una idea que pasó al pecho, y fue opresión, y llegó a la boca hecho himno que le encendía la lengua y hacía entrechocar los dientes. Fue la visión de todos los mendigos, de todos los desamparados, de todos los miserables, de todos los suicidas, de todos los borrachos, del harapo y de la llaga, de todos los que viven —¡Dios mío!— en perpetua noche, tanteando la sombra, cayendo al

The Hymn to Gold

On that day, a ragged man, a beggar from the looks of him, perhaps a pilgrim, perhaps a poet, reached the shade of the tall poplars on the great street of palaces, where onyx and porphyry, agate and marble vie for haughty supremacy; where the tall columns, the beautiful friezes, the gilded domes, receive the pale caress of the dying sun.

Behind the window panes, in the vast dwelling places of wealth, there were faces of elegant women or charming children. Behind the iron gates could be discerned extensive gardens, large green areas dotted with roses and boughs swaying gently and regularly as if subject to some rhythm. And there in the great salons there were surely purple tapestries shot through with gold, white statues, Chinese bronzes, Oriental vases painted with blue fields and dense rice paddies, large curtains pulled back like skirts, decorated with opulent flowers, where the Oriental ocher makes the light vibrate on the gleaming silk. Then, the Venetian mirrors, the rosewood and cedar, the mother-of-pearl and ebony, and the dark piano, opened and smiling, displaying its keys like beautiful teeth; and the crystal chandeliers in which the numerous tapers hold aloft their white wax aristocratically. Oh, and farther along! Farther along, the expensive paintings, gilded by time, portraits signed by Duran or Bonnat, and precious watercolors in which the rosy tone seems to emerge from a pure sky to envelop everything in one wave of sweetness, from the distant horizon to the humble, quivering ivy. And even farther along . . .

(Evening is dying.
At the palace gates a brand-new, varnished open carriage arrives. From it descend a couple who enter the mansion so haughtily that the beggar thinks: Surely, the eagle and his mate are returning to their nest. The team, noisy and restless, pulls the carriage forward, at one stroke of the whip, making the cobblestones flash with sparks. Night.)

Then, in that madman's brain covered by a threadbare hat, there welled up something like the germ of an idea; traveling to his breast, it caused difficulty in breathing; arriving on his lips, it became a hymn that burned his tongue and made his teeth clash. It was the vision of all beggars, all the forsaken, all the wretched, all suicides, all drunks, of tatters and sores, of all those who live (my God!) in perpetual night, groping in the dark, falling into the abyss for want of a crust to fill their

abismo por no tener un mendrugo para llenar el estómago. Y después la turba feliz, el lecho blando, la trufa y el áureo vino que hierve, el raso y el muaré que con su roce ríen; el novio rubio y la novia morena cubierta de pedrería y blonda; y el gran reloj que la suerte tiene para medir la vida de los felices opulentos, y que, en vez de granos de arena, deja caer escudos de oro.

Aquella especie de poeta sonrió; pero su faz tenía aire dantesco. Sacó de su bolsillo un pan moreno, comió y dio al viento su himno. Nada más cruel que aquel canto tras el mordisco.

¡Cantemos el oro!

Cantemos el oro, rey del mundo, que lleva dicha y luz por donde va, como los fragmentos de un sol despedazado.

Cantemos el oro, que nace del vientre fecundo de la madre Tierra; inmenso tesoro, leche rubia de ubre gigantesca.

Cantemos el oro, río caudaloso, fuente de la vida, que hace jóvenes y bellos a los que se bañan en sus corrientes maravillosas, y envejece a aquellos que no gozan de sus raudales.

Cantemos el oro, porque de él se hacen las tiaras de los pontífices, las coronas de los reyes y los cetros imperiales; y porque se derrama por los montes como un fuego sólido, e inunda las capas de los arzobispos, y refulge en los altares y sostiene al Dios eterno en las custodias radiantes.

Cantemos el oro, porque podemos ser unos perdidos y él nos pone mamparas para cubrir las locuras abyectas de la taberna y las vergüenzas de las alcobas adúlteras.

Cantemos el oro, porque al saltar del cuño lleva en su disco un perfil soberbio de los césares, y va a repletar cajas de sus vastos templos, los bancos, y mueve las máquinas, y da la vida, y hace engordar los tocinos privilegiados.

Cantemos el oro, porque él da los palacios y los carruajes, los vestidos a la moda, y los frescos senos de las mujeres garridas; y las genuflexiones de espinazos aduladores y las muecas de los labios eternamente sonrientes.

Cantemos el oro, padre del pan.

Cantemos el oro, porque es, en las orejas de las lindas damas, sostenedor del rocío del diamante, el extremo de tan sonrosado y bello caracol; porque en los pechos siente el latido de los corazones, y en las manos a veces es símbolo de amor y de santa promesa.

Cantemos el oro, porque tapa las bocas que nos insultan; detiene

stomachs with. Then he saw the throng of the fortunate, soft beds, truffles and bubbling golden wine, satins and moirés that smile as they touch you; a blond fiancé and a dark-haired fiancée covered with jewels and lace; and the big hourlgass with which Fortune measures the lives of the fortunate wealthy, one that, instead of grains of sand, drops gold coins.

That (sort of) poet smiled; but his face wore an expression like Dante's. He drew a dark loaf from his pocket, ate it, and poured out his hymn to the winds. Nothing could be more cruel than that song following that nibble.

Let us sing to gold!

Let us sing to gold, king of the world, which brings felicity and light wherever it goes, like the fragments of a shattered sun.

Let us sing to gold, which is born in the fertile womb of mother earth; a vast treasure, the yellow milk of a gigantic udder.

Let us sing to gold, a copious river, fountain of life, which makes those who bathe in its miraculous current young and beautiful, and makes those old who do not enjoy its torrents.

Let us sing to gold, because of it are made the tiaras of pontiffs, the crowns of kings, and the scepters of emperors; and because it flows through the mountains like solid fire and inundates the copes of archbishops, and gleams on altars and supports eternal God in radiant monstrances.

Let us sing to gold, because we may be lost souls and it provides us with screens to cloak the abject madness of the tavern and the shameful deeds of adulterous bedrooms.

Let us sing to gold, because when it leaves the mint it bears on its disk a haughty profile of some Caesar; and it fills tills in its vast temples, the banks, and sets machines in motion, and dispenses life, and fattens privileged bacon.

Let us sing to gold, because it bestows palaces and carriages, fashionable dresses, and the cool breasts of pretty women; and the genuflections of flattering backs, and the grimaces of eternally smiling lips.

Let us sing to gold, father of bread.

Let us sing to gold, because, in the ears of lovely ladies, it holds up the dew of the diamond, the tip of such a pink, beautiful shell; because on bosoms it feels the beating of hearts, and on hands it is sometimes the symbol of love and a sacred promise.

Let us sing to gold, because it shuts the mouths that insult us; it

las manos que nos amenazan, y pone vendas a los pillos que nos sirven.

Cantemos el oro, porque su voz es música encantada; porque es heroico y luce en las corazas de los héroes homéricos, y en las sandalias de las diosas y en los coturnos trágicos y en las manzanas del Jardín de las Hespérides.

Cantemos el oro, porque de él son las cuerdas de las grandes liras, la cabellera de las más tiernas amadas, los granos de la espiga y el peplo que al levantarse viste la olímpica aurora.

Cantemos el oro, premio y gloria del trabajador y pasto del bandido.

Cantemos el oro, que cruza por el carnaval del mundo disfrazado de papel, de plata, de cobre y hasta de plomo.

Cantemos el oro, amarillo como la muerte.

Cantemos el oro, calificado de vil por los hambrientos; hermano del carbón, oro negro que incuba el diamante; rey de la mina, donde el hombre lucha y la roca se desgarra; poderoso en el poniente, donde se tiñe de sangre; carne de ídolo, tela de que Fidias hace el traje de Minerva.

Cantemos el oro, en el arnés del caballo, en el carro de guerra, en el puño de la espada, en el laurel que ciñe cabezas luminosas, en la copa del festín dionisíaco, en el alfiler que hiere el seno de la esclava, en el rayo del astro y en el champaña que burbujea como una disolución de topacios hirvientes.

Cantemos el oro, porque nos hace gentiles, educados y pulcros.

Cantemos el oro, porque es la piedra de toque de toda amistad.

Cantemos el oro, purificado por el fuego, como el hombre por el sufrimiento; mordido por la lima, como el hombre por la envidia; golpeado por el martillo, como el hombre por la necesidad; realzado por el estuche de seda, como el hombre por el palacio de mármol.

Cantemos el oro, esclavo, despreciado por Jerónimo, arrojado por Antonio, vilipendiado por Macario, humillado por Hilarión, maldecido por Pablo el Ermitaño, quien tenía por alcázar una cueva bronca, y por amigos las estrellas de la noche, los pájaros del alba y las fieras hirsutas y salvajes del yermo.

Cantemos el oro, dios becerro, tuétano de roca misterioso y callado en su entraña, bullicioso cuando brota a pleno sol y a toda vida, sonante como un coro de tímpanos; feto de astros, residuo de luz, encarnación del éter.

Cantemos el oro, hecho sol, enamorado de la noche, cuya camisa de crespón riega de estrellas brillantes, después del último beso, como con una gran muchedumbre de libras esterlinas.

restrains the hands that threaten us; and it blindfolds the rogues who wait on us.

Let us sing to gold, because its voice is enchanted music; because it is heroic and shines in the breastplates of Homeric heroes, and in the sandals of the gods and in the buskins of tragedians and in the apples of the garden of the Hesperides.

Let us sing to gold, because it is the material of the strings of great lyres, of the hair of our tenderest sweethearts, of the ears of grain, and of the peplum that Olympian dawn wears when she arises.

Let us sing to gold, reward and glory of the worker and nourishment of the bandit.

Let us sing to gold, which wanders through the world's carnival disguised as paper, silver, copper, and even lead.

Let us sing to gold, yellow as death.

Let us sing to gold, characterized as vile by the hungry; brother to coal, that black gold which incubates diamonds; king of the mine in which man labors and rock is rended; powerful in the sunset, where it is tinged with blood; an idol of flesh, the cloth from which Phidias makes Minerva's garment.

Let us sing to gold, in the horse's trappings, in the war chariot, on the sword hilt, on the laurel that wreathes luminous heads, in the goblet of the Dionysiac feast, in the pin that wounds the slave girl's breast, in the beams of the heavenly body, and in the champagne that bubbles like seething topazes in solution.

Let us sing to gold, because it makes us genteel, well brought up, and neat.

Let us sing to gold, because it is the touchstone of every friendship.

Let us sing to gold, purified by fire, as men are by their suffering; gnawed by the file, as men are by envy; beaten by the mallet, as men are by need; enhanced by its silk casing, as men are by marble palaces.

Let us sing to gold, a slave, belittled by Saint Jerome, rejected by Saint Anthony, reviled by Macarius, scorned by Hilarion, cursed by Paul the Hermit, whose fortress was a rough cave and whose friends were the night stars, the dawn birds, and the shaggy, fierce beasts of the desert.

Let us sing to gold, a god in the form of a calf, a rock-marrow mysterious and silent in the bowels of the earth, but noisy when it emerges into daylight and the stream of life, resonant as a chorus of kettledrums; fetus of stars, residuum of light, incarnation of ether.

Let us sing to gold, which has become a sun, in love with night, whose crepe chemise it sprinkles with shining stars, after their last kiss, as if with a great multitude of sterling pound coins.

¡Eh!, miserables beodos, pobres de solemnidad, prostitutas, mendigos, vagos, rateros, bandidos, pordioseros peregrinos, y vosotros los desterrados, y vosotros los holgazanes y, sobre todo, vosotros, ¡oh poetas!

¡Unámonos a los felices, a los poderosos, a los banqueros, a los semidioses de la Tierra!

¡Cantemos el oro!

Y el eco se llevó aquel himno, mezcla de gemido, ditirambo y carcajada, y como ya la noche oscura y fría había entrado, el eco resonaba en las tinieblas.

Pasó una vieja y pidió limosna.

Y aquella especie de harapiento, por las trazas un mendigo, tal vez un peregrino, quizá un poeta, le dio su último mendrugo de pan petrificado, y se marchó por la terrible sombra, rezongando entre dientes.

El pájaro azul

París es teatro divertido y terrible. Entre los concurrentes al café Plombier, buenos y decididos muchachos —pintores, escultores, escritores, poetas; sí, ¡todos buscando el viejo laurel verde!—, ninguno más querido que aquel pobre Garcín triste casi siempre, buen bebedor de ajenjo, soñador que nunca se emborrachaba y, como bohemio intachable, bravo improvisador.

En el cuartucho destartalado de nuestras alegres reuniones, guardaba el yeso de las paredes, entre los esbozos de rasgos de futuros Clays, versos, estrofas enteras escritas en letra echada y gruesa de nuestro *pájaro azul*.

El pájaro azul era el pobre Garcín. ¿No sabéis por qué se llamaba, así? Nosotros le bautizamos con ese nombre.

Ello no fue un simple capricho. Aquel excelente muchacho tenía el vino triste. Cuando le preguntábamos por qué, cuando todos reíamos como insensatos o como chicuelos, él arrugaba el ceño y miraba fijamente al cielo raso, nos respondía sonriendo con cierta amargura:

—Camaradas: habéis de saber que tengo un pájaro azul en el cerebro; por consiguiente . . .

Sucedió también que gustaba de ir a las campiñas nuevas, al entrar la primavera. El aire del bosque hacía bien a sus pulmones, según nos decía el poeta.

De sus excursiones solía traer ramos de violetas y gruesos

Ah, wretched drunks, penniless paupers, prostitutes, beggars, tramps, pickpockets, bandits, pilgrims asking for alms, and you the exiled, and you the idlers, and, above all, you the poets!

Let us join the fortunate, the mighty, the bankers, the demigods of the earth!

Let us sing to gold!

And the echoes carried off that hymn, a combination of a moan, a dithyramb, and a horselaugh; and, since dark, cold night had already fallen, the echoes rang in the blackness.

An old woman passed by and asked for alms.

And that (sort of) ragged man, a beggar from the looks of him, perhaps a pilgrim, perhaps a poet, gave away his last hardened crust of bread and departed in the fearful darkness, grumbling to himself.

The Blue Bird

Paris is an amusing and terrible spectacle. Among the habitués of the Café Plombier, good and resolute fellows—painters, sculptors, writers, poets, and all of them in quest of that old green laurel!—none was better liked than that poor Garcín, almost always sad, a heavy drinker of absinthe, a dreamer who never got drunk and, irreproachable bohemian that he was, a talented improviser.

In the ramshackle little room where our jolly gatherings took place, the plaster of the walls, amid sketchy outlines drawn by future Clays, retained entire strophes written in the slanting, thick hand of our "blue bird."

The blue bird was poor Garcín. Don't you know why he was called that? We were the ones who baptized him with that name.

It wasn't a mere caprice. That excellent fellow became sad when he drank. Whenever we asked him why he knitted his brow and stared fixedly at the clear sky while we were laughing like fools, or little boys, he'd reply, smiling with a touch of bitterness:

"Comrades: I'll have you know that there's a blue bird in my brain; therefore . . ."

Moreover, he sometimes liked to visit the fresh countryside at the beginning of spring. The forest air was good for his lungs, the poet told us.

From his excursions he usually brought back bunches of violets and

cuadernillos de madrigales, escritos al ruido de las hojas y bajo el ancho cielo sin nubes. Las violetas eran para Niní, su vecina, una muchacha fresca y rosada, que tenía los ojos muy azules.

Los versos eran para nosotros. Nosotros los leíamos y los aplaudíamos. Todos teníamos una alabanza para Garcín. Era un ingenio que debía brillar. El tiempo vendría. ¡Oh, el pájaro azul volaría muy alto! ¡Bravo! ¡Bien! ¡Eh, mozo, más ajenjo!

Principios de Garcín:
De las flores, las lindas campánulas.
Entre las piedras preciosas, el zafiro.
De las inmensidades, el cielo y el amor; es decir, las pupilas de Niní.
Y repetía el poeta: Creo que siempre es preferible la neurosis a la estupidez.

A veces Garcín estaba más triste que de costumbre.

Andaba por los bulevares; veía pasar, indiferente, los lujosos carruajes, los elegantes, las hermosas mujeres. Frente al escaparate de un joyero sonreía; pero cuando pasaba cerca de un almacén de libros, se llegaba a las vidrieras, husmeaba, y al ver las lujosas ediciones, se declaraba decididamente envidioso, arrugaba la frente; para desahogarse, volvía el rostro hacia el cielo y suspiraba. Corría al café en busca de nosotros, conmovido, exaltado, pedía su vaso de ajenjo, y nos decía:

—Sí; dentro de la jaula de mi cerebro está preso un pájaro azul que quiere su libertad . . .

Hubo algunos que llegaron a creer en un descalabro de razón.

Un alienista a quien se le dio la noticia de lo que pasaba, calificó el caso como una monomanía especial. Sus estudios patológicos no dejaban lugar a duda.

Decididamente, el desgraciado Garcín estaba loco.

Un día recibió de su padre, un viejo provinciano de Normandía, comerciante en trapos, una carta que decía lo siguiente, poco más o menos:

«Sé tus locuras en París. Mientras permanezcas de ese modo no tendrás de mí un solo *sou*. Ven a llevar los libros de mi almacén, y cuando hayas quemado, gandul, tus manuscritos de tonterías, tendrás mi dinero.»

Esta carta se leyó en el café Plombier.

—¿Y te irás?

thick notebooks filled with madrigals written as he heard the leaves rustling beneath the wide, cloudless sky. The violets were for Nini, his neighbor, a healthy, pink young woman with very blue eyes.

The poetry was for us. We would read it and applaud it. We all had praises for Garcín. He had a talent that would surely shine forth. His day would come. Oh, the blue bird was going to fly very high! Bravo! Good! Hey, waiter, more absinthe!

Garcín's favorites:
Among flowers, pretty bluebells.
Among precious stones, sapphires.
Among infinite things, the sky and love—that is, Nini's eyes.
And the poet used to repeat: "I think that being neurotic is always preferable to being stupid."

At certain times Garcín was sadder than usual.

He'd walk along the boulevards; with indifference he saw luxurious carriages, elegant men, and beautiful women go by. In front of a jeweler's window he'd smile; but when he came near a bookstore, he'd walk right up to the windows and sniff, and when he saw luxury editions he admitted he was really envious and he'd wrinkle his brow; to let off steam, he'd turn his face skyward and sigh. He'd run to the café looking for us, moved, excited; he'd order his glass of absinthe, and he'd say:

"Yes, inside the cage of my brain there's a captive blue bird longing to be free. . . ."

There were some who came to believe that his mind was unhinged.

An alienist who was informed of what was going on characterized the case as a special form of fixation. His pathological studies left no room for doubt.

Decidedly, the unfortunate Garcín was mad.

One day he received from his father, an old provincial from Normandy in the "rag" trade, a letter that read as follows, more or less:

"I know about your wild doings in Paris. As long as you keep it up that way, you won't get a single sou from me. Come home and be the bookkeeper in my shop, and when you've burned your foolish manuscripts, good-for-nothing, you'll get my money."

This letter was read in the Café Plombier.
"And will you go?"

—¿No te irás?

—¿Aceptas?

—¿Desdeñas?

¡Bravo, Garcín! Rompió la carta y soltando el trapo a la vena, improvisó unas cuantas estrofas, que acababan, si mal no recuerdo:

> ¡Sí; seré siempre un gandul,
> lo cual aplaudo y celebro
> mientras sea mi cerebro
> jaula del pájaro azul!

Desde entonces Garcín cambió de carácter. Se volvió charlador, se dio un baño de alegría, compró una levita nueva y comenzó un poema en tercetos titulado: *El pájaro azul*.

Cada noche se leía en nuestra tertulia algo nuevo de la obra. Aquello era excelente, sublime, disparatado.

Allí había un cielo muy hermoso, una campiña muy fresca, países brotados como por la magia del pincel de Corot, rostros de niños asomados entre flores, los ojos de Niní húmedos y grandes; y, por añadidura, el buen Dios que envía, volando, volando, sobre todo aquello un pájaro azul que, sin saber cómo ni cuándo, anida dentro del cerebro del poeta, en donde queda aprisionado. Cuando el pájaro canta, se hacen versos alegres y rosados. Cuando el pájaro quiere volar y abre las alas y se da contra las paredes del cráneo, se alzan los ojos al cielo, se arruga la frente y se bebe ajenjo con poca agua, fumando, además, por remate, un cigarrilo de papel.

He aquí el poema.

Una noche llegó Garcín riendo mucho y, sin embargo, muy triste. La bella vecina había sido conducida al cementerio.

—¡Una noticia! ¡Una noticia! Canto último de mi poema. Niní ha muerto. Viene la primavera y Niní se va. Ahorro de violetas para la campiña. Ahora falta el epílogo del poema. Los editores no se dignan siquiera leer mis versos. Vosotros, muy pronto, tendréis que dispersaros. La ley del tiempo. El epílogo se debe titular así: *De cómo el pájaro azul alza el vuelo al cielo azul*.

¡Plena primavera! ¡Los árboles florecidos, las nubes rosadas en el alba y pálidas por la tarde; el aire suave que mueve las hojas y hace

"Won't you go?"

"Do you accept?"

"Do you reject it?"

Bravo, Garcín! He tore up the letter and, starting to write furiously,[3] he improvised a few stanzas, which ended, if my memory doesn't fail me:

> Yes, I'll always be a good-for-nothing,
> A condition that I'll applaud and celebrate
> As long as my brain is
> A cage for the blue bird!

From that time on, Garcín's character changed. He became talkative, he bathed in cheerfulness, he bought a new frock coat, and began a long poem in terza rima called *The Blue Bird*.

Every night some new part of the work was read at our gathering. It was excellent, sublime, eccentric.

In it there was a very beautiful sky, a very fresh countryside, landscapes that seemed to have been created by Corot's magic brush, children's faces peeping out of clusters of flowers, Nini's large, liquid eyes; and, in addition, God, who sends flying, flying, over all this a blue bird, which, without knowing how or when, builds a nest in the poet's brain and is imprisoned there. When the bird sings, the poet writes cheerful, pink verses. When the bird wants to fly, spreads its wings, and dashes itself against the walls of his skull, the poet raises his eyes skyward, wrinkles his brow, and drinks absinthe with not much water, topping this off, in addition, by smoking a cigarette.

That was the content of the poem.

One night Garcín arrived laughing frequently but nevertheless very sad. His beautiful neighbor had been taken to the cemetery.

"News! News! Last canto of my poem. Nini has died. Spring comes and Nini goes. Which means that the countryside can hold onto more of its violets. Now only the epilogue of the poem is missing. Publishers don't even deign to read my verse. Very soon, your group will have to split up. It's the law of time. The epilogue should bear the title: 'How the Blue Bird Wings Its Way to the Blue Sky.'"

Springtime in full force! The trees in blossom, the clouds pink at dawn and pale in the evening; gentle breezes stirring the leaves and

---

[3]The Spanish phrase is obscure and has been interpreted and amended in various ways.

aletear las cintas de los sombreros de paja con especial ruido! Garcín
no ha ido al campo.

He ahí; viene con un traje nuevo, a nuestro amado café Plombier,
pálido, con una sonrisa triste.

—¡Amigos míos, un abrazo! Abrazadme todos, así, fuerte; decidme
adiós, con todo el corazón, con toda el alma . . . El pájaro azul vuela . . .

Y el pobre Garcín lloró, nos estrechó, nos apretó las manos con
todas sus fuerzas y se fue.

Todos dijimos: Garcín, el hijo pródigo, busca a su padre, el viejo
normando. —Musas, adiós; adiós, Gracias. ¡Nuestro poeta se decide a
medir trapos! ¡Eh! ¡Una copa por Garcín!

Pálidos, asustados, entristecidos, al día siguiente todos los parro-
quianos del café Plombier, que metíamos tanta bulla en aquel cuartu-
cho destartalado, nos hallábamos en la habitación de Garcín. Él estaba
en su lecho sobre las sábanas ensangrentadas, con el cráneo roto de
un balazo. Sobre la almohada había fragmentos de masa cerebral . . .
¡Horrible!

Cuando, repuestos de la impresión, pudimos llorar ante el cadáver
de nuestro amigo, encontramos que tenía consigo el famoso poema.
En la última página había escrito estas palabras: *Hoy, en plena pri-
mavera, dejo abierta la puerta de la jaula al pájaro azul.*

¡Ay, Garcín, cuántos llevan en el cerebro tu misma enfermedad!

Palomas blancas y garzas morenas

Mi prima Inés era rubia como una alemana. Fuimos criados juntos,
desde muy niños, en casa de la buena abuelita, que nos amaba mucho
y nos hacía vernos como hermanos, vigilándonos cuidadosamente,
viendo que no riñésemos. ¡Adorable la viejecita, con sus trajes a
grandes flores, y sus cabellos crespos y recogidos, como una vieja mar-
quesa de Boucher!

Inés era un poco mayor que yo. No obstante, yo aprendí a leer antes
que ella; y comprendía —lo recuerdo muy bien— lo que ella recitaba
de memoria, maquinalmente, en una pastorela, donde bailaba y
cantaba delante del niño Jesús, la hermosa María y el Señor San José;
todo con el gozo de las sencillas personas mayores de la familia, que
reían con risa de miel, alabando el talento de la actrizuela.

fluttering the ribbons on straw hats with that special sound! Garcín hasn't gone to the country.

Here he is; he arrives at our beloved Café Plombier in a new suit, pale, with a sad smile.

"My friends, an embrace! All of you embrace me, like this, hard; say good-bye to me with all your heart, with all your soul. . . . The blue bird is flying. . . ."

And poor Garcín wept, hugged us, shook hands with us with all his might, and left.

We all said: "Garcín, the prodigal son, is returning to his old father in Normandy. Muses, farewell; farewell, Graces. Our poet has decided to measure out cloth! Hey! A glass for Garcín!"

The next day, our whole flock from the Café Plombier, the same ones who raised such a row in that ramshackle little room, were in Garcín's apartment, pale, frightened, saddened. He was lying on his bed on top of the blood-stained sheets, his skull split open by a bullet. On the pillow there were bits of brain tissue. . . . Horrible!

When we got over our first shock and were able to weep over our friend's body, we found that he had that much-discussed poem with him. On the last page he had written these words: "Today, while spring-time is in full force, I am leaving the cage door open for the blue bird."

Ah, Garcín, how many people there are with the same sickness as yours in their minds!

White Doves and Brown Herons

My cousin Inés was as blond as a German woman. We were brought up together from early childhood in the home of my good grandmother, who loved us dearly and led us to regard each other as brother and sister, keeping careful watch over us and making sure we didn't fight. How adorable that little old lady was, with her dresses patterned with big flowers, and her curly hair tied back, like an old marquise in a Boucher painting!

Inés was a little older than I. All the same, I learned to read before she did; and I understood (I remember this clearly) the lines she used to recite from memory, mechanically, in a Christmas playlet in which she danced and sang in front of the Christ Child, the beautiful Virgin, and Saint Joseph; all to the joy of the simple adults in the family who gave honeyed laughs, praising the little actress's talent.

Inés crecía. Yo también; pero no tanto como ella. Yo debía entrar a un colegio, en internado terrible y triste, a dedicarme a los áridos estudios del bachillerato, a comer los platos clásicos de los estudiantes, a no ver el mundo —¡mi mundo de mozo!— y mi casa, mi abuela, mi prima, mi gato, un excelente romano que se restregaba cariñosamente en mis piernas y me llenaba los trajes negros de pelos blancos.

Partí.

Allá, en el colegio, mi adolescencia se despertó por completo. Mi voz tomó timbres aflautados y roncos; llegué al período ridículo del niño que pasa a joven. Entonces, por un fenómeno especial, en vez de preocuparme de mi profesor de matemáticas, que no logró nunca hacer que yo comprendiese el binomio de Newton, pensé —todavía vaga y misteriosamente— en mi prima Inés.

Luego tuve revelaciones profundas. Supe muchas cosas. Entre ellas, que los besos eran un placer exquisito.

Tiempo.

Leí *Pablo y Virginia.* Llegó un fin de año escolar y salí de vacaciones, rápido como una saeta camino de mi casa. ¡Libertad!

Mi prima —¡pero Dios Santo, en tan poco tiempo!— se había hecho una mujer completa. Yo delante de ella me hallaba como avergonzado, un tanto serio. Cuando me dirigía la palabra, me ponía a sonreírle con una sonrisa simple.

Ya tenía quince años y medio Inés. La cabellera dorada y luminosa al sol, era un tesoro. Blanca y levemente amapolada, su cara era una creación murillesca, si se veía de frente. A veces, contemplando su perfil, pensaba en una soberbia medalla siracusana, en un rostro de princesa. El traje, corto antes, había descendido. El seno, firme y esponjado, era un ensueño oculto y supremo; la voz clara y vibrante, las pupilas azules inefables, la boca llena de fragancia, de vida y de color de púrpura. ¡Sana y virginal primavera!

La abuelita me recibió con los brazos abiertos. Inés se negó a abrazarme, me tendió la mano. Después, no me atreví a invitarla a los juegos de antes. Me sentía tímido. ¡Y qué! Ella debía de sentir algo de lo que yo.

¡Yo amaba a mi prima!

Inés, los domingos, iba con la abuela a misa muy de mañana.

Mi dormitorio estaba vecino al de ellas. Cuando cantaban los campanarios su sonora llamada matinal, ya estaba yo despierto.

Oía, oreja atenta, el ruido de las ropas. Por la puerta entreabierta veía salir la pareja que hablaba en voz alta. Cerca de mí pasaba el

Inés grew. So did I; but not as fast as she did. I was to enter school, a terrible, gloomy boarding school, to devote my time to the arid studies for a high-school diploma, to eat the time-honored food of students, and no longer see the world—my adolescent world!—or my home, my grandmother, my cousin, or my cat, a fine Roman breed, which used to rub up against my legs affectionately and cover my dark suits with white hairs.

I left.

There, at school, my puberty was completely awakened. My voice took on high-pitched and hoarse timbres; I had arrived at the ludicrous phase of a boy becoming a young man. Then, by a special phenomenon, instead of concerning myself with my mathematics teacher, who never succeeded in making me understand Newton's binomial, my thoughts turned—still vaguely and mysteriously—to my cousin Inés.

Next, I had profound revelations. I learned many things. Among them, that kisses were an exquisite pleasure.

Time passed.

I read *Paul et Virginie*. A school year came to an end, and I left on vacation, heading homeward as swiftly as an arrow. Freedom!

My cousin (dear God, how quickly!) had become a full-fledged woman. In her presence I felt somewhat ashamed, a little over-serious. When she spoke to me, I started to smile at her with a mindless smile.

Inés was already fifteen and a half. With her luminous golden hair in the sunshine she was a treasure. Fair-skinned with a touch of red, her face was like a painting by Murillo, when looked at head on. At times while gazing at her profile, I was reminded of a splendid coin from ancient Syracuse, a princess's visage. Her dress, formerly short, was now longer. Her breasts, firm and spongy, were a hidden, supreme dream; her voice was clear and vibrant, her eyes were indescribably blue, her fragrant purple lips were full of life. A healthy, virginal springtime!

My grandmother welcomed me with open arms. Inés refused to hug me; she held out her hand. Afterward, I didn't dare invite her to the games we used to play. I felt shy. Why not? She must have shared some of my feelings.

I was in love with my cousin!

On Sundays Inés used to go to Mass with my grandmother at a very early hour.

My bedroom was near theirs. When the church bells rang out their resonant morning call, I'd be already awake.

All ears, I'd hear the rustle of their clothing. Through the slightly opened door I'd see the pair go out, speaking aloud. Near me passed

frufrú de las polleras antiguas de mi abuela y del traje de Inés, co-
queto, ajustado, para mí siempre revelador.

¡Oh, Eros!

—Inés . . .

—¿ . . . ?

Y estábamos solos, a la luz de una luna argentina dulce, ¡una bella
luna de aquellas del país de Nicaragua!

Le dije todo lo que sentía, suplicante, balbuciente, echando las
palabras, ya rápidas, ya contenidas, febril y temeroso. Sí, se lo dije
todo: las agitaciones sordas y extrañas que en mí experimentaba
cerca de ella, el amor, el ansia, los tristes insomnios del deseo, mis
ideas fijas en ella allá en mis meditaciones del colegio; y repetía
como una oración sagrada la gran palabra: amor: ¡Oh, ella debía
recibir gozosa mi adoración! Creceríamos más. Seríamos marido y
mujer . . .

Esperé.

La pálida claridad celeste nos iluminaba. El ambiente nos llevaba
perfumes tibios que a mí se me imaginaban propicios para los fogosos
amores.

¡Cabellos áureos, ojos paradisíacos, labios encendidos y entreabier-
tos!

De repente, y con un mohín:

—¡Ve! La tontería . . .

Y corrió como una gata alegre adonde se hallaba la abuela, rezando
a las calladas sus rosarios y responsorios.

Con risa descocada de educanda maliciosa, con aire de locuela:

—¡Eh, abuelita, ya me dijo! . . .

¡Ellas, pues, sabían que yo debía «decir»! . . .

Con su reír interrumpió el rezo de la anciana, que se quedó pen-
sativa, acariciando las cuentas de su camándula. ¡Y yo que todo lo veía
a la husma, de lejos, lloraba, sí, lloraba lágrimas amargas, las primeras
de mis desengaños de hombre!

Los cambios fisiológicos que en mí se sucedían y las agitaciones de
mi espíritu me conmovían hondamente. ¡Dios mío! Soñador, un pe-
queño poeta como me creía, al comenzarme el bozo, sentía llenas de
ilusiones la cabeza, de versos los labios, y mi alma y mi cuerpo de
púber tenían sed de amor. ¿Cuándo llegaría el momento soberano en
que alumbraría una celeste mirada el fondo de mi ser, y aquel en que
se rasgaría el velo del enigma atrayente?

the frou-frou of my grandmother's old-fashioned petticoats and of Inés's dress, stylish, form-fitting, always a revelation to me.

O Eros!

"Inés?"

"Hmm?"

We were alone, in the light of a soft, silvery moon, one of those beautiful moons that shine in Nicaragua!

I told her all I was feeling, beseechingly, stammeringly, blurting out the words, now rapidly, now with constraint; I was feverish and timid. Yes, I told her everything: the strange obscure excitement I felt inside me when I was near her, my love, my anxiety, the sad nights when my desire kept me awake, the fixation of my thoughts on her there in my meditations at school; and I repeated, as if it were a holy prayer, the great word: love. Oh, she'd surely be glad to accept my adoration! We'd grow up to be adults. We'd be man and wife. . . .

I stopped and waited.

The pale brightness from the sky illumined us. The gardens around us wafted warm fragrance to us that I imagined was auspicious for ardent romance.

Golden hair, heavenly eyes, burning lips slightly parted!

Suddenly, making a face, she said:

"Oh, how stupid! . . ."

And she ran like a jolly cat to where my grandmother sat, quietly saying her rosaries and responsories.

With the brazen laughter of a naughty schoolgirl and with a madcap air, Inés said:

"Well, Grandmother, he's come out with it! . . ."

And so they knew I was bound to "come out with it"! . . .

Inés's laughter interrupted the old woman's prayers, and my grandmother became thoughtful, caressing the beads of her rosary. And I, who saw all this by conjecture, from afar, I was crying, yes, crying bitter tears, the first tears of my grown-up disappointments!

The bodily changes I kept on undergoing, and the troubles of my mind, affected me deeply. My God! A dreamer, a young poet as I imagined myself, when my first facial hair was sprouting, I felt my head full of ambitious dreams and my lips full of verses, and my adolescent soul and body were thirsting for love. When would that supreme moment come in which a heavenly gaze would light up the depths of my being, the moment when the veil of the alluring enigma would be torn?

Un día, a pleno sol, Inés estaba en el jardín regando trigo, entre los arbustos y las flores, a las que llamaba sus amigas: unas palomas albas, arrulladoras, con sus buches níveos y amorosamente musicales. Llevaba un traje —siempre que con ella he soñado la he visto con el mismo— gris, azulado, de anchas mangas, que dejaban ver casi por entero los satinados brazos alabastrinos; los cabellos los tenía recogidos y húmedos y el vello alborotado de su nuca blanca y rosa era para mí como luz crespa. Las aves andaban a su alrededor, e imprimían en el suelo oscuro la estrella acarminada de sus patas.

Hacía calor. Yo estaba oculto tras los ramajes de unos jazmines. La devoraba con los ojos. ¡Por fin se acercó por mi escondite, la prima gentil! Me vio trémulo, enrojecida la faz, en mis ojos una llama viva y rara y acariciante, y se puso a reír cruelmente, terriblemente. ¡Y bien! ¡Oh, aquello no era posible! Me lancé con rapidez frente a ella. Audaz, formidable debía estar cuando retrocedió, como asustada, un paso.

—¡Te amo!

Entonces tornó a reír. Una paloma voló a uno de sus brazos. Ella la miró dándole granos de trigo entre las perlas de su boca fresca y sensual. Me acerqué más. Mi rostro estaba junto al suyo. Los cándidos animales nos rodeaban. Me turbaba el cerebro una onda invisible y fuerte de aroma femenil. ¡Se me antojaba Inés una paloma hermosa y humana, blanca y sublime, y al propio tiempo llena de fuego, de ardor, un tesoro de dichas! No dije más. Le tomé la cabeza y le di un beso en una mejilla, un beso rápido, quemante, de pasión furiosa. Ella, un tanto enojada, salió en fuga. Las palomas se asustaron y alzaron el vuelo formando un opaco ruido de alas sobre los arbustos temblorosos. Yo, abrumado, quedé inmóvil.

Al poco tiempo partía a otra ciudad. La paloma blanca y rubia no había, ¡ay!, mostrado a mis ojos el soñado paraíso del misterioso deleite.

¡Musa ardiente y sacra para mi alma, el día había de llegar! Elena, la graciosa, la alegre, ella fue el nuevo amor. ¡Bendita sea aquella boca que murmuró por primera vez cerca de mí las inefables palabras!

¡Era allá, en una ciudad que está a la orilla de un lago de mi tierra, un lago encantador lleno de islas floridas, con pájaros de colores!

Los dos solos, estábamos cogidos de las manos, sentados en el viejo muelle, debajo del cual el agua glauca y oscura chapoteaba musicalmente. Había un crepúsculo acariciador, de aquellos que son la

One day, in broad daylight, Inés was in the garden, amid the shrubs and flowers, scattering grain to those she called her friends: a group of cooing white doves, with their snowy, amorously musical throats. She was wearing a dress—every time I've dreamed of her, I've seen her in that dress—which was a bluish gray, with wide sleeves that permitted an almost complete view of her satiny, alabaster arms; her hair was tied back and damp, and the ruffled down on her white-and-pink nape was to me like crinkled light. The birds were walking around her, imprinting the carmine star of their feet on the dark soil.

It was a hot day. I was hidden behind the branches of some jasmine plants. I was devouring her with my eyes. Finally she approached my hiding place, my sweet cousin! She saw me trembling, my face all red, a vivid, strange, caressing flame in my eyes, and she started to laugh cruelly, horribly. Well! That just wasn't possible! I rapidly darted toward her. I must have looked bold and terrifying when she took a step backward, as if frightened.

"I love you!"

Then she laughed again. A dove flew up to one of her arms. She looked at it and fed it wheat grains from between the pearly teeth in her cool, sensual mouth. I came closer. My face was next to hers. The white birds were all around us. My brain was confused by a strong, invisible wave of the smell of woman. I imagined Inés as a beautiful human dove, white and sublime, but at the same time full of fire and ardor, a treasure of bliss! I said no more. I took her head and kissed her on one cheek; it was a quick kiss, burning, furious with passion. Somewhat angry, she ran away. The doves got scared and flew upward, creating a dense fluttering of wings over the trembling shrubs. Overwhelmed, I remained stock-still.

Not long after that, I left for another town. Alas, the white, blond dove hadn't given my eyes a glimpse of that paradise of mysterious delight I dreamed of.

Ardent muse, sacred to my soul, that day was to come! Elena, the graceful, the cheerful—she was my new love. Blessings on the lips that first murmured those indescribable words in my ear!

It was yonder, in a city beside a lake in my country, an enchanting lake full of flowering islands, with brightly colored birds!

The two of us were alone, holding hands and seated on the old wharf, under which the dark blue-green water was lapping musically. It was a caressing dusk, of the kind that are among the delights of

delicia de los enamorados tropicales. En el cielo opalino se veía una diafanidad apacible que disminuía hasta cambiarse en tonos de violeta oscuro, por la parte del Oriente, y aumentaba convirtiéndose en oro sonrosado en el horizonte profundo, donde vibraban oblicuos, rojos y desfallecientes, los últimos rayos solares. Arrastrada por el deseo, me miraba la adorada mía y nuestros ojos se decían cosas ardorosas y extrañas. En el fondo de nuestras almas cantaban un unísono embriagador como dos invisibles y divinas Filomelas.

Yo, extasiado, veía a la mujer tierna y ardiente; con su cabellera castaña que acariciaba con mis manos, su rostro color de canela y rosa, su boca cleopatrina, su cuerpo gallardo y virginal, y oía su voz queda, muy queda, que me decía frases cariñosas, tan bajo, como que sólo eran para mí, temerosa quizá de que se las llevase el viento vespertino. Fijos en mí, me inundaban de felicidad sus ojos de Minerva, ojos verdes, ojos que deben siempre gustar a los poetas. Luego erraban nuestras miradas por el lago todavía lleno de vaga claridad. Cerca de la orilla se detuvo un gran grupo de garzas. Garzas blancas, garzas morenas, de esas que cuando el día calienta llegan a las riberas a espantar a los cocodrilos, que con las anchas mandíbulas abiertas beben sol sobre las rocas negras. ¡Bellas garzas! Algunas ocultaban los largos cuellos en la onda, o bajo el ala, y semejaban grandes manchas de flores vivas y sonrosadas, móviles y apacibles. A veces una, sobre una pata, se alisaba con el pico las plumas, o permanecía inmóvil, escultural y hieráticamente, o varias daban un corto vuelo, formando en el fondo de la ribera llena de verde, o en el cielo, caprichosos dibujos, como las bandadas de grullas de un parasol chino.

Me imaginaba junto a mi amada, que de aquel país de la altura me traerían las garzas muchos versos desconocidos y soñadores. Las garzas blancas las encontraba más puras y más voluptuosas, con la pureza de la paloma y la voluptuosidad del cisne; garridas, con sus cuellos reales, parecidos a los de las damas inglesas que junto a los pajecillos rizados se ven en aquel cuadro en que Shakespeare recita en la corte de Londres. Sus alas, delicadas y albas, hacen pensar en desfallecientes sueños nupciales, todas —bien dice un poeta— como cinceladas en jaspe.

¡Ah, pero las otras tenían algo de más encantador para mí! Mi Elena se me antojaba como semejante a ellas, con su color de canela y de rosa, gallarda y gentil.

Ya el sol desaparecía, arrastrando toda su púrpura opulenta de rey oriental. Yo había halagado a la amada tiernamente con mis juramen-

lovers in the tropics. In the opaline sky there was a peaceful trans-
parency that graded off until it changed to tones of dark violet toward
the east, and grew brighter until changing to rosy gold at the deep
horizon, where the last beams of the sun were vibrating, oblique, red,
and losing their strength. Spurred by desire, my adored one was look-
ing at me, and our eyes exchanged ardent, strange messages. Deep in
our souls, two invisible, divine nightingales seemed to be singing in in-
toxicating unison.

In ecstasy I gazed at the tender, ardent woman, with her chestnut
hair that I was stroking with my hands, her face the color of cinnamon
and roses, her mouth like Cleopatra's, her elegant, virginal body; and I
listened to her low, very low voice speaking affectionate words, as qui-
etly as if they were meant for me alone—she was afraid, perhaps, that
the evening breeze might carry them away. Fixed on me, her Minerva-
like eyes were drowning me in bliss, green eyes, eyes that poets must al-
ways like. Then our glances strayed over the lake, which was still full of
a vague glow. Near the shore a big flock of herons had halted. White
herons, brown herons, the type that come to shorelines on hot, sunny
days to frighten the crocodiles that lie on the black rocks drinking in the
sunshine with their gaping jaws open. Beautiful herons! Some of them
were hiding their long necks in the water, or under one wing, and they
resembled big blotches of living, pink flowers, endowed with motion
but peaceful. At times one of them, standing on one leg, would preen
its feathers with its bill, or would remain motionless, sculpturally and hi-
eratically; or else a few of them would take a brief flight, creating whim-
sical designs against the background of the greenery-filled shoreline, or
against the sky, like the flocks of cranes on a Chinese parasol.

Sitting there next to my loved one, I imagined that the herons
would bring back many unknown, dreamy verses for me from that
land high aloft. I found the white herons more pure and voluptuous,
with the purity of the dove and the voluptuousness of the swan; pretty,
with their regal necks, like those of the English ladies who are seen
alongside little curly-haired pages in that painting where Shakespeare
is reciting at the royal court in London. Their wings, delicate and
white, are reminiscent of fading nuptial dreams; they all seem—as a
poet well says—to be carved out of jasper.

Oh, but the other herons held greater enchantment for me! My
Elena appeared to me to resemble *them*, with her cinnamon-and-rose
complexion, her elegance and charm.

And the sun was disappearing, drawing away all its opulent purple,
like that of an Eastern monarch. I had tenderly flattered my loved one

tos y frases melifluas y cálidas; y juntos seguíamos en un lánguido dúo de pasión inmensa. Habíamos sido hasta ahí dos amantes soñadores, consagrados místicamente uno a otro.

De pronto, y como atraídos por una fuerza secreta, en un momento inexplicable, nos besamos la boca, todo trémulos, con un beso para mí sacratísimo y supremo: el primer beso recibido de labios de mujer. ¡Oh, Salomón, bíblico y real poeta, tú lo dijiste como nadie: *Mel et lac sub lingua tua!*

Aquel día no soñamos más.

¡Ah, mi adorable, mi bella, mi querida garza morena! ¡Tú tienes en los recuerdos que en mi alma forman lo más alto y sublime, una luz inmortal!

Porque tú me revelaste el secreto de las delicias divinas en el inefable primer instante de amor.

La muerte de la emperatriz de la China

Delicada y fina como una joya humana, vivía aquella muchachita de carne rosada en la pequeña casa que tenía un saloncito con los tapices de color azul desfalleciente. Era su estuche.

¿Quién era el dueño de aquel delicioso pájaro alegre, de ojos negros y boca roja? ¿Para quién cantaba su canción divina, cuando la señorita Primavera mostraba en el triunfo del sol su bello rostro riente, abría las flores del campo, y alborotaba la nidada? Suzette se llamaba la avecilla que había puesto en jaula de seda, peluches y encajes, un soñador artista cazador, que la había cazado una mañana de mayo en que había mucha luz en el aire y muchas rosas abiertas.

Recaredo —capricho paternal, él no tenía la culpa de llamarse Recaredo— se había casado hacía año y medio.

—¿Me amas?

—Te amo. ¿Y tú?

—Con toda el alma.

Hermoso el día dorado, después de lo del cura.

Habían ido luego al campo nuevo, a gozar libres del gozo del amor. Murmuraban allá en sus ventanas de hojas verdes, las campanillas y las violetas silvestres que olían cerca del riachuelo, cuando pasaban los dos amantes, el brazo de él en la cintura de ella, el brazo de ella en la cintura de él, los rojos labios en flor dejando escapar los besos.

with my vows and my warm, honeyed phrases; and together we remained in a languid duet of immense passion. Up till then we had been two dream lovers, mystically devoted to each other.

Suddenly, as if drawn by some secret force, at an unexplainable moment, we joined our lips, all a-tremble, in a kiss that was to me most holy and supreme: the first kiss I had received from a woman's lips. O Solomon, biblical and royal poet, you said it better than anyone else: "Honey and milk are under thy tongue!"

That day we no longer merely dreamed.

Oh, my adorable, my beautiful, my beloved brown heron! In the memories that constitute the loftiest and most sublime part of my soul, you retain an immortal light!

Because you revealed to me the secret of the divine delights at the indescribable first moment of love.

The Death of the Empress of China

Delicate and fine as a human jewel, that pink-fleshed girl lived in the little house that had a salon tapestried in faded blue. It was her jewel case.

Who was the owner of that delightful merry bird with dark eyes and red lips? For whom did she sing her divine song when Miss Springtime showed her beautiful smiling face as the sun triumphed, opened the flowers in the fields, and created a disturbance in the nest? Suzette was the name of the little songbird that had been placed in a silk, plush, and lace cage by an artist, a dreamer and a huntsman who had captured her one May morning when the air was full of light and many rosebuds had opened.

Recaredo—it was his parents' whim, it wasn't his fault that his name was Recaredo—had been married about a year and a half.

"Love me?"

"Love you. And you?"

"With all my soul."

That golden day had been beautiful, after the parish priest's business was over.

First they had gone to the fresh countryside to enjoy the joy of love at liberty. There, in their windows of green leaves, came the murmur of the bellflowers and the wild violets that gave off their fragrance near the brook when the two lovers passed by, his arm around her waist, her arm around his waist, their red lips in blossom letting kisses

Después, fue la vuelta a la gran ciudad, al nido lleno de perfume, de juventud y de calor dichoso.

¿Dije ya que Recaredo era escultor? Pues si no lo he dicho, sabedlo.

Era escultor. En la pequeña casa tenía su taller, con profusión de mármoles, yesos, bronces y terracotas. A veces, los que pasaban oían a través de las rejas y persianas una voz que cantaba y un martilleo vibrante y metálico. Suzette, Recaredo, la boca que emergía el cántico, y el golpe del cincel.

Luego el incesante idilio nupcial. En puntillas, llegar donde él trabajaba, e inundándole de cabellos la nuca, besarle rápidamente. Quieto, quietecito, llegar donde ella duerme en su *chaise longue,* los piececitos calzados y con medias negras, uno sobre otro, el libro abierto sobre el regazo, medio dormida; y allí el beso es en los labios, beso que sorbe el aliento y hace que se abran los ojos inefablemente luminosos. Y a todo esto, las carcajadas del mirlo, un mirlo enjaulado que cuando Suzette toca de Chopin, se pone triste y no canta. ¡Las carcajadas del mirlo! No era poca cosa.

—¿Me quieres?

—¿No lo sabes?

—¡Te adoro!

Ya estaba el animalucho echando toda la risa del pico. Se le sacaba de la jaula, revolaba por el saloncito azulado, se detenía en la cabeza de un Apolo de yeso, o en la frámea de un viejo germano de bronce oscuro. Tiiiiiirit . . . rrrrrrich . . . fiii . . . ¡Vaya que a veces era malcriado e insolente en la algarabía! Pero era lucido sobre la mano de Suzette, que le mimaba, le apretaba el pico entre sus dientes hasta hacerlo desesperar, y le decía a veces con una voz severa que temblaba de terneza:

—¡Señor mirlo, es usted un picarón!

Cuando los dos amados estaban juntos, se arreglaban uno al otro el cabello. «Canta», decía él. Y ella cantaba lentamente; y aunque no eran sino pobres muchachos enamorados, se veían hermosos, gloriosos y reales; él la miraba como a una Elsa, y ella le miraba como a un Lohengrin. Porque el Amor, ¡oh, jóvenes llenos de sangre y de sueños!, pone un azul cristal ante los ojos y da infinitas alegrías.

¡Cómo se amaban! Él la contemplaba sobre las estrellas de Dios; su amor recorría toda la escala de la pasión, y era ya contenido, ya tempestuoso en su querer, a veces casi místico. En ocasiones dijérase aquel artista un teósofo que veía en la amada mujer algo supremo y

escape. Afterward, they returned to the big city, to their fragrant nest full of youth and happy warmth.

Have I already said that Recaredo was a sculptor? If not, I now inform you of that fact.

He was a sculptor. In the little house he had his studio, with a profusion of marble statues, plaster casts, bronzes, and terra-cottas. Sometimes passersby heard through the window grilles and shutters a voice singing and vibrant, metallic mallet strokes. Suzette, Recaredo, the lips that emitted the canticle, and the blow of the chisel.

Then, the unceasing marital idyll. She'd walk on tiptoes to where he was working and flood the back of his neck with her hair, giving him quick kisses. Quietly, very quietly, he'd go up to where she was sleeping on her chaise longue, her little feet in their shoes and black stockings, one foot over the other, the open book on her lap as she drowsed; and there he'd kiss her lips with a kiss that draws in her breath and makes her indescribably luminous eyes open. And on top of all that, the laughter of the blackbird, a caged blackbird that becomes sad and stops singing whenever Suzette plays Chopin. The blackbird's laughter! It was no trifle.

"Love me?"

"Don't you know?"

"I adore you!"

By now the little creature was emitting all the laughter its beak contained. It was taken out of the cage, it flew around the little bluish salon, it paused on the head of a plaster Apollo, or on the dark bronze javelin of some ancient Teuton. Trrr . . . riii . . . fiii . . . Yes, at times its gibberish was impolite and insolent! But it was splendid on the hand of Suzette, who pampered it, squeezing its beak between her teeth until it became desperate, and at times saying to it in a severe voice that trembled with tenderness:

"Mister Blackbird, you're a great rogue!"

When the two lovers were together, they used to arrange each other's hair. "Sing," he'd say. And she sang slowly; and though they were only poor youngsters in love, they saw themselves as good-looking, glorious, and regal; he looked on her as on an Elsa, and she looked on him as on a Lohengrin. Because, O young people full of vitality and dreams, Love places a blue crystal before one's eyes and gives infinite pleasures.

How they loved each other! He regarded her as loftier than God's stars; his love ran the whole gamut of passion; in his affection he was now restrained, now stormy, sometimes almost mystical. On occasions you might imagine that that artist was a theosophist who saw in the beloved

extrahumano como la Ayesha de Rider Haggard; y se sentía soberbia-
mente vencedor al estrechar contra su pecho aquella adorable cabeza,
que cuando estaba pensativa y quieta era comparable al perfil
hierático de la medalla de una emperatriz bizantina.

Recaredo amaba su arte. Tenía la pasión de la forma; hacía brotar
del mármol gallardas diosas desnudas de ojos blancos, serenos y sin
pupilas; su taller estaba poblado de un pueblo de estatuas silen-
ciosas, animales de metal, gárgolas terroríficas, grifos de largas colas
vegetales, creaciones góticas quizá inspiradas por el ocultismo. ¡Y,
sobre todo, la gran afición! Japonerías y chinerías. Recaredo era en
esto un original. No sé qué habría dado por hablar chino o japonés.
Conocía los mejores álbumes; había leído buenos exotistas, adoraba
a Loti y a Judith Gautier, y hacía sacrificios por adquirir trabajos
legítimos de Yokohama, de Nagasaki, de Kioto o de Nankín o Pekín;
los cuchillos, las pipas, las máscaras feas y misteriosas, como las caras
de los sueños hípnicos, los mandarinitos enanos con panzas de cur-
bitáceas y ojos circunflejos, los monstruos de grandes bocas de ba-
tracios, abiertas y dentadas, y diminutos soldados de Tartaria, con
faces foscas.

—¡Oh —le decía Suzette—, aborrezco tu casa de brujo, ese terri-
ble taller, arca extraña que te roba a mis caricias!

Él sonreía, dejaba su lugar de labor, su templo de raras chucherías
y corría al pequeño salón azul, a ver y mimar su gracioso dije vivo, y
oír cantar y reír al loco mirlo jovial.

Aquella mañana cuando entró, vio que estaba su dulce Suzette,
soñolienta y tendida, cerca de un tazón de rosas que sostenía un
trípode. ¿Era la Bella durmiente del bosque? Medio dormida, el de-
licado cuerpo modelado bajo una bata blanca, la cabellera castaña
apelotonada sobre uno de los hombros, toda ella exhalando un suave
olor femenino, era como una deliciosa figura de los amables cuentos
que empiezan: «Éste era un rey . . .»

La despertó:

—¡Suzette; mi bella!

Traía la cara alegre; le brillaban los ojos negros bajo su fez rojo de
labor; llevaba una carta en la mano.

—Carta de Robert, Suzette. ¡El bribonazo está en China! «Hong
Kong, 18 de enero . . .»

Suzette, un tanto amodorrada, se había sentado y le había quitado
el papel. ¡Conque aquel andariego había llegado tan lejos! «Hong
Kong, 18 de enero . . .» Era gracioso. ¡Un excelente muchacho el tal

woman something supreme and superhuman like Rider Haggard's Ayesha; and he considered himself a proud conqueror when he pressed to his bosom that adorable head, which, when quiet and thoughtful, was comparable to the hieratic profile on a Byzantine empress's coin.

Recaredo loved his art. He had a passion for form; he caused to emerge from the marble block elegant nude goddesses with white, serene, pupilless eyes; his studio was peopled by a population of silent statues, metal animals, terrifying gargoyles, griffins with long, plant-like tails, gothic creations perhaps inspired by his studies of the occult. And above all, his greatest hobby: collecting Japanese and Chinese art objects. In this Recaredo was an original. I don't know what he wouldn't have given to be able to speak Chinese or Japanese. He was familiar with the best art books; he had read the works of experts in exotica, and he worshipped Loti and Judith Gautier; he made sacrifices in order to acquire authentic items from Yokohama, Nagasaki, and Kyoto, or from Nanking and Peking: knives, pipes, ugly, mysterious masks like the faces in hypnotic dreams, dwarf mandarins with gourd bellies and curved eyes, monsters with big mouths like toads, open and filled with teeth, and tiny soldiers from Tartary with dark faces.

"Oh," Suzette would say, "I abhor your wizard's house, that awful studio, a strange ark that steals you from my caresses!"

He would smile and would leave his workplace, his temple of rare knickknacks, and he'd run into the little blue salon to visit and pamper his graceful living jewel, and hear the mad, jovial blackbird sing and laugh.

When he entered that morning, he saw his sweet Suzette lying drowsily near a bowlful of roses supported by a tripod. Was she Sleeping Beauty? Half-asleep, the form of her delicate body clearly perceptible under her white robe, her chestnut hair heaped up on one shoulder, and her whole person emitting a sweet female fragrance, she was like a delightful character in those lovable folktales that begin: "There once was a king. . . ."

He awakened her.

"Suzette, darling!"

His face was cheerful; his dark eyes shone below the red fez he wore while working; he had a letter in his hand.

"A letter from Robert, Suzette. The scoundrel is in China! 'Hong Kong, January 18th . . .'"

Suzette, a little drowsy, had sat up and had taken the sheet of paper from him. And so that gadabout had gotten that far! "Hong Kong, January 18th . . ." It was funny. A likeable fellow, that Robert, with his

Robert, con la manía de viajar! Llegaría al fin del mundo. ¡Robert, un grande amigo! Le veían como de la familia. Había partido hacía dos años para San Francisco de California. ¡Habríase visto loco igual!

Comenzó a leer.

«Hong Kong, 18 de enero de 1888.

«Mi buen Recaredo:

«Vine y vi. No he vencido aún.

«En San Francisco supe vuestro matrimonio y me alegré. Di un salto y caí en la China. He venido como agente de una casa californiana, importadora de sedas, lacas, marfiles y demás chinerías. Junto con esta carta debes recibir un regalo mío que, dada tu afición por las cosas de este país amarillo, te llegará de perlas. Ponme a los pies de Suzette, y conserva el obsequio en memoria de tu

Robert.»

Ni más, ni menos. Ambos soltaron la carcajada. El mirlo, a su vez, hizo estallar la jaula en una explosión de gritos musicales.

La caja había llegado, una caja de regular tamaño, llena de marchamos, de números y de letras negras que decían y daban a entender que el contenido era muy frágil. Cuando la caja se abrió, apareció el misterio. Era un fino busto de porcelana, un admirable busto de mujer sonriente, pálido y encantador. En la base tenía tres inscripciones, una en caracteres chinescos, otra en inglés y otra en francés: ¡*La emperatriz de la China!* ¡La emperatriz de la China! ¿Qué manos de artista asiático habían moldeado aquellas formas atrayentes de misterio? Era una cabellera recogida y apretada, una faz enigmática, ojos bajos y extraños, de princesa celeste, sonrisa de esfinge, cuello erguido sobre los hombros columbinos, cubiertos por una onda de seda bordada de dragones, todo dando magia a la porcelana blanca, con tonos de cera, inmaculada y cándida. ¡La emperatriz de la China! Suzette pasaba sus dedos de rosa sobre los ojos de aquella graciosa soberana, un tanto inclinados, con sus curvos epicantus bajo los puros y nobles arcos de las cejas. Estaba contenta. Y Recaredo sentía orgullo de poseer su porcelana. Le haría un gabinete especial, para que viviese y reinase sola, como en el Louvre la Venus de Milo, triunfadora, cobijada imperialmente por el plafón de su recinto sagrado.

Así lo hizo. En un extremo del taller formó un gabinete minúsculo, con biombos cubiertos de arrozales y de grullas.

wanderlust! He'd reach the end of the world. Robert, a true friend!
They considered him one of the family. He had departed two years ear-
lier for San Francisco in California. Was there ever such a madcap?!
    She began to read.

                                        "Hong Kong, January 18, 1888.

"Dear Recaredo,
    "I came. I saw. I haven't conquered yet.
    "While in San Francisco I heard that you two had gotten married,
and I was glad. I made a hop and landed in China. I've come here as
representative of a California firm that imports silks, lacquers, ivories,
and other Chinese articles. At the same time as this letter you should
be receiving a gift from me which, given your passion for objects from
this yellow land, will suit you to a T. Tell Suzette I fall at her feet, and
keep the present in memory of your friend,

                                                            Robert."

    There was no more or less than that. Both of them laughed out
loud. The blackbird, when its turn came, made the cage explode with
musical cries.
    The packing case had arrived, a case of normal size, full of customs
stamps, numbers, and black lettering which stated and made known that
the contents were very fragile. When the case was open, the mystery ap-
peared. It was a delicate porcelain bust, an admirable bust of a smiling
woman, pale and enchanting. On the base were three inscriptions, one
in Chinese characters, one in English, and one in French: "The Empress
of China." The Empress of China! What Asian artist's hands had mod-
eled those forms, alluring in their mystery? The hair was compact and
pulled back, the expression was enigmatic, the eyes low and strange, like
those of a celestial princess, the smile like that of a sphinx, the neck erect
on dovelike shoulders which were covered with a wave of silk embroi-
dered with dragons, all this lending magic to the white porcelain with
waxy tints, immaculate and snowy. The Empress of China! Suzette ran
her pink fingers over that graceful sovereign's eyes, which were a little
slanted, with their curved epicanthus, below the pure and noble arches
of the eyebrows. She was pleased. And Recaredo felt proud to own that
porcelain. He would build a special cabinet for the empress to live and
reign in all by herself, like the Venus de Milo in the Louvre, triumphant,
imperially sheltered by the ceiling of her sacred precinct.
    And so he did. At one end of the studio he built a tiny cabinet, with
folding screens covered with rice paddies and cranes. The yellow note

Predominaba la nota amarilla. Toda la gama, oro, fuego, ocre de Oriente, hoja de otoño hasta el pálido que agoniza fundido en la blancura. En el centro, sobre un pedestal dorado y negro, se alzaba riendo la exótica imperial. Alrededor de ella había colocado Recaredo todas sus japonerías y curiosidades chinas. Las cubría con un gran quitasol nipón, pintado de camelias y de anchas rosas sangrientas. Era cosa de risa, cuando el artista soñador, después de dejar la pipa y los cinceles, llegaba frente a la emperatriz, con las manos cruzadas sobre el pecho, a hacer zalemas. Una, dos, diez, veinte veces la visitaba. Era una pasión. En un plato de laca yoko- hamesa le ponía flores frescas todos los días. Tenía, en momentos, verdaderos arrobos delante del busto asiático que le conmovía en su deleitable e inmóvil majestad. Estudiaba sus menores detalles, el caracol de la oreja, el arco del labio, la nariz pulida, el epicantus del párpado. ¡Un ídolo, la famosa emperatriz! Suzette le llamaba de lejos:

—¡Recaredo!

—¡Voy! —y seguía en la contemplación de su obra de arte. Hasta que Suzette llegaba a llevárselo a rastras y a besos.

Un día, las flores del plato de laca desaparecieron como por encanto.

—¿Quién ha quitado las flores? —gritó el artista desde el taller.

—Yo —dijo una voz vibradora.

Era Suzette, que entreabría una cortina, toda sonrosada y haciendo relampaguear sus ojos negros.

Allá en lo hondo de su cerebro se decía el señor Recaredo, artista escultor:

—¿Qué tendrá mi mujercita? ¿Qué tendrá mi mujercita?

No comía casi. Aquellos buenos libros desflorados por su espátula de marfil estaban en el pequeño estante negro con sus hojas cerradas sufriendo la nostalgia de las blancas manos de rosa y del tibio regazo perfumado. El señor Recaredo la veía triste. ¿Qué tendrá mi mujercita? En la mesa no quería comer. Estaba seria. ¡Qué seria! Le miraba a veces con el rabo del ojo y el marido veía aquellas pupilas oscuras, húmedas, como que querían llorar. Y ella al responder, hablaba como los niños a quienes se ha negado un dulce. ¿Qué tendrá mi mujercita? ¡Nada! Aquel «nada» lo decía ella con voz de queja, y entre sílaba y sílaba había lágrimas.

¡Oh señor Recaredo! Lo que tiene vuestra mujercita es que sois un hombre abominable. ¿No habéis notado que desde que esa buena de

was predominant. The entire gamut, gold, fire, Oriental ocher, autumn-leaf, down to the pallor that dies away into whiteness. In the center, on a gilded and black pedestal, stood the exotic empress, smiling. Around her Recaredo had placed all his articles of japonaiserie and his Chinese curiosities. He covered them with a large Nipponese parasol painted with camellias and broad, blood-red roses. It was amusing when the artistic dreamer, after leaving his pipe and his chisels, came before the empress, his hands folded across his chest, and kowtowed to her. He'd visit her once, twice, ten or twenty times a day. It was a passion with him. Every day he'd make her an offering of fresh flowers on a lacquer platter from Yokohama. At times he became literally enraptured before that Asian bust, which affected him with its charming, motionless majesty. He'd study its smallest details, the shell of its ear, the arc of its lips, the refined nose, the epicanthus of the eyelid. An idol, that notorious empress! Suzette would call to him from the distance:

"Recaredo!"

"Coming!" But he'd remain, gazing at the art work he owned, until Suzette came to fetch him, pulling him away and kissing him.

One day, the flowers disappeared from the lacquer platter as if by magic.

"Who took away the flowers?" the artist shouted from his studio.

"I did," replied a vibrant voice.

It was Suzette, who slightly parted a curtain; her face was suffused with pink, and her dark eyes were flashing.

At the very bottom of his mind, the sculptor Recaredo asked himself:

"What can be wrong with my little wife? What can be wrong with my little wife?"

She was hardly eating. Those good books deflowered by her ivory page-cutter lay on the little black shelf with their closed leaves painfully longing for those white-and-rose hands and that warm, fragrant lap. Recaredo found her always sad. What can be wrong with my little wife? At table she didn't want to eat. She was always grave. Why should she be? At times he looked at her out of the corner of his eye, and her husband saw that her eyes were dark and moist, as if ready to weep. And whenever she answered, she spoke like a child that has been refused a candy. What can be wrong with my little wife? Nothing! She uttered that "Nothing!" in a querulous tone, and there were tears between the syllables.

Oh, Recaredo! What's wrong with your little wife is that you're an abominable man. Haven't you noticed that, ever since that good

la emperatriz de la China ha llegado a vuestra casa, el saloncito azul se
ha entristecido, y el mirlo no canta ni ríe con su risa perlada? Suzette
despierta a Chopin, y lentamente hace brotar la melodía enferma y
melancólica del negro piano sonoro. ¡Tiene celos, señor Recaredo!
Tiene el mal de los celos, ahogador y quemante, como una serpiente
encendida que aprieta el alma. ¡Celos!

Quizá él lo comprendía, porque una tarde dijo a la muchachita de
su corazón estas palabras, frente a frente, a través del humo de una
taza de café:

—Eres demasiado injusta. ¿Acaso no te amo con toda mi alma?
¿Acaso no sabes leer en mis ojos lo que hay dentro de mi corazón?

Suzette rompió a llorar. ¡Que le amaba! No, ya no la amaba. Habían
huido las buenas y radiantes horas, y los besos que chasqueaban tam-
bién eran idos, como pájaros en fuga. Ya no la quería. Y a ella, a la que
en él veía su religión, su delicia, su sueño, su rey, a ella, a su Suzette,
la había dejado por otra.

¡La otra! Recaredo dio un salto. Estaba engañada. ¿Lo diría por la
rubia Eulogia, a quien en un tiempo había dirigido madrigales?

Ella movió la cabeza:

—No.

¿Por la ricachona Gabriela, de largos cabellos negros, blanca como
un alabastro, y cuyo busto había hecho? ¿O por aquella Luisa, la dan-
zarina, que tenía una cintura de avispa, un seno de buena nodriza y
unos ojos incendiarios? ¿O por la viudita Andrea, que al reír sacaba la
punta de la lengua, roja y felina, entre sus dientes brillantes y amarfi-
lados?

No, no era ninguna de esas. Recaredo quedó con gran asombro.

—Mira chiquilla, dime la verdad. ¿Quién es ella? Sabes cuánto te
adoro, mi Elsa, mi Julieta, amor mío.

Temblaba tanta verdad de amor en aquellas palabras entrecortadas
y trémulas, que Suzette, con los ojos enrojecidos, secos ya de lágrimas,
se levantó irguiendo su linda cabeza heráldica.

—¿Me amas?

—¡Bien lo sabes!

—Deja, pues, que me vengue de mi rival. Ella o yo, escoge. Si es
cierto que me adoras, ¿querrás permitir que la aparte para siempre de
tu camino, que quede yo sola, confiada en tu pasión?

—Sea —dijo Recaredo.

Y viendo irse a su avecita celosa y terca, prosiguió sorbiendo el café
negro como la tinta.

empress of China arrived in your house, the little blue salon has grown sad, and the blackbird hasn't sung or laughed its pearly laughs? Suzette awakens Chopin, and slowly lets the sickly, melancholy melody emerge from the black, resonant piano. She's jealous, Recaredo! She's sick with jealousy, that stifling, burning ailment, like a fiery serpent crushing the soul. Jealousy!

Maybe he understood, because one day, face to face with the girl of his heart, across the steam from a cup of coffee, he pronounced these words:

"You're too unfair. Don't I love you with all my soul? Can't you read in my eyes what's in my heart?"

Suzette burst into tears. He loved her! No, he didn't love her anymore. They had fled, those happy, radiant hours, and the noisy kisses had also departed, like escaping birds. He no longer loved her. He had left her, though she saw in him her religion, her delight, her dream, her king, he had left her, his Suzette, for another woman.

Another woman! Recaredo jumped. She was mistaken. Was she talking about the blond Eulogia, to whom he had once addressed madrigals?

She shook her head:

"No."

Did she mean the wealthy Gabriela, with the long, black hair and skin as white as alabaster, whose portrait bust he had sculpted? Or that Luisa, the dancer, who had a wasp waist, a bosom like a healthy wetnurse, and incendiary eyes? Or the little widow Andrea, who, when she laughed, thrust out the tip of her tongue, red and feline, between her shining, ivorylike teeth?

No, it was none of those. Recaredo was left quite dumbfounded.

"See here, dearest, tell me the truth. Who is she? You know how much I worship you, my Elsa, my Juliet, my love."

So much true love vibrated in those choppy, trembling words that Suzette, with eyes that were reddened but now free of tears, stood up, straightening her pretty, heraldic head.

"You love me?"

"You know I do!"

"Then, let me avenge myself on my rival. It's her or me: choose. If it's true that you worship me, will you let me get her out of your life for good, so I can remain as your only woman and I can trust in your passion?"

"All right," said Recaredo.

And watching his jealous and stubborn little bird walk away, he continued to sip the ink-black coffee.

No había tomado tres sorbos cuando oyó un gran ruido de fracaso en el recinto de su taller.

Fue: ¿Qué miraron sus ojos? El busto había desaparecido del pedestal de negro y oro, y entre minúsculos mandarines caídos y descolgados abanicos, se veían por el suelo pedazos de porcelana que crujían bajo los pequeños zapatos de Suzette, quien toda encendida y con el cabello suelto, aguardando los besos, decía entre carcajadas argentinas al maridito asustado:

—Estoy vengada. ¡Ha muerto ya para ti la emperatriz de la China!

Y cuando comenzó la ardiente reconciliación de los labios, en el saloncito azul, todo lleno de regocijo, el mirlo, en su jaula, se moría de risa.

El caso de la señorita Amelia

Que el doctor Z es ilustre, elocuente, conquistador; que su voz es profunda y vibrante al mismo tiempo, y su gesto avasallador y misterioso, sobre todo después de la publicación de su obra sobre *La plástica de ensueño,* quizás podríais negármelo o aceptármelo con restricción; pero que su calva es única, insigne, hermosa, solemne, lírica si gustáis, ¡oh, eso nunca, estoy seguro! ¿Cómo negaríais la luz del sol, el aroma de las rosas y las propiedades narcóticas de ciertos versos? Pues bien; esta noche pasada, poco después que saludamos el toque de las doce con una salva de doce taponazos del más legítimo Roederer, en el precioso comedor rococó de ese sibarita de judío que se llama Lowensteinger, la calva del doctor alzaba, aureolada de orgullo, su bruñido orbe de marfil, sobre el cual, por un capricho de la luz, se veían sobre el cristal de un espejo las llamas de dos bujías que formaban, no sé cómo, algo así como los cuernos luminosos de Moisés. El doctor enderezaba hacia mí sus grandes gestos y sus sabias palabras. Yo había soltado de mis labios, casi siempre silenciosos, una frase banal cualquiera. Por ejemplo, ésta:

—¡Oh, si el tiempo pudiera detenerse!

La mirada que el doctor me dirigió y la clase de sonrisa que decoró su boca después de oír mi exclamación, confieso que hubiera turbado a cualquiera.

—Caballero —me dijo saboreando el champaña—; si yo no estuviese completamente desilusionado de la juventud; si no supiese que todos los que hoy empezáis a vivir estáis ya muertos, es decir, muertos del alma, sin fe, sin entusiasmo, sin ideales, canosos por dentro; que

He hadn't taken three sips when he heard a loud noise of breakage in the confines of his studio.

He went there. What did his eyes behold? The bust had vanished from the black-and-gold pedestal, and in the midst of tiny fallen mandarins and fans detached from the wall, there could be seen on the floor pieces of porcelain creaking under Suzette's little shoes. She, all aflame and with her hair undone, was waiting for kisses, and was saying to her frightened hubby, with silvery laughter:

"I've had my revenge. Now the Empress of China is dead to you!"

And when their lips began their ardent reconciliation, in the little blue salon the blackbird, full of joy there in his cage, was rocking with laughter.

The Case of Miss Amelia

You may possibly deny, or accept my saying so only with provisos, that Doctor Z. is famous, eloquent, and a conqueror; that his voice is deep and vibrant at the same time, while his expression is overpowering and mysterious, especially ever since his work on *The Sculpture of Dreams* was published. But that his bald head is unique, remarkable, beautiful, solemn, lyrical if you like, that I am absolutely sure of! How could you deny the sunlight, the fragrance of roses, and the narcotic properties of certain poems? Well, then, last night, shortly after we greeted the stroke of midnight with a salute of twelve popping corks of the most authentic Roederer, in the precious Rococo dining room of that sybaritic Jew named Lowensteinger, the doctor's bald pate, with its nimbus of pride, raised its polished ivory sphere, over which, through a caprice of the light, there could be seen in the glass of a mirror the flames of two candles, which somehow or other took the form of something like Moses's shining horns. The doctor was addressing his broad gestures and his scholarly words to me. I had just emitted from my lips, which are almost always silent, some banal phrase or other. This, for example:

"Oh, if time could only stand still!"

The look that the doctor gave me, and the kind of smile that adorned his mouth after hearing my exclamation, would have upset anyone, I admit.

"Sir," he said to me, tasting the champagne, "if I weren't completely disillusioned with youth; if I didn't know that all those of you who are beginning to live today are already dead—that is, dead in your soul, without faith, without enthusiasm, without ideals, gray-headed inside;

no sois sino máscaras de vida, nada más . . . sí, si no supiese eso, si
viese en vos algo más que un hombre de fin de siglo, os diría que esa
frase que acabáis de pronunciar: «¡Oh, si el tiempo pudiera dete-
nerse!», tiene en mí la respuesta más satisfactoria.

—¡Doctor!

—Sí, os repito que vuestro escepticismo me impide hablar, como
hubiera hecho en otra ocasión.

—Creo —contesté con voz firme y serena— en Dios y su Iglesia.
Creo en los milagros. Creo en lo sobrenatural.

—En ese caso, voy a contaros algo que os hará sonreír. Mi narración
espero que os hará pensar.

En el comedor habíamos quedado cuatro convidados, a más de
Minna, la hija del dueño de casa; el periodista Riquet, el abate
Pureau, recién enviado por Hirch, el doctor y yo. A lo lejos oíamos
en la alegría de los salones la palabrería usual de la hora primera
del año nuevo: *Happy new year! Happy new year!* ¡Feliz Año
Nuevo!

El doctor continuó:

—¿Quién es el sabio que se atreve a decir *esto es así?* Nada se
sabe. *Ignoramus et ignorabimus.* ¿Quién conoce a punto fijo la no-
ción del tiempo? ¿Quién sabe con seguridad lo que es el espacio?
Va la ciencia a tanteo, caminando como una ciega, y juzga a veces
que ha vencido cuando logra advertir un vago reflejo de la luz ver-
dadera. Nadie ha podido desprender de su círculo uniforme la
culebra simbólica. Desde el tres veces más grande, el Hermes,
hasta nuestros días, la mano humana ha podido apenas alzar una
línea del manto que cubre a la eterna Isis. Nada ha logrado saberse
con absoluta seguridad en las tres grandes expresiones de la
Naturaleza: hechos, leyes, principios. Yo que he intentado profun-
dizar en el inmenso campo del misterio, he perdido casi todas mis
ilusiones.

Yo que he sido llamado sabio en Academias ilustres y libros volu-
minosos; yo que he consagrado toda mi vida al estudio de la hu-
manidad, sus orígenes y sus fines; yo que he penetrado en la cábala,
en el ocultismo y en la teosofía, que he pasado del plano material del
sabio al plano astral del *mágico* y al plano espiritual del *mago,* que sé
cómo obraba Apolonio el Thianense y Paracelso, y que he ayudado en
su laboratorio, en nuestros días, al inglés Crookes; yo que ahondé en
el Karma búdhico y en el misticismo cristiano, y sé al mismo tiempo
la ciencia desconocida de los fakires y la teología de los sacerdotes ro-
manos, yo os digo que *no hemos visto los sabios ni un solo rayo de la*

that you are merely masks of life and nothing more; . . . if, if I didn't know this, if I saw in you something more than a fin-de-siècle man, I'd tell you that the phrase you've just pronounced—'Oh, if time could only stand still'—has its most satisfactory reply in me."

"Doctor!"

"Yes, I repeat: your skepticism prevents me from speaking as I might have done on a different occasion."

I answered in a steady, calm voice: "I believe in God and His Church. I believe in miracles. I believe in the supernatural."

"In that case, I shall tell you a story that will make you smile. I hope my narrative will make you think."

Four of us guests were left in the dining room, in addition to Minna, the daughter of the master of the house: the journalist Riquet, the Abbé Pureau, who had recently been sent over by Hirsch, the doctor, and myself. In the distance we heard, amid the merriment in the sitting rooms, the phrases usually uttered during the first hour of the new year: "Happy New Year" in both English and Spanish.

The doctor continued:

"Where is the sage bold enough to say 'This is the way it is'? Nothing is known for certain. We are ignorant and shall remain ignorant. Who has a precise notion of time? Who knows beyond a doubt what space is? Science gropes its way along, walking like the blind, and sometimes deems that it has conquered when it manages to discern a vague reflection of the true light. No one has been able to uncoil the symbolic snake from its perfect circle of infinity. From the time of Hermes Trismegistus down to our time, human hands have scarcely been able to raise by a tenth of an inch the veil that covers eternal Isis. No one has succeeded in learning anything with absolute certainty in the three great categories of Nature: facts, laws, and principles. I, a man who has tried to delve into the vast field of mystery, have lost nearly all my illusions.

"I, a man who has been called a scholar in famous academies and voluminous treatises; I, who have devoted my entire life to the study of mankind, its origins, and its goals; I, who have gone deeply into the Kabbala, occultism, and theosophy, who have ascended from the material plane of the 'sage' to the astral plane of the 'magician' and the spiritual plane of the 'magus'; I, who understand the operations of Apollonius of Tyana and Paracelsus, and in our own times have aided the Englishman Crookes in his laboratory; I, who have plunged deeply into Buddhist karma and Christian mysticism, and also know the unfamiliar knowledge of Muslim fakirs and the theology of the Roman priests—I tell you that *we scholars haven't seen even a single ray of*

luz suprema, y que la inmensidad y la eternidad del *misterio* forman la única y pavorosa verdad.

Y dirigiéndose a mí:

—¿Sabéis cuáles son los principios del hombre? Grupa, jiba, linga, sharira, kama, rupa, manas, buddhi, atma, es decir: el cuerpo, la fuerza vital, el cuerpo astral, el alma animal, el alma humana, la fuerza espiritual y la esencia espiritual . . .

Viendo a Minna poner una cara un tanto desolada, me atreví a interrumpir al doctor:

—Me parece que íbais a demostrarnos que el tiempo . . .

—Y bien —dijo—, puesto que no os placen las disertaciones por prólogo, vamos al cuento que debo contaros, y es el siguiente:

Hace veintitrés años, conocí en Buenos Aires a la familia Revall, cuyo fundador, un excelente caballero francés, ejerció un cargo consular en tiempo de Rosas. Nuestras casas eran vecinas, era yo joven y entusiasta, y las tres señoritas Revall hubieran podido hacer competencia a las tres Gracias. De más está decir que muy pocas chispas fueron necesarias para encender una hoguera de amor . . .

Amoor, pronunciaba el sabio obeso, con el pulgar de la diestra metido en la bolsa del chaleco, y tamborileando sobre su potente abdomen con los dedos ágiles y regordetes, y continuó:

—Puedo confesar francamente que no tenía predilección por ninguna, y que Luz, Josefina y Amelia ocupaban en mi corazón el mismo lugar. El mismo, tal vez no; pues los dulces al par que ardientes ojos de Amelia, su alegre y roja risa, su picardía infantil . . . diré que era ella mi preferida. Era la menor; tenía doce años apenas, y yo ya había pasado de los treinta. Por tal motivo, y por ser la chicuela de carácter travieso y jovial, tratábala yo como niña que era, y entre las otras dos repartía mis miradas incendiarias, mis suspiros, mis apretones de manos y hasta mis serias promesas de matrimonio, en una, os lo confieso, atroz y culpable bigamia de pasión. ¡Pero la chiquilla Amelia! . . . Sucedía que, cuando ya llegaba a la casa, era ella quien primero corría a recibirme, llena de sonrisas y zalamerías: «¿Y mis bombones?» He aquí la pregunta sacramental. Yo me sentaba regocijado, después de mis correctos saludos, y colmaba las manos de la niña de ricos caramelos de rosas y de deliciosas grajeas de chocolate, los cuales, ella, a plena boca, saboreaba con una sonora música palatinal, lingual y dental. El porqué de mi apego a aquella muchachita de vestido a media pierna y de ojos lindos, no os lo podré explicar; pero es el caso que, cuando por causa de mis estudios tuve que dejar Buenos Aires, fingí alguna emoción al despedirme de Luz, que me

the supreme light, and that the immensity and eternity of the *mystery* constitute the only—terrifying—truth."

And, addressing me:

"Do you know what the principles of man are? *Grupa, jiba, linga, sharira, kama, rupa, manas, buddhi, atma:* that is, the body, the life force, the astral body, the animal soul, the human soul, spiritual force, and spiritual essence. . . ."

Seeing Minna's expression becoming a little desolate, I ventured to interrupt the doctor:

"I thought you were going to prove to us that time—"

"All right," he said, "seeing that you don't like lectures for a preamble, let's proceed to the story I promised to tell you, which goes as follows:

"Twenty-three years ago in Buenos Aires I met the Revall family, the founder of which, an excellent French gentleman, filled a consular post in the days of Rosas. Our houses were near each other, I was young and enthusiastic, and the three Misses Revall could have competed with the three Graces. Needless to say, very few sparks were necessary to ignite a bonfire of love."

The fat scholar drawled the word as "lo-o-ove," his right thumb hitched in his vest pocket as he drummed on his prominent stomach with his chubby, agile fingers. He continued:

"I can admit frankly that I had no preference for any particular one; Luz, Josefina, and Amelia occupied the same place in my heart. No, maybe not the same place; because Amelia's eyes, as sweet as they were ardent, her happy, rosy smile, her childish roguishness—I'll say that she was my favorite. She was the youngest; she was scarcely twelve, and I was past thirty. For that reason, and because the girl was mischievous and jolly by nature, I treated her like the child that she was, and distributed between the other two my burning gazes, my sighs, my squeezing of hands, and even my serious proposals of marriage, indulging in what I confess was an atrocious, blameworthy bigamy of passion. But little Amelia! . . . At times when I visited their house, she was the first to run over and welcome me, full of smiles and ceremonies: 'And my candy?' That was the sacrosanct question. I would sit down cheerfully after my polite greetings, and I'd fill the child's hands with delicious rose-water bonbons and tasty chocolate-coated almonds, which she'd taste voraciously, with a loud smacking of her palate, tongue, and teeth. I can't explain to you why I was so attracted to that little girl, whose dress extended only to mid-calf, and who had pretty eyes; but the fact is that when, to pursue my studies, I had to leave Buenos Aires, I feigned some emotion when saying good-bye to Luz,

miraba con anchos ojos doloridos y sentimentales; di un falso apretón de manos a Josefina, que tenía entre los dientes, por no llorar, un pañuelo de batista, y en la frente de Amelia incrusté un beso, el más puro y el más encendido, el más casto y el más ardiente ¡qué sé yo! de todos los que he dado en mi vida. Y salí en barco para Calcuta, ni más ni menos que como vuestro querido y admirado general Mansilla cuando fue a Oriente, lleno de juventud y de sonoras y flamantes esterlinas de oro. Iba yo, sediento ya de las ciencias ocultas, a estudiar entre los mahatmas de la India lo que la pobre ciencia occidental no puede enseñarnos todavía. La amistad epistolar que mantenía con madama Blavatsky, habíame abierto ancho campo en el país de los fakires, y más de un gurú, que conocía mi sed de saber, se encontraba dispuesto a conducirme por buen camino a la fuente sagrada de la verdad, y si es cierto que mis labios creyeron saciarse en sus frescas aguas diamantinas, mi sed no se pudo aplacar. Busqué, busqué con tesón lo que mis ojos ansiaban contemplar, el Keherpas de Zoroastro, el Kalep persa, el Kovei-Khan de la filosofía india, el archoeno de Paracelso, el limbuz de Swedenborg; oí la palabra de los monjes budhistas en medio de las florestas del Thibet; estudié los diez sephiroth de la Kabala, desde el que simboliza el espacio sin límites hasta el que, llamado Malkuth, encierra el principio de la vida. Estudié el espíritu, el aire, el agua, el fuego, la altura, la profundidad, el Oriente, el Occidente, el Norte y el Mediodía; y llegué casi a comprender y aun a conocer íntimamente a Satán, Lucifer, Astharot, Beelzebutt, Asmodeo, Belphegor, Mabema, Lilith, Adrameleh y Baal. En mis ansias de comprensión; en mi insaciable deseo de sabiduría; cuando juzgaba haber llegado al logro de mis ambiciones, encontraba los signos de mi debilidad y las manifestaciones de mi pobreza, y estas ideas, Dios, el espacio, el tiempo, formaban la más impenetrable bruma delante de mis pupilas . . . Viajé por Asia, Africa, Europa y América. Ayudé al coronel Olcott a fundar la rama teosófica de Nueva York. Y a todo esto —recalcó de súbito el doctor, mirando fijamente a la rubia Minna—, ¿sabéis lo que es la ciencia y la inmortalidad de todo? ¡Un par de ojos azules . . . o negros!

—¿Y el fin del cuento? —gimió dulcemente la señorita.

El doctor, más serio que nunca, dijo:

—Juro, señores, que lo que estoy refiriendo es de una absoluta verdad. ¿El fin del cuento? Hace apenas una semana he vuelto a la Argentina, después de veintitrés años de ausencia. He vuelto gordo, bastante gordo, y calvo como una rodilla; pero en mi corazón he man-

who looked at me with pained and sentimental wide eyes; I deceitfully squeezed Josefina's hand, while, to keep from crying, she clamped a cambric handkerchief in her teeth; whereas on Amelia's forehead I imprinted a kiss, the purest and most fiery, the most chaste and most ardent, for all I know, of any that I ever gave in my whole life. And I sailed away to Calcutta, exactly like your beloved and admired General Mansilla when he went to the East, laden with youth and brand-new, ringing gold sovereigns. Already thirsting for occult knowledge, I was going to study with the mahatmas of India that which our poor Western science is still unable to teach us. The friendship I maintained through letters with Madame Blavatsky had opened a wide field for me in the land of the fakirs, and more than one guru, aware of my thirst for knowledge, was willing to lead me along the proper path to the sacred fount of truth; and though it's a fact that my lips thought they were sated by its cool, diamantine waters, my thirst couldn't be assuaged. I sought, I tenaciously sought that which my eyes longed to behold, Zoroaster's Keherpas, the Persian Kalep, the Kovei-Khan of Indian philosophy, Paracelsus's Archoen, Swedenborg's Limbuz; I heard the words of Buddhist monks amid the forests of Tibet; I studied the ten sephiroth of the Kabbala, from the one symbolizing limitless space to the one called Malkuth, which embodies the principle of life. I studied spirit, air, water, fire, height, depth, the Orient, the Occident, the North, and the South; and I nearly came to understand, and even become intimately acquainted with, Satan, Lucifer, Ashtareth, Beelzebub, Asmodeus, Belphegor, Mabema, Lilith, Adrammelech, and Baal. In my yearning to understand, in my insatiable desire for knowledge, when I thought I had achieved my ambitions, I found the signs of my weakness and the indications of my poverty of spirit; and these ideas, God, space, time, created the most impenetrable fog in front of my eyes. . . . I traveled through Asia, Africa, Europe, and the Americas. I helped Colonel Olcott found the New York chapter of theosophy. And after all that," the doctor suddenly stated with emphasis, gazing fixedly at blond Minna, "do you know what the science and immortality of everything is? A pair of blue eyes . . . or of dark ones!"

"And the end of the story?" the young lady moaned softly.

The doctor, more serious than ever, said:

"Gentlemen, I swear that what I am now recounting to you is the unvarnished truth. The end of the story? Barely a week ago, I returned to Argentina, after being away for twenty-three years. I came back fat, quite fat, and as bald as a kneecap; but in my heart I have kept burning

tenido ardiente el fuego del amor, la vestal de los solterones. Y, por tanto, lo primero que hice fue indagar el paradero de la familia Revall. «¡Las Revall —me dijeron—, las del caso de Amelia Revall!», y estas palabras acompañadas con una especial sonrisa. Llegué a sospechar que la pobre Amelia, la pobre chiquilla . . . Y buscando, buscando, di con la casa. Al entrar, fui recibido por un criado negro y viejo, que llevó mi tarjeta, y me hizo pasar a una sala donde todo tenía un vago tinte de tristeza. En las paredes, los espejos estaban cubiertos con velos de luto, y dos grandes retratos, en los cuales reconocía a las dos hermanas mayores, se miraban melancólicos y oscuros sobre el piano. A poco, Luz y Josefina:

—¡Oh amigo mío, oh amigo mío!

Nada más. Luego, una conversación llena de reticencias y de timideces, de palabras entrecortadas y de sonrisas de inteligencia tristes, muy tristes. Por todo lo que logré entender, vine a quedar en que ambas no se habían casado. En cuanto a Amelia, no me atreví a preguntar nada . . . Quizá mi pregunta llegaría a aquellos pobres seres, como una amarga ironía, a recordar tal vez una irremediable desgracia y una deshonra . . . En esto vi llegar saltando a una niña, cuyo cuerpo y rostro eran iguales en todo a los de mi pobre Amelia. Se dirigió a mí, y con su misma voz exclamó:

—¿Y mis bombones?

Yo no hallé qué decir.

Las dos hermanas se miraban pálidas, pálidas, y movían la cabeza desoladamente . . .

Mascullando una despedida y haciendo una zurda genuflexión, salí a la calle, como perseguido por algún soplo extraño. Luego lo he sabido todo. La niña que yo creía fruto de amor culpable es Amelia, la misma que yo dejé hace veintitrés años, la cual se ha quedado en la infancia, ha contenido su carrera vital. Se ha detenido para ella el reloj del Tiempo, en una hora señalada ¡quién sabe con qué designio del desconocido Dios!

El doctor Z era en este momento todo calvo . . .

the flame of love, vestal virgin of bachelors. Therefore, the first thing I did was to inquire after the whereabouts of the Revall family. 'The Revall women,' people said to me, 'the ones involved in the case of Amelia Revall!' And those words were accompanied by a special smile. I came to suspect that poor Amelia, the poor little thing . . . And searching, searching, I came across the house. On entering I was welcomed by an old black servant who took my card and showed me into a parlor in which everything was vaguely tinged with sadness. On the walls the mirrors were covered with mourning veils, and two large portraits, in which I recognized the two older sisters, gazed at each other, dark and melancholy, over the piano. Soon Luz and Josefina were there, saying:

"'Oh, my friend, oh, my friend!'

"And nothing more. There followed a conversation full of reticence and timidity, choppy words and sad, very sad meaningful smiles. From all I was able to gather, I concluded that neither of them had married. As regards Amelia, I didn't have the courage to ask any questions. . . . My question might strike those poor creatures as a bitter irony, perhaps reminding them of an irremediable misfortune or disgrace. . . . At this point I saw a little girl come skipping in, her body and face exactly like those of my poor Amelia. She turned to me, and in that same voice, exclaimed:

"'And my candy?'

"I didn't know what to say.

"The two sisters were terribly pale as they looked at each other, and they shook their heads desolately. . . .

"Murmuring a good-bye and making a clumsy bow, I went out into the street, as if pursued by some strange gust of wind. Afterward, I learned everything. The child that I thought was the offspring of an illicit love affair is really Amelia, the same girl I left behind twenty-three years ago. She has remained a child, she has halted the progress of her life. For her the clock of time has stood still at a predestined hour, by who knows what plan of the unknown God!"

At that moment Doctor Z. was entirely bald. . . .

Poesías
Poems

Caupolicán

A Enrique Hernández Miyares

Es algo formidable que vio la vieja raza;
robusto tronco de árbol al hombro de un campeón
salvaje y aguerrido, cuya fornida maza
blandiera el brazo de Hércules, o el brazo de Sansón.

Por casco sus cabellos, su pecho por coraza,
pudiera tal guerrero, de Arauco en la región,
lancero de los bosques, Nemrod que todo caza,
desjarretar un toro, o estrangular un león.

Anduvo, anduvo, anduvo. Le vio la luz del día,
le vio la tarde pálida, le vio la noche fría,
y siempre el tronco de árbol a cuestas del titán.

«¡El Toqui, el Toqui!», clama la conmovida casta.
Anduvo, anduvo. La aurora dijo: «Basta»,
e irguióse la alta frente del gran Caupolicán.

Venus

En la tranquila noche, mis nostalgias amargas sufría.
En busca de quietud bajé al fresco y callado jardín.
En el oscuro cielo Venus bella temblando lucía,
como incrustado en ébano un dorado y divino jazmín.

A mi alma enamorada, una reina oriental parecía,
que esperaba a su amante, bajo el techo de su camarín,
o que, llevada en hombros, la profunda extensión recorría,
triunfante y luminosa, recostada sobre un palanquín.

Caupolicán

To Enrique Hernández Miyares

It's a tremendous feat seen by our ancestors:
a heavy tree trunk on the shoulder of a champion
wild and warlike; such a mighty mace
could have been brandished by the arm of Hercules or Samson.

For a helmet, his hair; his breast as breastplate,
such a warrior, in the Araucanian territory,
lancer of the forests, Nimrod who hunts all beasts,
could have hamstrung a bull or strangled a lion.

He walked, walked, walked. The daylight saw him,
the dusky evening saw him, the cold night saw him,
and always the tree trunk was on the titan's back.

"The chief, the chief!" his thrilled clan acclaims him.
He walked, he walked. Dawn said: "Enough!"
and the tall brow of great Caupolicán was lifted up.

Venus

In the tranquil night, I suffered from my bitter longing for home.
In search of peace I descended to the cool, silent garden.
In the dark sky, beautiful Venus was twinkling
like a divine golden jasmine inlaid in ebony.

To my amorous soul it was like an Oriental queen
awaiting her lover beneath the ceiling of her alcove,
or traversing deep space, borne on men's shoulders,
triumphant and luminous, lying on a palanquin.

«¡Oh reina rubia! —díjele—, mi alma quiere dejar su crisálida
y volar hacia ti, y tus labios de fuego besar;
y flotar en el nimbo que derrama en tu frente luz pálida,

y en siderales éxtasis no dejarte un momento de amar.»
El aire de la noche refrescaba la atmósfera cálida.
Venus, desde el abismo, me miraba con triste mirar.

Walt Whitman

En un país de hierro vive el gran viejo,
bello como un patriarca, sereno y santo.
Tiene en la arruga olímpica de su entrecejo
algo que impera y vence con noble encanto.

Su alma del infinito parece espejo;
son sus cansados hombros dignos del manto;
y con arpa labrada de un roble añejo,
como un profeta nuevo canta su canto.

Sacerdote, que alienta soplo divino,
anuncia en el futuro tiempo mejor.
Dice al águila: «¡Vuela!» «¡Boga!», al marino,

y «¡Trabaja!», al robusto trabajador.
¡Así va ese poeta por su camino
con su soberbio rostro de emperador!

"Era un aire suave . . ."

Era un aire suave, de pausados giros;
el hada Harmonía ritmaba sus vuelos;
e iban frases vagas y tenues suspiros
entre los sollozos de los violoncelos.

Sobre la terraza, junto a los ramajes,
diríase un trémolo de liras eolias
cuando acariciaban los sedosos trajes
sobre el tallo erguidas las blancas magnolias.

La marquesa Eulalia risas y desvíos
daba a un tiempo mismo para dos rivales:

"O blond queen," I said, "my soul wishes to leave its chrysalis
and fly up to you, and kiss your lips of fire,
and float in the halo that bathes your brow with pale light,

and, in starry ecstasy, never stop loving you for a moment."
The night air refreshed the warm atmosphere.
Venus, from the gulf of the sky, gazed on me with a sad gaze.

Walt Whitman

In a land of iron lives the grand old man,
handsome as a patriarch, serene and holy.
In the Olympian furrows between his eyebrows he has
something that commands and conquers with noble enchantment.

His soul is like a mirror of the infinite;
his weary shoulders are worthy of a prophet's mantle;
and with a harp fashioned from an old oak tree,
like a modern prophet he sings his song.

A priest inspired by divine breath,
he proclaims better days in the future.
He bids the eagle "Fly!," the seaman "Sail!,"

and the sturdy worker "Work!"
Thus does this poet proceed along his way
with his proud face, like an emperor's!

"The Air Was Gentle . . ."

The air was gentle, circulating calmly;
the fairy Harmony made rhythmical flights;
and vague phrases and soft sighs mingled
with the sobs of the violoncellos.

On the terrace, beside the tree branches,
it was like a tremolo of Aeolian lyres
when the silken dresses were caressed
by the white magnolias tall on their stalks.

The marquise Eulalia was uttering laughter and cold remarks
at one and the same time to two rivals:

el vizconde rubio de los desafíos
y el abate joven de los madrigales.

Cerca, coronado con hojas de viña,
reía en su máscara Término barbudo,
y, como un efebo que fuese una niña,
mostraba una Diana su mármol desnudo.

Y bajo un boscaje del amor palestra,
sobre rico zócalo al modo de Jonia,
con un candelabro prendido en la diestra
volaba el Mercurio de Juan de Bolonia.

La orquesta perlaba sus mágicas notas,
un coro de sones alados se oía;
galantes pavanas, fugaces gavotas
cantaban los dulces violines de Hungría.

Al oír las quejas de sus caballeros
ríe, ríe, ríe la divina Eulalia,
pues son su tesoro las flechas de Eros,
el cinto de Cipria, la rueca de Onfalia.

¡Ay de quien sus mieles y frases recoja!
¡Ay de quien del canto de su amor se fíe!
Con sus ojos lindos y su boca roja,
la divina Eulalia ríe, ríe, ríe.

Tiene azules ojos, es maligna y bella;
cuando mira vierte viva luz extraña;
se asoma a sus húmedas pupilas de estrella
el alma del rubio cristal de Champaña.

Es noche de fiesta, y el baile de trajes
ostenta su gloria de triunfos mundanos.
La divina Eulalia, vestida de encajes,
una flor destroza con sus tersas manos.

El teclado harmónico de su risa fina
a la alegre música de un pájaro iguala,
con los *staccati* de una bailarina
y las locas fugas de una colegiala.

¡Amoroso pájaro que trinos exhala
bajo el ala a veces ocultando el pico;

the blond viscount fond of issuing challenges
and the young abbé who composed madrigals.

Nearby, garlanded with vineleaves,
the bearded statue of the god Terminus laughed into his mask,
and like an ephebe who proved to be a girl,
a Diana was displaying her marble nudity.

And in a grove that was an exercise ground for love,
on a rich pedestal of the Ionian order,
with a candleholder grasped in his right hand
Giambologna's Mercury was flying.

The orchestra poured out its magic notes like pearls,
a chorus of winged sounds could be heard;
gallant pavans, fleeting gavottes
were sung by the sweet Hungarian violins.

On hearing the laments of her suitors,
divine Eulalia laughs, laughs, laughs,
because in her own treasury she possesses the arrows of Eros,
the girdle of Cypris, the spinning wheel of Omphale.

Woe is the man who gathers the honey of her speech!
Woe is the man who trusts her song of love!
With her pretty eyes and red lips
divine Eulalia laughs, laughs, laughs.

She has blue eyes, she is malicious and beautiful;
when she gazes she sheds a strange vibrant light;
from her moist, starlike pupils there peers out
the soul of the yellow glass of champagne.

It is a festive night, and the fancy-dress ball
blazons forth its glory of social triumphs.
Divine Eulalia, dressed in lace,
picks apart a flower with her smooth hands.

The harmonious keyboard of her elegant laughter
is equal to the merry music of a bird,
combined with a ballerina's *staccati*
and the madcap pranks of a schoolgirl.

Amorous bird that utters its warbling,
sometimes hiding its beak under its wing!

que desdenes rudos lanza bajo el ala,
bajo el ala aleve del leve abanico!

Cuando a medianoche sus notas arranque
y en arpegios áureos gima Filomela,
y el ebúrneo cisne, sobre el quieto estanque
como blanca góndola imprima su estela,

la marquesa alegre llegará al boscaje,
boscaje que cubre la amable glorieta,
donde han de estrecharla los brazos de un paje,
que siendo su paje será su poeta.

Al compás de un canto de artista de Italia
que en la brisa errante la orquesta deslíe,
junto a los rivales la divina Eulalia,
la divina Eulalia ríe, ríe, ríe.

¿Fue acaso en el tiempo del rey Luis de Francia,
sol con corte de astros, en campos de azur?
¿Cuando los alcázares llenó de fragancia
la regia y pomposa rosa Pompadour?

¿Fue cuando la bella su falda cogía
con dedos de ninfa, bailando el minué,
y de los compases el ritmo seguía
sobre el tacón rojo, lindo y leve el pie?

¿O cuando pastoras de floridos valles
ornaban con cintas sus albos corderos,
y oían, divinas Tirsis de Versalles,
las declaraciones de sus caballeros?

¿Fue en ese buen tiempo de duques pastores,
de amantes princesas y tiernos galanes,
cuando entre sonrisas y perlas y flores
iban las casacas de los chambelanes?

¿Fue acaso en el Norte o en el Mediodía?
Yo el tiempo y el día y el país ignoro,
pero sé que Eulalia ríe todavía,
¡y es cruel y eterna su risa de oro!

It hurls rough words of disdain from under its wing,
under the perfidious wing of its light fan!

When Philomel heaves forth her song at midnight,
moaning in golden arpeggios,
and the ivory swan imprints its wake
on the still pool, like a white gondola,

the merry marquise will come to the coppice,
the coppice awninged by the charming arbor,
where the arms of a page will hold her close;
only her page, but he will be her poet.

To the beat of a song sung by an Italian performer,
which the orchestra diffuses into the wandering breeze,
beside the rivals divine Eulalia,
divine Eulalia laughs, laughs, laughs.

Was it perchance in the days of King Louis of France,
a sun with a court of stars, in an azure field?
When palaces were filled with fragrance
by the royal, pompous Pompadour rose?

Was it when that beauty gathered up her skirts
with nymphlike fingers, dancing the minuet,
and followed the rhythm of the musicians' beat
on her high red heels, lovely and light of foot?

Or when shepherdesses in blossoming valleys
adorned their white lambs with ribbons,
and, like divine Thyrsises of Versailles, listened
to their suitors' declarations of love?

Was it in the good old days of ducal shepherds,
amorous princesses and tender wooers,
when the dress coats of the chamberlains walked
amid smiles and pearls and flowers?

Was it perchance in the North or the South?
I don't know the time or day or country,
but I know that Eulalia is still laughing,
and her golden laughter is cruel and eternal!

Divagación

¿Vienes? Me llega aquí, pues que suspiras,
un soplo de las mágicas fragancias
que hicieran los delirios de las liras
en las Grecias, las Romas y las Francias.

¡Suspira así! Revuelen las abejas
al olor de la olímpica ambrosía,
en los perfumes que en el aire dejas;
y el dios de piedra se despierte y ría,

y el dios de piedra se despierte y cante
la gloria de los tirsos florecientes
en el gesto ritual de la bacante
de rojos labios y nevados dientes;

en el gesto ritual que en las hermosas
ninfalias guía a la divina hoguera,
hoguera que hace llamear las rosas
en las manchadas pieles de pantera.

Y pues amas reír, ríe, y la brisa
lleve el son de los líricos cristales
de tu reír, y haga temblar la risa
la barba de los Términos joviales.

Mira hacia el lado del boscaje, mira
blanquear el muslo de marfil de Diana,
y después de la Virgen, la Hetaíra
diosa, su blanca, rosa y rubia hermana,

pasa en busca de Adonis; sus aromas
deleitan a las rosas y los nardos;
síguela una pareja de palomas
y hay tras ella una fuga de leopardos.

✻

¿Te gusta amar en griego? Yo las fiestas
galantes busco, en donde se recuerde
al suave són de rítmicas orquestas
la tierra de la luz y el mirto verde.

Digression

Are you coming? I feel here, now that you are sighing,
a breath of the magical fragrance
that would have delighted the lyres
of Greece, Rome, and France.

Keep sighing that way! Let the bees circle around
in the scent of Olympian ambrosia,
in the perfume that you leave on the air;
and let the stone god awaken and laugh,

and let the stone god awaken and sing
the glory of blossoming thyrsi
in the ritual gesture of the bacchante
with red lips and snowy teeth;

in the ritual gesture which in the beautiful
festival of nymphs guides the divine bonfire,
bonfire that makes roses blaze
on the spotted panther skins.

And, since you like to laugh, laugh, and let the breeze
carry off the sound of the lyrical crystals
of your laughter, and let laughter shake
the beard of the jovial statues of Terminus.

Gaze in the direction of the grove, see
Diana's ivory thigh grow white,
and, beyond that virgin, the courtesan
goddess, her white, pink, blond sister,

is going in search of Adonis; her fragrance
delights the roses and the spikenard;
she is accompanied by a pair of doves
and, behind her, leopards race.

❁

Do you enjoy love in a Greek mode? As for me, I seek
the *fêtes galantes,* which retain the memory—
to the soft sound of rhythmical orchestras—
of the land of light and the green myrtle.

(Los abates refieren aventuras
a las rubias marquesas. Soñolientos
filósofos defienden las ternuras
del amor, con sutiles argumentos,

mientras que surge de la verde grama,
en la mano el acanto de Corinto,
una ninfa a quien puso un epigrama
Beaumarchais, sobre el mármol de su plinto.

Amo más que la Grecia de los griegos
la Grecia de la Francia, porque en Francia
el eco de las risas y los juegos,
su más dulce licor Venus escancia.

Demuestran más encantos y perfidias
coronadas de flores y desnudas,
las diosas de Clodión que las de Fidias.
Unas cantan francés, otras son mudas.

Verlaine es más que Sócrates; y Arsenio
Houssaye supera al viejo Anacreonte.
En París reinan el Amor y el Genio:
ha perdido su imperio el dios bifronte.

Monsieur Prudhomme y Homais no saben nada.
Hay Chipres, Pafos, Tempes y Amatuntes,
donde al amor de mi madrina, un hada,
tus frescos labios a los míos juntes.)

Sones de bandolín. El rojo vino
conduce un paje rojo. ¿Amas los sones
del bandolín, y un amor florentino?
Serás la reina en los decamerones.

(Un coro de poetas y pintores
cuenta historias picantes. Con maligna
sonrisa alegre aprueban los señores.
Clelia enrojece. Una dueña se signa.)

¿O un amor alemán? —que no han sentido
jamás los alemanes—: la celeste
Gretchen; claro de luna; el aria; el nido
del ruiseñor; y en una roca agreste,

(The abbés recount adventurous tales
to the blond marquises. Drowsy
philosophers defend the tender feelings
of love with subtle arguments,

while there emerges from the green sward,
in her hand the Corinthian acanthus,
a nymph, for whom an epigram was placed
by Beaumarchais on the marble of her plinth.

More than the Greece of the Greeks I love
the Greece of France, because in France
Venus serves her sweetest beverage,
the echo of laughter and jollity.

Nude and garlanded with flowers,
Clodion's goddesses display more charm and deceit
than those of Phidias.
One group sings in French, the other is mute.

Verlaine is more than Socrates; and Arsène
Houssaye is superior to ancient Anacreon.
In Paris, Love and Genius reign:
the two-faced god has lost his authority.

Monsieur Prudhomme and Homais know nothing.
There are Cypruses, Paphoses, Tempes, and Amathuntes
where, to the love spell of my fairy godmother,
you can join your cool lips to mine.)

Mandolin tones. The red wine
is brought by a red-clad page. Do you like the tones
of the mandolin, and a Florentine love?
You'll be the queen in the decamerons.

(A chorus of poets and painters
narrates spicy stories. With a mischievous,
merry smile the gentlemen approve.
Clelia blushes. A duenna crosses herself.)

Or a German love? (Which the Germans
have never felt.) The heavenly
Gretchen; moonlight; an aria; the nest
of the nightingale; and, on a wild crag,

la luz de nieve que del cielo llega
y baña a una hermosura que suspira,
la queja vaga que a la noche entrega
Loreley en la lengua de la lira.

Y sobre el agua azul el caballero
Lohengrín; y su cisne, cual si fuese
un cincelado témpano viajero,
con su cuello enarcado en forma de S.

Y del divino Enrique Heine un canto,
a la orilla del Rhin; y del divino
Wolfgang la larga cabellera, el manto;
y de la uva teutona el blanco vino.

O amor lleno de sol, amor de España,
amor lleno de púrpuras y oros;
amor que da el clavel, la flor extraña
regada con la sangre de los toros;

flor de gitanas, flor que amor recela,
amor de sangre y luz, pasiones locas;
flor que trasciende a clavo y a canela,
roja cual las heridas y las bocas.

✿

¿Los amores exóticos acaso? . . .
Como rosa de Oriente me fascinas:
me deleitan la seda, el oro, el raso.
Gautier adoraba a las princesas chinas.

¡Oh bello amor de mil genuflexiones;
torres de kaolín, pies imposibles,
tazas de té, tortugas y dragones,
y verdes arrozales apacibles!

Amame en chino, en el sonoro chino
de Li-Tai-Pe. Yo igualaré a los sabios
poetas que interpretan el destino;
madrigalizaré junto a tus labios.

Diré que eres más bella que la luna;
que el tesoro del cielo es menos rico

the snowy light that comes from the sky
to bathe a sighing beauty,
the vague lament consigned to the night
by Lorelei on the tongue of the lyre.

And on the blue waters the knight
Lohengrin; and his swan, which resembles
a chiseled, floating ice floe,
with its neck arched in the form of an S.

And a poem by the divine Heinrich Heine
by the banks of the Rhine; and the divine
Wolfgang's long hair and mantle,
and the white wine from the Germanic grape.

O love full of sunshine, love in Spain,
love full of purple and gold;
love given by the carnation, the strange flower
watered with the blood of bulls,

the flower of Gypsy women, flower that excites love,
love of blood and light, mad passions;
flower that smells of clove and cinnamon,
red as wounds and lips.

✿

Exotic loves, perhaps? . . .
You fascinate me like an Oriental rose:
I am delighted by silk, gold, satin.
Gautier adored Chinese princesses.

Oh, beautiful love with a thousand kowtows;
kaolin towers, incredibly small feet,
teacups, tortoises, and dragons,
and peaceful green rice paddies!

Love me in Chinese, in the sonorous Chinese
of Li Bai. I shall be a match for the sage
poets who interpret destiny;
I shall write madrigals next to your lips.

I shall say you're more beautiful than the moon;
that the treasure of heaven is less rich

que el tesoro que vela la importuna
caricia de marfil de tu abanico.

✿

Amame, japonesa, japonesa
antigua, que no sepa de naciones
occidentales: tal una princesa
con las pupilas llenas de visiones,

    que aun ignorase en la sagrada Kioto,
en su labrado camarín de plata,
ornado al par de crisantemo y loto,
la civilización de Yamagata.

    O con amor hindú que alza sus llamas
en la visión suprema de los mitos,
y hace temblar en misteriosas bramas
la iniciación de los sagrados ritos,

    en tanto mueven tigres y panteras
sus hierros, y en los fuertes elefantes
sueñan con ideales bayaderas
las rajahs constelados de brillantes.

    O negra, negra como la que canta
en su Jerusalem el rey hermoso,
negra que haga brotar bajo su planta
la rosa y la cicuta del reposo . . .

    Amor, en fin, que todo diga y cante,
amor que encante y deje sorprendida
a la serpiente de ojos de diamante
que está enroscada al árbol de la vida.

    Amame así, fatal, cosmopolita,
universal, inmensa, única, sola
y todas; misteriosa y erudita:
ámame mar y nube, espuma y ola.

    Sé mi reina de Saba, mi tesoro;
descansa en mis palacios solitarios.
Duerme. Yo encenderé los incensarios.
Y junto a mi unicornio cuerno de oro,
tendrán rosas y miel tus dromedarios.

than the treasure guarded by the vexing
ivory caress of your fan.

❀

    Love me, Japanese woman, Japanese woman
of olden days, you that know nothing about Occidental
nations: like a princess
whose eyes are filled with visions,

    who in her sacred Kyoto,
in her alcove fashioned of silver
and adorned on an equal footing with chrysanthemum and lotus,
is unaware even of the civilization of Yamagata.

    Or with a Hindu love that raises its flames
in the supreme vision of myths,
and makes the sacred initiatory rites
tremble with a mysterious rutting,

    while tigers and panthers shake
their chains, and on strong elephants
diamond-bedecked rajahs
dream of ideal bayadères.

    Oh, swarthy woman, as swarthy as the one
that the handsome king sang of in his Jerusalem,
a swarthy woman who will cause to spring up beneath her soles
the rose and the hemlock that grants repose. . . .

    In short, a love that will say and sing everything,
a love that will enchant and leave in surprise
the serpent with diamond eyes
that is coiled around the tree of life.

    Love me in that way, my predestined, cosmopolitan woman,
universal, immense, unique, a single person
comprising all women; mysterious and learned:
love me as sea and cloud, foam and waves.

    Be my queen of Sheba, my treasure;
rest in my lonely palaces.
Sleep. I shall light the censers.
And, alongside my golden-horned unicorn,
your dromedaries shall bear roses and honey.

Sonatina

La princesa está triste . . . ¿qué tendrá la princesa?
Los suspiros se escapan de su boca de fresa,
que ha perdido la risa, que ha perdido el color.
La princesa está pálida en su silla de oro,
está mudo el teclado de su clave sonoro;
y en un vaso olvidada se desmaya una flor.

El jardín puebla el triunfo de los pavos-reales.
Parlanchina, la dueña dice cosas banales,
y, vestido de rojo, piruetea el bufón.
La princesa no ríe, la princesa no siente;
la princesa persigue por el cielo de Oriente
la libélula vaga de una vaga ilusión.

¿Piensa acaso en el príncipe de Golconda o de China,
o en el que ha detenido su carroza argentina
para ver de sus ojos la dulzura de luz?
¿O en el rey de las Islas de las Rosas fragantes,
o en el que es soberano de los claros diamantes,
o en el dueño orgulloso de las perlas de Ormuz?

¡Ay! La pobre princesa de la boca de rosa
quiere ser golondrina, quiere ser mariposa,
tener alas ligeras, bajo el cielo volar,
ir al sol por la escala luminosa de un rayo,
saludar a los lirios con los versos de mayo,
o perderse en el viento sobre el trueno del mar.

Ya no quiere el palacio, ni la rueca de plata,
ni el halcón encantado, ni el bufón escarlata,
ni los cisnes unánimes en el lago de azur.
Y están tristes las flores por la flor de la corte;
los jazmines de Oriente, los nelumbos del Norte,
de Occidente las dalias y las rosas del Sur.

¡Pobrecita princesa de los ojos azules!
Está presa en sus oros, está presa en sus tules,
en la jaula de mármol del palacio real,
el palacio soberbio que vigilan los guardas,
que custodian cien negros con sus cien alabardas,
un lebrel que no duerme y un dragón colosal.

Sonatina

The princess is sad . . . what can be ailing the princess?
Sighs escape her strawberry lips,
which have lost their laughter, which have lost their color.
The princess is pale on her golden chair,
the keyboard of her resonant harpsichord is mute;
and, forgotten in a vase, a flower swoons.

The garden is peopled by the triumph of the peacocks.
Talkative, the duenna says banal things,
and, dressed in red, the jester pirouettes.
The princess doesn't laugh, the princess doesn't react;
in the Eastern sky the princess pursues
the vague dragonfly of a vague hopeful dream.

Can she be thinking about the prince of Golconda or China,
or the one who has halted his silvery coach
to see the sweetness of light with his own eyes?
Or about the king of the Isles of Fragrant Roses,
or the one who possesses the bright diamonds,
or the proud owner of the pearls of Ormuz?

Alas! The poor princess with the rose lips
wishes to be a swallow, wishes to be a butterfly,
to have light wings, to fly beneath the sky,
to travel to the sun on the luminous ladder of a beam,
to greet the lilies with the verses of May,
or to be lost in the wind over the thunder of the sea.

She no longer cares for her palace, nor the silver spinning wheel,
nor the magical falcon, nor the scarlet-clad jester,
nor the unanimous swans on the azure lake.
And the flowers are sad for the flower of the court;
the jasmines of the East, the water lilies of the North,
the dahlias of the West, and the roses of the South.

Poor blue-eyed princess!
She's a captive of her gold, she's a captive of her tulle,
in the marble cage of the royal palace,
the proud palace policed by guards,
watched over by a hundred blacks with their hundred halberds,
a greyhound that never sleeps, and a colossal dragon.

¡Oh quién fuera hipsipila que dejó la crisálida!
(La princesa está triste. La princesa está pálida)
¡Oh visión adorada de oro, rosa y marfil!
¡Quién volara a la tierra donde un príncipe existe
(La princesa está pálida. La princesa está triste)
más brillante que el alba, más hermoso que abril!

—¡Calla, calla, princesa —dice el hada madrina—,
en caballo con alas, hacia acá se encamina,
en el cinto la espada y en la mano el azor,
el feliz caballero que te adora sin verte,
y que llega de lejos, vencedor de la Muerte,
a encenderte los labios con su beso de amor!

Blasón

Para la condesa de Peralta

El olímpico cisne de nieve
con el ágata rosa del pico
lustra el ala eucarística y breve
que abre al sol como un casto abanico.

En la forma de un brazo de lira
y del asa de un ánfora griega
es su cándido cuello que inspira
como prora ideal que navega.

Es el cisne, de estirpe sagrada,
cuyo beso, por campos de seda,
ascendió hasta la cima rosada
de las dulces colinas de Leda.

Blanco rey de la fuente Castalia,
su victoria ilumina el Danubio;
Vinci fue su barón en Italia;
Lohengrín es su príncipe rubio.

Su blancura es hermana del lino,
del botón de los blancos rosales
y del albo toisón diamantino
de los tiernos corderos pascuales.

Oh, to be a butterfly that has emerged from its chrysalis!
(The princess is sad, the princess is pale.)
O adored vision of gold, rose, and ivory!
If she could only fly to the land where a prince lives
(the princess is pale, the princess is sad)
who is brighter than the dawn, handsomer than April!

"Be silent, silent, princess," says her fairy godmother;
"on a winged horse there is heading this way,
sword in belt and hawk in hand,
the fortunate knight who worships you though he has never seen you;
he comes from afar, having conquered Death,
to ignite your lips with his kiss of love!"

Coat-of-Arms

For the Countess de Peralta

The Olympian, snowy swan
with the pink agate of his bill
preens his short eucharistic wing,
which he opens to the sun like a chaste fan.

Shaped like the arm of a lyre,
or the ear of a Greek amphora,
is his white neck, which inspires one
like a sailing prow from the realm of Ideas.

He is the swan, of sacred lineage,
whose kiss, on fields of silk,
ascended to the pink summit
of Leda's gentle hills.

White king of the Castalian spring,
his victory illumines the Danube;
Vinci was his baron in Italy;
Lohengrin is his blond prince.

His whiteness is sister to flax,
to the bud of white rosebushes,
and the diamondlike white fleece
of tender Easter lambs.

Rimador de ideal florilegio,
es de armiño su lírico manto,
y es el mágico pájaro regio
que al morir rima el alma en un canto.

El alado aristócrata muestra
lises albos en campo de azur,
y ha sentido en sus plumas la diestra
de la amable y gentil Pompadour.

Boga y boga en el lago sonoro
donde el sueño a los tristes espera,
donde aguarda una góndola de oro
a la novia de Luis de Baviera.

Dad, Condesa, a los cisnes cariño,
dioses son de un país halagüeño
y hechos son de perfume, de armiño,
de lux alba, de seda y de sueño.

Ite, missa est

A Reynaldo de Rafael

Yo adoro a una sonámbula con alma de Eloísa,
virgen como la nieve y honda como la mar;
su espíritu es la hostia de mi amorosa misa,
y alzo al son de una dulce lira crepuscular.

Ojos de evocadora, gesto de profetisa,
en ella hay la sagrada frecuencia del altar:
su risa es la sonrisa suave de Monna Lisa;
sus labios son los únicos labios para besar.

Y he de besarla un día con rojo beso ardiente;
apoyada en mi brazo como convaleciente
me mirará asombrada con íntimo pavor;

la enamorada esfinge quedará estupefacta;
apagaré la llama de la vestal intacta
¡y la faunesa antigua me rugirá de amor!

Rhymer of an ideal anthology,
he has a lyrical mantle of ermine;
he is the magical, royal bird
who, when dying, rhymes his soul in a song.

This winged aristocrat displays
white fleurs-de-lis on an azure field,
and has felt on his feathers the right hand
of the lovable, charming Pompadour.

He sails and sails on the resounding lake
where dreams await those who are sad,
where a golden gondola is waiting
for the fiancée of Ludwig of Bavaria.

Countess, give the swans your affection;
they are gods of a pleasing land
and they are compounded of perfume, ermine,
white light, silk, and dreams.

Ite, Missa Est

To Reynaldo de Rafael

I adore a somnambulist who has a soul like that of Heloise,
virginal as snow and deep as the sea;
her spirit is the Host of my loving Mass,
and I raise it to the sound of a sweet, crepuscular lyre.

Eyes of a woman who conjures up spirits, face of a prophetess;
in her there is the holy frequentation of the altar;
her laughter is the gentle smile of Mona Lisa;
her lips are the only lips for kissing.

And one day I shall kiss her with a burning red kiss;
leaning on my arm like a convalescent,
she will look at me with awe and deep-seated fear;

the loving sphinx will remain stupefied;
I shall extinguish the flame of the spotless vestal
and the ancient female Faun will roar to me with love!

Coloquio de los centauros

A Paul Groussac

En la isla en que detiene su esquife el argonauta
del inmortal Ensueño, donde la eterna pauta
de las eternas liras se escucha —isla de oro
en que el tritón elige su caracol sonoro
y la sirena blanca va a ver el sol— un día
se oye un tropel vibrante de fuerza y de harmonía.

Son los Centauros. Cubren la llanura. Les siente
la montaña. De lejos, forman son de torrente
que cae; su galope al aire que reposa
despierta, y estremece la hoja del laurel-rosa.

Son los Centauros. Unos enormes, rudos; otros
alegres y saltantes como jóvenes potros;
unos con largas barbas como los padres-ríos;
otros imberbes, ágiles y de piafantes bríos,
y de robustos músculos, brazos y lomos aptos
para portar las ninfas rosadas en los raptos.

Van en galope rítmico. Junto a un fresco boscaje,
frente al gran Oceano, se paran. El paisaje
recibe de la urna matinal luz sagrada
que el vasto azul suaviza con límpida mirada.
Y oyen seres terrestres y habitantes marinos
la voz de los crinados cuadrúpedos divinos.

QUIRÓN
Calladas las bocinas a los tritones gratas,
calladas las sirenas de labios escarlatas,
los carrillos de Eolo desinflados, digamos
junto al laurel ilustre de florecidos ramos
la gloria inmarcesible de las Musas hermosas
y el triunfo del terrible misterio de las cosas.
He aquí que renacen los lauros milenarios;
vuelven a dar su lumbre los viejos lampadarios;
y anímase en mi cuerpo de Centauro inmortal
la sangre del celeste caballo paternal.

Dialogue of the Centaurs

To Paul Groussac

On the island where the argonaut of the immortal Dream
halts on his voyage, where the eternal pattern
of eternal lyres is heard—a golden island
on which the triton chooses his resonant seashell
and the white siren comes to see the sun—one day
there is heard a troop vibrant with strength and harmony.

It is the Centaurs. They cover the plain. They are felt
by the mountain. From afar, they create the roar of a torrent
falling from cliffs; their gallop awakens the resting
air, and shakes the leaves of the rose-laurel.

It is the Centaurs. Some are huge, rough; others
merry and frisking like young colts;
some have long beards like river gods;
others are beardless, agile, and paw the ground energetically,
with sturdy muscles, arms and loins fitted
for carrying rosy nymphs when they abduct them.

They proceed at a rhythmical gallop. Beside a cool grove,
facing the great Ocean, they halt. The landscape
receives from the urn of morning holy light
softened by the limpid gaze of the immense blue sky.
And terrestrial beings and inhabitants of the sea hear
the voices of the long-maned divine quadrupeds.

CHIRON
Now that the trumpets pleasing to the tritons are silent,
now that the sirens with scarlet lips are silent,
and Aeolus's cheeks no longer puffed out, let us speak,
beside the illustrious laurel's flowering branches,
of the unfading glory of the beautiful Muses
and the triumph of the awesome mystery of nature.
Behold, the age-old laurels are growing once more;
the old lamps are giving their light again;
and in my immortal Centaur body there stirs
the blood of the heavenly horse that sired me.

RETO

Arquero luminoso, desde el Zodíaco llegas;
aun presas en las crines tienes abejas griegas;
aun del dardo herakleo muestras la roja herida
por do salir no pudo la esencia de tu vida.
¡Padre y Maestro excelso! Eres la fuente sana
de la verdad que busca la triste raza humana:
aun Esculapio sigue la vena de tu ciencia;
siempre el veloz Aquiles sustenta su existencia
con el manjar salvaje que le ofreciste un día,
y Herakles, descuidando su maza, en la harmonía
de los astros, se eleva bajo el cielo nocturno . . .

QUIRÓN

La ciencia es flor del tiempo: mi padre fue Saturno.

ABANTES

Himnos a la sagrada Naturaleza; al vientre
de la tierra y al germen que entre las rocas y entre
las carnes de los árboles, y dentro humana forma,
es un mismo secreto y es una misma norma,
potente y sutilísimo, universal resumen
de la suprema fuerza, de la virtud del Numen.

QUIRÓN

¡Himnos! Las cosas tienen un ser vital; las cosas
tienen raros aspectos, miradas misteriosas;
toda forma es un gesto, una cifra, un enigma;
en cada átomo existe un incógnito estigma;
cada hoja de cada árbol canta un propio cantar
y hay un alma en cada una de las gotas del mar;
el vate, el sacerdote, suele oír el acento
desconocido; a veces enuncia el vago viento
un misterio; y revela una inicial la espuma
o la flor; y se escuchan palabras de la bruma;
y el hombre favorito del Numen, en la linfa
o la ráfaga encuentra mentor —demonio o ninfa.

FOLO

El biforme ixionida comprende de la altura,
por la materna gracia, la lumbre que fulgura,

RHOETUS
Luminous archer, you have come from the Zodiac;
you still have Greek bees caught in your mane;
you still show the red wound from Herakles's arrow
through which the essence of your life was unable to issue.
Father and lofty Master! You are the healthful fountain
of the truth that the sad human race is seeking:
even Aesculapius follows the course of your knowledge;
swift Achilles always sustains his existence
with the food of the wilds that you offered him one day,
and Herakles, neglecting his cudgel, in the harmony
of the spheres, rises beneath the night sky. . . .

CHIRON
Knowledge is the flower of time: my father was Saturn.

ABAS
Hymns to holy Nature; to the womb
of the earth and the seed that among rocks and among
the flesh of trees, and in human form,
is one-and-the-same secret and one-and-the-same norm,
potent and most subtle, a universal summary
of the supreme force, of the powers of the Godhead.

CHIRON
Hymns! Things possess a vital essence; things
have strange aspects, mysterious gazes;
every form is a face, a code, an enigma;
in every atom an unknown sign exists;
every leaf on every tree sings its own song
and there is a soul in every one of the drops in the sea;
the bard, the priest, is accustomed to hear the unknown
accent; at times the unsubstantial wind proclaims
a mystery; and an initial is revealed by froth
or flower; and words are heard in the mist;
and the man favored by the Godhead finds a mentor—
demon or nymph—in water or wind gusts.

PHOLUS
Through his mother's grace, the double-formed son of Ixion
understands the light that flashes from the high heavens,

la nube que se anima de luz y que decora
el pavimento en donde rige su carro Aurora,
y la banda de Iris que tiene siete rayos
cual la lira en sus brazos siete cuerdas, los mayos
en la fragante tierra llenos de ramos bellos,
y el Polo coronado de cándidos cabellos.
El ixionida pasa veloz por la montaña
rompiendo con el pecho de la maleza huraña
los erizados brazos, las cárceles hostiles;
escuchan sus orejas los ecos más sutiles:
sus ojos atraviesan las intrincadas hojas
mientras sus manos toman para sus bocas rojas
las frescas bayas altas que el sátiro codicia;
junto a la oculta fuente su mirada acaricia
las curvas de las ninfas del séquito de Diana;
pues en su cuerpo corre también la esencia humana
unida a la corriente de la savia divina
y a la salvaje sangre que hay en la bestia equina.
Tal el hijo robusto de Ixión y de la Nube.

QUIRÓN
   Sus cuatro patas bajan; su testa erguida sube.

ORNEO
   Yo comprendo el secreto de la bestia. Malignos
seres hay y benignos. Entre ellos se hacen signos
de bien y mal, de odio o de amor, o de pena
o gozo: el cuervo es malo y la torcaz es buena.

QUIRÓN
   Ni es la torcaz benigna, ni es el cuervo protervo:
son formas del Enigma la paloma y el cuervo.

ASTILO
   El Enigma es el soplo que hace cantar la lira.

NESO
   ¡El Enigma es el rostro fatal de Deyanira!
Mi espalda aún guarda el dulce perfume de la bella;
aún mis pupilas llaman su claridad de estrella.

the cloud that is animated by light and that adorns
the pavement over which Aurora drives her chariot,
and Iris's bow, which has seven rays
just as the lyre encloses seven strings between its arms, and Maytimes
full of beautiful boughs on sweet-smelling earth,
and the Pole crowned with gleaming-white hair.
The son of Ixion passes rapidly through the mountains,
breaking with his breast the prickly arms
of the surly underbrush, its hostile prisons;
his ears hear the slightest of echoes:
his eyes penetrate the tangled leaves
while his hands take for his red mouth
the lofty fresh berries that the satyr covets;
beside the hidden fountain his gaze caresses
the curves of the nymphs from Diana's retinue;
for in his body human essence also flows
united with the current of godlike sap
and the savage blood that exists in the equine animal.
Such is the sturdy son of Ixion and the Cloud.

CHIRON
    His four legs touch the ground; his uplifted head soars.

ORNEUS
    I comprehend the secret of animals. There are malevolent
beings and benevolent ones. Between them are exchanged signals
of good and evil, hate or love, or else pain
or joy: the raven is evil and the ringdove is good.

CHIRON
    The ringdove is not good, nor is the raven vicious:
both dove and raven are different forms of the same Enigma.

ASTYLUS
    The Enigma is the breath of air that makes the lyre sing.

NESSUS
    The Enigma is the fateful face of Dejanira!
My back still retains that beauty's sweet fragrance;
my eyes still call for her starlike brightness.

¡Oh aroma de su sexo! ¡Oh rosas y alabastros!
¡Oh envidia de las flores y celos de los astros!

QUIRÓN
   Cuando del sacro abuelo la sangre luminosa
con la marina espuma formara nieve y rosa,
hecha de rosa y nieve nació la Anadiomena.
Al cielo alzó los brazos la lírica sirena,
los curvos hipocampos sobre las verdes ondas
levaron los hocicos; y caderas redondas,
tritónicas melenas y dorsos de delfines
junto a la Reina nueva se vieron. Los confines
del mar llenó el grandioso clamor; el universo
sintió que un nombre harmónico sonoro como un verso
llenaba el hondo hueco de la altura; ese nombre
hizo gemir la tierra de amor: fue para el hombre
más alto que el de Jove; y los númenes mismos
lo oyeron asombrados; los lóbregos abismos
tuvieron una gracia de luz. ¡VENUS impera!
Ella es entre las reinas celestes la primera,
pues es quien tiene el fuerte poder de la Hermosura.
¡Vaso de miel y mirra brotó de la amargura!
Ella es la más gallarda de las emperatrices;
princesa de los gérmenes, reina de las matrices,
señora de las savias y de las atracciones,
señora de los besos y de los corazones.

EURITO
   ¡No olvidaré los ojos radiantes de Hipodamia!

HIPEA
   Yo sé de la hembra humana la original infamia.
Venus anima artera sus máquinas fatales;
tras sus radiantes ojos ríen traidores males;
de su floral perfume se exhala sutil daño;
su cráneo obscuro alberga bestialidad y engaño.
Tiene las formas puras del ánfora, y la risa
del agua que la brisa riza y el sol irisa;
mas la ponzoña ingénita su máscara pregona:
mejores son el águila, la yegua y la leona.
De su húmeda impureza brota el calor que enerva

Oh, the smell of her sex! Oh, rose and alabaster!
Oh, envy of the flowers and jealousy of the heavenly bodies!

CHIRON
   When the luminous blood of the sacred ancestor
had created snow and rose in conjunction with the sea foam,
Anadyomene was born, made of rose and snow.
The lyrical sirens raised their arms to heaven,
the curved hippocamps lifted their muzzles
above the green waves; and rounded hips,
tritons' tousled hair, and the backs of dophins
were seen beside the new Queen. The confines
of the sea were filled with the grandiose shout; the universe
felt a harmonious name, resonant as poetry,
filling the hollow summit of the heavens; that name
made the earth moan with love; for mankind
it was loftier than Jupiter's; and the gods themselves
heard it with awe; the gloomy depths
were touched by the grace of light. VENUS rules!
Among heavenly queens she is the foremost,
because it is she who possesses the strong power of Beauty.
A vessel of honey and myrrh emerged from the bitter element!
She is the most elegant of empresses;
princess of vital seeds, queen of wombs,
mistress of sap and mutual attraction,
mistress of kisses and hearts.

EURYTUS
   I shall never forget Hippodamia's radiant eyes!

HIPPEA
   I know the primordial infamy of human females.
Crafty Venus sets their fateful machinery in motion;
behind their radiant eyes treacherous evil laughs;
secret harm is exhaled by their flowery fragrance;
their dark skulls harbor bestiality and deceit.
They have the pure shape of the amphora, and the laughter
of water rippled by the breeze and made iridescent by the sun;
but their inborn venom proclaims that they wear a mask:
the eagle, mare, and lioness are kinder.
From their damp impurity there springs the heat that enervates

los mismos sacros dones de la imperial Minerva;
y entre sus duros pechos, lirios del Aqueronte,
hay un olor que llena la barca de Caronte.

ODITES
    Como una miel celeste hay en su lengua fina;
su piel de flor aún húmeda está de agua marina.
Yo he visto de Hipodamia la faz encantadora,
la cabellera espesa, la pierna vencedora;
ella de la hembra humana fuera ejemplar augusto;
ante su rostro olímpico no habría rostro adusto;
las Gracias junto a ella quedarían confusas,
y las ligeras Horas y las sublimes Musas
por ella detuvieran sus giros y su canto.

HIPEA
    Ella la causa fuera de inenarrable espanto:
por ella el ixionida dobló su cuello fuerte.
La hembra humana es hermana del Dolor y la Muerte.

QUIRÓN
    Por suma ley un día llegará el himeneo
que el soñador aguarda: Cenis será Ceneo;
claro será el origen del femenino arcano:
la Esfinge tal secreto dirá a su soberano.

CLITO
    Naturaleza tiende sus brazos y sus pechos
a los humanos seres; la clave de los hechos
conócela el vidente; Homero con su báculo,
en su gruta Deifobe, la lengua del Oráculo.

CAUMANTES
    El monstruo expresa un ansia del corazón del Orbe,
en el Centauro el bruto la vida humana absorbe,
el sátiro es la selva sagrada y la lujuria,
une sexuales ímpetus a la harmoniosa furia.
Pan junta la soberbia de la montaña agreste
al ritmo de la inmensa mecánica celeste;
la boca melodiosa que atrae en Sirenusa
es de la fiera alada y es de la suave musa;

even the sacred gifts of imperial Minerva;
and between their firm breasts, lilies of Acheron,
there is a perfume that fills Charon's boat.

ODITES
    There is something like heavenly honey on their delicate tongues;
their flowery skin is still moist with sea water.
I have seen Hippodamia's enchanting face,
thick hair, conquering legs;
she was an outstanding example of the human female;
when her Olympian face appeared there couldn't be any severe face;
alongside her the Graces would be embarrassed,
and the light-footed Hours and the sublime Muses
would cease their rounds and songs for her sake.

HIPPEA
    She was the cause of unspeakable horror:
for her the son of Ixion bent his mighty neck.
The human female is sister to Sorrow and Death.

CHIRON
    One day the supreme law will arrive in the form of a marriage
that dreamers await: Caenis will be Caeneus;
the origin of the feminine mystery will be clear:
the Sphinx will tell that secret to her sovereign.

CLYTUS
    Nature holds out her arms and breasts
to human beings; the key to facts
is known to seers: Homer with his blind man's staff,
Deiphobe in her grotto, the tongue of the Oracle.

CAUMAS
    A monstrous birth represents an anxiety of the World's heart;
in the Centaur, the brute beast absorbs the human element;
the satyr is both the sacred forest and lust,
he combines the sexual urge with the rage of music.
Pan joins the haughtiness of the wild mountains
to the rhythm of the immense celestial machine;
the melodious lips that draw seafarers to the sirens' islands
are those of the winged creature and the gentle muse;

con la bicorne bestia Pasifae se ayunta,
Naturaleza sabia formas diversas junta,
y cuando tiende al hombre la gran Naturaleza,
el monstruo, siendo el símbolo, se viste de belleza.

GRINEO
    Yo amo lo inanimado que amó el divino Hesiodo.

QUIRÓN
    Grineo, sobre el mundo tiene un ánima todo.

GRINEO
    He visto, entonces, raros ojos fijos en mí:
los vivos ojos rojos del alma del rubí;
los ojos luminosos del alma del topacio
y los de la esmeralda que del azul espacio
la maravilla imitan; los ojos de las gemas
de brillos peregrinos y mágicos emblemas.
Amo el granito duro que el arquitecto labra
y el mármol en que duermen la línea y la palabra . . .

QUIRÓN
    A Deucalión y a Pirra, varones y mujeres
las piedras aún intactas dijeron: «¿Qué nos quieres?»

LÍCIDAS
    Yo he visto los lemures flotar, en los nocturnos
instantes, cuando escuchan los bosques taciturnos
el loco grito de Atis que su dolor revela
o la maravillosa canción de Filomela.
El galope apresuro, si en el boscaje miro
manes que pasan, y oigo su fúnebre suspiro.
Pues de la Muerte el hondo, desconocido Imperio,
guarda el pavor sagrado de su fatal misterio.

ARNEO
    La Muerte es de la Vida la inseparable hermana.

QUIRÓN
    La Muerte es la victoria de la progenie humana.

Pasiphae cohabits with the two-horned beast,
wise Nature combines various forms,
and when great Nature turns her hand toward man,
the monster, which is the symbol, is clothed with beauty.

GRYNEUS
  I love the inanimate existence which divine Hesiod loved.

CHIRON
  Gryneus, everything in the world is animate, and has a soul.

GRYNEUS
  In that case, I have seen strange eyes staring at me:
the vivid red eyes of the soul of the ruby;
the luminous eyes of the soul of the topaz
and those of the emerald, which imitate the marvel
of blue space; the eyes of gems
with exotic brightness and magical emblems.
I love the hard granite that the architect fashions
and the marble in which lines and words slumber. . . .

CHIRON
  Deucalion and Pyrrha were asked by the as yet untouched stones,
future men and women: "What do you want of us?"

LYCIDAS
  I have seen phantoms hovering, at moments
of night, when the silent forests listen to
the mad cry of Atys revealing his sorrow
or to the wonderful song of Philomel.
I gallop more swiftly, if in the grove I espy
shades of the dead passing, and I hear their funereal sighs.
Because the deep, unknown Realm of Death
retains the sacred fear of its fatal mystery.

ARNEUS
  Death is the inseparable sister of Life.

CHIRON
  Death is the victory of mankind.

MEDÓN

¡La Muerte! Yo la he visto. No es demacrada y mustia
ni ase corva guadaña, ni tiene faz de angustia.
Es semejante a Diana, casta y virgen como ella;
en su rostro hay la gracia de la núbil doncella
y lleva una guirnalda de rosas siderales.
En su siniestra tiene verdes palmas triunfales,
y en su diestra una copa con agua del olvido.
A sus pies, como un perro, yace un amor dormido.

AMICO

Los mismos dioses buscan la dulce paz que vierte.

QUIRÓN

La pena de los dioses es no alcanzar la Muerte.

EURITO

Si el hombre —Prometeo— pudo robar la vida,
la clave de la muerte seréle concedida.

QUIRÓN

La virgen de las vírgenes es inviolable y pura.
Nadie su casto cuerpo tendrá en la alcoba obscura,
ni beberá en sus labios el grito de victoria,
ni arrancará a su frente las rosas de su gloria . . .

✿

Mas he aquí que Apolo se acerca al meridiano.
Sus truenos prolongados repite el Oceano.
Bajo el dorado carro del reluciente Apolo
vuelve a inflar sus carrillos y sus odres Eolo.
A lo lejos, un templo de mármol se divisa
entre laureles-rosa que hace cantar la brisa.
Con sus vibrantes notas de Céfiro desgarra
la veste transparente la helénica cigarra,
y por el llano extenso van en tropel sonoro
los Centauros, y al paso, tiembla la Isla de Oro.

MEDON
Death! I've seen her. She isn't gaunt and withered,
she doesn't grip a curved scythe, nor does she have a frightening face.
She resembles Diana, she is just as chaste and virginal;
in her face there is the grace of a marriageable maiden,
and she wears a garland of starry roses.
In her left hand she carries green palm leaves of triumph,
and in her right a goblet of the water of forgetfulness.
At her feet, like a dog, lies a sleeping cupid.

AMYCUS
The gods themselves seek the sweet peace that she dispenses.

CHIRON
The punishment of the gods is never to attain death.

EURYTUS
If man—Prometheus—was able to steal life,
the key to death will be granted to him as well.

CHIRON
The virgin of virgins is inviolable and pure.
No one will possess her chaste body in the dark alcove,
or drink the cry of victory from her lips,
or tear from her brow the roses of her glory. . . .

✿

But, behold, Apollo is approaching the meridian.
Ocean repeats its prolonged thundering.
Beneath the gilded chariot of gleaming Apollo,
Aeolus once more inflates his cheeks and his bags.
Far off, a marble temple can be discerned
amid rose-laurels that the breeze causes to sing.
With its vibrant notes the Hellenic cicada
rends the transparent robe of Zephyr,
and across the broad plain, in a sonorous troop, go
the Centaurs, and, as they pass, the Golden Island shakes.

El poeta pregunta por Stella

Lirio divino, lirio de las Anunciaciones;
lirio, florido príncipe,
hermano perfumado de las estrellas castas,
joya de los abriles.

A ti las blancas Dianas de los parques ducales;
los cuellos de los cisnes,
las místicas estrofas de cánticos celestes
y en el sagrado empíreo la mano de las vírgenes.

Lirio, boca de nieve donde sus dulces labios
la primavera imprime:
en tus venas no corre la sangre de las rosas pecadoras,
sino el ícor excelso de las flores insignes.

Lirio real y lírico
que naces con la albura de las hostias sublimes,
de las cándidas perlas
y del lino sin mácula de las sobrepellices:
¿Has visto acaso el vuelo del alma de mi Stella,
la hermana de Ligeia, por quien mi canto a veces es tan triste?

Sinfonía en gris mayor

El mar como un vasto cristal azogado
refleja la lámina de un cielo de zinc;
lejanas bandadas de pájaros manchan
el fundo bruñido de pálido gris.

El sol como un vidrio redondo y opaco
con paso de enfermo camina al cenit;
el viento marino descansa en la sombra
teniendo de almohada su negro clarín.

Las ondas que mueven su vientre de plomo
debajo del muelle parecen gemir.
Sentado en un cable, fumando su pipa,
está un marinero pensando en las playas
de un vago, lejano, brumoso país.

The Poet Asks About Stella

Divine lily, lily of Annunciations;
lily, flowery prince,
fragrant brother to the chaste stars,
jewel of Aprils.

For you, the white Dianas in ducal parks;
the necks of swans,
the mystic strophes of celestial canticles
and the hands of virgins in the holy empyrean.

Lily, snowy mouth on which springtime presses
her sweet lips:
in your veins there flows not the blood of sinful roses,
but the lofty ichor of renowned flowers.

Royal, lyrical lily,
you that are born with the whiteness of consecrated Hosts,
of gleaming pearls,
and the spotless linen of surplices:
Have you by any chance seen in its flight the soul of my Stella,
sister to Ligeia, on whose account my song is at times so sad?

Symphony in Gray Major

The sea, like a vast silvered mirror,
reflects the sky's sheet of zinc;
distant flocks of birds stain
the polished pale-gray background.

The sun, like an opaque glass sphere,
mounts to the zenith with a sick man's gait;
the ocean breeze is resting in the shade,
using its black bugle for a pillow.

The waves that shake their leaden bellies
under the wharf seem to be moaning.
Seated on a cable, smoking his pipe,
is a sailor thinking about the beaches
of a vague, distant, misty land.

Es viejo ese lobo. Tostaron su cara
los rayos de fuego del sol del Brasil;
los recios tifones del mar de la China
le han visto bebiendo su frasco de *gin*.

La espuma impregnada de yodo y salitre
ha tiempo conoce su roja nariz,
sus crespos cabellos, sus bíceps de atleta,
su gorra de lona, su blusa de dril.

En medio del humo que forma el tabaco
ve el viejo el lejano, brumoso país,
adonde una tarde caliente y dorada
tendidas las velas partió el bergantín . . .

La siesta del trópico. El lobo se aduerme.
Ya todo lo envuelve la gama del gris.
Parece que un suave y enorme esfumino
del curvo horizonte borrara el confín.

La siesta del trópico. La vieja cigarra
ensaya su ronca guitarra senil,
y el grillo preludia un solo monótono
en la única cuerda que está en su violín.

†

Verlaine

A Angel Estrada, poeta

Responso

Padre y maestro mágico, liróforo celeste
que al instrumento olímpico y a la siringa agreste
         diste tu acento encantador;
¡Panida! Pan tú mismo, que coros condujiste
hacia el propíleo sacro que amaba tu alma triste,
         ¡al son del sistro y del tambor!

Que tu sepulcro cubra de flores Primavera,
que se humedezca el áspero hocico de la fiera
         de amor si pasa por allí;

That sea wolf is old. His face was tanned
by the fiery rays of the Brazilian sun;
the violent typhoons of the China seas
have seen him drinking his bottle of gin.

The spray impregnated with iodine and saltpeter
has long been familiar to his red nose,
his curly hair, his athletic biceps,
his canvas cap, his duck blouse.

Amid the smoke formed by the tobacco
the old man sees the distant, misty land
for which, on one hot, golden afternoon,
his brigantine set sail, with all canvas spread. . . .

Siesta in the tropics. The sea wolf falls asleep.
Now the gamut of gray envelops him entirely.
It is as if a soft, enormous stumped drawing
blurred the edge of the curved horizon.

Siesta in the tropics. The old cicada
tries out its hoarse, senile guitar,
and the cricket plays, as prelude, a monotonous solo
on the only string his violin possesses.

†

Verlaine

To Angel Estrada, poet

Response

Father and magical master, celestial lyrebearer
who, to the music of that Olympian instrument and the rustic reed flute,
        uttered your bewitching words;
Son of Pan! You yourself Pan, leading choirs
up to the sacred propylaeon that your sad soul loved,
        to the sound of the sistrum and the drum!

May Spring cover your grave with flowers,
may the harsh muzzle of the beast of love
        be moistened if it passes that way;

que el fúnebre recinto visite Pan bicorne;
que de sangrientas rosas el fresco abril te adorne
　　　　y de claveles de rubí.

Que si posarse quiere sobre la tumba el cuervo,
ahuyenten la negrura del pájaro protervo
　　　　el dulce canto de cristal
que Filomela vierta sobre tus tristes huesos,
o la harmonía dulce de risas y de besos
　　　　de culto oculto y florestal.

Que púberes canéforas te ofrenden el acanto,
que sobre tu sepulcro no se derrame el llanto,
　　　　sino rocío, vino, miel;
que el pámpano allí brote, las flores de Citeres,
y que se escuchen vagos suspiros de mujeres
　　　　¡bajo un simbólico laurel!

Que si un pastor su pífano bajo el frescor del haya,
en amorosos días, como en Virgilio, ensaya,
　　　　tu nombre ponga en la canción;
y que la virgen náyade, cuando ese nombre escuche,
con ansias y temores entre las linfas luche,
　　　　llena de miedo y de pasión.

De noche, en la montaña, en la negra montaña
de las Visiones, pase gigante sombra extraña,
　　　　sombra de un Sátiro espectral;
que ella al centauro adusto con su grandeza asuste;
de una extra-humana flauta la melodía ajuste
　　　　a la harmonía sideral.

Y huya el tropel equino por la montaña vasta;
tu rostro de ultratumba bañe la luna casta
　　　　de compasiva y blanca luz;
y el Sátiro contemple sobre un lejano monte
una cruz que se eleve cubriendo el horizonte
　　　　¡y un resplandor sobre la cruz!

may two-horned Pan visit the cemetery grounds;
may fresh April adorn you with blood-red roses
        and ruby carnations.

And if the raven wishes to perch on your tomb,
may the blackness of the evil bird be frightened away
        by the sweet, crystalline song
that Philomel pours forth onto your unhappy bones,
or by the sweet harmony of laughter and kisses
        of some secret forest cult.

May nubile basket-bearing maidens bring you an offering of acanthus,
may no tears be shed over your grave,
        but only dew, wine, honey;
may the grapevine grow there, and the flowers of Cythera,
and may the soft sighs of women be heard
        beneath a symbolic laurel!

And if a shepherd tries out his fife in the shade of the beech,
on days when he is in love, as in the poems of Vergil,
        may he place your name in his song;
and may the virgin naiad, on hearing that name,
struggle in the water with anxieties and fears,
        filled with terror and passion.

At night, in the mountains, in the black mountains
of Visions, may a strange gigantic shadow pass,
        the shadow of a spectral Satyr;
may it frighten the grim centaur by its great size;
may it tune the melody of a more than human flute
        to the harmony of the stars.

And may the equine troop flee across the vast mountain;
may your face beyond the tomb be bathed by the chaste moon
        with compassionate white light;
and may the Satyr, on a distant hill, contemplate
a cross that rises till it covers the horizon,
        and a bright glow above the cross!

El reino interior

A Eugenio de Castro

. . . with Psychis, my soul.
POE

Una selva suntuosa
en el azul celeste su rudo perfil calca.
Un camino. La tierra es de color de rosa,
cual la que pinta fra Doménico Cavalca
en sus Vidas de santos. Se ven extrañas flores
de la flora gloriosa de los cuentos azules,
y entre las ramas encantadas, papemores
cuyo canto extasiara de amor a los bulbules.
(*Papemor:* ave rara; *Bulbules:* ruiseñores.)

    ❁

Mi alma frágil se asoma a la ventana obscura
de la torre terrible en que ha treinta años sueña.
La gentil Primavera primavera le augura.
La vida le sonríe rosada y halagüeña.
Y ella exclama: «¡Oh fragante día! ¡Oh sublime día!
Se diría que el mundo está en flor; se diría
que el corazón sagrado de la tierra se mueve
con un ritmo de dicha; luz brota, gracia llueve.
¡Yo soy la prisionera que sonríe y que canta!»
Y las manos liliales agita, como infanta
real en los balcones del palacio paterno.

    ❁

¿Qué son se escucha, son lejano, vago y tierno?
Por el lado derecho del camino adelanta
el paso leve una adorable teoría
virginal. Siete blancas doncellas, semejantes
a siete blancas rosas de gracia y de harmonía
que el alba constelara de perlas y diamantes.
¡Alabastros celestes habitados por astros:
Dios se refleja en esos dulces alabastros!
Sus vestes son tejidos del lino de la luna.
Van descalzas. Se mira que posan el pie breve
sobre el rosado suelo, como una flor de nieve.

The Inner Kingdom

To Eugenio de Castro

. . . with Psyche, my Soul.
POE

A sumptuous forest
traces its ragged profile on the blue of the sky.
A path. The earth is rose-colored,
like that painted by Fra Domenico Cavalca
in his Lives of Saints. One sees strange flowers,
from the glorious flora of fairy tales,
and, amid the enchanted boughs, "papemors"
whose song would enrapture the bulbuls with love.
("Papemor": rare bird. "Bulbuls": nightingales.)
✿

My fragile soul looks out at the dark window
of the frightful tower in which it has been dreaming for thirty years.
Lovely Springtime predicts springtime for it.
Life smiles to it rosily and flatteringly.
And my soul exclaims: "Oh, fragrant day! Oh, sublime day!
It's as if the whole world were in blossom; it's as if
the sacred heart of the earth were beating
to a rhythm of good fortune; light germinates, grace rains down.
I am the captive who smiles and sings!"
And it waves its lily hands, like a royal
princess on the balconies of her father's palace.
✿

What sound is heard, what distant, vague, tender sound?
Along the righthand side of the path there moves forward
the light step of a charming procession
of virgins. Seven white maidens, resembling
seven white roses of grace and harmony
studded with pearls and diamonds by the dawn.
Heavenly alabasters inhabited by stars:
God is reflected in those sweet alabasters!
Their robes are woven of the moon's linen.
They walk barefoot. One sees them set their small feet
on the pink ground like flowers of snow.

Y los cuellos se inclinan, imperiales, en una
manera que lo excelso pregona de su origen.
Como al compás de un verso su suave paso rigen.
Tal el divino Sandro dejara en sus figuras
esos graciosos gestos en esas líneas puras.
Como a un velado son de liras y laúdes,
divinamente blancas y castas pasan esas
siete bellas princesas. Y esas bellas princesas
son las siete Virtudes.

✿

Al lado izquierdo del camino y paralela-
mente, siete mancebos —oro, seda, escarlata,
armas ricas de Oriente— hermosos, parecidos
a los satanes verlenianos de Ecbatana,
vienen también. Sus labios sensuales y encendidos,
de efebos criminales, son cual rosas sangrientas;
sus puñales, de piedras preciosas revestidos
—ojos de víboras de luces fascinantes—,
al cinto penden; arden las púrpuras violentas
en los jubones; ciñen las cabezas triunfantes
oro y rosas; sus ojos, ya lánguidos, ya ardientes,
son dos carbunclos mágicos de fulgor sibilino,
y en sus manos de ambiguos príncipes decadentes
relucen como gemas las uñas de oro fino.
Bellamente infernales,
llenan el aire de hechiceros veneficios
esos siete mancebos. Y son los siete vicios,
los siete poderosos pecados capitales.

✿

Y los siete mancebos a las siete doncellas
lanzan vivas miradas de amor. Las Tentaciones.
De sus liras melifluas arrancan vagos sones.
Las princesas prosiguen, adorables visiones
en su blancura de palomas y de estrellas.

✿

Unos y otras se pierden por la vía de rosa,
y el alma mía queda pensativa a su paso.
—¡Oh! ¿Qué hay en ti, alma mía?

And their imperial necks are bent in a
manner that proclaims the loftiness of their birth.
Their soft steps move as if to the beat of poetry.
The divine Sandro gave his figures
just such gracious expressions with just such pure lines.
As if to a muffled sound of lyres and lutes,
those seven beautiful princesses pass by,
divinely white and chaste. And those beautiful princesses
are the seven Virtues.

      ❁

On the lefthand side of the path, parallel
to them, seven young men—gold, silk, scarlet,
richly adorned Oriental weapons—handsome, looking like
the Satans whom Verlaine places in Ecbatana,
also come. Their sensual, fiery lips,
those of criminal ephebes, are like blood-red roses;
their daggers, encrusted with precious stones—
vipers' eyes with fascinating glints—
hang at their belt; violent purples burn
in their doublets; their triumphant heads are wreathed
in gold and roses; their eyes, now languid, now ardent,
are two magical garnets of sibylline radiance,
and in their hands—those of ambiguous, decadent princes—
the fingernails of fine gold shine like gems.
Infernally handsome,
they fill the air with spellbinding enchantments,
those seven lads. And they are the seven vices,
the seven powerful deadly sins.

      ❁

And the seven lads dart vivid glances of love
at the seven maidens. Temptations.
From their melodious lyres they wring indefinable sounds.
The princesses continue on their way, charming visions
in their whiteness of doves and stars.

      ❁

Both groups are lost to sight down the pink path,
and my soul remains pensive as they pass.
"Oh! What is going on in you, my soul?

¡Oh! ¿Qué hay en ti, mi pobre infanta misteriosa?
¿Acaso piensas en la blanca teoría?
¿Acaso
los brillantes mancebos te atraen, mariposa?

✿

Ella no me responde.
Pensativa se aleja de la obscura ventana
—pensativa y risueña,
de la Bella-durmiente-del-bosque tierna hermana—,
y se adormece en donde
hace treinta años sueña.

✿

Y en sueño dice: «¡Oh dulces delicias de los cielos!
¡Oh tierra sonrosada que acarició mis ojos!
—¡Princesas, envolvedme con vuestros blancos velos!
—¡Príncipes, estrechadme con vuestros brazos rojos!»

"Ama tu ritmo . . ."

Ama tu ritmo y ritma tus acciones
bajo su ley, así como tus versos;
eres un universo de universos
y tu alma una fuente de canciones.

La celeste unidad que presupones
hará brotar en ti mundos diversos,
y al resonar tus números dispersos
pitagoriza en tus constelaciones.

Escucha la retórica divina
del pájaro del aire y la nocturna
irradiación geométrica adivina;

mata la indiferencia taciturna
y engarza perla y perla cristalina
en donde la verdad vuelca su urna.

Oh! What is going on in you, my poor mysterious princess?
Can you be thinking about the white procession?
Or perhaps
the brilliant boys attract you, you butterfly?"

✿

She doesn't answer me.
Pensively she withdraws from the dark window—
pensively and smilingly,
a tender sister to Sleeping Beauty—
and falls asleep in the same place where
she has been dreaming for thirty years.

✿

And in her dream she says: "Oh, sweet delights of the skies!
Oh, rosy-red land that caressed my eyes!
—Princesses, wrap me in your white veils!
—Princes, clasp me in your red arms!"

"Love Your Rhythm . . ."

Love your rhythm and rhythm your actions
in obedience to its law, and your poetry as well;
you are a universe of universes,
and your soul a fountain of song.

The celestial unity that you presuppose
will make varied worlds germinate within you,
and, as your scattered poems resound,
philosophize like Pythagoras among your constellations.

Listen to the divine rhetoric
of the bird in the air, and divine
the geometric radiation of the night;

slay silent indifference
and string pearl on crystalline pearl
there where truth pours out her urn.

Alma mía

Alma mía, perdura en tu idea divina;
todo está bajo el signo de un destino supremo;
sigue en tu rumbo, sigue hasta el ocaso extremo
por el camino que hacia la Esfinge te encamina.

Corta la flor al paso, deja la dura espina;
en el río de oro lleva a compás el remo;
saluda el rudo arado del rudo Triptolemo,
y sigue como un dios que sus sueños destina . . .

Y sigue como un dios que la dicha estimula,
y mientras la retórica del pájaro te adula
y los astros del cielo te acompañan, y los

ramos de la Esperanza surgen primaverales,
atraviesa impertérrita por el bosque de males
sin temer las serpientes, y sigue, como un dios . . .

"Yo persigo una forma . . ."

Yo persigo una forma que no encuentra mi estilo,
botón de pensamiento que busca ser la rosa;
se anuncia con un beso que en mis labios se posa
al abrazo imposible de la Venus de Milo.

Adornan verdes palmas el blanco peristilo;
los astros me han predicho la visión de la Diosa;
y en mi alma reposa la luz como reposa
el ave de la luna sobre un lago tranquilo.

Y no hallo sino la palabra que huye,
la iniciación melódica que de la flauta fluye
y la barca del sueño que en el espacio boga;

y bajo la ventana de mi Bella-Durmiente,
el sollozo continuo del chorro de la fuente
y el cuello del gran cisne blanco que me interroga.

My Soul

My soul, persevere in your divine ideals;
all things are under the sign of a supreme destiny;
follow in your chosen path, follow to the farthest west
along the way that leads you to the Sphinx.

Pick the flower as you go, leave the tough thorn;
on the golden river ply your oar to a regular beat;
greet the primitive plow of primitive Triptolemus,
and continue on like a god who destines his own dreams. . . .

And continue on like a god stimulated by good fortune,
and while the rhetoric of the bird praises you
and the stars in the sky accompany you, and the

branches of Hope sprout forth in springtime beauty,
cross the forest of evils undismayed,
without fearing the serpents, and continue on, like a god. . . .

"I Pursue a Form . . ."

I pursue a form that my stylus cannot find,
a bud of thought that seeks to be a rose;
it is announced by a kiss imprinted on my lips
during the impossible embrace of the Venus de Milo.

Green palm leaves adorn the white peristyle;
the stars have predicted to me a vision of the Goddess;
and in my soul light reposes as the bird
of the moon reposes on a tranquil lake.

And I find nothing but the fleeing word,
the initiatory melody that flows from the flute,
and the boat of dreams that sails through space;

and below the window of my Sleeping Beauty,
the constant sobbing of the fountain jet
and the neck of the great white swan questioning me.

"Yo soy aquel . . ."

Yo soy aquel que ayer no más decía
el verso azul y la canción profana,
en cuya noche un ruiseñor había
que era alondra de luz por la mañana.

El dueño fui de mi jardín de sueño,
lleno de rosas y de cisnes vagos;
el dueño de las tórtolas, el dueño
de góndolas y liras en los lagos;

y muy siglo diez y ocho y muy antiguo
y muy moderno; audaz, cosmopolita;
con Hugo fuerte y con Verlaine ambiguo,
y una sed de ilusiones infinita.

Yo supe de dolor desde mi infancia;
mi juventud . . . , ¿fue juventud la mía?
Sus rosas aún me dejan su fragancia . . . ,
una fragancia de melancolía . . .

Potro sin freno se lanzó mi instinto,
mi juventud montó potro sin freno;
iba embriagada y con puñal al cinto;
si no cayó, fue porque Dios es bueno.

En mi jardín se vio una estatua bella,
se juzgó mármol y era carne viva;
una alma joven habitaba en ella,
sentimental, sensible, sensitiva.

Y tímida ante el mundo, de manera
que, encerrada en silencio, no salía
sino cuando en la dulce primavera
era la hora de la melodía . . .

Hora de ocaso y de discreto beso;
hora crepuscular y de retiro;
hora de madrigal y de embeleso,
de «te adoro», de «¡ay!» y de suspiro.

Y entonces era en la dulzaina un juego
de misteriosas gamas cristalinas,

"I Am That Man . . ."

I am that man who only yesterday uttered
the blue verses and the worldly songs,
in whose night there was a nightingale
that became a lark of light in the mornings.

I was the owner of my dream garden,
filled with roses and idle swans;
the owner of the turtle-doves, the owner
of gondolas and lyres on the lakes;

and very eighteenth-century and very Greco-Roman
and very modern; audacious, cosmopolitan;
powerful with Hugo and ambiguous with Verlaine,
and with an infinite thirst for hopeful dreams.

I had known of sorrow ever since childhood;
my youth . . . was that a youth I had?
Its roses still leave their fragrance with me . . . ,
a fragrance of melancholy. . . .

My instinct darted forth like an unbridled colt,
my youth rode an unbridled colt;
it went about intoxicated, a dagger in its belt;
if it didn't fall off, it was because God is good.

In my garden a beautiful statue was to be seen,
it was thought to be marble but it was living flesh;
a youthful soul dwelt in it,
sentimental, sensitive, sentient.

And shy in society, so that
it was enclosed in silence and didn't venture out
except in sweet springtime
at the hour of melody. . . .

The hour of sunset and discreet kisses;
the hour of twilight and withdrawal;
the hour of madrigals and enchantment,
of "I adore you," "Ah!," and sighs.

And then on the shawm there was a playing
of mysterious, crystalline scales,

un renovar de notas del Pan griego
y un desgranar de músicas latinas,

con aire tal y con ardor tan vivo,
que a la estatua nacían de repente
en el muslo viril patas de chivo
y dos cuernos de sátiro en la frente.

Como la Galatea gongorina
me encantó la marquesa verleniana,
y así juntaba a la pasión divina
una sensual hiperestesia humana;

todo ansia, todo ardor, sensación pura
y vigor natural; y sin falsía,
y sin comedia y sin literatura . . .
si hay una alma sincera, ésa es la mía.

La torre de marfil tentó mi anhelo,
quise encerrarme dentro de mí mismo,
y tuve hambre de espacio y sed de cielo
desde las sombras de mi propio abismo.

Como la esponja que la sal satura
en el jugo del mar, fue el dulce y tierno
corazón mío, henchido de amargura
por el mundo, la carne y el infierno.

Mas, por gracia de Dios, en mi conciencia
el Bien supo elegir la mejor parte;
y si hubo áspera hiel en mi existencia,
melificó toda acritud el Arte.

Mi intelecto libré de pensar bajo,
bañó el agua castalia el alma mía,
peregrinó mi corazón y trajo
de la sagrada selva la armonía.

¡Oh, la selva sagrada! ¡Oh, la profunda
emanación del corazón divino
de la sagrada selva! ¡Oh, la fecunda
fuente cuya virtud vence al destino!

Bosque ideal que lo real complica,
allí el cuerpo arde y vive y Psiquis vuela;

a renewal of the tones of the Greek Pan,
and a reeling off of Latin music,

with such allure and with such vivid ardor
that the statue suddenly grew
goat's feet from its virile thighs
and two satyr's horns on its forehead.

Like Góngora's Galatea
Verlaine's marquise also delighted me,
thus joining to the divine passion
a sensual human hyperesthesia;

all anxiety, all ardor, pure sensation
and natural vigor; and without hypocrisy,
without playacting, without literary poses . . .
if there's a sincere soul anywhere, it's mine.

The ivory tower tempted my longings,
I wished to lock myself up inside myself,
but I hungered for space and thirsted for sky
in the shadows of my own abyss.

Like a sponge saturated by salt
in the waters of the sea: such was my gentle,
tender heart, swollen with bitterness
because of society, the flesh, and hell.

But, thank God, in my conscience
the Good was able to choose the better part;
and if there was raw gall in my existence,
Art honeyed all its sharpness.

I freed my intellect from low thoughts,
the Castalian spring bathed my soul,
my heart went on pilgrimage and brought back
harmony from the holy forest.

Oh, the holy forest! Oh, the profound
emanation from the divine heart
of the holy forest! Oh, the ever-flowing
fountain whose power conquers destiny!

Forest of ideality which involves reality:
there the body burns and lives, and Psyche flies;

mientras abajo el sátiro fornica,
ebria de azul deslíe Filomela

perla de ensueño y música amorosa
en la cúpula en flor del laurel verde;
Hipsipila sutil liba en la rosa,
y la boca del fauno el pezón muerde.

Allí va el dios en celo tras la hembra,
y la caña de Pan se alza del lodo;
la eterna vida sus semillas siembra,
y brota la armonía del gran Todo.

El alma que entra allí debe ir desnuda,
temblando de deseo y fiebre santa,
sobre cardo heridor y espina aguda:
así sueña, así vibra y así canta.

Vida, luz y verdad, tal triple llama
produce la interior llama infinita.
El Arte puro como Cristo exclama:
Ego sum lux et veritas et vita!

Y la vida es misterio, la luz ciega
y la verdad inaccesible asombra;
la adusta perfección jamás se entrega,
y el secreto ideal duerme en la sombra.

Por eso ser sincero es ser potente;
de desnuda que está, brilla la estrella;
el agua dice el alma de la fuente
en la voz de cristal que fluye de ella.

Tal fue mi intento, hacer del alma pura
mía una estrella, una fuente sonora,
con el horror de la literatura
y loco de crepúsculo y de aurora.

Del crepúsculo azul que da la pauta
que los celestes éxtasis inspira,
bruma y tono menor —¡toda la flauta!
y Aurora, hija del Sol— ¡toda la lira!

Pasó una piedra que lanzó una honda;
pasó una flecha que aguzó un violento.

while on its floor the satyr fornicates,
Philomel, drunken with light, pours out

her pearls of dream, her amorous music,
on the blossoming cupola of the green laurel;
the subtle butterfly drinks nectar from the rose,
while the Faun's mouth nibbles its stalk.

There, the god goes lusting after the female,
while Pan's reed rises from the mud;
eternal life sows its seeds,
and the harmony of the great All germinates.

The soul that enters there must walk naked,
trembling with desire and sacred fever,
over wounding thistles and sharp thorns:
thus it dreams, thus it vibrates, and thus it sings.

Life, light, and truth: that triple flame
engenders the infinite inner flame.
Pure Art exclaims, as Christ did:
"I am the light, the truth, and the life!"

And life is mystery, light blinds you,
and unreachable truth casts shadow on you;
severe perfection never surrenders itself to you,
and the secret ideal slumbers in the shadows.

Therefore, to be sincere is to be powerful;
it is in its nudity that the star shines;
water tells of the fountain's soul
with the crystal voice that flows from it.

Such was my intent, to make of my
pure soul a star, a sounding fountain,
with a loathing for literary formulas,
and a yearning for twilight and dawn.

For the blue twilight that sets the pattern
by which heavenly ecstasy is inspired,
mist and the minor mode—the flute's full range!—
and Dawn, daughter of the Sun—all the lyre contains!

A stone whizzed by, hurled from a sling;
An arrow whizzed by that a violent man had sharpened.

La piedra de la honda fue a la onda,
y la flecha del odio fuese al viento.

La virtud está en ser tranquilo y fuerte;
con el fuego interior todo se abrasa;
se triunfa del rencor y de la muerte,
y hacia Belén . . . ¡la caravana pasa!

Salutación del optimista

Ínclitas razas ubérrimas, sangre de Hispania fecunda,
espíritus fraternos, luminosas almas, ¡salve!
Porque llega el momento en que habrán de cantar nuevos himnos
lenguas de gloria. Un vasto rumor llena los ámbitos; mágicas
ondas de vida van renaciendo de pronto;
retrocede el olvido, retrocede engañada la muerte;
se anuncia un reino nuevo, feliz sibila sueña
y en la caja pandórica, de que tantas desgracias surgieron,
encontramos de súbito, talismánica, pura, riente,
cual pudiera decirla en su verso Virgilio divino,
la divina reina de luz, ¡la celeste Esperanza!

Pálidas indolencias, desconfianzas fatales que a tumba
o a perpetuo presidio condenasteis al noble entusiasmo,
ya veréis el salir del sol en un triunfo de liras,
mientras dos continentes, abonados de huesos gloriosos,
del Hércules antiguo la gran sombra soberbia evocando,
digan al orbe: la alta virtud resucita
que a la hispana progenie hizo dueña de siglos.

Abominad la boca que predice desgracias eternas,
abominad los ojos que ven sólo zodíacos funestos,
abominad las manos que apedrean las ruinas ilustres,
o que la tea empuñan o la daga suicida.
Siéntense sordos ímpetus en las entrañas del mundo,
la inminencia de algo fatal hoy conmueve a la Tierra;
fuertes colosos caen, se desbandan bicéfalas águilas,
y algo se inicia como vasto social cataclismo
sobre la faz del orbe. ¿Quién dirá que las savias dormidas
no despiertan entonces en el tronco del roble gigante

The slingstone fell into the water,
and the arrow of hatred was carried off by the wind.

Virtue consists of being calm and strong;
by the inner fire everything is set ablaze;
you triumph over rancor, over death,
and in the direction of Bethlehem . . . the caravan passes!

Greetings from an Optimist

Renowned, fertile clans, prolific blood of Hispania,
fraternal spirits, luminous souls, hail!
For the moment is coming when new hymns are to be sung
by glorious tongues. An immense rumbling fills the atmosphere; magical
waves of life will soon be reborn;
forgetfulness is retreating, disappointed death is retreating;
a new kingdom is proclaimed, a happy Sibyl is dreaming
and in Pandora's box, from which so many misfortunes emerged,
we suddenly find, talismanic, pure, laughing,
and just as divine Vergil might have described her in his verses,
the divine queen of light, heavenly Hope!

Pallid indolence, fatal mistrust, which condemned
noble enthusiasm to the tomb or to perpetual imprisonment,
now you shall see the sun rise to the triumphant sound of lyres,
while two continents, their soil enriched by the remains of heroes,
will conjure up the great, proud shade of ancient Hercules
and will tell the world: that lofty virtue is recalled to life
which made the offspring of Hispania mistress of centuries.

Loathe the lips that predict everlasting misfortune,
loathe the eyes that see nothing but gloomy horoscopes,
loathe the hands that cast stones at hallowed ruins,
or which grasp the torch and the suicidal dagger.
Indefinable stirrings are felt in the bowels of the earth,
the imminence of something fateful is agitating the world today;
strong colossi fall, two-headed eagles are fleeing in disorder,
and something like a vast social cataclysm is beginning
on the face of the globe. Who can say that the sleeping sap
will not then awaken in the trunk of the gigantic oak

bajo el cual se exprimió la ubre de la loba romana?
¿Quién será el pusilánime que al vigor español niegue músculos
y que al alma española juzgase áptera y ciega y tullida?
No es Babilonia ni Nínive enterrada en olvido y en polvo
ni entre momias y piedras reina que habita el sepulcro,
la nación generosa, coronada de orgullo inmarchito,
que hacia el lado del alba fija las miradas ansiosas,
ni la que tras los mares en que yace sepultada la Atlántida,

tiene su coro de vástagos, altos, robustos y fuertes.
Únanse, brillen, secúndense tantos vigores dispersos;
formen todos un solo haz de energía ecuménica.
Sangre de Hispania fecunda, sólidas, ínclitas razas,
muestren los dones pretéritos que fueron antaño su triunfo.
Vuelva el antiguo entusiasmo, vuelva el espíritu ardiente
que regará lenguas de fuego en esa epifanía.
Juntas las testas ancianas ceñidas de líricos lauros
y las cabezas jóvenes que la alta Minerva decora,
así los manes heroicos de los primitivos abuelos,
de los egregios padres que abrieron el surco pristino,
sientan los soplos agrarios de primaverales retornos
y el rumor de espigas que inició la labor triptolémica.

Un continente y otro renovando las viejas prosapias,
en espíritu unidos, en espíritu y ansias y lengua,
ven llegar el momento en que habrán de cantar nuevos himnos.
La latina estirpe verá la gran alba futura,
y en un trueno de música gloriosa, millones de labios
saludarán la espléndida luz que vendrá del Oriente,
Oriente augusto en donde todo lo cambia y renueva
la eternidad de Dios, la actividad infinita.
Y así sea esperanza la visión permanente en nosotros.
¡Ínclitas razas ubérrimas, sangre de Hispania fecunda!

beneath which the Roman she-wolf's udder yielded its milk?
Who will be so small-minded as to deny that Spanish vigor has muscles,
or to deem the Spanish soul to be wingless, blind, and maimed?
This is not Babylon or Nineveh, buried in oblivion and dust,
this is not a queen inhabiting the tomb amid mummies and stones,
but a high-hearted nation, crowned with unwithered pride,
fixing its eager gaze in the direction of the dawn,
and the same holds for the lands beyond the sea in which Atlantis lies
        buried,
which have their choir of descendants, tall, sturdy, and strong.
Let all those scattered forces unite and shine;
let them all form a single bundle of worldwide energy.
Fertile blood of Hispania, solid, renowned clans,
let them display the past gifts which were their triumph in time gone by.
Let the old enthusiasm return, and the ardent spirit
that will rain down tongues of fire in that Pentecost.
When the ancient brows wreathed with lyrical laurel are combined
with the youthful heads adorned by lofty Minerva,
then let the heroic shades of our primitive forefathers,
of our noble fathers who dug the first furrows,
feel the rural gusts of returning springtime
and the sound of waving grain, which the labor of Triptolemus first
        created.

    One and another continent, renewing the old lineages,
united in spirit, in spirit, concerns, and language,
see the moment coming when new hymns are to be sung.
The Latin race will see the great dawn of the future,
and in a thunder of glorious music, millions of lips
will greet the splendid light that will come from the East,
the august East where everything is transformed and renewed
by God's eternity, infinite activity.
And thus let hope be the permanent vision within us.
Renowned fertile clans, prolific blood of Hispania!

Al rey Óscar

Le roi de Suède et de Norvège, après avoir visité Saint-Jean-
de-Luz s'est rendu à Hendaye et à Fonterrabie. En arrivant
sur le sol espagnol, il a crié: «Vive l'Espagne!»
Le Figaro, mars 1899.

Así, sire, en el aire de la Francia nos llega
la paloma de plata de Suecia y de Noruega,
que trae en vez de olivo una rosa de fuego.

Un búcaro latino, un noble vaso griego
recibirá el regalo del país de la nieve.
¡Que a los reinos boreales el patrio viento lleve
otra rosa de sangre y de luz españolas;
pues sobre la sublime hermandad de las olas,
al brotar tu palabra, un saludo le envía
al sol de medianoche el sol de Mediodía!

Si Segismundo siente pesar, Hamlet se inquieta.
El Norte ama las palmas; y se junta el poeta
del fiord con el del carmen, porque el mismo oriflama
es de azur. Su divina cornucopia derrama
sobre el polo y el trópico la paz; y el orbe gira
en un ritmo uniforme por una propia lira:
el Amor. Allá surge Sigurd que al Cid se aúna.
Cerca de Dulcinea brilla el rayo de luna,
y la musa de Bécquer del ensueño es esclava
bajo un celeste palio de luz escandinava.

Sire de ojos azules, gracias: por los laureles,
de cien bravos vestidos de honor; por los claveles
de la tierra andaluza y la Alhambra del moro;
por la sangre solar de una raza de oro;
por la armadura antigua y el yelmo de la gesta;
por las lanzas que fueron una vasta floresta
de gloria y que pasaron Pirineos y Andes;
por Lepanto y Otumba; por el Perú, por Flandes;
por Isabel que cree, por Cristóbal que sueña
y Velázquez que pinta y Cortés que domeña;
por el país sagrado en que Herakles afianza
sus macizas columnas de fuerza y esperanza,

To King Oscar

*The king of Sweden and Norway, after a visit to Saint-Jean-
de-Luz, proceeded to Hendaye and Fuenterrabia. Upon arriv-
ing on Spanish soil, he shouted: "Long live Spain!"*
                                                     Le Figaro, March 1899.

Thus, Sire, on the winds from France we receive
the silver dove of Sweden and Norway,
which bears not an olive branch, but a fiery rose.

A Roman clay vase, a noble Greek urn,
will receive the gift from the land of snow.
May the breeze of our land bear to the northern kingdoms
another rose of Spanish blood and light;
for, across the sublime brotherhood of the ocean waves,
on the utterance of your words, a greeting is sent
to the midnight sun by the sun of the South!

If Segismundo feels sorrow, Hamlet is troubled.
The North loves palms; and the poet of the fjord
joins with the poet of the Granadan villa, because their oriflamme
is of the same azure. Peace empties her divine cornucopia
over both the pole and the tropics; and the world turns
in a uniform rhythm to the music of one lyre:
Love. There behold Sigurd joining forces with the Cid.
Near Dulcinea the moonbeam shines,
and Bécquer's muse is a slave to dreams
beneath a celestial canopy of Scandinavian light.

Blue-eyed Majesty, thanks: on behalf of the laurels
of a hundred brave men clothed in honor; on behalf of the carnations
of the Andalusian soil and the Moor's Alhambra;
speaking for the solar blood of a golden race;
for the ancient armor and the epic helmet;
for the lances that formed a vast forest
of glory and crossed the Pyrenees and the Andes;
for Lepanto and Otumba; for Peru, for Flanders;
for Isabella who believes, for Christopher who dreams,
and Velázquez who paints, and Cortés who subdues;
for the sacred country in which Herakles establishes
his massive pillars of strength and hope,

mientras Pan trae el ritmo con la egregia siringa
que no hay trueno que apague ni tempestad que extinga;
por el león simbólico y la Cruz, gracias, sire.

¡Mientras el mundo aliente, mientras la esfera gire,
mientras la onda cordial aliente un sueño,
mientras haya una viva pasión, un noble empeño,
un buscado imposible, una imposible hazaña,
una América oculta que hallar, vivirá España!

Y pues tras la tormenta vienes de peregrino
real, a la morada que entristeció el destino,
la morada que viste luto su puerta abra
al purpúreo y ardiente vibrar de tu palabra:
¡Y que sonría, oh rey Oscar, por un instante;
y tiemble en la flor áurea el más puro brillante
para quien sobre brillos de corona y de nombre,
con labios de monarca lanza un grito de hombre!

Cyrano en España

He aquí que Cyrano de Bergerac traspasa
de un salto el Pirineo. Cyrano está en su casa.
¿No es en España, acaso, la sangre vino y fuego?
Al gran gascón saluda y abraza el gran manchego.

¿No se hacen en España los más bellos castillos?
Roxanas encarnaron con rosas los Murillos,
y la hoja toledana que aquí Quevedo empuña
conócenla los bravos cadetes de Gascuña.
Cyrano hizo su viaje a la Luna; mas, antes,
ya el divino lunático de don Miguel Cervantes
pasaba entre las dulces estrellas de su sueño
jinete en el sublime pegaso Clavileño.
Y Cyrano ha leído la maravilla escrita,
y al pronunciar el nombre de Quijote, se quita
Bergerac el sombrero; Cyrano Balazote
siente que es lengua suya la lengua del Quijote.
Y la nariz heroica del gascón se diría
que husmea los dorados vinos de Andalucía.
Y la espada francesa, por él desenvainada,

while Pan supplies the rhythm with his superb reed flute
that no thunder can quell, or storm extinguish;
for the symbolic lion and the Cross, thanks, Sire.

For as long as the world breathes, as long as the sphere turns,
for as long as the tonic waves foment a dream,
for as long as there exists a vivid passion, a noble task,
an impossible quest, an impossible exploit,
a hidden America to discover, Spain shall live!

And since you come after the tempest, as a royal
pilgrim, to the dwelling saddened by destiny,
let the dwelling that wears mourning open its door
to the purple, ardent stirring of your speech:
And may it smile, O King Oscar, for a moment;
and may the purest diamond tremble on the golden flower
for the man who, in addition to the glory of his crown and his name,
utters the cry of a man with the lips of a monarch!

Cyrano in Spain

Behold, Cyrano de Bergerac has crossed
the Pyrenees with one jump. Cyrano is now at home.
Isn't Spanish blood wine and fire, after all?
The great Gascon is greeted and embraced by the great man of La
      Mancha.
Aren't the most beautiful castles built in Spain?
Roxanes were given rosy complexions by painters like Murillo,
and the Toledan blade that Quevedo wields here among us
is familiar to the brave cadets of Gascony.
Cyrano made his journey to the moon; but, before that,
the divine madman created by Don Miguel Cervantes was already
riding among the sweet stars of his dream
mounted on that sublime winged horse Clavileño.
And Cyrano read that wonderful writing,
and when he pronounces the name of Quixote, Bergerac
doffs his hat; Cyrano, as embodied by Balazote,
senses that the tongue of Quixote is his own tongue.
And the Gascon's heroic nose seems to be
sniffing the golden wines of Andalusia.
And the French sword that he unsheathes

brilla bien en la tierra de la capa y la espada.
¡Bien venido, Cyrano de Bergerac! Castilla
te da su idioma, y tu alma, como tu espada, brilla
al sol que allá en tus tiempos, no se ocultó en España.
Tu nariz y penacho no están en tierra extraña,
pues vienes a la tierra de la Caballería.
Eres el noble huésped de Calderón. María
Roxana te demuestra que lucha la fragancia
de las rosas de España con las rosas de Francia,
y sus supremas gracias, y sus sonrisas únicas,
y sus miradas, astros que visten negras túnicas,
y la lira que vibra en su lengua sonora
te dan una Roxana de España, encantadora.
¡Oh poeta! ¡Oh celeste poeta de la facha
grotesca! Bravo y noble y sin miedo y sin tacha,
príncipe de locuras, de sueños y de rimas:
Tu penacho es hermano de las más altas cimas,
del nido de tu pecho una alondra se lanza,
un hada es tu madrina, y es la Desesperanza;
y en medio de la selva del duelo y del olvido
las nueve musas vendan tu corazón herido.
¿Allá en la Luna hallaste algún mágico prado
donde vaga el espíritu de Pierrot desolado?
¿Viste el palacio blanco de los locos del Arte?
¿Fue acaso la gran sombra de Píndaro a encontrarte?
¿Contemplaste la mancha roja que entre las rocas
albas forma el castillo de las Vírgenes locas?
¿Y en un jardín fantástico de misteriosas flores
no oíste al melodioso Rey de los ruiseñores?
No juzgues mi curiosa demanda inoportuna,
pues todas esas cosas existen en la Luna.
¡Bien venido, Cyrano de Bergerac! Cyrano
de Bergerac, cadete y amante, y castellano
que trae los recuerdos que Durandal abona
al país en que aún brillan las luces de Tizona.
El Arte es el glorioso vencedor. Es el Arte
el que vence el espacio y el tiempo; su estandarte,
pueblos, es del espíritu el azul oriflama.
¿Qué elegido no corre si su trompeta llama?
Y a través de los siglos se contestan, oíd:
la Canción de Rolando y la Gesta del Cid.

gleams appropriately in the land of cloak-and-dagger.
Welcome, Cyrano de Bergerac! Castile
lends you its language, and your soul, like your sword, shines
in the sunlight which, back in your time, wasn't hidden in Spain.
Your nose and your plume are not in a foreign country,
since you have come to the land of Chivalry.
You are the noble guest of Calderón. María,
as Roxane, proves to you that the fragrance
of Spanish roses can vie with the roses of France,
and her supreme grace, and her unique smiles,
and her glances, stars that wear black tunics,
and the lyre that vibrates on her resonant tongue,
give you an enchanting Roxane of Spain.
O poet! O heavenly poet with the grotesque
appearance! Brave, noble, fearless, blameless,
prince of mad doings, dreams, and rhymes:
Your plume is brother to the loftiest peaks,
from the nest of your bosom a lark darts out,
you have a fairy godmother, who is Despair;
and amid the forest of sorrow and oblivion
the nine muses bandage your wounded heart.
Up there on the Moon, did you find some magical meadow
where the desolate spirit of Pierrot strays?
Did you see the white palace of those mad for Art?
Did the great shade of Pindar come to meet you, perchance?
Did you look upon the red stain amid the white
rocks which is formed by the castle of the Foolish Virgins?
And, in a fantasy garden of mysterious flowers,
didn't you hear the melodious king of the nightingales?
Don't think my inquisitive questions out of place,
because all those things exist on the Moon.
Welcome, Cyrano de Bergerac! Cyrano
de Bergerac, cadet and lover, and a Castilian
who brings the memories that Durandal vouches for
to the country in which the light of Tizona still gleams.
Art is the glorious conqueror. It is Art
that conquers space and time; its banner,
O nations, is the blue oriflamme of the spirit.
What chosen man fails to run when his trumpet calls?
And, across the centuries they answer each other, listen:
the Song of Roland and the epic of the Cid.

Cyrano va marchando, poeta y caballero,
al redoblar sonoro del grave Romancero.
Su penacho soberbio tiene nuestra aureola.
Son sus espuelas finas de fábrica española.
Y cuando en su balada Rostand teje el envío,
creeríase a Quevedo rimando un desafío.
¡Bien venido, Cyrano de Bergerac! No seca
el tiempo el lauro; el viejo Corral de la Pacheca
recibe al generoso embajador del fuerte
Molière. En copa gala Tirso su vino vierte.
Nosotros exprimimos las uvas de Champaña
para beber por Francia y en un cristal de España.

A Roosevelt

¡Es con voz de la Biblia, o verso de Walt Whitman,
que habría que llegar hasta ti, Cazador!
Primitivo y moderno, sencillo y complicado,
con un algo de Washington y cuatro de Nemrod.
Eres los Estados Unidos,
eres el futuro invasor
de la América ingenua que tiene sangre indígena,
que aún reza a Jesucristo y aún habla en español.

Eres soberbio y fuerte ejemplar de tu raza;
eres culto, eres hábil; te opones a Tolstoy.
Y domando caballos, o asesinando tigres,
eres un Alejandro-Nabucodonosor.
(Eres un profesor de energía,
como dicen los locos de hoy.)

Crees que la vida es incendio,
que el progreso es erupción;
en donde pones la bala
el porvenir pones.
          No.

Los Estados Unidos son potentes y grandes.
Cuando ellos se estremecen hay un hondo temblor
que pasa por las vértebras enormes de los Andes.
Si clamáis, se oye como el rugir del león.

Cyrano is marching, a poet and a knight,
to the resonant drumbeat of the austere Spanish ballads.
His haughty plume has our aureole.
His elegant spurs are of Spanish make.
And when Rostand weaves the *envoi* to his *ballade,*
you'd think it was Quevedo rhyming a challenge.
Welcome, Cyrano de Bergerac! Time
does not wither laurels; the old Pacheca courtyard
welcomes the noble ambassador of powerful
Molière. Into a Gallic goblet Tirso pours his wine.
We are pressing grapes from Champagne
in order to drink to France from a Spanish glass.

To Roosevelt

It's with a biblical voice, or with a verse by Walt Whitman,
that it would be fitting to approach you, Hunter!
Primitive and modern, simple and complex,
with a touch of Washington and four touches of Nimrod.
You are the United States,
you are the future invader
of that ingenuous America which has Indian blood,
which still prays to Jesus Christ, and still speaks Spanish.

You are a splendid, strong specimen of your breed;
you are cultured, you are able; you oppose Tolstoy.
And, when breaking horses or killing tigers,
you are both Alexander and Nebuchadnezzar.
(You're a professor of energy,
as modern fools say.)

You believe that life is a burning building,
that progress is a volcanic eruption;
where you place your bullet
you place the future.
                    No.

The United States is powerful and great.
When it shakes there is a deep-seated tremor
that moves down the enormous vertebrae of the Andes.
If you yell, it sounds like a lion's roar.

Ya Hugo a Grant le dijo: «Las estrellas son vuestras.»
(Apenas brilla, alzándose, el argentino sol
y la estrella chilena se levanta . . .) Sois ricos.
Juntáis al culto de Hércules el culto de Mammón;
y alumbrando el camino de la fácil conquista,
la Libertad levanta su antorcha en Nueva York.

Mas la América nuestra, que tenía poetas
desde los viejos tiempos de Netzahualcoyotl,
que ha guardado las huellas de los pies del gran Baco,
que el alfabeto pánico en un tiempo aprendió;
que consultó los astros, que conoció la Atlántida,
cuyo nombre nos llega resonando en Platón,
que desde los remotos momentos de su vida
vive de luz, de fuego, de perfume, de amor,
la América del gran Moctezuma, del Inca,
la América fragante de Cristóbal Colón,
la América católica, la América española,
la América en que dijo el noble Guatemoc:
«Yo no estoy en un lecho de rosas»; esa América
que tiembla de huracanes y que vive de Amor,
hombres de ojos sajones y alma bárbara, vive.
Y sueña. Y ama, y vibra; y es la hija del Sol.
Tened cuidado. ¡Vive la América española!
Hay mil cachorros sueltos del León Español.
Se necesitaría, Roosevelt, ser por Dios mismo,
el Riflero terrible y el fuerte Cazador,
para poder tenernos en vuestras férreas garras.

Y, pues contáis con todo, falta una cosa: ¡Dios!

"¡Torres de Dios! . . ."

¡Torres de Dios! ¡Poetas!
¡Pararrayos celestes,
que resistís las duras tempestades,
como crestas escuetas,
como picos agrestes,
rompeolas de las eternidades!

Even back then, Hugo said to Grant: "The stars belong to you."
(The sun of Argentina, getting higher, is hardly shining yet,
and the star of Chile is rising. . . .) Your people are wealthy.
You combine the worship of Hercules with the worship of Mammon;
and, lighting the path of easy conquests,
Liberty raises her torch in New York.

    But our America, which has had poets
ever since the ancient days of Netzahualcoyotl,
which has retained the footprints of great Bacchus,
and which once learned the alphabet invented by Pan;
which consulted the stars, which knew Atlantis
(whose name comes down to us in the pages of Plato);
which from the remotest stages of its life
has lived on light, fire, fragrance, love,
the America of the great Moctezuma, of the Inca,
the sweet-smelling America of Christopher Columbus,
Catholic America, Spanish America,
the America where noble Cuauhtemoc said
"I'm not on a bed of roses"—that America
which is shaken by hurricanes and lives on Love:
it is alive, O man of Anglo-Saxon eyes and barbarous soul.
And it dreams. And it loves, and stirs; and is the daughter of the Sun.
Watch out! Spanish America lives!
There are a thousand cubs of the Spanish Lion on the loose.
Roosevelt, it would have to be the will of God Himself,
the awesome Rifleman and the mighty Hunter,
for you to be able to hold us in your iron talons.

    And, since you have everything at your disposal, one thing is
      missing: God!

"Towers of God! . . ."

    Towers of God! Poets!
Heavenly lightning rods
that withstand heavy storms,
like bare mountain crests,
like wild peaks,
breakwaters of eternity!

La mágica esperanza anuncia un día
en que sobre la roca de armonía
expirará la pérfida sirena.
¡Esperad, esperemos todavía!

Esperad todavía.
El bestial elemento se solaza
en el odio a la sacra poesía
y se arroja baldón de raza a raza.

La insurrección de abajo
tiende a los Excelentes.
El caníbal codicia su tasajo
con roja encía y afilados dientes.

Torres, poned al pabellón sonrisa.
Poned ante ese mal y ese recelo
una soberbia insinuación de brisa
y una tranquilidad de mar y cielo . . .

Canto de esperanza

Un gran vuelo de cuervos mancha el azul celeste.
Un soplo milenario trae amagos de peste.
Se asesinan los hombres en el extremo Este.

¿Ha nacido el apocalíptico Anticristo?
Se han sabido presagios y prodigios se han visto
y parece inminente el retorno de Cristo.

La Tierra está preñada de dolor tan profundo
que el soñador, imperial meditabundo,
sufre con las angustias del corazón del mundo.

Verdugos de ideales afligieron la Tierra,
en un pozo de sombra la humanidad se encierra
con los rudos molosos del odio y de la guerra.

¡Oh, Señor Jesucristo! ¿Por qué tardas, qué esperas
para tender tu mano de luz sobre las fieras
y hacer brillar al sol tus divinas banderas?

Surge de pronto y vierte la esencia de la vida
sobre tanta alma loca, triste o empedernida
que, amante de tinieblas, tu dulce aurora olvida.

Magical hope proclaims a day
when, on her musical rock,
the treacherous siren will perish.
Hope! Let us keep hoping!

Keep hoping!
The bestial element takes comfort
in its hatred for sacred poetry,
and insults are hurled from race to race.

The insurrection from below
is directed against the Outstanding.
The cannibal covets his jerked meat
with red gums and sharp teeth.

Towers, paint a smile on your flags.
Confront this evil and this fear
with a proud hint of breeze
and a calmness in sea and sky. . . .

Song of Hope

A long flight of crows blots the blue of the sky.
A wind from the gulf of ages is bearing signs of plague.
Men are being murdered in the Far East.

Has the Antichrist of the Apocalypse been born?
Omens have been learned of, and wonders have been seen,
and the return of Christ seems imminent.

The Earth is charged with a grief so deep
that the dreamer, the imperial pensive man,
is suffering the anxieties of the heart of the world.

Executioners of ideals have afflicted the Earth,
mankind is imprisoned in a well of darkness
along with the violent mastiffs of hatred and war.

O Lord Jesus Christ! Why do You delay, why do You wait
before extending Your luminous hand over the wild beasts
and making Your divine banners shine in the sunlight?

Arise soon and pour the essence of life
into all these insane, sad, or hardened souls
which love darkness and forget Your sweet dawn.

Ven, Señor, para hacer la gloria de ti mismo,
ven con temblor de estrellas y horror de cataclismo,
ven a traer amor y paz sobre el abismo.

Y tu caballo blanco, que miró el visionario,
pase. Y suene el divino clarín extraordinario.
Mi corazón será brasa de tu incensario.

Marcha triunfal

  ¡Ya viene el cortejo!
¡Ya viene el cortejo! Ya se oyen los claros clarines.
La espada se anuncia con vivo reflejo;
ya viene, oro y hierro, el cortejo de los paladines.

  Ya pasa debajo los arcos ornados de blancas Minervas y Martes,

los arcos triunfales en donde las Famas erigen sus largas trompetas,
la gloria solemne de los estandartes
llevados por manos robustas de heroicos atletas.
Se escucha el ruido que forman las armas de los caballeros,
los frenos que tascan los fuertes caballos de guerra,
los cascos que hieren la tierra
y los timbaleros,
que el paso acompasan con ritmos marciales.
¡Tal pasan los fieros guerreros
debajo los arcos triunfales!

  Los claros clarines de pronto levantan sus sones,
su canto sonoro,
su cálido coro,
que envuelve en un trueno de oro
la augusta soberbia de los pabellones.
Él dice la lucha, la herida venganza,
las ásperas crines,
los rudos penachos, la pica, la lanza,
la sangre que riega de heroicos carmines
la tierra;
los negros mastines
que azuza la muerte, que rige la guerra.

Come, Lord, to achieve Your own glory,
come with a shaking of stars and the terror of a cataclysm,
come bringing love and peace over the abyss.

And let Your white horse, which the visionary beheld,
pass by. And let the miraculous divine trumpet sound.
My heart will be an ember in Your censer.

Triumphal March

The parade is coming!
The parade is coming! The bright bugles can already be heard.
The swords proclaim their presence with vivid reflections of light;
now, all gold and steel, the parade of paladins is coming.

Now it passes under the arches adorned with white images of
        Minerva and Mars,
triumphal arches where figures of Fame raise long trumpets,
the solemn glory of the banners
borne by the sturdy hands of heroic athletes.
You can hear the sound made by the weapons of the cavalry,
the bits at which the strong warhorses champ,
the hooves striking the ground,
and the kettledrummers
setting the beat for the procession with martial rhythms.
That is how fierce warriors
march under triumphal arches!

The bright bugles soon increase their sound,
their sonorous song,
their warm chorus,
which envelops in golden thunder
the august pride of the national flags.
That music speaks of battle, vengeange for injury,
rough manes,
brutal plumes, the pike, the lance,
the blood that drenches the earth
with heroic red;
the black mastiffs
egged on by death, which rules war.

Los áureos sonidos
anuncian el advenimiento
triunfal de la Gloria;
dejando el picacho que guarda sus nidos,
tendiendo sus alas enormes al viento,
los cóndores llegan. ¡Llegó la victoria!

Ya pasa el cortejo.
Señala el abuelo los héroes al niño.
Ved cómo la barba del viejo
los bucles de oro circunda de armiño.
Las bellas mujeres aprestan coronas de flores,
y bajo los pórticos vense sus rostros de rosa;
y la más hermosa
sonríe al más fiero de los vencedores.
¡Honor al que trae cautiva la extraña bandera;
honor al herido y honor a los fieles
soldados que muerte encontraron por mano extranjera!
¡Clarines! ¡Laureles!

Las nobles espadas de tiempos gloriosos,
desde sus panoplias saludan las nuevas coronas y lauros: —
Las viejas espadas de los granaderos, más fuertes que osos,
hermanos de aquellos lanceros que fueron centauros. —
Las trompas guerreras resuenan;
de voces los aires se llenan . . .
— A aquellas antiguas espadas,
a aquellos ilustres aceros,
que encarnan las glorias pasadas . . .
Y al sol que hoy alumbra las nuevas victorias ganadas,
y al héroe que guía su grupo de jóvenes fieros,
al que ama la insignia del suelo materno,
al que ha desafiado, ceñido el acero y el arma en la mano,
los soles del rojo verano,
las nieves y vientos del gélido invierno,
la noche, la escarcha
y el odio y la muerte, por ser por la patria inmortal,
¡saludan con voces de bronce las trompas de guerra que tocan la marcha
triunfal! . . .

The golden sounds
announce the triumphal
advent of Glory;
abandoning the rugged peak that guards their nests,
and spreading their enormous wings to the wind,
the condors come. Victory has come!

Now the parade is passing by.
A grandfather points out the heroes to a child.
See how the old man's beard
surrounds the golden curls with ermine.
Beautiful women prepare garlands of flowers,
and under the porticos their rose faces are seen;
and the most beautiful one
smiles to the fiercest of the conquerors.
Honor to the man who carries the foreign flag prisoner;
honor to the wounded and honor to the loyal
soldiers who met death at foreign hands!
Bugles! Laurels!

The noble swords of glorious days
from their panoplies salute the new wreaths and laurels:
the old swords of the grenadiers, who are stronger than bears,
brothers to those mighty lancers, the centaurs.
The warlike trumpets blow;
the air is filled with shouts . . .
—Those old-fashioned swords,
that illustrious steel
which embodies the glories of the past . . .
and the sun that shines today on the new victories won,
and the hero who guides his group of fierce young men,
the man who loves the banner of his native soil,
the man who, steel girded on and weapon in hand, has defied
the suns of red summer,
the snows and winds of freezing winter,
night, frost,
hatred, and death, to win immortality for his country's sake—
all these are saluted with bronze voices by the war trumpets that play
the triumphal march! . . .

(Cisnes) I

¿Qué signo haces, ¡oh Cisne!, con tu encorvado cuello
al paso de los tristes y errantes soñadores?
¿Por qué tan silencioso de ser blanco y ser bello,
tiránico a las aguas e impasible a las flores?

Yo te saludo ahora como en versos latinos
te saludara antaño Publio Ovidio Nasón.
Los mismos ruiseñores cantan los mismos trinos,
y en diferentes lenguas es la misma canción.

A vosotros mi lengua no debe ser extraña.
A Garcilaso visteis, acaso, alguna vez . . .
Soy un hijo de América, soy un nieto de España . . .
Quevedo pudo hablaros en verso en Aranjuez . . .

Cisnes, los abanicos de vuestras alas frescas
den a las frentes pálidas sus caricias más puras
y alejen vuestras blancas figuras pintorescas
de nuestras mentes tristes las ideas oscuras.

Brumas septentrionales nos llenan de tristezas,
se mueren nuestras rosas, se agostan nuestras palmas,
casi no hay ilusiones para nuestras cabezas,
y somos los mendigos de nuestras pobres almas.

Nos predican la guerra con águilas feroces,
gerifaltes de antaño revienen a los puños,
mas no brillan las glorias de las antiguas hoces,
ni hay Rodrigos ni Jaimes, ni hay Alfonsos ni Nuños.

Faltos de los alientos que dan las grandes cosas,
¿qué haremos los poetas sino buscar tus lagos?
A falta de laureles son muy dulces las rosas,
y a falta de victorias busquemos los halagos.

La América Española como la España entera
fija está en el Oriente de su fatal destino;
yo interrogo a la Esfinge que el porvenir espera
con la interrogación de tu cuello divino.

¿Seremos entregados a los bárbaros fieros?
¿Tantos millones de hombres hablaremos inglés?

(Swans) I

What sign are you forming, O Swan, with your curving neck
as these sad, wandering dreamers go by?
Why are you so silent in your whiteness and your beauty,
tyrannical to the waters and indifferent to the flowers?

I greet you now, as in Latin verses
Publius Ovidius Naso greeted you long ago.
The same nightingales are singing the same trills,
and in different languages it is the same song.

To you my language should not sound foreign.
You may have caught sight of Garcilaso at some time. . . .
I am a son of America, I am a grandchild of Spain. . . .
Quevedo may have addressed you in verse at Aranjuez. . . .

Swans, let the fans of your cool wings
give pale brows their purest caresses,
and let your picturesque white figures dispel
dark ideas from our sad minds.

Northern fogs fill us with sadness,
our roses are dying, our palm trees are withering;
there are virtually no hopeful dreams left in our heads,
and we are the mendicants of our poor souls.

War with ferocious eagles is preached to us,
the gerfalcons of yesteryear are returning to their owners' fists,
but the glories of bygone sickles no longer shine,
there is no Rodrigo or Jaime, no Alfonso or Nuño.

Bereft of the enthusiasm generated by great events,
what can we poets do except seek out your lakes?
When laurels are lacking, roses are very sweet,
and when conquests are absent, let us seek pleasures.

Spanish America, like Spain as a whole,
keeps its eyes fixed on the East of its fateful destiny;
I question the Sphinx that awaits the future
with the question mark of your divine neck.

Will we be handed over to the fierce barbarians?
Will all our millions of people speak English?

¿Ya no hay nobles hidalgos ni bravos caballeros?
¿Callaremos ahora para llorar después?

He lanzado mi grito, Cisnes, entre vosotros,
que habéis sido los fieles en la desilusión,
mientras siento una fuga de americanos potros
y el estertor postrero de un caduco león . . .

. . . Y un cisne negro dijo: «La noche anuncia el día.»
Y uno blanco: «¡La aurora es inmortal, la aurora
es inmortal!» ¡Oh tierras de sol y de armonía,
aún guarda la Esperanza la caja de Pandora!

(Cisnes) II: En la muerte de Rafael Núñez

Que sais-je?

El pensador llegó a la barca negra;
y le vieron hundirse
en las brumas del lago del Misterio
los ojos de los Cisnes.

Su manto de poeta
reconocieron los ilustres lises
y el laurel y la espina entremezclados
sobre la frente triste.

A lo lejos alzábanse los muros
de la ciudad teológica, en que vive
la sempiterna Paz. La negra barca
llegó a la ansiada costa, y el sublime
espíritu gozó la suma gracia;
y ¡oh Montaigne! Núñez vio la cruz erguirse,
y halló al pie de la sacra Vencedora
el helado cadáver de la Esfinge.

(Cisnes) III

Por un momento, ¡oh Cisne!, juntaré mis anhelos
a los de tus dos alas que abrazaron a Leda,

Are there no more noble hidalgos or brave knights?
Shall we remain silent now, only to weep later?

I have uttered my cry, Swans, in your midst,
since you have been faithful to me in my disappointment,
while I sense a runaway stampede of American colts
and the last death rattle of a decrepit lion. . . .

And a black swan said: "Night announces day."
And a white one said. "Dawn is immortal, dawn
is immortal!" Oh, lands of sunshine and harmony,
Pandora's box still has Hope left in it!

(Swans) II: On the Death of Rafael Núñez

What do I know?

The thinker arrived at the black boat;
and the eyes of the Swans
saw him submerge
in the mists of the lake of Mystery.

His poet's mantle
was recognized by the illustrious irises,
and the laurels and thorns intermingled
on his sad brow.

In the distance loomed the walls
of the theological city, in which lives
eternal Peace. The black boat
arrived at the longed-for shore, and his sublime
spirit enjoyed the highest grace;
and, O Montaigne, Núñez saw the Cross looming up,
and at the foot of that holy Conqueror he found
the frozen corpse of the Sphinx.

(Swans) III

For one moment, O Swan, I shall add my longings
to those of your two wings, which embraced Leda,

y a mi maduro ensueño, aún vestido de seda,
dirás, por los Dioscuros, la gloria de los cielos.

Es el otoño. Ruedan de la flauta consuelos.
Por un instante, ¡oh Cisne!, en la oscura alameda
sorberé entre dos labios lo que el Pudor me veda,
y dejaré mordidos Escrúpulos y Celos.

Cisne, tendré tus alas blancas por un instante,
y el corazón de rosa que hay en tu dulce pecho
palpitará en el mío con su sangre constante.

Amor será dichoso, pues estará vibrante
el júbilo que pone al gran Pan en acecho
mientras su ritmo esconde la fuente de diamante.

(Cisnes) IV

¡Antes de todo, gloria a ti, Leda!;
tu dulce vientre cubrió de seda
el Dios. ¡Miel y oro sobre la brisa!
Sonaban alternativamente
flauta y cristales, Pan y la fuente.
¡Tierra era canto, Cielo sonrisa!

Ante el celeste, supremo acto,
dioses y bestias hicieron pacto.
Se dio a la alondra la luz del día,
se dio a los búhos sabiduría,
y melodías al ruiseñor.
A los leones fue la victoria,
para las águilas toda la gloria,
y a las palomas todo el amor.

Pero vosotros sois los divinos
príncipes. Vagos como las naves,
inmaculados como los linos,
maravillosos como las aves.

En vuestros picos tenéis las prendas
que manifiestan corales puros.
Con vuestros pechos abrís las sendas
que arriba indican los Dioscuros.

and to my ripened dream, which is still clad in silk,
you shall tell, through the agency of the Dioscuri, the glory of the heavens.

It is autumn. Solace pours around me from the flute.
For one instant, O Swan, in the dark poplar grove
I shall sip between two lips that which Shamefulness forbids me,
and I shall leave Scruples and Jealousy wounded.

Swan, I shall have your white wings for an instant,
and the heart of rose that is in your sweet breast
shall beat within mine with its constant blood.

Love will be fortunate, because there shall vibrate
the jubilation that makes great Pan remain on the lookout,
while the diamondlike fountain conceals its rhythm.

(Swans) IV

First and foremost, glory to you, Leda!
Your sweet womb was covered with silk
by the god. Honey and gold in the breeze!
There was the sound, in alternation,
of flute and crystal waters, Pan and the fountain.
The Earth was song, Heaven was smiles!

In view of that celestial, supreme act
gods and animals struck a pact.
The lark was given the light of day,
the owls were given wisdom,
and the nightingale melodies.
To the lions went victory,
to the eagles all glory,
and to the doves all love.

But you are the divine
princes. Wandering like ships,
immaculate as linen,
marvelous as birds.

In your beaks you hold the pledges of love
which display pure corals.
With your breasts you open the paths
which, up above, point out the Dioscuri.

Las dignidades de vuestros actos,
eternizadas en lo infinito,
hacen que sean ritmos exactos,
voces de ensueño, luces de mito.

De orgullo olímpico sois el resumen,
¡oh, blancas urnas de la armonía!
Ebúrneas joyas que anima un numen
con su celeste melancolía.

¡Melancolía de haber amado,
junto a la fuente de la arboleda,
el luminoso cuello estirado
entre los blancos muslos de Leda!

"La dulzura del ángelus . . ."

La dulzura del ángelus matinal y divino
que diluyen ingenuas campanas provinciales,
en un aire inocente a fuerza de rosales,
de plegaria, de ensueño de virgen y de trino

de ruiseñor, opuesto todo al rudo destino
que no cree en Dios . . . El áureo ovillo vespertino
que la tarde devana tras opacos cristales
por tejer la inconsútil tela de nuestros males

todos hechos de carne y aromados de vino . . .
Y esta atroz amargura de no gustar de nada,
de no saber adónde dirigir nuestra prora

mientras el pobre esquife en la noche cerrada
va en las hostiles olas huérfano de la aurora . . .
(¡Oh, suaves campanas entre la madrugada!)

Tarde del trópico

Es la tarde gris y triste.
Viste el mar de terciopelo
y el cielo profundo viste
de duelo.

The dignity of your actions,
which becomes eternal in infinity,
causes them to be precise rhythms,
dream voices, mythical light.

You are the epitome of Olympian pride,
O white urns of harmony!
Ivory treasures which a godhead animates
with his celestial melancholy.

The melancholy of having loved,
beside the fountain in the copse,
with his luminous neck stretched tautly
between Leda's white thighs!

"The Sweetness of the Angelus . . ."

The sweetness of the divine morning Angelus
diffused by ingenuous country church bells
in the air innocent by dint of roses,
of prayer, virginal dreams, and trills

of nightingales, completely opposed to the rough destiny
which doesn't believe in God . . . The golden twilight ball of yarn
which evening reels behind opaque panes
with which to weave the seamless web of our misfortunes

all made of flesh and flavored with wine . . .
And that atrocious bitterness of not enjoying anything,
of not knowing where to direct our prow

while in the blackness of the night our poor vessel
rides the hostile waves, an orphan of the dawn . . .
(Oh, gentle bells at daybreak!)

Evening in the Tropics

It is the gray, sad evening.
The sea is garbed in velvet
and the deep sky is garbed
in grief.

Del abismo se levanta
la queja amarga y sonora.
La onda, cuando el viento canta,
llora.

Los violines de la bruma
saludan al sol que muere.
Salmodia la blanca espuma:
miserere.

La armonía el cielo inunda,
y la brisa va a llevar
la canción triste y profunda
del mar.

Del clarín del horizonte
brota sinfonía rara,
como si la voz del monte
vibrara.

Cual si fuese lo invisible . . .
cual si fuese el rudo son
que diese al viento un terrible
león.

Nocturno

Quiero expresar mi angustia en versos que abolida
dirán mi juventud de rosas y de ensueños,
y la desfloración amarga de mi vida
por un vasto dolor y cuidados pequeños.

Y el viaje a un vago Oriente por entrevistos barcos,
y el grano de oraciones que floreció en blasfemia,
y los azoramientos del cisne entre los charcos,
y el falso azul nocturno de inquerida bohemia.

Lejano clavicordio que en silencio y olvido
no diste nunca al sueño la sublime sonata,
huérfano esquife, árbol insigne, oscuro nido
que suavizó la noche de dulzura de plata . . .

Esperanza olorosa a hierbas frescas, trino
del ruiseñor primaveral y matinal,

From the abyss arises
the bitter, resonant lament.
The waves, when the wind sings,
weep.

The violins of the mist
greet the dying sun.
The white foam chants:
"Miserere."

Music drowns the sky,
and the breeze will soon bear
the sad, profound song
of the sea.

From the trumpet of the horizon
a strange symphony emerges,
as if the voice of the mountain
vibrated.

As if it were the invisible . . .
as if it were the wild sound
unleashed on the wind by a fearful
lion.

Nocturne

I wish to express my anxiety in verses which will proclaim
that my youth of roses and dreams is abrogated,
which will proclaim the bitter deflowering of my life
by an immense sorrow and by petty cares.

And the voyage to a vague East on glimpsed ships,
and the seed of prayer that blossomed into blasphemy,
and the swan's frights amid the pools,
and the specious nighttime blue of an unloved bohemian life.

You distant clavichord that, in silence and oblivion,
never gave the dream its sublime sonata,
orphaned boat, renowned tree, dark nest
that the night softened with silvery sweetness . . .

Hope redolent of fresh grass, warbling
of the springtime morning nightingale,

azucena tronchada por un fatal destino,
rebusca de la dicha, persecución del mal . . .

El ánfora funesta del divino veneno
que ha de hacer por la vida la tortura interior,
la conciencia espantable de nuestro humano cieno
y el horror de sentirse pasajero, el horror

de ir a tientas, en intermitentes espantos,
hacia lo inevitable, desconocido, y la
pesadilla brutal de este dormir de llantos
¡de la cual no hay más que Ella que nos despertará!

Canción de otoño en primavera

A Martínez Sierra

Juventud, divino tesoro,
¡ya te vas para no volver!
Cuando quiero llorar, no lloro . . .
Y a veces lloro sin querer . . .

Plural ha sido la celeste
historia de mi corazón.
Era una dulce niña, en este
mundo de duelo y aflicción.

Miraba como el alba pura;
sonreía como una flor.
Era su cabellera oscura
hecha de noche y de dolor.

Yo era tímido como un niño.
Ella, naturalmente, fue,
para mi amor hecho de armiño,
Herodías y Salomé . . .

Juventud, divino tesoro,
¡ya te vas para no volver!
Cuando quiero llorar, no lloro . . .
Y a veces lloro sin querer . . .

Y más consoladora y más
halagadora y expresiva,

lily broken by a fatal destiny,
the search for happiness, the grim pursuit by misfortune . . .

The funereal amphora of divine poison
that will create inner torture throughout life,
the awful consciousness of our human mire,
and the horror of feeling oneself to be transient, the horror

of proceeding gropingly, frightened at intermittent intervals,
toward the inevitable, the unknown, and the
brutal nightmare of that sleep of tears
from which only Death will awaken us!

Autumnal Song in Springtime

To Martínez Sierra

Youth, divine treasure,
you are now departing, never to return!
When I wish to weep, I cannot . . .
and at times I weep without wanting to. . . .

The celestial history
of my heart has been plural.
She was like a sweet girl, in this
world of sorrow and affliction.

Her gaze was as pure as the dawn;
she smiled like a flower.
Her dark hair was
compounded of night and sorrow.

I was as bashful as a little boy.
To my love made of ermine,
she naturally was
Herodias and Salome. . . .

Youth, divine treasure,
you are now departing, never to return!
When I wish to weep, I cannot . . .
and at times I weep without wanting to. . . .

More consoling, more
flattering and expressive,

la otra fue más sensitiva
cual no pensé encontrar jamás.

Pues a su continua ternura
una pasión violenta unía.
En un peplo de gasa pura
una bacante se envolvía . . .

En brazos tomó mi ensueño
y lo arrulló como a un bebé . . .
y le mató, triste y pequeño,
falto de luz, falto de fe . . .

Juventud, divino tesoro,
¡ya te vas para no volver!
Cuando quiero llorar, no lloro . . .
Y a veces lloro sin querer . . .

Otra juzgó que era mi boca
el estuche de su pasión;
y que me roería, loca,
con sus dientes el corazón,

poniendo en un amor de exceso
la mira de su voluntad,
mientras eran abrazo y beso
síntesis de la eternidad;

y de nuestra carne ligera
imaginó siempre un Edén,
sin pensar que la Primavera
y la carne acaban también . . .

Juventud, divino tesoro,
¡ya te vas para no volver!
Cuando quiero llorar, no lloro . . .
Y a veces lloro sin querer . . .

¡Y las demás! En tantos climas,
en tantas tierras siempre son,
si no pretextos de mis rimas,
fantasmas de mi corazón.

En vano busqué a la princesa
que estaba triste de esperar.

the next woman was more sensitive,
the sort I never expected to meet.

For, to her constant tenderness
she joined a violent passion.
In a peplum of pure gauze
a bacchante was draped. . . .

She took my dreams in her arms
and sang them to sleep like a baby . . .
and she killed the unhappy little thing
for want of light, for want of faithfulness. . . .

Youth, divine treasure,
you are now departing, never to return!
When I wish to weep, I cannot . . .
and at times I weep without wanting to. . . .

The next woman thought that my lips
were a jewel case for her passion,
and that in her madness she would gnaw
my heart with her teeth,

aiming her willpower
at an excessive love,
while embraces and kisses
were a synthesis of eternity;

and she always imagined that our
light flesh was a garden of Eden,
without stopping to think that Springtime
and the flesh also come to an end. . . .

Youth, divine treasure,
you are now departing, never to return!
When I wish to weep, I cannot . . .
and at times I weep without wanting to. . . .

And the rest of the women! In so many climes,
in so many lands, they are always,
if not a pretext for my rhymes,
at least phantoms of my heart.

In vain I sought the princess
who was sad with waiting.

La vida es dura. Amarga y pesa.
¡Ya no hay princesa que cantar!

Mas a pesar del tiempo terco,
mi sed de amor no tiene fin;
con el cabello gris, me acerco
a los rosales del jardín . . .

Juventud, divino tesoro,
¡ya te vas para no volver!
Cuando quiero llorar, no lloro . . .
Y a veces lloro sin querer . . .

¡Mas es mía el Alba de oro!

Trébol

I: De don Luis de Góngora y Argote
   a don Diego de Silva Velázquez

Mientras el brillo de tu gloria augura
ser en la eternidad sol sin poniente,
fénix de viva luz, fénix ardiente,
diamante parangón de la pintura,

de España está sobre la veste oscura
tu nombre, como joya reluciente;
rompe la Envidia el fatigado diente,
y el Olvido lamenta su amargura.

Yo en equívoco altar, tú en sacro fuego,
miro a través de mi penumbra el día
en que al calor de tu amistad, Don Diego,

jugando de la luz con la armonía,
con la alma luz, de tu pincel el juego
el alma duplicó de la faz mía.

II: De don Diego de Silva Velázquez
    a don Luis de Góngora y Argote

Alma de oro, fina voz de oro,
al venir hacia mí, ¿por qué suspiras?

Life is hard. It embitters you and weighs you down.
There is no longer any princess to sing of!

But despite the obstinacy of time,
my thirst for love is endless;
now gray-haired, I approach
the rose bushes in the garden. . . .

Youth, divine treasure,
you are now departing, never to return!
When I wish to weep, I cannot . . .
and at times I weep without wanting to. . . .

But the golden Dawn is mine!

Cloverleaf

I: FROM DON LUIS DE GÓNGORA Y ARGOTE
TO DON DIEGO DE SILVA VELÁZQUEZ

While the radiance of your glory promises
to remain eternally a never-setting sun,
phoenix of vivid light, burning phoenix,
perfect diamond of painting,

the dark robe of Spain wears
your name like a glistening jewel;
Envy wears out and breaks her teeth,
and Oblivion laments its own bitterness.

I on an altar of equivocation, you amid the sacred flames,
I see through my penumbra the day
when, in the warmth of your friendship, Don Diego,

the play of your brush, playing with the harmonies
of light, with nourishing light,
duplicated the soul of my face.

II: FROM DON DIEGO DE SILVA VELÁZQUEZ
TO DON LUIS DE GÓNGORA Y ARGOTE

Golden soul, elegant golden voice,
when coming toward me, why do you sigh?

Ya empieza el noble coro de las liras
a preludiar el himno a tu decoro;

ya al misterioso son del noble coro
calma el Centauro sus grotescas iras,
y con nueva pasión que les inspiras,
tornan a amarse Angélica y Medoro.

A Teócrito y Poussin la Fama dote
con la corona de laurel supremo;
que en donde da Cervantes el Quijote

y yo las telas con mis luces gemo;
para Don Luis de Góngora y Argote
traerá una nueva palma Polifemo.

III

En tanto «pace estrellas» el Pegaso divino,
y vela tu hipogrifo, Velázquez, la Fortuna,
en los celestes parques al Cisne gongorino
deshoja sus sutiles margaritas la Luna.

Tu castillo, Velázquez, se eleva en el camino
del Arte como torre que de águilas es cuna,
y tu castillo, Góngora, se alza al azul cual una
jaula de ruiseñores labrada en oro fino.

Gloriosa la península que abriga tal colonia.
¡Aquí bronce corintio y allá mármol de Jonia!
Las rosas a Velázquez, y a Góngora claveles.

De ruiseñores y águilas se pueblen las encinas,
y mientras pasa Angélica sonriendo a las Meninas,
salen las nueve musas de un bosque de laureles.

Leda

El cisne en la sombra parece de nieve;
su pico es de ámbar, del alba al trasluz;
el suave crepúsculo que pasa tan breve
las cándidas alas sonrosa de luz.

The noble chorus of lyres is now beginning
its prelude to the hymn in your honor;

now, to the mysterious sound of the noble chorus,
the Centaur calms his grotesque wrath,
and with the new passion you inspire in them
Angelica and Medoro fall in love again.

Let Fame endow Theocritus and Poussin
with the wreath of loftiest laurel;
for where Cervantes gives us his Quixote,

I too begem canvases with my light;
for Don Luis de Góngora y Argote
Polyphemus will bring a new palm.

III

While divine Pegasus is "grazing on stars,"
and Fortune is guarding your hippogriff, Velázquez,
in the parks of heaven for Góngora's swan
the Moon is pulling the petals off her subtle daisies.

Your castle, Velázquez, looms above the road
of Art like a tower that is a cradle for eagles,
and your castle, Góngora, rises into the blue like a
cage of nightingales fashioned of fine gold.

Glorious is the peninsula that shelters such a colony.
Here Corinthian bronze and there Ionian marble!
Roses to Velázquez, and to Góngora carnations.

The ilexes are peopled with nightingales and eagles,
and while Angelica passes by, smiling to *Las Meninas,*
the nine muses emerge from a laurel wood.

Leda

The swan in the shadow resembles snow;
its bill is of amber, in the reflected light of daybreak;
the gentle dawn that passes so quickly
sheds rosy light on its white wings.

Y luego, en las ondas del lago azulado,
después que la aurora perdió su arrebol,
las alas tendidas y el cuello enarcado,
el cisne es de plata, bañado de sol.

Tal es cuando esponja las plumas de seda,
olímpico pájaro herido de amor,
y viola en las linfas sonoras a Leda,
buscando su pico los labios en flor.

Suspira la bella desnuda y vencida,
y en tanto que al aire sus quejas se van,
del fondo verdoso de fronda tupida
chispean turbados los ojos de Pan.

"Divina Psiquis . . ."

¡Divina Psiquis, dulce mariposa invisible
que desde los abismos has venido a ser todo
lo que en mi ser nervioso y en mi cuerpo sensible
forma la chispa sacra de la estatua de lodo!

Te asomas por mis ojos a la luz de la Tierra
y prisionera vives en mí de extraño dueño;
te reducen a esclava mis sentidos en guerra
y apenas vagas libre por el jardín del sueño.

Sabia de la Lujuria que sabe antiguas ciencias,
te sacudes a veces entre imposibles muros,
y más allá de todas las vulgares conciencias
exploras los recodos más terribles y oscuros.

Y encuentras sombra y duelo. Que sombra y duelo
          encuentres
bajo la viña en donde nace el vino del Diablo.
Te posas en los senos, te posas en los vientres
que hicieron a Juan loco e hicieron cuerdo a Pablo.

A Juan virgen y a Pablo militar y violento,
a Juan que nunca supo del supremo contacto;
a Pablo el tempestuoso que halló a Cristo en el viento,
y a Juan ante quien Hugo se queda estupefacto.

And then, in the waters of the bluish lake,
after dawn has lost its ruddy glow,
its wings spread and its neck arched,
the swan is silvery, and bathed in sunshine.

Such it is when it sponges its silken feathers,
an Olympian bird smitten with love,
and when it violates Leda in the noisy waters,
its bill seeking her blossoming lips.

The naked, vanquished beauty sighs,
and while her laments fly off in the breeze,
from the verdant depths of dense foliage
Pan's eyes sparkle in confusion.

"Divine Psyche . . ."

Divine Psyche, sweet invisible butterfly
that has come from the abyss to be everything
that, in my nervous being and sensitive body,
forms the holy spark in the mud statue!

You peer out through my eyes at the light of the Earth
and in me you live as the captive of a foreign master;
my warring senses reduce you to slavery
and you scarcely take a free step in the gardens of my dreams.

Wise with the Lust that is full of ancient knowledge,
at times you are jolted against impossible walls,
and beyond the realm of all common consciousness
you explore all the darkest and most terrible recesses.

And you encounter shadow and grief. May you encounter shadow
        and grief
beneath the grapevine that furnishes the Devil's wine.
You alight on the breasts, you alight on the bellies
that made John mad and Paul prudent.

John the virgin and Paul the violent soldier,
John who never knew the supreme contact;
tempestuous Paul who found Christ in the wind,
and John, before whom Hugo remains dumbfounded.

Entre la catedral y las ruinas paganas
vuelas, ¡oh Psiquis, oh alma mía!
—Como decía
aquel celeste Edgardo,
que entró en el paraíso entre un son de campanas
y un perfume de nardo—.
Entre la catedral
y las paganas ruinas
repartes tus dos alas de cristal,
tus dos alas divinas.
Y de la flor
que al ruiseñor
canta en su griego antiguo, de la rosa,
vuelas, ¡oh, Mariposa!,
a posarte en un clavo de nuestro Señor.

A Phocás el campesino

Phocás el campesino, hijo mío, que tienes,
en apenas escasos meses de vida, tantos
dolores en tus ojos que esperan tantos llantos
por el fatal pensar que revelan tus sienes . . .

Tarda en venir a este dolor adonde vienes,
a este mundo terrible en duelos y en espantos;
duerme bajo los Ángeles, sueña bajo los Santos,
que ya tendrás la Vida para que te envenenes . . .

Sueña, hijo mío, todavía, y cuando crezcas,
perdóname el fatal don de darte la vida
que yo hubiera querido de azul y rosas frescas;

pues tú eres la crisálida de mi alma entristecida,
y te he de ver en medio del triunfo que merezcas
renovando el fulgor de mi psique abolida.

"¡Carne, celeste carne . . . !"

¡Carne, celeste carne de la mujer! Arcilla
—dijo Hugo—, ambrosía más bien, ¡oh maravilla!,

Between the cathedral and the pagan ruins
you fly, O Psyche, O my soul!
—as that heavenly
Edgar said,
who entered into paradise between a peal of bells
and a fragrance of spikenard.—
Between the cathedral
and the pagan ruins
you share your two crystal wings,
your two divine wings.
And from the flower
that sings to the nightingale
in its ancient Greek, from the rose,
you fly, O Butterfly,
and alight on a nail of Our Lord's Cross.

To Phocas the Peasant

Phocas the peasant—my son—you that have,
though barely a few months old, so many
sorrows in your eyes, which expect so many tears
because of the fateful thoughts which your temples reveal . . .

Be slow in arriving at that sorrow to which you are heading,
that world terrible in its griefs and scares;
sleep in the Angels' care, dream in the Saints' care,
for later you will have Life with which to poison yourself . . .

Keep dreaming, my son, and when you grow up,
forgive me for the fatal gift of bestowing life upon you,
a life I would have wanted to be of blue and of new roses;

because you are the chrysalis of my saddened soul,
and I shall see you amid the triumph that you deserve,
renewing the resplendence of my abolished psyche.

"Flesh, Heavenly Flesh . . ."

Flesh, heavenly flesh of woman! Clay,
Hugo called it, but really ambrosia, a miracle!

la vida se soporta,
tan doliente y tan corta,
solamente por eso:
¡roce, mordisco o beso
en ese pan divino
para el cual nuestra sangre es nuestro vino!
En ella está la lira,
en ella está la rosa,
en ella está la ciencia armoniosa,
en ella se respira
el perfume vital de toda cosa.

Eva y Cipris concentran el misterio
del corazón del mundo.
Cuando el áureo Pegaso
en la victoria matinal se lanza
con el mágico ritmo de su paso
hacia la vida y hacia la esperanza,
si alza la crin y las narices hincha
y sobre las montañas pone el casco sonoro
y hacia la mar relincha,
y el espacio se llena
de un gran temblor de oro,
es que ha visto desnuda a Anadiomena.

Gloria, ¡oh Potente a quien las sombras temen!
¡Que las más blancas tórtolas te inmolen!
¡Pues por ti la floresta está en el polen
y el pensamiento en el sagrado semen!

Gloria, ¡oh sublime que eres la existencia
por quien siempre hay futuros en el útero eterno!
¡Tu boca sabe al fruto del árbol de la Ciencia
y al torcer tus cabellos apagaste el infierno!

Inútil es el grito de la legión cobarde
del interés, inútil el progreso
yankee, si te desdeña.
Si el progreso es de fuego, por ti arde.
¡Toda lucha del hombre va a tu beso,
por ti se combate o se sueña!

Life can be abided,
though so painful and brief,
because of that alone:
a caress, a bite, or a kiss
on that divine bread
for which our blood is our wine!
In it is the lyre,
in it is the rose,
in it is the science of music,
in it we breathe
the vital fragrance of all things.

Eve and Cypris concentrate the mystery
of the heart of the world.
When golden Pegasus
takes flight in the morning's victory
to the magical rhythm of his movement
toward life and toward hope,
if he erects his mane and distends his nostrils
and sets his ringing hooves on the mountains
and whinnies in the direction of the sea,
and space is filled
with a great golden tremor,
it is because he has seen Anadyomene naked.

Glory to you, powerful one whom the shades fear!
May they sacrifice the whitest turtle-doves to you!
Because it is on your account that the forest is latent in the pollen,
and human thought in the sacred semen!

Glory to you, sublime one who are the existence
through which there is always a future in the eternal womb!
Your mouth has the flavor of the fruit of the Tree of Knowledge,
and when you twisted your hair, you extinguished Hell!

Useless is the cry of the cowardly legion
of self-interest, useless is Yankee
progress, if it disdains you.
If progress is made of fire, it burns because of you.
All of man's struggles have your kiss as their goal,
for you man fights or dreams!

Pues en ti existe Primavera para el triste,
labor gozosa para el fuerte,
néctar, Ánfora, dulzura amable.
¡Porque en ti existe
el placer de vivir hasta la muerte
y ante la eternidad de lo probable! . . .

"En el país de las Alegorías . . ."

En el país de las Alegorías
Salomé siempre danza,
ante el tiarado Herodes,
eternamente.
Y la cabeza de Juan el Bautista,
ante quien tiemblan los leones,
cae al hachazo. Sangre llueve.

Pues la rosa sexual
al entreabrirse
conmueve todo lo que existe,
con su efluvio carnal
y con su enigma espiritual.

Augurios

A E. Díaz Romero

Hoy pasó un águila
sobre mi cabeza;
lleva en sus alas
la tormenta,
lleva en sus garras
el rayo que deslumbra y aterra.
¡Oh águila!
Dame la fortaleza
de sentirme en el lodo humano
con alas y fuerzas
para resistir los embates
de las tempestades perversas,

Because in you Springtime exists for the sad,
enjoyable toil for the strong,
nectar, Amphora, lovable sweetness.
Because in you there exists
the pleasure of living until death
and face to face with the eternity of the probable! . . .

"In the Land of Allegories . . ."

In the land of Allegories
Salome is always dancing
before Herod with his tiara,
eternally.
And the head of John the Baptist,
before whom lions tremble,
falls as the axe strikes it. Blood rains down.

Because the rose of sex,
when it begins to open,
excites all that exists
with its carnal effluvia
and its spiritual enigma.

Omens

To E. Díaz Romero

Today an eagle flew
over my head;
it bears in its wings
the storm,
it bears in its talons
the lightning that dazzles and terrifies.
O eagle!
Give me the fortitude
to feel in this human mire of mine
sufficiently winged and strong
to resist the attacks
of evil tempests,

y de arriba las cóleras
y de abajo las roedoras miserias.

   Pasó un búho
sobre mi frente.
Yo pensé en Minerva
y en la noche solemne.
¡Oh búho!
Dame tu silencio perenne,
y tus ojos profundos en la noche
y tu tranquilidad ante la muerte.
Dame tu nocturno imperio
y tu sabiduría celeste,
y tu cabeza cual la de Jano,
que, siendo una, mira a Oriente y Occidente.

   Pasó una paloma
que casi rozó con sus alas mis labios.
¡Oh paloma!
Dame tu profundo encanto
de saber arrullar, y tu lascivia
en campo tornasol; y en campo
de luz tu prodigioso
ardor en el divino acto.
(Y dame la justicia en la naturaleza,
pues, en este caso,
tú serás la perversa
y el chivo será el casto.)

   Pasó un gerifalte. ¡Oh gerifalte!
Dame tus uñas largas
y tus ágiles alas cortadoras de viento,
y tus ágiles patas,
y tus uñas que bien se hunden
en las carnes de la caza.
Por mi cetrería
irás en giras fantásticas,
y me traerás piezas famosas
y raras,
palpitantes ideas,
sangrientas almas.

the anger from above
and the gnawing miseries from below.

   An owl flew
over my brow.
I thought of Minerva
and the solemn night.
O owl!
Give me your perennial silence,
and your deep eyes in the night,
and your tranquillity in the face of death.
Give me your command of the night
and your heavenly wisdom,
and your head like Janus's,
which, though only one, can look to the East and the West.

   A dove flew by,
nearly brushing my lips with its wings.
O dove!
Give me your deep magic
of knowing how to coo, and your lasciviousness
in the iridescent field, and in the field
of light your prodigious
ardor in the divine act.
(And give me justice in Nature,
because, in this case,
you will be the lewd party
and the goat will be the chaste one.)

   A gerfalcon flew by. O gerfalcon!
Give me your long nails
and your agile wings that cut the wind,
and your agile legs,
and your nails that sink deeply
into the flesh of your prey.
By way of my falconry
you will go on fantastic excursions,
and you will bring me wonderful
and rare game,
palpitating ideas,
bloodstained souls.

Pasa el ruiseñor.
¡Ah divino doctor!
No me des nada. Tengo tu veneno,
tu puesta de sol
y tu noche de luna y tu lira,
y tu lírico amor.
(Sin embargo, en secreto,
tu amigo soy,
pues más de una vez me has brindado,
en la copa de mi dolor,
con el elixir de la luna
celestes gotas de Dios . . .)

Pasa un murciélago.
Pasa una mosca. Un moscardón.
Una abeja en el crepúsculo.
No pasa nada.
La muerte llegó.

Melancolía

A Domingo Bolívar

Hermano, tú que tienes la luz, dame la mía.
Soy como un ciego. Voy sin rumbo y ando a tientas.
Voy bajo tempestades y tormentas,
ciego de ensueño y loco de armonía.

Ése es mi mal. Soñar. La poesía
es la camisa férrea de mil puntas cruentas
que llevo sobre el alma. Las espinas sangrientas
dejan caer las gotas de mi melancolía.

Y así voy, ciego y loco, por este mundo amargo;
a veces me parece que el camino es muy largo,
y a veces que es muy corto . . .

Y en este titubeo de aliento y agonía,
cargo lleno de penas lo que apenas soporto.
¿No oyes caer las gotas de mi melancolía?

The nightingale flies by.
Ah, divine teacher!
Don't give me anything. I possess your poison,
your sunset
and your moonlight night and your lyre,
and your lyrical love.
(All the same, in secret,
I am your friend,
because more than once you have poured for me,
into the goblet of my sorrow,
along with the elixir of the moon,
heavenly drops of God. . . .)

A bat flies by.
A fly goes by. A hornet.
A bee in the twilight.
Nothing flies by.
Death has come.

Melancholy

To Domingo Bolívar

Brother, you who possess light, give me mine.
I am like a blind man. I have no fixed course, and I grope about.
My path lies beneath tempests and storms,
I am blind with dreaming and mad with music.

That's my trouble. Dreaming. Poetry
is the iron shirt with a thousand bloodied points
that I wear over my soul. The blood-stained thorns
let fall the drops of my melancholy.

And so I go on, blind and mad, through this bitter world;
at times it seems to me that the way is very long,
and at times that it is very short. . . .

And in this staggering between enthusiasm and agony,
filled with pain, I shoulder a load I can scarcely carry.
Don't you hear the drops of my melancholy falling?

Nocturno

A Mariano de Cavia

Los que auscultasteis el corazón de la noche,
los que por el insomnio tenaz habéis oído
el cerrar de una puerta, el resonar de un coche
lejano, un eco vago, un ligero ruido . . .

En los instantes del silencio misterioso,
cuando surgen de su prisión los olvidados,
en la hora de los muertos, en la hora del reposo,
sabréis leer estos versos de amargor impregnados . . .

Como en un vaso vierto en ellos mis dolores
de lejanos recuerdos y desgracias funestas,
y las tristes nostalgias de mi alma, ebria de flores,
y el duelo de mi corazón, triste de fiestas.

Y el pesar de no ser lo que yo hubiera sido,
la pérdida del reino que estaba para mí,
el pensar que un instante pude no haber nacido,
y el sueño que es mi vida desde que yo nací.

Todo esto viene en medio del silencio profundo
en que la noche envuelve la terrena ilusión,
y siento como un eco del corazón del mundo
que penetra y conmueve mi propio corazón.

Letanía de nuestro señor don Quijote

A Navarro Ledesma

Rey de los hidalgos, señor de los tristes,
que de fuerza alientas y de ensueños vistes,
coronado de áureo yelmo de ilusión;
que nadie ha podido vencer todavía,
por la adarga al brazo, toda fantasía,
y la lanza en ristre, toda corazón.

Noble peregrino de los peregrinos,
que santificaste todos los caminos

Nocturne

To Mariano de Cavia

You who have auscultated the heart of the night,
you who in your tenacious insomnia have heard
the shutting of a door, the clatter of a carriage
in the distance, a vague echo, a slight noise . . .

In the moments of mysterious silence,
when forgotten men emerge from their prison,
at the hour of the dead, in the hour of rest,
you will know how to read these verses impregnated with bitterness. . . .

I pour into them, as into a vessel, my sorrows
due to distant memories and disastrous misfortunes,
and the sad nostalgia of my soul that is drunk with flowers,
and the grief of my heart that is sad with merrymaking.

And the vexation of not being what I might have been,
the loss of the kingdom that was meant for me,
the thought that, at one moment, I might have avoided being born,
and the dream which my life has been ever since birth.

All this comes to me amid the deep silence
in which night envelops our earthly hopes,
and I seem to feel an echo of the world's heart
penetrating and agitating my own heart.

Litany of Our Lord Don Quixote

To Navarro Ledesma

King of hidalgos, lord of the sad,
you that inspire us with strength and clothe us in dreams,
crowned with your golden helmet of fanciful hope;
you whom no one has yet been able to conquer,
thanks to the shield on your arm, a shield that is entirely imagination,
and to your couched lance, which is entirely heart.

Noble pilgrim among pilgrims,
you that sanctified all roads

con el paso augusto de tu heroicidad,
contra las certezas, contra las conciencias
y contra las leyes y contra las ciencias,
contra la mentira, contra la verdad . . .

¡Caballero errante de los caballeros,
varón de varones, príncipe de fieros,
par entre los pares, maestro, salud!
¡Salud, porque juzgo que hoy muy poca tienes,
entre los aplausos o entre los desdenes,
y entre las coronas y los parabienes
y las tonterías de la multitud!

¡Tú, para quien pocas fueron las victorias
antiguas y para quien clásicas glorias
serían apenas de ley y razón,
soportas elogios, memorias, discursos,
resistes certámenes, tarjetas, concursos,
y, teniendo a Orfeo, tienes a orfeón!

Escucha, divino Rolando del sueño,
a un enamorado de tu Clavileño,
y cuyo Pegaso relincha hacia ti;
escucha los versos de estas letanías,
hechas con las cosas de todos los días
y con otras que en lo misterioso vi.

¡Ruega por nosotros, hambrientos de vida,
con el alma a tientas, con la fe perdida,
llenos de congojas y faltos de sol,
por advenedizas almas de manga ancha,
que ridiculizan el ser de la Mancha,
el ser generoso y el ser español!

¡Ruega por nosotros, que necesitamos
las mágicas rosas, los sublimes ramos
de laurel! *Pro nobis ora,* gran señor.
¡Tiembla la floresta del laurel del mundo,
y antes que tu hermano vago, Segismundo,
el pálido Hamlet te ofrece una flor!

Ruega generoso, piadoso, orgulloso,
ruega casto, puro, celeste, animoso;
por nos intercede, suplica por nos,

by the august passage of your heroism,
against all certainties, against consciences,
and against laws and sciences,
against lies, against truth. . . .

Knight errant among knights,
champion among champions, prince of the fierce,
peer among peers, master, here's health to you!
Health, because I think you enjoy very little of it nowadays,
amid the applause or amid the scorn,
and amid the garlands and congratulations
and follies of the multitude!

You, for whom the victories of ancient days
were scanty in comparison, and for whom classical glories
would hardly be logical and reasonable,
you now have to put up with praises, memorials, speeches,
you have to combat contests, inscribed tablets, competitions,
and, possessing something of Orpheus, you get an *Orphéon!*

Listen, divine Roland of dreams,
to a man who loves your Clavileño,
and whose own Pegasus whinnies to you;
listen to the verses of this litany,
composed of everyday things
and of other things, which I saw in the realm of mystery.

Pray for us, because we hunger for life,
our souls are groping blindly, our faith is lost,
we are filled with complaints and short of sunshine,
because of upstart souls of lax morality
which turn to ridicule the essence of La Mancha,
noblemindedness and the Spanish spirit!

Pray for us, because we stand in need of
the magical roses, the sublime boughs
of laurel! *Pro nobis ora,* great lord.
The forest of the world's laurel is shaking,
and, before your idle brother Segismundo does so,
pale Hamlet offers you a flower!

Pray nobly, piously, proudly,
pray chastely, purely, celestially, courageously;
intercede for us, supplicate for us,

pues casi ya estamos sin savia, sin brote,
sin alma, sin vida, sin luz, sin Quijote,
sin pies y sin alas, sin Sancho y sin Dios.

De tantas tristezas, de dolores tantos,
de los superhombres de Nietzsche, de cantos
áfonos, recetas que firma un doctor,
de las epidemias, de horribles blasfemias
de las Academias,
¡líbranos, Señor!

De rudos malsines,
falsos paladines,
y espíritus finos y blandos y ruines,
del hampa que sacia
su canallocracia
con burlar la gloria, la vida, el honor,
del puñal con gracia,
¡líbranos, Señor!

Noble peregrino de los peregrinos,
que santificaste todos los caminos,
con el paso augusto de tu heroicidad,
contra las certezas, contra las conciencias
y contra las leyes y contra las ciencias,
contra la mentira, contra la verdad . . .

¡Ora por nosotros, señor de los tristes,
que de fuerza alientas y de ensueños vistes,
coronado de áureo yelmo de ilusión!;
¡que nadie ha podido vencer todavía,
por la adarga al brazo, toda fantasía,
y la lanza en ristre, toda corazón!

Lo fatal

A René Pérez

Dichoso el árbol que es apenas sensitivo,
y más la piedra dura, porque ésa ya no siente,
pues no hay dolor más grande que el dolor de ser vivo,
ni mayor pesadumbre que la vida consciente.

for we are virtually without sap, without shoots,
without soul, without life, without light, without Quixote,
without feet and without wings, without Sancho, and without God.

From so many afflictions, from so many sorrows,
from Nietzsche's supermen, from hoarse
songs, prescriptions signed by a doctor,
from epidemics, from the horrible blasphemies
of the Academies,
deliver us, Lord!

From coarse backbiters,
false paladins,
and subtle, cajoling, base minds,
from the underworld that nourishes
its canaille-ocracy
by mocking glory, life, and honor,
from the dagger wielded with grace,
deliver us, Lord!

Noble pilgrim among pilgrims,
you that sanctified all roads
by the august passage of your heroism,
against all certainties, against consciences,
and against laws and sciences,
against lies, against truth. . . .

Pray for us, lord of the sad,
you that inspire us with strength and clothe us in dreams,
crowned with your golden helmet of fanciful hope!
You whom no one has yet been able to conquer,
thanks to the shield on your arm, a shield that is entirely imagination,
and to your couched lance, which is entirely heart!

Fatality

To René Pérez

Fortunate is the tree, which hardly has feeling,
and more so the stone, because it has none,
because there is no greater sorrow than the sorrow of being alive,
nor greater sadness than conscious life.

Ser, y no saber nada, y ser sin rumbo cierto,
y el temor de haber sido y un futuro terror . . .
Y el espanto seguro de estar mañana muerto,
y sufrir por la vida y por la sombra y por

lo que no conocemos y apenas sospechamos,
y la carne que tienta con sus frescos racimos,
y la tumba que aguarda con sus fúnebres ramos,
¡y no saber adónde vamos,
ni de dónde venimos! . . .

Momotombo

O vieux Momotombo, colosse chauve et nu . . .
                                            V. H.

El tren iba rodando sobre sus rieles. Era
en los días de mi dorada primavera
y era en mi Nicaragua natal.
De pronto, entre las copas de los árboles, vi
un cono gigantesco, «calvo y desnudo», y
lleno de antiguo orgullo triunfal.

Ya había yo leído a Hugo y la leyenda
que Squire le enseñó. Como una vasta tienda
vi aquel coloso negro ante el sol,
maravilloso de majestad. Padre viejo
que se duplica en el armonioso espejo
de un agua perla, esmeralda, col.

Agua de un vario verde y de un gris tan cambiante,
que discernir no deja su ópalo y su diamante,
a la vasta llama tropical.
¡Momotombo se alzaba lírico y soberano,
yo tenía quince años: una estrella en la mano!
Y era en mi Nicaragua natal.

Ya estaba yo nutrido de Oviedo y de Gomara,
y mi alma florida soñaba historia rara,
fábula, cuento, romance, amor
de conquistas, victorias de caballeros bravos,

To be, and yet know nothing, and to be without a fixed course,
and the fear of having been, and terrors about the future . . .
And the guaranteed horror of being dead tomorrow,
and to suffer from life and from darkness and from

what we don't yet know and barely suspect,
and the flesh that tempts us with its fresh clusters of grapes,
and the tomb that awaits us with its funereal wreaths,
and not knowing where we are bound,
or where we have come from!

Momotombo

O ancient Momotombo, bald and naked colossus . . .
V. H.

The train went rolling on its rails. It was
in the days of my golden springtime,
and it was in my native Nicaragua.
Soon, between the treetops, I saw
a gigantic cone, "bald and naked," and
filled with ancient triumphal pride.

I had already read Hugo and the legend
that Squier taught him. Like a vast tent
I saw that black colossus against the sun,
marvelous in its majesty. An aged father
duplicated in the harmonious mirror
of waters of pearl, emerald, cabbage-green.

Waters of various shades of green and a gray so changeable
that its opal and its diamond keep you from making out
the vast tropical blaze.
Momotombo loomed up, lyrical and sovereign;
I was fifteen, a star in my hands!
And it was in my native Nicaragua.

I was already well up in Oviedo and Gómara,
and my flowering soul dreamt of strange stories,
fables, tales, ballads, love
of conquest, the victories of brave knights,

incas y sacerdotes, prisioneros y esclavos,
plumas y oro, audacia, esplendor.

Y llegué y vi en las nubes la prestigiosa testa
de aquel cono de siglos, de aquel volcán de gesta,
que era ante mí de revelación.
Señor de las alturas, emperador del agua,
a sus pies el divino lago de Managua,
con islas todas de luz y canción.

¡Momotombo! —exclamé—, ¡oh nombre de epopeya!
Con razón Hugo, el grande, en su onomatopeya
ritmo escuchó que es de eternidad.
Dijérase que fueses para las sombras dique,
desde que oyera el blanco la lengua del cacique
en sus discursos de libertad.

Padre de fuego y piedra, yo te pedí ese día
tu secreto de llamas, tu arcano de armonía,
la iniciación que podías dar;
por ti pensé en lo inmenso de Osas y Peliones,
en que arriba hay titanes en las constelaciones
y abajo dentro la tierra y el mar.

¡Oh Momotombo ronco y sonoro! Te amo
porque a tu evocación vienen a mí otra vez,
obedeciendo a un íntimo reclamo,
perfumes de mi infancia, brisas de mi niñez.

¡Los estandartes de la tarde y de la aurora!
Nunca los vi más bellos que alzados sobre ti,
toda zafir la cúpula sonora
sobre los triunfos de oro, de esmeralda y rubí.

Cuando las babilonias del Poniente
en purpúreas catástrofes hacia la inmensidad
rodaban tras la augusta soberbia de tu frente,
eras tú como el símbolo de la Serenidad.

En tu incesante hornalla vi la perpetua guerra,
en tu roca unidades que nunca acabarán.
Sentí en tus terremotos la brama de la tierra
y la inmortalidad de Pan.

Incas and priests, prisoners and slaves,
feathers and gold, boldness, splendor.

And I came and saw in the clouds the far-famed summit
of that age-old cone, that epic volcano,
which was a revelation to my eyes.
Lord of heights, emperor of waters,
at its feet the divine lake of Managua,
with islands all compact of light and song.

"Momotombo!" I exclaimed. "Name out of an epic poem!
The great Hugo was right when in its onomatopoeia
he heard a rhythm of eternity.
You seem to have been a barrier against the darkness
ever since the white man heard the tongue of the cacique
discoursing on liberty."

Father of fire and stone, I asked you that day
for your secret of flames, your mystery of harmony,
the initiation that you could grant;
you made me think of the immensity of Ossa and Pelion,
in which, above, there are titans in the constellations
and, below, within, the earth and sea.

O hoarse, sonorous Momotombo! I love you
because when I evoke your memory there come to me once more,
in obedience to an inner call,
aromas from my childhood, breezes from my boyhood.

The banners of evening and dawn!
I never saw them lovelier than when raised over you,
your sounding dome all sapphire
above the triumphs of gold, emerald, and ruby.

When the Babylons of the West
rushed into immense eternity in purple catastrophes
behind the august pride of your brow,
you were like the symbol of Serenity.

In your unresting furnace I saw perpetual strife,
in your rock I saw never-ending unities.
In your earthquakes I felt the rut of the earth
and the immortality of Pan.

¡Con un alma volcánica entré en la dura vida,
Aquilón y huracán sufrió mi corazón,
y de mi mente mueven la cimera encendida
huracán y Aquilón!

Tu voz escuchó un día Cristóforo Colombo;
Hugo cantó tu gesta legendaria. Los dos
fueron, como tú, enormes, Momotombo,
montañas habitadas por el fuego de Dios.

¡Hacia el misterio caen poetas y montañas;
y romperáse el cielo de cristal
cuando luchen sonando de Pan las siete cañas
y la trompeta del Juicio final!

Salutación al águila

. . . May this grand Union have no end!
FONTOURA XAVIER

Bien vengas, mágica Águila de alas enormes y fuertes,
a extender sobre el Sur tu gran sombra continental,
a traer en tus garras, anilladas de rojos brillantes,
una palma de gloria, del color de la inmensa esperanza,
y en tu pico la oliva de una vasta y fecunda paz.

Bien vengas, ¡oh mágica Águila, que amara tanto Walt Whitman!,
quien te hubiera cantado en esta olímpica gira,
Águila que has llevado tu noble, y magnífico símbolo
desde el trono de Júpiter hasta el gran continente del Norte.

Ciertamente, has estado en las rudas conquistas del orbe.
Ciertamente, has tenido que llevar los antiguos rayos.
Si tus alas abiertas la visión de la paz perpetúan,
en tu pico y tus uñas está la necesaria guerra.

¡Precisión de la fuerza! ¡Majestad adquirida del trueno!
Necesidad de abrirle el gran vientre fecundo a la tierra
para que en ella brote la concreción del oro de la espiga,
y tenga el hombre el pan con que mueve su sangre.

No es humana la paz con que sueñan ilusos profetas,
la actividad eterna hace precisa la lucha,

With a volcanic soul I entered into this hard life;
my heart suffered from north winds and hurricanes;
and the blazing helmet-crest of my mind is shaken
by hurricanes and north winds!

One day Christopher Columbus listened to your voice;
Hugo sang your legendary epic. Both of them
were as enormous as you, Momotombo,
mountains inhabited by God's fire.

Into the mystery, poets and mountains fall;
and the crystalline sky will be shattered
when Pan's seven-reeded pipe vies musically
with the trumpet of the Last Judgment!

Greetings to the Eagle

. . . May this grand Union have no end!
FONTOURA XAVIER

Welcome, magical Eagle with enormous, strong wings,
as you come to spread your great continental shadow over the South,
bearing in your talons, with their rings of red diamonds,
a palm leaf of glory, of the color of boundless hope,
and in your bill the olive branch of a long, prosperous peace.

Welcome, magical Eagle loved so dearly by Walt Whitman,
who would have sung of you on this Olympian excursion,
you Eagle that have brought your noble, magnificent symbol
from Jupiter's throne to the great continent of the North.

Surely, you have participated in the violent conquests of the globe.
Surely, you have had to wield the ancient thunderbolts.
If your open wings perpetuate the vision of peace,
your bill and your claws are weapons of war, when necessary.

The need for strength! The acquired majesty of thunder!
The necessity to open the earth's vast, prolific womb
so that, in it, may germinate the golden concretion of the grain,
and man may have the bread to make his blood circulate.

The peace that deluded prophets dream of is beyond human capacity,
eternal activity makes struggle necessary,

y desde tu etérea altura tú contemplas, divina Águila,
la agitación combativa de nuestro globo vibrante.

Es incidencia la historia. Nuestro destino supremo
está más allá del rumbo que marcan fugaces las épocas.
Y Palenque y la Atlántida no son más que momentos soberbios
con que puntúa Dios los versos de su augusto Poema.

Muy bien llegada seas a la tierra pujante y ubérrima,
sobre la cual la Cruz del Sur está, que miró Dante
cuando, siendo Mesías, impulsó en su intuición sus bajeles,
que antes que los del Sumo Cristóbal supieron nuestro cielo.

E pluribus unum! ¡Gloria, victoria, trabajo!
Tráenos los secretos de las labores del Norte,
y que los hijos nuestros dejen de ser los retores latinos,
y aprendan de los yanquis la constancia, el vigor, el carácter.

¡Dinos, Águila ilustre, la manera de hacer multitudes
que hagan Romas y Grecias con el jugo del mundo presente,
y que potentes y sobrias, extiendan su luz y su imperio
y que, teniendo el Águila y el Bisonte y el Hierro y el Oro,
tengan un áureo día para darle las gracias a Dios!

Águila, existe el Cóndor. Es tu hermano en las grandes alturas.
Los Andes le conocen y saben, que, cual tú, mira
        al Sol.
May this grand Union have no end!, dice el poeta.
Puedan ambos juntarse, en plenitud, concordia y esfuerzo.

Águila, que conoces desde Jove hasta Zarathustra
y que tienes en los Estados Unidos tu asiento,
que sea tu venida fecunda para estas naciones
que el pabellón admiran constelado de bandas y estrellas.

¡Águila, que estuviste en las horas sublimes de Pathmos,
Águila prodigiosa, que te nutres de luz y de azul,
como una Cruz viviente, vuela sobre estas naciones,
y comunica al globo la victoria feliz del futuro!

Por algo eres la antigua mensajera jupiterina,
por algo has presenciado cataclismos y luchas de
        razas,
por algo estás presente en los sueños del Apocalipsis,
por algo eres el ave que han buscado los fuertes imperios.

and from your ethereal heights, divine Eagle, you observe
the combative restlessness of our vibrant globe.

History is chance. Our supreme destiny
lies beyond the course charted by fleeting eras.
And Palenque and Atlantis are no more than proud moments
with which God punctuates the lines of his august Poem.

You are most welcome in the vigorous, very fertile land
over which hangs the Southern Cross, which Dante saw
when, as a Messiah, he drove forward the ships of his intuition,
which came to know our sky before those of lofty Christopher.

E pluribus unum! Glory, victory, toil!
Bring us the secrets of the labors of the North,
and let our sons cease to be Latin rhetoricians,
and learn from the Yankees perseverance, vigor, and character.

Illustrious Eagle, tell us how to create multitudes
that can create Romes and Greeces with the essence of the present world;
how, in power and sobriety, they can extend their light and dominance,
and how, possessing the Eagle, Bison, Iron, and Gold,
they can possess a golden day in which to give thanks to God!

Eagle, the Condor exists. He is your brother in the great heights.
The Andes are familiar with him and they know that, like you, he
        gazes at the Sun.
"May this grand Union have no end!" the poet says.
May both sides join forces, in plenty, concord, and efforts.

Eagle, you that are familiar with all from Jupiter to Zarathustra
and have your seat in the United States,
may your coming be productive for these nations
which admire the flag spangled with stripes and stars.

Eagle, you that were present during the sublime hours of Patmos,
miraculous Eagle who feed on light and the blue,
fly over these nations like a living Cross,
and communicate to the globe the happy victory of the future!

For a good reason you are Jupiter's ancient messenger,
for a good reason you have witnessed cataclysms and battles between
        races,
for a good reason you are present in the dreams of the Apocalypse,
for a good reason you are the bird that mighty empires have sought.

¡Salud, Águila, extensa virtud a tus inmensos revuelos!;
reina de los azures, ¡salud!, ¡gloria!, ¡victoria y encanto!
¡Que la Latina América reciba tu mágica influencia
y que renazca nuevo Olimpo, lleno de dioses y héroes!

¡Adelante, siempre adelante! ¡Excelsior! ¡Vida! ¡Lumbre!
¡Que se cumpla lo prometido en los destinos terrenos,
y que vuestra obra inmensa las aprobaciones recoja
del mirar de los astros, y de lo que hay más allá!

Río de Janeiro, 1906.

¡Eheu!

Aquí, junto al mar latino,
digo la verdad:
Siento en roca, aceite y vino
yo mi antigüedad.

¡Oh, qué anciano soy, Dios santo,
oh, qué anciano soy! . . .
¿De dónde viene mi canto?
Y yo, ¿adónde voy?

El conocerme a mí mismo
ya me va costando
muchos momentos de abismo
y el cómo y el cuándo . . .

Y esta claridad latina,
¿de qué me sirvió
a la entrada de la mina
del yo y el no yo . . . ?

Nefelibata contento,
creo interpretar
las confidencias del viento,
la tierra y el mar . . .

Unas vagas confidencias
del ser y el no ser,
y fragmentos de conciencias
de ahora y ayer.

Health to you, Eagle, much power to your immense circling flights!
Queen of the blue, health, glory, victory, and enchantment!
May Latin America receive your magical influence
and may a new Olympus be born, filled with gods and heroes!

Forward, ever forward! Excelsior! Life! Light!
May the promise be fulfilled in earthly destinies,
and may your immense work gather the approval
of the gaze of the stars and all that lies beyond them!

Rio de Janeiro, 1906.

Eheu!

Here, beside the Latin sea,
I speak the truth:
In rock, olive oil, and wine I feel
my antiquity.

Oh, how ancient I am, holy God,
oh, how ancient I am! . . .
Where does my song come from?
And I, where am I going?

The knowledge of myself
is already costing me
many moments of dejection,
and the how and the when. . . .

And this Latin clarity and brightness,
what good was it to me
at the entrance to the mine
of the self and the nonself? . . .

A contented cloudwalker,
I believe I can interpret
the secrets of the wind,
the land and the sea. . . .

Vague secrets
about being and nonbeing,
and fragments of awareness
about now and yesterday.

Como en medio de un desierto
me puse a clamar;
y miré el sol como muerto
y me eché a llorar.

Nocturno

Silencio de la noche, doloroso silencio
nocturno . . . ¿Por qué el alma tiembla de tal manera?
Oigo el zumbido de mi sangre,
dentro de mi cráneo pasa una suave tormenta.
¡Insomnio! No poder dormir, y, sin embargo,
soñar. Ser la auto-pieza
de disección espiritual, ¡el auto-Hamlet!
Diluir mi tristeza
en un vino de noche
en el maravilloso cristal de las tinieblas . . .
Y me digo: ¿a qué hora vendrá el alba?
Se ha cerrado una puerta . . .
Ha pasado un transeúnte . . .
Ha dado el reloj tres horas . . . ¡Si será Ella! . . .

Epístola

A la señora de Leopoldo Lugones

1

Madame Lugones, *j'ai commencé ces vers*
en écoutant la voix d'un carillon d'Anvers . . .
¡Así empecé, en francés, pensando en Rodenbach
cuando hice hacia el Brasil una fuga . . . de Bach!

En Río de Janeiro iba yo a proseguir,
poniendo en cada verso el oro y el zafir
y la esmeralda de esos pájaros-moscas
que melifican entre las áureas siestas foscas
que temen los que temen el cruel vómito negro.
Ya no existe allá fiebre amarilla. ¡Me alegro!

As if in the midst of a wilderness,
I began to cry out;
and I gazed at the seemingly dead sun
and I burst into tears.

Nocturne

Silence of the night, sorrowful nighttime
silence . . . Why does my soul tremble this way?
I hear the humming of my blood,
a gentle storm passes by inside my skull.
Insomnia! To be unable to sleep, and yet
to keep dreaming. To be the self-subject
of spiritual dissection, the self-Hamlet!
To diffuse my sadness
into a night wine
in the miraculous crystal goblet of the darkness. . . .
And I ask myself: "At what hour will the dawn come?"
A door has closed. . . .
Someone has walked by outside. . . .
The clock has struck three.[4]. . . What if it's Death?! . . .

Epistle

To Mrs. Leopoldo Lugones

1

Mrs. Lugones, "I began these verses
while listening to the sound of a carillon in Antwerp—"
That's how I began, in French, thinking of Rodenbach,
when I dashed off to Brazil, fugacious as . . . a Bach fugue!

In Rio de Janeiro I was going to continue,
placing in every verse the gold, sapphire,
and emerald of those hummingbirds
which sip nectar during the golden, sullen siesta hours
feared by those who fear the cruel "black vomit."
Yellow fever no longer exists there. I'm glad of it!

---

[4]At least one editor of Darío reads *trece* ("thirteen").

Et pour cause. Yo pan-americanicé
con un vago temor y con muy poca fe
en la tierra de los diamantes y la dicha
tropical. Me encantó ver la vera machicha,
mas encontré también un gran núcleo cordial
de almas llenas de amor, de ensueños, de ideal.
Y si había un calor atroz, también había
todas las consecuencias y ventajas del día,
en panorama igual al de los cuadros y hasta
igual al que pudiera imaginarse . . . Basta.
Mi ditirambo brasileño es ditirambo
que aprobaría tu marido. *Arcades ambo.*

2

   Mas al calor de ese Brasil maravilloso,
tan fecundo, tan grande, tan rico, tan hermoso,
a pesar de Tijuca y del cielo opulento,
a pesar de ese foco vivaz de pensamiento,
a pesar de Nabuco, embajador, y de
los delegados panamericanos que
hicieron lo posible por hacer cosas buenas,
saboreé lo ácido del saco de mis penas;
quiero decir que me enfermé. La neurastenia
es un don que me vino con mi obra primigenia.
¡Y he vivido tan mal, y tan bien, como tanto!
¡Y tan buen comedor guardo bajo mi manto!
¡Y tan buen bebedor guardo bajo mi capa!
¡Y he gustado bocados de cardenal y papa . . . !
Y he exprimido la ubre cerebral tantas veces,
que estoy grave. Esto es mucho ruido y pocas nueces,
según dicen doctores de una sapiencia suma.
Mis ilusiones se van en ilusión y espuma.
Me recetan que no haga nada ni piense nada,
que me retire al campo a ver la madrugada
con las alondras y con Garcilaso, y con
el *sport.* ¡Bravo! Sí. Bien. Muy bien. ¿Y *La Nación*?
¿Y mi trabajo diario y preciso y fatal?
¿No se sabe que soy cónsul como Stendhal?
Es preciso que el médico que eso recete, dé
también libros de cheques para el Crédit Lyonnais,

"And with good reason." I Pan-Americanized
with a vague fear and with very little trust
in the land of diamonds and tropical
bliss. I was enchanted to see the real maxixe,
but I also came across a large cordial group
of souls filled with love, dreams, and ideals.
And, though the heat was atrocious, there were also
all the consequences and benefits of the day,
in the form of a panorama equal to that of paintings and even
equal to any that can be imagined. . . . Enough.
My Brazilian dithyramb is a dithyramb
that your husband would approve of. We have the same tastes.

2

But in the heat of that wonderful Brazil,
so fertile, so big, so rich, so beautiful,
despite Tijuca and the splendid sky,
despite that lively focus of thought,
despite Ambassador Nabuco and
the Pan-American delegates who
did their best to do their business well,
I tasted the sourness of the bag of my pains;
I mean, I got sick. Neurasthenia
is a gift that came to me along with my earliest efforts.
And I've lived just as badly and well as many another!
And I have such a hearty eater under my mantle!
And I have such a hearty drinker under my cape!
And I've tasted mouthfuls fit for a cardinal or pope! . . .
And I've squeezed my mental udder dry so often
that I'm in serious condition. This is much ado about nothing,
according to the opinion of highly skilled doctors.
My hopeful dreams are fading into illusions and foam.
They prescribe doing nothing and not thinking,
they say I should go to the country and watch the sun rise
along with the larks and a volume of Garcilaso, while partaking in
sports. Fine! Yes. Good. Very good. But what about *La Nación*?
What about my daily work, both needful and predestined?
Don't they know I'm a consul like Stendhal?
The doctor who prescribes this must also give me
checkbooks that can be drawn on the Crédit Lyonnais,

y envíe un automóvil devorador de viento,
en el cual se pasee mi egregio aburrimiento,
harto de profilaxis, de ciencia y de verdad.

3

En fin, convaleciente, llegué a nuestra ciudad
de Buenos Aires, no sin haber escuchado
a míster Root a bordo del *Charleston* sagrado;
mas mi convalecencia duró poco. ¿Qué digo?
Mi emoción, mi entusiasmo y mi recuerdo amigo,
y el banquete de *La Nación,* que fue estupendo,
y mis viejas siringas con su pánico estruendo,
y ese fervor porteño, ese perpetuo arder,
y el milagro de gracia que brota en la mujer
argentina, y mis ansias de gozar de esa tierra,
me pusieron de nuevo con mis nervios en guerra.
Y me volví a París. Me volví al enemigo
terrible, centro de la neurosis, ombligo
de la locura, foco de todo *surmenage*
donde hago buenamente mi papel de *sauvage*
encerrado en mi celda de la rue Marivaux,
confiando sólo en mí y resguardando el yo.
¡Y si lo resguardara, señora, si no fuera
lo que llaman los parisienses una *pera!*
A mi rincón me llegan a buscar las intrigas,
las pequeñas miserias, las traiciones amigas,
y las ingratitudes. Mi maldita visión
sentimental del mundo me aprieta el corazón,
y así cualquier tunante me explotará a su gusto.
Soy así. Se me puede burlar con calma. Es justo.
Por eso los astutos, los listos, dicen que
no conozco el valor del dinero. ¡Lo sé!
Que ando, nefelibata, por las nubes . . . Entiendo.
Que no soy hombre práctico en la vida . . . ¡Estupendo!
Sí, lo confieso: soy inútil. No trabajo
por arrancar a otro su pitanza; no bajo
a hacer la vida sórdida de ciertos previsores.
Yo no ahorro ni en seda, ni en champaña, ni en flores.
No combino sutiles pequeñeces, ni quiero
quitarle de la boca su pan al compañero.

And send me an automobile that devours the wind,
in which I can ride to get rid of my colossal boredom,
fed up as I am with prophylaxis, science, and truth.

3

In short, I was a convalescent when I arrived in our city
of Buenos Aires, not without having listened to
Mr. Root on board that execrable *Charleston;*
but my convalescence didn't last long. What am I saying?
My emotion, my enthusiasm, and my kindly memories,
and the banquet given by *La Nación,* which was stupendous,
and my old reed-flutes with their Pan-like racket,
and that Buenos Aires fervor, that constant seething,
and the miracle of grace that springs from Argentine
women, and my eagerness to enjoy that land,
set me at war with my nerves again.
And I returned to Paris. I returned to the terrible
enemy, center of neurosis, focal point
of madness, midpoint of all overexertion,
where I duly act out my role as a "savage"
shut up in my cell on the Rue Marivaux,
trusting only in myself and protecting my ego.
And how I'd protect it, ma'am, if I weren't
what Parisians call "an easy mark"!
Intrigues come and seek me out in my corner,
petty troubles, betrayals by friends,
and ingratitude. My accursed sentimental
view of the world tugs at my heart,
and so any con man can exploit me at will.
That's how I am. People can fool me and be carefree. It's only fair.
Therefore, astute, clever people say that
I don't know the value of money. I know that!
That I'm a dreamer with my head in the clouds. . . . I understand.
That I'm not practical in the business of life. . . . Wonderful!
Yes, I admit: I'm useless. I don't work
in order to steal someone else's daily bread; I don't stoop
to live the sordid life of certain people with foresight.
I don't cut corners on silk, champagne, or flowers.
I don't make little clever schemes, nor do I wish
to take my friend's food out of his mouth.

Me complace en los cuellos blancos ver los diamantes.
Gusto de gentes de maneras elegantes
y de finas palabras y de nobles ideas.
Las gentes sin higiene ni urbanidad, de feas
trazas, avaros, torpes, o malignos y rudos,
mantienen, lo confieso, mis entusiasmos mudos.
No conozco el valor del oro . . . ¿Saben esos
que tal dicen lo amargo del jugo de mis sesos,
del sudor de mi alma, de mi sangre y mi tinta,
del pensamiento en obra y de la idea encinta?
¿He nacido yo acaso hijo de millonario?
¿He tenido yo Cirineo en mi Calvario?

4

    Tal continué en París lo empezado en Anvers.
Hoy, heme aquí en Mallorca, *la terra dels foners,*
como dice Mossen Cinto, el gran Catalán.
Y desde aquí, señora, mis versos a ti van,
olorosos a sal marina y azahares,
al suave aliento de las islas Baleares.
Hay un mar tan azul como el Partenopeo.
Y al azul celestial, vasto como un deseo,
su techo cristalino bruñe con el sol de oro.
Aquí todo es alegre, fino, sano y sonoro.
Barcas de pescadores sobre la mar tranquila
descubro desde la terraza de mi *villa,*
que se alza entre las flores de su jardín fragante,
con un monte detrás y con la mar delante.

5

    A veces me dirijo al mercado, que está
en la Plaza Mayor. (¿Qué Coppée, no es verdad?)
Me rozo con un núcleo crespo de muchedumbre
que viene por la carne, la fruta y la legumbre.
Las mallorquinas usan una modesta falda,
pañuelo en la cabeza y la trenza a la espalda.
Esto, las que yo he visto, al pasar, por supuesto.
Y las que no la lleven no se enojen por esto.
He visto unas payesas con sus negros corpiños,

I like seeing diamonds on white throats.
I enjoy people with elegant manners,
witty words, and noble ideas.
Unhygienic, impolite people, with an ugly
appearance, miserly, clumsy, malevolent, and coarse people,
I admit, fail to arouse my enthusiasm.
I don't know the value of gold. . . . Do the ones
who say that know the bitterness of the pith of my brains,
of the sweat of my soul, my blood, and my ink,
my thought processes at work, and my pregnant ideas?
Was I perhaps born the son of a millionaire?
Did I have a Simon of Cyrene at my Calvary?

4

Thus I continued in Paris what I had begun in Antwerp.
Today, here I am on Majorca, "the land of slingsmen,"
as that great Catalan, "Mossen Cinto," says.
And from here, ma'am, my verses travel to you,
redolent of sea salt and orange blossoms,
on the gentle breeze of the Balearic Islands.
There's a sea as blue as at Naples.
And it burnishes with a golden sun the crystal ceiling
of the blue of the sky, vast as desire.
Here all is cheerful, elegant, healthy, and musical.
I discover fishing boats on the calm sea
from the terrace of my villa,
which rises amid the flowers of its fragrant garden,
with a mountain behind it and the sea in front.

5

Sometimes I head for the market, which is located
in the Plaza Mayor. (Just like Coppée, isn't it?)
I rub elbows with an intricate throng of people
who come to buy meat, fruit, and vegetables.
Majorcan women wear a simple skirt,
a kerchief on their head, and a braid down their back.
Of course, this applies to the ones I've seen on my walks.
I hope that the ones who dress differently won't get angry.
I've seen some local peasant women in their black sleeveless bodices,

con cuerpos de odaliscas y con ojos de niños;
y un velo que les cae por la espalda y el cuello,
dejando al aire libre lo oscuro del cabello.
Sobre la falda clara, un delantal vistoso.
Y saludan con un *bon di tengui* gracioso,
entre los cestos llenos de patatas y coles,
pimientos de corales, tomates de arreboles,
sonrosadas cebollas, melones y sandías,
que hablan de las Arabias y las Andalucías.
Calabazas y nabos para ofrecer asuntos
a madame Noailles y Francis Jammes juntos.

A veces me detengo en la plaza de abastos
como si respirase soplos de vientos vastos,
como si se me entrase con el respiro el mundo.
Estoy ante la casa en que nació Raimundo
Lulio. Y en ese instante mi recuerdo me cuenta
las cosas que le dijo la Rosa a la Pimienta . . .
¡Oh, cómo yo diría el sublime destierro
y la lucha y la gloria del mallorquín de hierro!
¡Oh, cómo cantaría en un carmen sonoro
la vida, el alma, el numen, del mallorquín de oro!
De los hondos espíritus es de mis preferidos.
Sus robles filosóficos están llenos de nidos
de ruiseñor. Es otro y es hermano del Dante.
¡Cuántas veces pensara su verbo de diamante
delante la Sorbona vieja del París sabio!
¡Cuántas veces he visto su infolio y su astrolabio
en una bruma vaga de ensueño, y cuántas veces
le oí hablar a los árabes cual Antonio a los peces,
en un imaginar de pretéritas cosas
que, por ser tan antiguas, se sienten tan hermosas!

6

    Hice una pausa.
                        El tiempo se ha puesto malo. El mar
a la furia del aire no cesa de bramar.
El temporal no deja que entren los vapores. Y
un *yacht* de lujo busca refugio en Porto-Pi.
Porto-Pi es una rada cercana y pintoresca.

with bodies like odalisques and eyes like children;
and a veil hangs over their neck and shoulders,
leaving their dark hair exposed.
Over their bright skirt, a colorful apron.
And they greet you with a gracious "Have a good day!"
amid their baskets full of potatoes and cabbages,
coral-red peppers, blushing tomatoes,
pink onions, melons, and watermelons
reminiscent of Arabia and Andalusia.
Gourds and turnips to furnish subjects
for Madame de Noailles and Francis Jammes put together.

    Sometimes I linger in the food market
as if I were inhaling the gusts of mighty winds,
as if the world were entering me with my breath.
I stand in front of the birth house of Ramón
Lull. And at that moment my memory relates to me
the things that the Rose said to the Red Pepper. . . .
Oh, how I could narrate the sublime exile
and the struggle and the glory of that iron Majorcan!
Oh, how I could sing in a resonant poem of
the life, soul, and divinity of that golden Majorcan!
Among profound minds he is a favorite of mine.
His philosophic oaks are full of nests
of nightingales. He is different from Dante but a brother to him.
How many times I had thought of his diamondlike words
in front of the old Sorbonne of scholarly Paris!
How many times I have seen his folio and his astrolabe
in a vague mist of dream, and how many times
I heard him talking to the Arabs, like Saint Anthony to the fish,
while I imagined bygone things,
which, because they are so old, appear so beautiful!

6

    Here I paused.
                  The weather has turned bad. The sea
doesn't cease bellowing in the fury of the wind.
The storm doesn't allow steamships to enter. And
a luxury yacht is seeking refuge at Porto-Pi.
Porto-Pi is a picturesque roadstead nearby.

Vista linda: aguas bellas, luz dulce y tierra fresca.
¡Ah, señora, si fuese posible a algunos el
dejar su Babilonia, su Tiro, su Babel,
para poder venir a hacer su vida entera
en esta luminosa y espléndida ribera!

Hay no lejos de aquí un archiduque austriaco
que las pomas de Ceres y las uvas de Baco
cultiva, en un retiro archiducal y egregio.
Hospeda como un monje —y el hospedaje es regio—.
Sobre las rocas se alza la mansión señorial
y la isla le brinda ambiente imperial.
Es un pariente de Jean Orth. Es un atrida
que aquí ha encontrado el cierto secreto de su vida.
Es un cuerdo. Aplaudamos al príncipe discreto
que aprovecha a la orilla del mar ese secreto.
La isla es florida y llena de encanto en todas partes.
Hay un aire propicio para todas las artes.
En Pollensa ha pintado Santiago Rusiñol
cosas de flor, de luz y de seda de sol.
Y hay villa de retiro espiritual famosa:
La literata Sand escribió en Valldemosa
un libro. Ignoro si vino aquí con Musset,
y si la vampiresa sufrió o gozó, no sé (1).

¿Por qué mi vida errante no me trajo a estas sanas
costas antes de que las prematuras canas
de alma y cabeza hicieran de mí la mezcolanza
formada de tristeza, de vida y esperanza?
¡Oh, qué buen mallorquín me sentiría ahora!
¡Oh, cómo gustaría sal de mar, miel de aurora,
al sentir como en un caracol en mi cráneo
el divino y eterno rumor mediterráneo!
Hay en mí un griego antiguo que aquí descansó un día,
después que le dejaron loco de melodía
las sirenas rosadas que atrajeron su barca.
Cuanto mi ser respira, cuanto mi vista abarca,
es recordado por mis íntimos sentidos;
los aromas, las luces, los ecos, los ruïdos,

---

(1)	He leído ya el libro que hizo Aurora Dupin.
	Fue Chopin el amante aquí. ¡Pobre Chopin!

A pretty view: beautiful water, gentle light, and verdant land.
   Oh, ma'am, if it were possible for some people to
leave behind their Babylon, their Tyre, their Babel,
to be able to come and live their entire life
on this luminous, splendid coast!

   Not far from here lives an Austrian archduke
who grows the apples of Ceres and the grapes of Bacchus
in a wonderful retreat befitting an archduke.
He lodges guests like a monk—and the hospice is regal.
His lordly mansion rises above the cliffs
and the island offers it surroundings worthy of an emperor.
He's a relative of Jean Orth. He is a descendant of Atreus
who has found here the true secret of existence.
He's a wise man. Let's applaud the discreet prince
who makes use of this secret beside the sea.
The island is full of flowers and enchantment everywhere.
There is an atmosphere propitious to all the arts.
At Pollensa, Santiago Rusiñol has painted
canvases of blossom, light, and sunlit silk.
And there's a famous intellectual-hideaway villa:
At Valldemosa the novelist Sand wrote
a book. I don't know whether she came here with Musset,
or whether that lady vampire had a good or bad time. (1)

   Why didn't my wandering life bring me to these healthful
shores before the premature gray hair
of my soul and head turned me into this mixture
of sadness, life, and hope?
Oh, what a good Majorcan I would feel like now!
Oh, how I'd enjoy the sea salt, the honey of dawn,
while I heard, as if in a seashell inside my skull,
the divine, eternal roar of the Mediterranean!
In me there's an ancient Greek who once rested here
after being driven mad by the melody
of the rosy sirens who allured his boat.
All that my being inhales, all that my eyes take in,
is remembered by my inmost senses:
the aromas, the play of light, the echoes, the sounds,

(1)   By now I've read the book written by Aurore Dupin.
       Her lover here was Chopin. Poor Chopin!
                                    [Darío's verse footnote.]

como en ondas atávicas me traen añoranzas
que forman mis ensueños, mis vidas y esperanzas.
Mas, ¿dónde está aquel templo de mármol y la gruta
donde mordí aquel seno dulce como una fruta?
¿Dónde los hombres ágiles que las piedras redondas
recogían para los cueros de sus hondas? . . .

   Calma, calma. Eso es mucha poesía, señora.
Ahora hay comerciantes muy modernos. Ahora
mandan barcos prosaicos la dorada Valencia,
Marsella, Barcelona y Génova. La ciencia
comercial es hoy fuerte y lo acapara todo.

   Entretanto, respiro mi salitre y mi yodo
brindados por las brisas de aqueste golfo inmenso,
y a un tiempo, como Kant y como el asno, pienso.
Es lo mejor.

7

          Y aquí mi epístola concluye.
Hay un ansia de tiempo que de mi pluma fluye
a veces, como hay veces de enorme economía.
«Si hay, he dicho, señora, alma clara, es la mía.»
Mírame transparentemente, con tu marido,
y guárdame lo que tú puedas del olvido.

Balada en honor de las musas de carne y hueso

A G. Martínez Sierra

   Nada mejor para cantar la vida,
y aun para dar sonrisas a la muerte,
que la áurea copa en donde Venus vierte
la esencia azul de su viña encendida.
Por respirar los perfumes de Armida
y por sorber el vino de su beso,
vino de ardor, de beso, de embeleso,
fuérase al cielo en la bestia de Orlando,
¡voz de oro y miel para decir cantando:
la mejor musa es la de carne y hueso!

as if in atavistic waves, bring me nostalgic yearnings
that form my dreams, life, and hopes.
But where is that marble temple and the grotto
in which I bit into that breast as sweet as a fruit?
Where are the agile men who used to gather
round stones for the leather straps of their slings? . . .

    Calm, calm. This is a lot of poetry, ma'am.
Now there are very modern businessmen. Now
prosaic cargo vessels are sent from golden Valencia,
Marseilles, Barcelona, and Genoa. Commercial
know-how is powerful today and monopolizes everything.

    In the meantime, I inhale my saltpeter and iodine
offered by the breezes of this immense bay,
and at the same time I think, like Kant and the donkey.
It's better that way.

7

                    And here my epistle ends.
There is an anxiety about time that flows from my pen
at times, just as there are other times of great economy.
"I've said it, ma'am, if any bright soul exists, mine is one."
Gaze on me transparently, along with your husband,
and do your best to keep from forgetting me.

Ballade in Honor of the Flesh-and-Blood Muses

To G. Martínez Sierra

    There's nothing better with which to sing of life,
and even to make death smile,
than the golden goblet into which Venus pours
the blue essence of her fiery grapevine.
If he could breathe the perfumes of Armida
and sip the wine of her kiss,
a wine of ardor, kisses, and enchantment,
a man would ride to heaven on Orlando's mount;
a voice of gold and honey with which to sing:
"The best muse is the one of flesh and blood!"

Cabellos largos en la buhardilla,
noches de insomnio al blancor del invierno,
pan de dolor con la sal de lo eterno
y ojos de ardor en que Juvencia brilla;
el tiempo en vano mueve su cuchilla,
el hilo de oro permanece ileso;
visión de gloria para el libro impreso
que en sueños va como una mariposa
y una esperanza en la boca de rosa.
¡La mejor musa es la de carne y hueso!

Regio automóvil, regia cetrería,
borla y muceta, heráldica fortuna,
nada son como a luz de la Luna
una mujer hecha una melodía.
Barca de amar busca la fantasía,
no el *yacht* de Alfonso o la barca de Creso.
Da al cuerpo llama y fortifica el seso
ese archivado y vital paraíso;
pasad de largo, Abelardo y Narciso.
¡La mejor musa es la de carne y hueso!

Clío está en esta fuente hecha de Aurora,
Euterpe canta en esta lengua fina,
Talía ríe en la boca divina,
Melpómene es ese gesto que implora;
en estos pies Terpsícore se adora,
cuello inclinado es de Erato embeleso,
Polymnia intenta a Caliope proceso
por esos ojos en que Amor se quema.
Urania rige todo ese sistema.
¡La mejor musa es la de carne y hueso!

No protestéis con celo protestante,
contra el panal de rosas y claveles
en que Tiziano moja sus pinceles
y gusta el cielo de Beatriz el Dante.
Por eso existe el verso de diamante,
por eso el iris tiéndese y por eso
humano genio es celeste progreso.
Líricos cantan y meditan sabios
por esos pechos y por esos labios:
¡La mejor musa es la de carne y hueso!

Long hair in the garret,
nights of insomnia in the whiteness of winter,
bread of sorrow with the salt of eternity
and ardent eyes in which Youth gleams;
time swings its blade in vain,
the golden thread remains unharmed;
a vision of glory for the printed book
that appears in dreams like a butterfly
and a hope on the lips of rose.
The best muse is the one of flesh and blood!

Royal automobile, royal falconry,
cap and gown, heraldic fortune,
are nothing in comparison to a woman
transformed into a melody in the moonlight.
Imagination seeks the boat of loving,
not Alfonso's yacht or Croesus's boat.
That storied, vital paradise
lends flame to the body and strengthens the mind;
pass by, Abelard and Narcissus.
The best muse is the one of flesh and blood!

Clio is in this fountain made of Dawn,
Euterpe sings on this witty tongue,
Thalia laughs on the divine lips,
that imploring expression is Melpomene;
in these feet Terpsichore is worshipped,
a sloping neck is an enchantment of Erato,
Polyhymnia is bringing a legal action against Calliope
over those eyes in which Love is burned.
Urania governs this entire system.
The best muse is the one of flesh and blood!

Don't protest with a protestant zeal
against the honeycomb of roses and carnations
in which Titian moistens his brushes
and Dante enjoys Beatrice's paradise.
It is for this that diamondlike verses exist,
it is for this that the rainbow stretches in the sky, for this
that human genius means celestial progress.
Lyric poets sing and sages meditate
because of those breasts and those lips:
The best muse is the one of flesh and blood!

ENVÍO

Gregorio: nada al cantor determina
como el gentil estímulo del beso.
Gloria al sabor de la boca divina.
¡La mejor musa es la de carne y hueso!

Poema del otoño

Tú, que estás la barba en la mano
meditabundo,
¿has dejado pasar, hermano,
la flor del mundo?

Te lamentas de los ayeres
con quejas vanas:
¡aún hay promesas de placeres
en los mañanas!

Aún puedes casar la olorosa
rosa y el lis,
y hay mirtos para tu orgullosa
cabeza gris.

El alma ahíta cruel inmola
lo que la alegra,
como Zingua, reina de Angola,
lúbrica negra.

Tú has gozado de la hora amable,
y oyes después
la imprecación del formidable
Eclesiastés.

El domingo de amor te hechiza;
mas mira cómo
llega el miércoles de ceniza;
Memento, homo . . .

Por eso hacia el florido monte
las almas van,
y se explican Anacreonte
y Omar Kayam.

ENVOI
Gregorio: nothing gives the singer resolve
like the kind stimulus of a kiss.
Glory to the taste of the divine lips!
The best muse is the one of flesh and blood!

Poem of Autumn

You whose chin is in your hand
as you meditate,
my brother, have you let
the flower of the world pass you by?

You lament about your yesterdays
with vain complaints:
there are still promises of pleasures
in our tomorrows!

You can still wed the fragrant
rose to the iris,
and there are myrtles for your proud
gray head.

The sated soul cruelly immolates
that which delights it,
like Zingua, queen of Angola,
the lustful African.

You have enjoyed the pleasurable hour,
and now, later, you hear
the imprecation of redoubtable
Ecclesiastes.

The Sunday of love bewitches you;
but observe that
Ash Wednesday is coming;
"Remember, O man . . ."

For this reason souls proceed
to the blossoming mountain,
and there is an explanation for Anacreon
and Omar Khayyam.

Huyendo del mal, de improviso
se entra en el mal,
por la puerta del paraíso
artificial.

Y, no obstante, la vida es bella,
por poseer
la perla, la rosa, la estrella
y la mujer.

Lucifer brilla. Canta el ronco
mar. Y se pierde
Silvano oculto tras el tronco
del haya verde.

Y sentimos la vida pura,
clara, real,
cuando la envuelve la dulzura
primaveral.

¿Para qué las envidias viles
y las injurias,
cuando retuercen sus reptiles
pálidas furias?

¿Para qué los odios funestos
de los ingratos?
¿Para qué los lívidos gestos
de los Pilatos?

¡Si lo terreno acaba, en suma,
cielo e infierno,
y nuestras vidas son la espuma
de un mar eterno!

Lavemos bien de nuestra veste
la amarga prosa;
soñemos en una celeste,
mística rosa.

Cojamos la flor del instante;
¡la melodía
de la mágica alondra cante
la miel del día!

Fleeing evil, one suddenly
enters evil,
through the gate of the artificial
paradise.

And yet, life is beautiful,
because it contains
the pearl, the rose, the star,
and woman.

The morning star shines. The hoarse sea
sings. And Sylvanus
is lost from sight behind the trunk
of the green beech tree.

And we feel that life is pure,
bright, regal,
when it is enveloped in the sweetness
of springtime.

What good are base envy
and slanders,
when pale Furies
twist their snaky hair?

What good are the baleful hatreds
of ungrateful people?
What good are the livid faces
of such as Pilate?

If earthly life ceases, in short,
Heaven and Hell,
and our lives are the foam
of an eternal ocean!

Let us cleanse our robe thoroughly
of bitter prose;
let us dream of a heavenly,
mystic rose.

Let us gather the flowers of the moment;
let the melody
of the magical lark sing
of the day's honey!

Amor a su fiesta convida
y nos corona.
Todos tenemos en la vida
nuestra Verona.

Aun en la hora crepuscular
canta una voz:
«¡Ruth, risueña, viene a espigar
para Booz!»

Mas coged la flor del instante,
cuando en Oriente
nace el alba para el fragante
adolescente.

¡Oh! Niño que con Eros juegas,
niños lozanos,
danzad como las ninfas griegas
y los silvanos.

El viejo tiempo todo roe
y va de prisa;
sabed vencerle, Cintia, Cloe
y Cidalisa.

Trocad por rosas, azahares,
que suena el son
de aquel Cantar de los Cantares
de Salomón.

Príapo vela en los jardines
que Cipris huella;
Hécate hace aullar los mastines;
mas Diana es bella,

y apenas envuelta en los velos
de la ilusión,
baja a los bosques de los cielos
por Endimión.

¡Adolescencia! Amor te dora
con su virtud;
goza del beso de la aurora,
¡oh juventud!

Love invites us to his feast
and garlands us.
All of us in our lives have
our own Verona.

Even at the twilight hour
a voice sings:
"Smiling Ruth, come and glean
for Boaz!"

But gather the flowers of the moment,
when in the East
the dawn breaks for the sweet-smelling
adolescent.

O you child who play with Eros,
lusty children,
dance like the Greek nymphs
and the Sylvani.

Old Time gnaws all things
and moves hurriedly;
have the skill to conquer him, Cynthia, Chloe,
and Cydalise.

Exchange orange blossoms for roses,
for the sound is heard
of that Song of Songs
of Solomon.

Priapus stands watch in the gardens
trodden by Cypris;
Hecate makes the mastiffs howl;
but Diana is beautiful,

and, only lightly wrapped in the veils
of hopeful dreams,
she descends to the forests of the skies
in search of Endymion.

Adolescence! Love gilds you
with his power;
enjoy the kiss of the dawn,
O youth!

¡Desventurado el que ha cogido
tarde la flor!
Y ¡ay de aquel que nunca ha sabido
lo que es amor!

Yo he visto en tierra tropical
la sangre arder,
como en un cáliz de cristal,
en la mujer.

Y en todas partes la que ama
y se consume
como una flor hecha de llama
y de perfume.

Abrasaos en esa llama
y respirad
ese perfume que embalsama
la Humanidad.

Gozad de la carne, ese bien
que hoy nos hechiza,
y después se tornará en
polvo y ceniza.

Gozad del sol, de la pagana
luz de sus fuegos;
gozad del sol, porque mañana
estaréis ciegos.

Gozad de la dulce armonía
que a Apolo invoca;
gozad del canto, porque un día
no tendréis boca.

Gozad de la tierra, que un
bien cierto encierra;
gozad, porque no estáis aún
bajo la tierra.

Apartad el temor que os hiela
y que os restringe;
la paloma de Venus vuela
sobre la Esfinge.

Unhappy is the man who has gathered
the flower too late!
And woe to the man who has never known
what love is!

In tropical lands I have seen
blood seething,
as if in a crystal chalice,
in woman.

And everywhere the woman who loves
and wastes away
like a flower compounded of flame
and fragrance.

Burn yourselves up in that flame
and inhale
that fragrance which perfumes
mankind.

Enjoy the flesh, that beneficial thing
which enchants us today,
and will later become
dust and ashes.

Enjoy the sun, the pagan
light of its fires;
enjoy the sun, for tomorrow
you will be blind.

Enjoy the sweet music
that invokes Apollo;
enjoy song, because one day
you will have no mouth.

Enjoy the earth, which
encloses undoubted benefits;
enjoy it because you are not yet
under the earth.

Dispel the fear that freezes you
and restrains you
Venus's dove flies
above the Sphinx.

Aún vencen muerte, tiempo y hado
las amorosas;
en las tumbas se han encontrado
mirtos y rosas.

Aún Anadiómena en sus lidias
nos da su ayuda;
aún resurge en la obra de Fidias
Friné desnuda.

Vive el bíblico Adán robusto,
de sangre humana,
y aún siente nuestra lengua el gusto
de la manzana.

Y hace de este globo viviente
fuerza y acción
la universal y omnipotente
fecundación.

El corazón del cielo late
por la victoria
de este vivir, que es un combate
y es una gloria.

Pues aunque hay pena y nos agravia
el sino adverso,
en nosotros corre la savia
del universo.

Nuestro cráneo guarda el vibrar
de tierra y sol,
como el ruido de la mar
el caracol.

La sal del mar en nuestras venas
va a borbotones;
tenemos sangre de sirenas
y de tritones.

A nosotros encinas, lauros,
frondas espesas;
tenemos carne de centauros
y satiresas.

Death, time, and fate are still conquered
by women in love;
myrtles and roses
have been found in tombs.

Even now Anadyomene in her combats
gives us her aid;
naked Phryne
still reappears in the work of Phidias.

He lives yet, that sturdy biblical Adam
of human blood,
and our tongue still senses the taste
of the apple.

And this living globe is turned into
force and action
by universal, omnipotent
fecundation.

The heart of heaven beats
because of the victory
of this life of ours, which is a combat
and a glory.

Because, even though there is pain and we are harmed
by adverse fate,
in us there flows the sap
of the universe.

Our skull retains the vibrancy
of earth and sun,
just as the seashell
retains the roar of the sea.

The sea salt in our veins
gushes furiously;
we have the blood of sirens
and tritons.

To us the ilexes, the laurels,
the dense foliage!
We have the flesh of centaurs
and female satyrs.

En nosotros la Vida vierte
fuerza y calor.
¡Vamos al reino de la Muerte
por el camino del Amor!

Into us Life pours
strength and heat.
We journey to the realm of Death
along the highway of Love!

Alphabetical List of Spanish Titles of Poems

*(Poems identified merely by their opening words
will be found in the list of first lines.)*

Alphabetical List of Spanish First Lines of Poems

A CATALOG OF SELECTED
DOVER BOOKS
IN ALL FIELDS OF INTEREST

A CATALOG OF SELECTED DOVER BOOKS IN ALL FIELDS OF INTEREST

100 BEST-LOVED POEMS, Edited by Philip Smith. "The Passionate Shepherd to His Love," "Shall I compare thee to a summer's day?" "Death, be not proud," "The Raven," "The Road Not Taken," plus works by Blake, Wordsworth, Byron, Shelley, Keats, many others. 96pp. 5$\frac{3}{16}$ x 8$\frac{1}{4}$. 0-486-28553-7

100 SMALL HOUSES OF THE THIRTIES, Brown-Blodgett Company. Exterior photographs and floor plans for 100 charming structures. Illustrations of models accompanied by descriptions of interiors, color schemes, closet space, and other amenities. 200 illustrations. 112pp. 8$\frac{3}{8}$ x 11. 0-486-44131-8

1000 TURN-OF-THE-CENTURY HOUSES: With Illustrations and Floor Plans, Herbert C. Chivers. Reproduced from a rare edition, this showcase of homes ranges from cottages and bungalows to sprawling mansions. Each house is meticulously illustrated and accompanied by complete floor plans. 256pp. 9$\frac{3}{8}$ x 12$\frac{1}{4}$. 0-486-45596-3

101 GREAT AMERICAN POEMS, Edited by The American Poetry & Literacy Project. Rich treasury of verse from the 19th and 20th centuries includes works by Edgar Allan Poe, Robert Frost, Walt Whitman, Langston Hughes, Emily Dickinson, T. S. Eliot, other notables. 96pp. 5$\frac{3}{16}$ x 8$\frac{1}{4}$. 0-486-40158-8

101 GREAT SAMURAI PRINTS, Utagawa Kuniyoshi. Kuniyoshi was a master of the warrior woodblock print — and these 18th-century illustrations represent the pinnacle of his craft. Full-color portraits of renowned Japanese samurais pulse with movement, passion, and remarkably fine detail. 112pp. 8$\frac{3}{8}$ x 11. 0-486-46523-3

ABC OF BALLET, Janet Grosser. Clearly worded, abundantly illustrated little guide defines basic ballet-related terms: arabesque, battement, pas de chat, relevé, sissonne, many others. Pronunciation guide included. Excellent primer. 48pp. 4$\frac{3}{16}$ x 5$\frac{3}{4}$. 0-486-40871-X

ACCESSORIES OF DRESS: An Illustrated Encyclopedia, Katherine Lester and Bess Viola Oerke. Illustrations of hats, veils, wigs, cravats, shawls, shoes, gloves, and other accessories enhance an engaging commentary that reveals the humor and charm of the many-sided story of accessorized apparel. 644 figures and 59 plates. 608pp. 6 $\frac{1}{8}$ x 9$\frac{1}{4}$. 0-486-43378-1

ADVENTURES OF HUCKLEBERRY FINN, Mark Twain. Join Huck and Jim as their boyhood adventures along the Mississippi River lead them into a world of excitement, danger, and self-discovery. Humorous narrative, lyrical descriptions of the Mississippi valley, and memorable characters. 224pp. 5$\frac{3}{16}$ x 8$\frac{1}{4}$. 0-486-28061-6

ALICE STARMORE'S BOOK OF FAIR ISLE KNITTING, Alice Starmore. A noted designer from the region of Scotland's Fair Isle explores the history and techniques of this distinctive, stranded-color knitting style and provides copious illustrated instructions for 14 original knitwear designs. 208pp. 8$\frac{3}{8}$ x 10$\frac{7}{8}$. 0-486-47218-3

CATALOG OF DOVER BOOKS

ALICE'S ADVENTURES IN WONDERLAND, Lewis Carroll. Beloved classic about a little girl lost in a topsy-turvy land and her encounters with the White Rabbit, March Hare, Mad Hatter, Cheshire Cat, and other delightfully improbable characters. 42 illustrations by Sir John Tenniel. 96pp. $5\frac{3}{16}$ x $8\frac{1}{4}$. 0-486-27543-4

AMERICA'S LIGHTHOUSES: An Illustrated History, Francis Ross Holland. Profusely illustrated fact-filled survey of American lighthouses since 1716. Over 200 stations — East, Gulf, and West coasts, Great Lakes, Hawaii, Alaska, Puerto Rico, the Virgin Islands, and the Mississippi and St. Lawrence Rivers. 240pp. 8 x $10\frac{3}{4}$. 0-486-25576-X

AN ENCYCLOPEDIA OF THE VIOLIN, Alberto Bachmann. Translated by Frederick H. Martens. Introduction by Eugene Ysaye. First published in 1925, this renowned reference remains unsurpassed as a source of essential information, from construction and evolution to repertoire and technique. Includes a glossary and 73 illustrations. 496pp. $6\frac{1}{8}$ x $9\frac{1}{4}$. 0-486-46618-3

ANIMALS: 1,419 Copyright-Free Illustrations of Mammals, Birds, Fish, Insects, etc., Selected by Jim Harter. Selected for its visual impact and ease of use, this outstanding collection of wood engravings presents over 1,000 species of animals in extremely lifelike poses. Includes mammals, birds, reptiles, amphibians, fish, insects, and other invertebrates. 284pp. 9 x 12. 0-486-23766-4

THE ANNALS, Tacitus. Translated by Alfred John Church and William Jackson Brodribb. This vital chronicle of Imperial Rome, written by the era's great historian, spans A.D. 14-68 and paints incisive psychological portraits of major figures, from Tiberius to Nero. 416pp. $5\frac{3}{16}$ x $8\frac{1}{4}$. 0-486-45236-0

ANTIGONE, Sophocles. Filled with passionate speeches and sensitive probing of moral and philosophical issues, this powerful and often-performed Greek drama reveals the grim fate that befalls the children of Oedipus. Footnotes. 64pp. $5\frac{3}{16}$ x $8\frac{1}{4}$. 0-486-27804-2

ART DECO DECORATIVE PATTERNS IN FULL COLOR, Christian Stoll. Reprinted from a rare 1910 portfolio, 160 sensuous and exotic images depict a breathtaking array of florals, geometrics, and abstracts — all elegant in their stark simplicity. 64pp. $8\frac{3}{8}$ x 11. 0-486-44862-2

THE ARTHUR RACKHAM TREASURY: 86 Full-Color Illustrations, Arthur Rackham. Selected and Edited by Jeff A. Menges. A stunning treasury of 86 full-page plates span the famed English artist's career, from *Rip Van Winkle* (1905) to masterworks such as *Undine, A Midsummer Night's Dream,* and *Wind in the Willows* (1939). 96pp. $8\frac{3}{8}$ x 11. 0-486-44685-9

THE AUTHENTIC GILBERT & SULLIVAN SONGBOOK, W. S. Gilbert and A. S. Sullivan. The most comprehensive collection available, this songbook includes selections from every one of Gilbert and Sullivan's light operas. Ninety-two numbers are presented uncut and unedited, and in their original keys. 410pp. 9 x 12. 0-486-23482-7

THE AWAKENING, Kate Chopin. First published in 1899, this controversial novel of a New Orleans wife's search for love outside a stifling marriage shocked readers. Today, it remains a first-rate narrative with superb characterization. New introductory Note. 128pp. $5\frac{3}{16}$ x $8\frac{1}{4}$. 0-486-27786-0

BASIC DRAWING, Louis Priscilla. Beginning with perspective, this commonsense manual progresses to the figure in movement, light and shade, anatomy, drapery, composition, trees and landscape, and outdoor sketching. Black-and-white illustrations throughout. 128pp. $8\frac{3}{8}$ x 11. 0-486-45815-6

Browse over 9,000 books at www.doverpublications.com

CATALOG OF DOVER BOOKS

THE BATTLES THAT CHANGED HISTORY, Fletcher Pratt. Historian profiles 16 crucial conflicts, ancient to modern, that changed the course of Western civilization. Gripping accounts of battles led by Alexander the Great, Joan of Arc, Ulysses S. Grant, other commanders. 27 maps. 352pp. 5⅜ x 8½. 0-486-41129-X

BEETHOVEN'S LETTERS, Ludwig van Beethoven. Edited by Dr. A. C. Kalischer. Features 457 letters to fellow musicians, friends, greats, patrons, and literary men. Reveals musical thoughts, quirks of personality, insights, and daily events. Includes 15 plates. 410pp. 5⅜ x 8½. 0-486-22769-3

BERNICE BOBS HER HAIR AND OTHER STORIES, F. Scott Fitzgerald. This brilliant anthology includes 6 of Fitzgerald's most popular stories: "The Diamond as Big as the Ritz," the title tale, "The Offshore Pirate," "The Ice Palace," "The Jelly Bean," and "May Day." 176pp. 5⅜ x 8½. 0-486-47049-0

BESLER'S BOOK OF FLOWERS AND PLANTS: 73 Full-Color Plates from Hortus Eystettensis, 1613, Basilius Besler. Here is a selection of magnificent plates from the Hortus Eystettensis, which vividly illustrated and identified the plants, flowers, and trees that thrived in the legendary German garden at Eichstätt. 80pp. 8⅜ x 11. 0-486-46005-3

THE BOOK OF KELLS, Edited by Blanche Cirker. Painstakingly reproduced from a rare facsimile edition, this volume contains full-page decorations, portraits, illustrations, plus a sampling of textual leaves with exquisite calligraphy and ornamentation. 32 full-color illustrations. 32pp. 9⅜ x 12¼. 0-486-24345-1

THE BOOK OF THE CROSSBOW: With an Additional Section on Catapults and Other Siege Engines, Ralph Payne-Gallwey. Fascinating study traces history and use of crossbow as military and sporting weapon, from Middle Ages to modern times. Also covers related weapons: balistas, catapults, Turkish bows, more. Over 240 illustrations. 400pp. 7¼ x 10⅛. 0-486-28720-3

THE BUNGALOW BOOK: Floor Plans and Photos of 112 Houses, 1910, Henry L. Wilson. Here are 112 of the most popular and economic blueprints of the early 20th century — plus an illustration or photograph of each completed house. A wonderful time capsule that still offers a wealth of valuable insights. 160pp. 8⅜ x 11. 0-486-45104-6

THE CALL OF THE WILD, Jack London. A classic novel of adventure, drawn from London's own experiences as a Klondike adventurer, relating the story of a heroic dog caught in the brutal life of the Alaska Gold Rush. Note. 64pp. 5³⁄₁₆ x 8¼. 0-486-26472-6

CANDIDE, Voltaire. Edited by Francois-Marie Arouet. One of the world's great satires since its first publication in 1759. Witty, caustic skewering of romance, science, philosophy, religion, government — nearly all human ideals and institutions. 112pp. 5³⁄₁₆ x 8¼. 0-486-26689-3

CELEBRATED IN THEIR TIME: Photographic Portraits from the George Grantham Bain Collection, Edited by Amy Pastan. With an Introduction by Michael Carlebach. Remarkable portrait gallery features 112 rare images of Albert Einstein, Charlie Chaplin, the Wright Brothers, Henry Ford, and other luminaries from the worlds of politics, art, entertainment, and industry. 128pp. 8⅜ x 11. 0-486-46754-6

CHARIOTS FOR APOLLO: The NASA History of Manned Lunar Spacecraft to 1969, Courtney G. Brooks, James M. Grimwood, and Loyd S. Swenson, Jr. This illustrated history by a trio of experts is the definitive reference on the Apollo spacecraft and lunar modules. It traces the vehicles' design, development, and operation in space. More than 100 photographs and illustrations. 576pp. 6¾ x 9¼. 0-486-46756-2

Browse over 9,000 books at www.doverpublications.com

A CHRISTMAS CAROL, Charles Dickens. This engrossing tale relates Ebenezer Scrooge's ghostly journeys through Christmases past, present, and future and his ultimate transformation from a harsh and grasping old miser to a charitable and compassionate human being. 80pp. 5³⁄₁₆ x 8¼.				0-486-26865-9

COMMON SENSE, Thomas Paine. First published in January of 1776, this highly influential landmark document clearly and persuasively argued for American separation from Great Britain and paved the way for the Declaration of Independence. 64pp. 5³⁄₁₆ x 8¼.				0-486-29602-4

THE COMPLETE SHORT STORIES OF OSCAR WILDE, Oscar Wilde. Complete texts of "The Happy Prince and Other Tales," "A House of Pomegranates," "Lord Arthur Savile's Crime and Other Stories," "Poems in Prose," and "The Portrait of Mr. W. H." 208pp. 5³⁄₁₆ x 8¼.				0-486-45216-6

COMPLETE SONNETS, William Shakespeare. Over 150 exquisite poems deal with love, friendship, the tyranny of time, beauty's evanescence, death, and other themes in language of remarkable power, precision, and beauty. Glossary of archaic terms. 80pp. 5³⁄₁₆ x 8¼.				0-486-26686-9

THE COUNT OF MONTE CRISTO: Abridged Edition, Alexandre Dumas. Falsely accused of treason, Edmond Dantès is imprisoned in the bleak Chateau d'If. After a hair-raising escape, he launches an elaborate plot to extract a bitter revenge against those who betrayed him. 448pp. 5³⁄₁₆ x 8¼.				0-486-45643-9

CRAFTSMAN BUNGALOWS: Designs from the Pacific Northwest, Yoho & Merritt. This reprint of a rare catalog, showcasing the charming simplicity and cozy style of Craftsman bungalows, is filled with photos of completed homes, plus floor plans and estimated costs. An indispensable resource for architects, historians, and illustrators. 112pp. 10 x 7.				0-486-46875-5

CRAFTSMAN BUNGALOWS: 59 Homes from "The Craftsman," Edited by Gustav Stickley. Best and most attractive designs from Arts and Crafts Movement publication — 1903–1916 — includes sketches, photographs of homes, floor plans, descriptive text. 128pp. 8¼ x 11.				0-486-25829-7

CRIME AND PUNISHMENT, Fyodor Dostoyevsky. Translated by Constance Garnett. Supreme masterpiece tells the story of Raskolnikov, a student tormented by his own thoughts after he murders an old woman. Overwhelmed by guilt and terror, he confesses and goes to prison. 480pp. 5³⁄₁₆ x 8¼.				0-486-41587-2

THE DECLARATION OF INDEPENDENCE AND OTHER GREAT DOCUMENTS OF AMERICAN HISTORY: 1775-1865, Edited by John Grafton. Thirteen compelling and influential documents: Henry's "Give Me Liberty or Give Me Death," Declaration of Independence, The Constitution, Washington's First Inaugural Address, The Monroe Doctrine, The Emancipation Proclamation, Gettysburg Address, more. 64pp. 5³⁄₁₆ x 8¼.				0-486-41124-9

THE DESERT AND THE SOWN: Travels in Palestine and Syria, Gertrude Bell. "The female Lawrence of Arabia," Gertrude Bell wrote captivating, perceptive accounts of her travels in the Middle East. This intriguing narrative, accompanied by 160 photos, traces her 1905 sojourn in Lebanon, Syria, and Palestine. 368pp. 5⅜ x 8½.				0-486-46876-3

A DOLL'S HOUSE, Henrik Ibsen. Ibsen's best-known play displays his genius for realistic prose drama. An expression of women's rights, the play climaxes when the central character, Nora, rejects a smothering marriage and life in "a doll's house." 80pp. 5³⁄₁₆ x 8¼.				0-486-27062-9